ndi Myers is the author of more than fifty
when she's not craftin
skiing, gardening, cook

A lover of small-town
and two spoiled dogs in

Jenna Kernan has penned over two dozen novels and received two RITA® Award nominations. Jenna is every bit as adventurous as her heroines. Her hobbies include recreational gold prospecting, scuba diving and gem hunting. Jenna grew up in the Catskills and currently lives in the Hudson Valley in New York State with her husband. Follow Jenna on Twitter, @jennakernan, on Facebook or at jennakernan.com

Also by Cindi Myers

Ice Cold Killer
Cold Conspiracy
Saved by the Sheriff
Avalanche of Trouble
Deputy Defender
Danger on Dakota Ridge
Murder in Black Canyon
Undercover Husband
Manhunt on Mystic Mesa

Also by Jenna Kernan

Defensive Action
Adirondack Attack
Surrogate Escape
Tribal Blood
Undercover Scout
Black Rock Guardian
Turquoise Guardian
Eagle Warrior Firewolf
The Warrior's Way
Shadow Wolf

SNOWBLIND JUSTICE

CINDI MYERS

WARNING SHOT

JENNA KERNAN

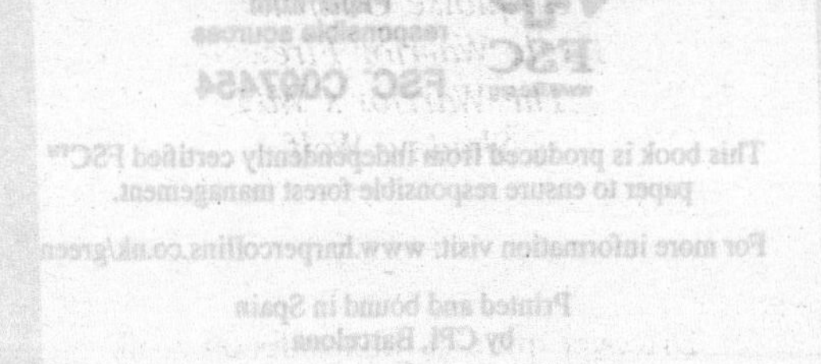

MILLS & BOON

First Published in Great Britain 2019
by Mills & Boon, an imprint of HarperCollins*Publishers*
1 London Bridge Street, London, SE1 9GF

ISBN: 978-0-263-27446-2

1119

SNOWBLIND JUSTICE

CINDI MYERS

For Gay and Reed.

Chapter One

Snow sifted down over the town like a downy blanket, turning trash piles into pristine drifts, transforming mine ruins into nostalgic works of art, hiding ugliness and danger beneath a dusting of wedding-cake white.

The murderer lurked behind a veil of snow, fresh flakes hiding his tracks, muffling the sound of his approach, covering up the evidence of his crimes. Deep cold and furious blizzards kept others indoors, but the killer reveled in his mastery over the landscape. His pursuers thought he was soft, like them. They couldn't find him because they assumed conditions were too harsh for him to survive in the wilderness.

And all the while he was waiting, striking when the right opportunity presented itself, his intellect as much of a weapon as his muscles. The woman who lay before him now was a prime example. She hadn't hesitated to stop when he had flagged her down on the highway. He was merely a stranded motorist who needed help. He was good-looking and charming—what woman wouldn't want to help him?

By the time she realized his purpose, it was too late. Like the officials who tracked him, she had underestimated him. The lawmen doubted his ability to instill trust in his victims, and were awed by his talent for killing quickly and efficiently while leaving no trace.

He lifted the woman's inert body into the car, arranging it into an artful tableau across the seat. There was very little blood—none in the vehicle— and no fingerprints or other evidence for the sheriff and his deputies to trace. They would search and examine and photograph and question—and they would find nothing.

He shut the door to the car and trudged away as the snow began to fall harder, a sifting of sugar over the bloodstains on the side of the road, and over his footprints, and over the signs of a struggle in the older snow beside the highway. The killer ducked behind a wall of ice, and disappeared out of sight of the empty road. Wind blew the snow sideways, the flakes sticking to the knit mask he had pulled up over his face, but he scarcely felt the cold, too absorbed in the details of his latest killing, reveling in his skill at pulling it off—again.

There were no witnesses to his crime, and none to his getaway. The lawmen thought they were closing in on him because they had linked his name to his crimes. But they didn't realize he was the one drawing nearer and nearer to his goal. Soon he would claim his final victim—the woman who had brought him to Eagle Mountain in the first place. After he had taken her, he would disappear, leaving his pursuers to wonder at his daring. They would hate him more than ever, but some part of them would have to admire his genius.

"I FEEL LIKE I should apologize for seventeen-year-old Emily's poor taste in prom dresses." Emily Walker looked down at the dress she had unearthed from the back of her closet that morning—too short in the front, too long in the back, entirely too many ruffles and a very bright shade of pink.

"It will be fine as soon as we straighten out the hem and maybe take off a few ruffles." Lacy Milligan looked up from her position kneeling on the floor beside the chair Emily stood on, and tucked a lock of her sleek brown hair behind one ear. "You'll look great."

"Everyone is supposed to be looking at you when you walk down the aisle in that gorgeous bridal gown—not at the clashing train wreck of attendants at the front of the room," Emily said. Watching Lacy wouldn't be a hardship—she was gorgeous, and so was her dress. The same couldn't be said for the bridesmaids' makeshift ensembles. "Let's hope the highway reopens and the dresses you chose for your wedding can be delivered."

"Not just the dresses," Lacy said. "The wedding favors and some of the decorations are waiting to be delivered, as well. Not to mention some of the guests." She returned to pinning the dress. "With less than a week to go, I can't risk waiting much longer to figure out how to use what we have here—including this dress." She inserted a pin in the hem of the skirt and sat back on her heels to study the results. "As it is, I may be going through the wedding shy one bridesmaid if the highway doesn't open soon."

"The road is going to open soon," Emily said. "The weather reports look favorable." Since the New Year, the southwest corner of Colorado had been hammered by a wave of snowstorms that had dumped more than six feet of snow in the mountains. The snow, and the avalanches that inevitably followed, had blocked the only road leading in and out of the small town of Eagle Mountain for most of the past month.

"Travis tried to talk me into delaying the wedding." Lacy sighed. "Not just because of the weather, but because of this serial killer business."

A serial murderer who had been dubbed the Ice Cold Killer had murdered six women in the area in the past few weeks. Lacy's fiancé—Emily's brother Sheriff Travis Walker—had been working practically 'round the clock to try to stop the elusive serial killer. Emily thought postponing the wedding until the killer was caught and the weather improved wasn't such a bad idea, but she wasn't a bride who had spent the past six months planning the ceremony and reception. "What did you tell him?" Emily asked.

"I told him I'm willing to postpone my honeymoon. I understand that being a sheriff's wife means putting my needs behind those of the town. And I've been patient—I really have. I haven't seen him in two days and I haven't complained at all. But Sunday is my wedding day. All I ask is that he be here for a few hours. The case will wait that long."

"It's not just Travis," Emily said. "Half the wedding party is law enforcement. There's Gage." Emily and Travis's brother was a sheriff's deputy. "Cody Rankin—he's technically on leave from the US Marshals office, but he's still working on the case. And Nate Harris—he's supposed to be off work from his job with the Department of Wildlife to recover from his ankle injury, but he's as busy as ever, from what I can tell. Oh, and Ryder Stewart—he's had plenty of time to help Travis, since most of his highway patrol territory is closed due to snow."

"Then they can be here for a few hours, too," Lacy said. "That may sound terribly selfish of me, but I put so much of my life on hold for the three years I was in prison. I don't want to wait any longer." Lacy had been wrongfully convicted of murdering her boss. She and Travis had fallen in love after he had worked to clear her name.

"Then you deserve the wedding you want, when you want it," Emily said. "I hope my brother was understanding."

"He was, after I whined and moaned a little bit." Lacy stood and walked around the chair to take in the dress from all sides. "I didn't tell him this, but another reason I want to go ahead with the wedding is that I'm beginning to be afraid the killer won't be caught. Travis and every other lawman in the area has been hunting this guy for weeks. It's like he's a ghost. Travis and Gage and the rest of them work so hard and the murderer just thumbs his nose at them."

"It's crazy." Emily climbed down off the chair and began helping Lacy gather up the sewing supplies. "At first I was terrified. Well, I guess I'm still terrified, but honestly, I'm also angry." She patted Lacy's shoulder. "Anyway, I'm not going to let the killer or the weather get me down. The weather is going to hold, the road will open and you'll have a beautiful wedding, without my fashion faux pas spoiling the day."

"I hope you're right and everyone I invited can be here," Lacy said.

"Who in the wedding party is still missing?" Emily asked.

"Paige Riddell. She recently moved to Denver with her boyfriend, Rob Allerton."

"Of course." Paige had run a bed-and-breakfast in town prior to moving away. "I never knew her well, but she seemed really nice."

"She is nice. And I really want her here for my wedding. But you can't fight nature, I guess, so we're going to make do no matter what." She turned to Emily. "Thank you so much for everything you've done to help," she said. "Not just with the wedding preparations, but all the work you've put into entertaining the wedding guests who are already here. I forget that the weather has forced you to put your own life on hold, too."

Like everyone else who had been in town when the first blizzard struck, Emily had been stuck in Eagle Mountain for most of the past month. "The first few weeks I was on my winter break," she said. She was working on her master's at Colorado State University and was employed by the university as a teaching assistant and researcher. "It's just the last ten days that I've missed. Fortunately, the university has been very understanding, letting me complete some of my coursework and research online, delaying some other work and arranging for another researcher to teach my undergrad class until I get back."

"I'm glad," Lacy said. "Can you imagine having to delay your master's degree because of snow?"

"Snow has its upsides, too," Emily said. "That sleigh ride last week was a blast, and I'm looking forward to the bonfire Wednesday."

"Every party you've thrown has been a big success," Lacy said. "I'm sure most brides don't entertain their guests so lavishly."

"Well, everything has gone well except the scavenger hunt," Emily said. "I wouldn't call that a success."

"It's not your fault Fiona was murdered during the party." Lacy hugged herself and shuddered. "I thought for sure Travis would catch the killer after that—he was so close, right here on the ranch."

Just like that, the conversation turned back to the Ice Cold Killer as the two friends remembered each of his victims—some of them locals they had known, a few tourists or newcomers they had never had a chance to meet. But every person who had fallen victim to the killer had been young and female, like Emily and Lacy. They didn't have to say it, but they were both keenly aware that they might have been one of the killer's victims—or they still might be.

Emily was relieved when the door to the sunroom, where they were working, opened and Bette Fuller, one of Lacy's best friends and the caterer for the wedding, breezed in. Blonde and curvy, Bette always lit up the room, and today she was all smiles. "Rainey just got back from town and she says the highway is open." Bette hugged Lacy. "I know this is what you've been waiting for."

"Is Rainey sure?" Lacy asked.

"Rainey isn't one for spreading rumors or telling lies," Emily said. The ranch cook was even more stone-faced and tight-lipped than Travis. Emily looked down at the dress she was wearing, now bristling with pins and marks made with tailor's chalk. "Maybe I won't have to wear this old thing after all."

"Rainey said there was a line of delivery trucks coming into town," Bette said. "Which is a good thing, since the stores are low on everything."

"I'm going to call Paige and tell her and Rob to drop everything and drive over right now—before another avalanche closes the road," Lacy said. "And I need to check with the florist and look at the tracking for the bridesmaids' dresses and the wedding favors and the guest book I ordered, too."

"I can help you with some of that," Bette said.

"You two go on," Emily said. "I'll finish cleaning up in here." The prom dress—pins and all—could go back in the closet. If she was lucky, she'd never have to put it on again.

As she gathered up the clutter from around the room, she thought of all the work that went into weddings. This was only her second time serving as a bridesmaid, and she was looking forward to the ceremony, though she was a little nervous, too. Mostly, she hoped she wouldn't get too emotional. Weddings were supposed to be hopeful occasions, but they always made her a little melancholy, wondering what her own wedding would have been like—and how different her life might have turned out if she had accepted the one proposal she had had.

Who was she kidding? If she had agreed to marry that man, it would have been a disaster. She had been far too young for marriage, and he certainly hadn't been ready to settle down, no matter what he said. At least she had had sense enough to see that.

She was stowing the last of the sewing supplies and looking forward to changing back into jeans and a sweater when the door to the sunroom opened again and a man entered, obscured from the waist up by a tower of brown boxes. "I met the UPS driver on the way in and he asked me to drop these off," said a deep, velvety voice that sent a hot tremor up Emily's spine and made her wonder if she was hallucinating. "Whoever answered the door told me to bring them back here."

"Thanks." Emily hurried to relieve the man of his burdens, then almost dropped the boxes as she came face-to-face with Brodie Langtry.

The man who had once proposed to her. She felt unsteady on her feet, seeing him here in this house again after so long. And if she was upset, her family was going to be furious.

"Hello, Emily." He grinned, his full lips curving over even, white teeth, eyes sparking with a blatant sex appeal that sent a bolt of remembered heat straight through her. "You're looking well." A single furrow creased his brow. "Though I have to ask—what is that you're wearing?"

She looked down at the prom dress, the hem lopped off and bristling with pins, one ruffle hanging loose where Lacy had started to detach it. She looked back up at Brodie, feeling a little like she had been hit on the head and was still reeling from the blow. "What are you doing here?" she asked.

"As it happens, the Colorado Bureau of Investigation sent me here to help your brother with a case," he said. "I hear you've got a serial murderer problem."

"Does Travis know you're coming?" Her brother hadn't said anything to her. Then again, he was probably trying to spare her feelings.

"He requested assistance from the CBI, though he doesn't know it's me. Is that going to be a problem?"

She bit her lower lip. "I don't know."

"It's been five years, Emily," he said.

Right. But it might have been five minutes for all the pain that was twisting her stomach. She hadn't expected to react like this. She was supposed to be over Brodie. "You never answered my letter," she said.

The crease across his brow deepened. "You sent me a letter?"

"You mean you don't even remember?" The words came out louder than she had intended, and she forced herself to lower her voice. "I tried calling, but your number had been changed. Travis found out you'd been transferred to Pueblo, so I wrote to you there."

He shook his head. "I never received your letter. Why did you write?"

Did he really not know? She pressed her hand to her stomach, hoping she wasn't going to be sick. This was too awful. "It doesn't matter now." She turned away and tried to make her voice light. "Like you said, it was five years ago. I'm sure Travis will appreciate your help with the case." Her brother was nothing if not a professional.

Brodie was silent, though she could feel his eyes boring into her. She began looking through the stack of packages. "I'll ask again," he said after a moment. "What is that you're wearing?"

"It's a prom dress," she managed.

"Isn't it the wrong time of year for prom? And aren't you in graduate school?"

Her eyes widened and she froze in the act of reaching for a package. "How did you know I'm in graduate school?"

"I might have checked up on you a time or two. They don't have proms in graduate school, do they?"

He'd *checked up* on her. Should she be flattered, or

creeped out? "It's the new thing. Haven't you heard?" She continued scanning the labels on the boxes. She picked up the one that surely held her bridesmaid's dress. Maybe instead of stuffing the prom dress back into her closet, she'd burn it at Wednesday night's bonfire. That would be appropriate, wouldn't it?

"What is all this?" Brodie swept his hand to indicate the piles of boxes, bits of tulle, sewing supplies, silk flowers and other flotsam piled around the room. "Are you getting ready for a big party?"

"Travis is getting married on Sunday," Emily said. "I guess you didn't know." Then again, why would he? He and Travis had stopped being friends five years ago.

"No, I didn't know. Good for him. Who's the lucky woman?"

"Her name is Lacy Milligan. I'm sure you don't know her."

"No, but I know of her. Now it's coming back to me." He grinned. "Lacy is the woman Travis arrested for murder—then after new evidence came to light, he worked to clear her name. I remember the story now, though I didn't know a wedding was in the offing."

It hadn't taken long for the media to latch onto the story of a wrongly accused woman falling in love with the law enforcement officer who had sent her to prison in the first place, then worked to clear her name. Most of the state was probably familiar with the story by now, but Emily didn't want to discuss it with Brodie. "Travis is at his office in town," she said, deciding it was past time to send Brodie on his way. "It's on Main. You can't miss it."

Before he could answer, her cell phone buzzed and she grabbed it off a nearby table. "Hello?"

"Hey." Travis's greeting was casual, but his voice carried the tension that never left him these days. "I was trying to get hold of Lacy, but I can't get through on her phone."

"I think she's talking to Paige, letting her know the highway is open."

"She's terrible about checking her messages, so do me a favor and tell her I'm not going to be able to take her to dinner today. I'm sorry, but we've had a break in the case."

Emily's heart leaped. "Have you made an arrest?"

"Not exactly, but we know who the killers are. One of them is dead, but the other is still on the loose."

"A second murderer?" Travis had long suspected the Ice Cold Killer might be more than one man. If he had caught one of the killers, surely that meant he was closing in on the second. Maybe the case would be solved before the wedding after all. "Lacy will be glad to hear it," Emily said.

"Maybe not so glad when you tell her I have to miss dinner. I need to focus on tracking down the second man."

Which meant he probably wouldn't be home to sleep, either. "Travis, you can't keep working around the clock like this."

"We're going to get some help. The Colorado Bureau of Investigation has agreed to loan us one of their investigators. Now that the road is open, he—or she—should be showing up anytime."

She glanced over her shoulder at Brodie, who was looking out the window. The past five years had been kind to him, filling out his shoulders, adding a few fine lines around his eyes. He wore his hair a little longer than when she'd last seen him, and sunlight through the window picked out the gold streaks in the brown. Add in chiseled cheekbones, a dimpled chin and a straight nose and it was no wonder he could be mistaken for a model or a movie star.

As if sensing her staring at him, he turned and met her gaze, then cocked one eyebrow, lips half-curved in a mocking smile.

"Emily? Are you still there?" Travis asked.

"Um, your help from the CBI is here," she said. "It's Brodie Langtry." Not waiting to hear Travis's reaction, she thrust the phone at Brodie. *It's Travis*, she mouthed.

Brodie took the phone. "Travis! It's been a long time. I'm looking forward to working with you on this case… Yes, I volunteered for the job. To tell you the truth, I thought it was past time we mended fences. I know we didn't part under the best of circumstances five years ago and I'd like to clear the air. I've been catching up with Emily."

She cringed at the words. She and Brodie didn't need to "catch up." They had had a fun time together once, and if it had ended badly, she took most of the blame for that. She'd been young and naive and had expected things from him that he had never promised to give. She wouldn't make that mistake again.

While he and Travis continued to talk about the case, she turned away and began opening the boxes, enjoying the way the scissors ripped through the tape, letting the sound drown out their conversation. As an investigator with the Colorado Bureau of Investigation, Brodie would no doubt bring a welcome extra pair of eyes to the hunt for the Ice Cold Killer. She needed to remember that he was here to help Travis and probably didn't have the least interest in her. So there was no need for her to feel awkward around him.

Brodie tapped her on the shoulder and held out her phone. "Travis didn't sound very happy to hear from me. Why is that, do you think?"

"You'll have to ask him." But she would make sure Travis didn't tell Brodie anything he didn't need to know. Best to leave the past in the past.

"I'm going to meet him in town and get caught up on this case," he said. "But I'm hoping to see more of you later."

Before she could think of an answer to this, he leaned forward and kissed her cheek. "It's great to see you again, Emily," he murmured, and she cursed the way her knees wobbled in response.

Then he strode from the room, the door shutting firmly behind him.

Emily groaned and snatched a pillow off the sofa. She hurled it at the door, half wishing Brodie was still standing there and she was aiming at his head. Brodie Langtry was the last person in the world she wanted to see right now. This next week with him was going to be her own version of hell.

Chapter Two

Brodie drove through a world so blindingly white it hurt even with sunglasses shading his eyes. Only the scarred trunks of aspen and the bottle-brush silhouettes of pine trees broke the expanse of glittering porcelain. If not for the walls of plowed snow on either side of the road, it would be difficult in places to distinguish the road from the surrounding fields. After five hours of similar landscape between here and Denver, Emily, in her crazy ruffled pink dress, had stood out like a bird of paradise, a welcome shock to the senses.

Shocking also was how much Travis's little sister had matured. She'd been pretty before—or maybe *cute* was the better word—vivacious and sweet and attractive in a lithe, youthful way. She had filled out since then, her curves more pronounced, her features sharpened into real beauty.

She seemed more serious, but then so was he. Life—and especially a life spent working in law enforcement—did that to people. He'd seen a dark side to people he couldn't forget. It was the kind of thing that left a mark. He couldn't say what had marked Emily, but he saw a new depth and gravity in her expression that hadn't been there before.

He had been such a rascal when they were together five years ago. He had thought Emily was just another fling. He had felt a little guilty about seducing one of his best friend's sisters, but she had been more than willing. And then he had fallen for her—hard. He hadn't been able to imagine a future without her, so he had laid his heart on the line and asked her to spend the rest of her life with him. And she had stomped his heart flat. The memory still hurt. He had offered her everything he had, but that hadn't been enough.

So yeah, that was in the past. He wasn't here to rehash any of it, though he hoped he was man enough to treat her with the respect and kindness she deserved. He owed that to her because she was Travis's sister, and because she had given him some good memories, even if things hadn't worked out.

And now there was this case—a serial killer in Eagle Mountain, of all places. Remote tourist towns weren't the usual hunting grounds for serial killers. They tended to favor big cities, where it was easy to hide and they had a wide choice of prey, or else they moved around a lot, making it tougher for law enforcement to find them. Yet this guy—this Ice Cold Killer—had targeted women in a limited population, during a time when the weather kept him trapped in a small geographic area.

Then again, maybe the killer had taken advantage of the road reopening today and was even now headed out of town.

Brodie steered his Toyota Tundra around an S-curve in the road and had to hit the brakes to avoid rear-ending a vehicle that was half-buried in the plowed snowbank on the right-hand side of the county road. Skid marks on the snow-packed surface of the road told the tale of the driver losing control while rounding the curve and sliding into the drift.

Brodie set his emergency brake, turned on his flashers and hurried out of his vehicle. The car in the snow was a white Jeep Wrangler with Colorado plates. Brodie couldn't see a driver from this angle. Maybe whoever this was had already flagged down another driver and was on the way into town. Boots crunching in the snow, Brodie climbed over a churned-up pile of ice and peered down into the driver's seat.

The woman didn't look like a woman anymore, sprawled across the seat, arms pinned beneath her, blood from the wound at her throat staining the front of her white fur coat. Brodie was reminded of going trapping with an uncle when he was a teenager. They'd come upon a trapped weasel in the snow, its winter-white coat splashed with crimson. Brodie hadn't had the stomach for trapping after that, and he hadn't thought of that moment in twenty years.

Taking a deep, steadying breath, he stepped away from the vehicle and marshaled his composure, then called Travis. "I'm on County Road Seven," he said. "On the way from the ranch into town. I pulled over to check on a car in a ditch. The driver is a woman, her throat's cut. I think we've got another victim."

BRODIE KNEW BETTER than to tell Travis that he looked ten years older since the two had last seen each other. Working a long case would do that to a man, and Travis was the kind who took things to heart more than most. Brodie was here to lift some of that burden. Not everyone liked the CBI interfering with local cases, but Travis had a small department and needed all the help he could get. "It's good to see you again," Brodie said, offering his hand.

Travis ignored the hand and focused on the vehicle in the ditch, avoiding Brodie's gaze. A chill settled somewhere in the pit of Brodie's stomach. So this really was going to be tougher than he had imagined. His old friend resented the way things had ended five years ago. They'd have to clear that up sooner or later, but for now, he'd take his cue from the sheriff and focus on the case.

"I called in the plate number," Brodie said as Travis approached the stranded Jeep. "It's registered to a Jonathan Radford."

Travis nodded. "I know the vehicle. It was stolen two days ago. It was driven by the killers."

"Killers? As in more than one?"

"We've learned the Ice Cold Killer isn't one man, but two. One of them, Tim Dawson, died last night, after kidnapping one of my deputies and her sister. The other—most likely Alex Woodruff—is still at large."

"And still killing." Brodie glanced toward the Jeep. "Most of that blood is still bright red. I think she wasn't killed that long ago."

Travis walked around the Jeep, studying it closely. "Before, Alex and Tim—the killers—always left the victims in their own vehicles."

"Except Fiona Winslow, who was killed at the scavenger hunt on your family's ranch." Brodie had familiarized himself with all the information Travis had sent to the CBI.

"They broke their pattern with Fiona because they were sending a message," Travis said. "Taunting me.

I think Alex is doing the same thing with this Jeep. He knows that we know it's the vehicle he was driving until recently."

"Do you think he's driving this woman's car now?" Brodie asked.

Travis shook his head. "That seems too obvious to me, but maybe, if he hasn't found another vehicle. He thinks he's smarter than we are, always one step ahead, but we know who he is now. It won't be as easy to hide. And it will be harder for him to kill alone, too. He's going to make mistakes. I can see it with this woman."

"What do you see?" Reading the case files Travis had emailed was no substitute for eyewitness experience.

"The woman's feet aren't bound. The others were. Maybe that's because he didn't have time, or without Tim's help he couldn't manage it." He moved closer to look into the car once more. "The collar of her fur coat is torn. I think she struggled and tried to fight him off. Maybe she marked him."

"The others didn't have time to put up a fight," Brodie said, recalling the case notes.

Travis opened the door and leaned into the car, being careful not to touch anything. With gloved hands, he felt gingerly around the edge of the seat and along the dash. When he withdrew and straightened, he held a small rectangle of card stock in his hand, the words *ICE COLD* printed across the front. "He's following his pattern of leaving the card," Brodie said.

"He doesn't want there to be any doubt about who's responsible," Travis said. He pulled out an evidence envelope and sealed the card inside. "It's another way to thumb his nose at us."

They turned at the sound of an approaching vehicle, or rather, a caravan of two sheriff's department SUVs and a black Jeep, traveling slowly up the snow-packed road. The vehicles parked on the opposite side of the road and two deputies and an older man bundled in a heavy coat got out.

"Hello, Gage," Brodie greeted one of the deputies, Travis's brother, Gage Walker.

"You're about the last person I expected to see here," Gage said. He seemed puzzled, but not unfriendly, and, unlike his brother, was willing to shake Brodie's hand. "Typical of CBI to show up when we have the case half-solved."

"Dwight Prentice." The second deputy, a tall, rangy blond, offered his hand and Brodie shook it.

"And this is Butch Collins, the county medical examiner." Travis introduced the older man, who nodded and moved on to the car. His face paled when he looked into the vehicle.

"Something wrong?" Travis asked, hurrying to the older man's side.

Collins shook his head. "I know her, that's all." He cleared his throat. "Lynn Wallace. She sings in the choir at my church."

"Do you know what kind of car she drives?" Brodie asked, joining them.

Collins stared at him, then back at the Jeep. "This isn't her car?"

"It was stolen from a local vacation home two days ago," Travis said. "We think the killer might have been driving it."

"I don't know what kind of car Lynn drove," Collins said. "Only that she was a lovely woman with a beautiful soprano voice. She didn't deserve this. But then, none of them did." He straightened his shoulders. "Are you ready for me to look at her?"

"Give us a few seconds to process the outside of the car, then you can have a look." Travis motioned to Gage and Dwight, who moved forward.

Travis indicated Brodie should follow him. "I need you to get to work on identifying Lynn Wallace's vehicle," he said. "I think Alex will ditch it as soon as he can, but he might not have had a chance yet. You can use my office."

"Tell me what you know about Alex," Brodie said.

"Alex Woodruff. A college student at the Colorado State University—or he was until recently. He doesn't have any priors, at least under that name, and that's the only name I've found for him."

"Emily goes to the Colorado State University, doesn't she?" Brodie asked. Knowing he was coming to Eagle Mountain, he'd checked her Facebook page. "Do they know each other?"

The lines around Travis's mouth tightened. "She says he participated in a research study she and her colleagues conducted, but they weren't friends, just acquaintances."

"What brought him to Eagle Mountain?"

"He and Tim supposedly came here to ice climb over their winter break and got stuck here when blizzards closed the highway. They were staying at an aunt's vacation cabin until recently."

"I'll get right on the search for the car," Brodie said. As he walked to his SUV, he considered the connection between Alex Woodruff and Emily Walker. His work investigating crimes had taught him to be skeptical of coincidence, but until he had further proof, he wasn't going to add to Travis's concerns by voicing the worry that now filled his mind. What if the thing that had brought Alex and Tim to Eagle Mountain wasn't ice climbing—but Emily?

Chapter Three

"Thank you, Professor. That would be so helpful. I'll review everything and be ready to discuss it when I see you next week after the wedding." Emily hung up the phone and mentally checked off one more item on her Tuesday to-do list. All her professors had agreed to excuse her for another week so that she could help with the preparations for Travis and Lacy's wedding. Though she could have made the six-hour drive back to Fort Collins to attend a few classes and try to catch up on all she had missed while stranded by the snow, the last thing she wanted was for the road to close again, forcing her to miss the wedding.

Instead, someone in her department had volunteered to make the drive out here to deliver files for Emily to review. She had protested that it was ridiculous to make such a long drive, but apparently more than one person had been eager for the excuse to get off campus for a while. The risk of getting stranded in Eagle Mountain if another storm system rolled in had only heightened the appeal.

She moved on to the next item on her list. She needed to check on her horse, Witchy. The mare had developed inflammation in one leg shortly after the first of the year and veterinarian Darcy Marsh had prescribed a course of treatment that appeared to be working, but Emily was supposed to exercise her lightly each day and check that there was no new swelling. Slipping on her barn coat—the same one she had worn as a teenager—she headed out the door and down the drive to the horse barn. Sunlight shimmered on the snow that covered everything like a starched white sheet. Every breath stung her nose, reminding her that temperatures hovered in the twenties. She still marveled that it could be so cold when the sun shone so brightly overhead, giving the air a clean, lemony light.

The barn's interior presented a sharp contrast to the outside world, its atmosphere warm from the breath of animals and smelling of a not-unpleasant mixture of molasses, hay and manure. A plaintive *meow!* greeted Emily, and a gray-striped cat trotted toward her, the cat's belly swollen with kittens soon to be born. "Aww, Tawny." Emily bent and gently stroked the cat, who started up a rumbling purr and leaned against Emily's legs. "It won't be long now, will it?" Emily crooned, feeling the kittens shift beneath her hand. She'd have to make sure Tawny had a warm, comfortable place to give birth.

She straightened and several of the family's horses poked their heads over the tops of their stalls. Witchy, in an end stall on the left-hand side, whinnied softly and stamped against the concrete floor of her stall.

Emily slipped into the stall and greeted Witchy, patting her neck, then bent to examine the bandaged front pastern. It no longer felt hot or swollen, though Darcy had recommended wrapping it for a few weeks longer to provide extra support. Emily breathed a sigh of relief. For a brief period during her childhood, she had considered studying to be a veterinarian, but had quickly ruled out any job that required dealing with animals' suffering.

"Are you contemplating climbing down out of your ivory tower and hiring on as the newest ranch hand?"

Emily froze as Brodie's oh-so-familiar teasing tone and velvety voice flowed around her like salted caramel—both sweet and biting. She was aware of her position, bent over with her backside facing the stall door, where she sensed him standing. She turned her head, and sure enough, Brodie had leaned over the top half of the stall door, grinning, the cat cradled in his arms.

With as much dignity as she could muster, she released her hold on the horse's leg and straightened. "Brodie, what are you doing here?" she asked.

He stroked the cat under the chin. Tawny closed her eyes and purred even louder. Emily had an uncomfortable memory of Brodie stroking *her*—eliciting a response not unlike that of the cat. "I was looking for you," he said. "Someone told me you're in charge of a bonfire and barbecue here Wednesday."

"Yes." She took a lead rope from a peg just outside the stall door and clipped it onto Witchy's halter. The mare regarded her with big gold-brown eyes like warm honey. "What about it?"

"I was hoping to wrangle an invite, since I'm staying on the ranch. It would be awkward if I felt the need to lock myself in my cabin for the evening."

She slid back the latch on the door and pushed it open, forcing Brodie to stand aside, then led the mare out. "I have to exercise Witchy," she said.

He gave the cat a last pat, then set her gently aside

and fell into step beside Emily, matching his long strides to her own shorter ones. "I didn't realize you were staying at the ranch," she said. He hadn't been at dinner last night, but then, neither had Travis. The two men had been working on the case. Frankly, she was shocked her parents had invited Brodie to stay. They certainly had no love lost for him, after what had happened between him and Emily.

"When the CBI agreed to send an investigator to help with the Ice Cold Killer case, Travis asked your parents if they could provide a place for the officer to stay. They were kind enough to offer up one of their guest cabins."

"Wouldn't it be more convenient for you in town?" she asked.

"There aren't any rooms in town," Brodie said. "They're all full of people stranded here by the road closure. I imagine that will change now that the avalanches have been cleared and it's safe to travel again, but in the meantime, your folks were gracious enough to let me stay." He fell silent, but she could feel his eyes on her, heating her neck and sending prickles of awareness along her arms. "Does it bother you, having me here?" he asked.

"Of course not."

She led Witchy out of the barn, along a fenced passage to a covered arena. Brodie moved forward to open the gate for her. "Are you going to ride her?" he asked.

Emily shook her head. "She's still recovering from an injury. But I need to walk her around the arena for a few laps."

"I'll walk with you." He didn't bother asking permission—men like Brodie didn't ask. He wasn't cruel or demanding or even particularly arrogant. He just accepted what people—women—had always given him—attention, time, sex. All he had to do was smile and flash those sea-blue eyes and most women would give him anything he wanted.

She had been like that, too, so she understood the magnetism of the man. But she wasn't that adoring girl anymore, and she knew to be wary. "Of course you can come to the bonfire," she said. "It's really no big deal."

She began leading the mare around the arena, watching the horse for any sign of pain or weakness, but very aware of the man beside her. "Tell me about Alex Woodruff," he said.

The question startled her, so much that she stumbled. She caught herself and continued on as if nothing had happened. "Why are you asking me about Alex?"

"I've been reviewing all the case notes. He was here, at the scavenger hunt the day Fiona Winslow was killed."

"Yes. He and his friend Tim were here. I invited them."

"Why did you do that?"

"I knew the road closure had stranded them here and I felt sorry for them, stuck in a small town where they didn't know many people. I figured the party would be something fun for them to do, and a way to meet some local people near their age." She cut her gaze over to him. "Why are you asking me about Alex?"

He did that annoying thing Travis sometimes did, answering a question with a question. "You knew Alex and Tim from the university?"

"I didn't really know them." She stopped and bent to run her hand down Witchy's leg, feeling for any warmth or swelling or sign of inflammation. "They both signed up as volunteers for research we were doing. Lots of students do. Most of the studies only pay five to ten dollars, but the work isn't hard and cash is cash to a broke student."

"What kind of research?" Brodie asked.

She straightened and looked him in the eye. She loved her work and could talk about it with almost anyone. If she talked long enough, maybe he'd get bored and leave. "I'm studying behavioral economics. It's sort of a melding of traditional psychology and economics. We look at how people make the buying decisions they make and why. Almost every choice has a price attached to it, and it can be interesting what motivates people to act one way versus another."

"How did Alex and Tim hear about your experiments?"

"We have flyers all over campus, and on social media." She shrugged. "They were both psychology majors, so I think the research appealed to them. I ran into Alex in a coffee shop on campus two days later and he had a lot of intelligent questions about what we were doing."

"Maybe he had studied so he'd have questions prepared so he could keep you talking," Brodie said. "Maybe he was flirting with you."

"Oh, please." She didn't hide her scorn for this idea. "He was not flirting. If anything, he was showing off."

One eyebrow rose a scant quarter inch—enough to make him look even cockier than usual. "Showing off is some men's idea of flirting."

"You would know about that, wouldn't you?"

His wicked grin sent a current of heat through her. "When you're good, it's not showing off," he said.

She wished she was the kind of woman who had a snappy comeback for a line like that, but it was taking all her concentration to avoid letting him see he was getting to her. So instead of continuing to flirt, she started forward with the horse once more and changed the subject. "Are you going to be able to help Travis catch the Ice Cold Killer?" she asked.

Brodie's expression sobered. Yes, nothing like a serial murderer to dampen the libido. "I'm going to do my best," he said. "We know who we're looking for now—we just have to find him."

She managed not to stumble this time, but she did turn to look at him. "You know who the killer is?"

He frowned. "Travis didn't tell you?"

"I haven't seen Travis in several days. He's either working or spending time with Lacy. He told me on the phone that one of the men he thought was involved is dead, but that there was another one he was after."

Brodie said nothing.

She stopped and faced him. "Tell me who it is," she said. "You know I won't go talking to the press."

"The man who died was Tim Dawson," Brodie said.

All the breath went out of her as this news registered. "Then the other man is Alex Woodruff." She grabbed his arm. "That's why you were asking me about him. But he and Tim left town when the road opened briefly a couple of weeks ago. Travis said so."

"They moved out of the cabin where they were staying, but now Travis believes they stayed in the area. If you have any idea where Alex might be hiding, or what he's likely to do next, you need to tell me." She released her hold on him and stepped back, the mare's warm bulk reassuring. If her suddenly weak legs gave out, she'd have the animal to grab on to. "I hardly know him," she said. "But a serial killer? Why would a smart, good-looking guy from a well-off family want to murder a bunch of women he doesn't even know?" And how could she have spent time with Alex and Tim and not seen that kind of evil in them?

"You're more likely to have an answer for that than I do," Brodie said. "You're conducting a lot of research on human behavior and motivation. Didn't you do one study on what motivates people to break rules or to cheat?"

"What did you do—run a background check on me? That's creepy."

"All I did was look at your public Facebook page," he said. "And there's nothing creepy about it. I knew I was coming here and I wanted to see how you were doing—as a friend. I guess you never did the same for me."

She couldn't keep color from flooding her cheeks. She had, in fact, perused Brodie's Facebook page more than once, as well as Googling his name for tidbits of information. Not because she still felt anything for him, simply because she was curious. "All right," she said. "As long as you're not being a creep."

"Such technical language from a psychologist."

"Behavioral economics is different," she said. "There's psychology involved, of course, but nothing that would give me insight into the mind of a serial killer."

"I think you're wrong," he said. "I think you probably can tell us things we don't know about Alex Woodruff. You've always been smart about people."

I wasn't smart about you. She bit her lip to hold back the words. "I'm sure the CBI has profilers who specialize in this kind of thing," she said.

"Yes, but they don't know Alex, and they don't know Eagle Mountain. You do."

She searched his face, trying to read his expression. He was focused on her in that intense way he had—a way that made her feel like she was the only person in the world he wanted to be with right this second. "What do you want from me?" she asked.

"I want you to think about Alex, and about this area, and see if you can come up with any ideas that might help us."

She shook her head. "I think you're grasping at straws. You need to consult a professional."

"We will. You're just another avenue for us to explore. You never know in a case like this what might be the key to a solution."

"Does Travis know you're asking me to help?"

"No, but I can't see why he'd object. I'm not asking you to do anything dangerous."

She nodded. "All right. I don't think it will do any good, but I'll think about it and see what I can come up with."

He clapped her on the shoulder. "Thanks. I knew I could count on you."

How had he known he could count on her? But she couldn't ask the question. He was already striding out of the arena, his boots making neat prints in the raked dirt.

Brodie had to know she would do anything to help

her brother. If Travis had asked her for help with the case, she wouldn't have hesitated. That she was less willing to cooperate with Brodie probably said more about her feelings for him than she cared to admit.

Never mind. She would try to come up with some ideas about Alex and—with her help or not—Travis and Brodie would catch him and put him in jail for a long time.

Then she could go back to her normal life, with no serial killers—and no former lovers—to unsettle her.

"YOUR SISTER HAS agreed to serve as a consultant on the case."

Travis was so even-keeled and unemotional that Brodie considered it a personal challenge to attempt to get a reaction from him. He'd scored a hit with this announcement.

Travis looked up from the file he'd been studying, eyes sparking with annoyance. "What could Emily possibly contribute to the case?" he asked.

Brodie moved out of the doorway where he'd been standing and dropped into one of the two chairs in front of Travis's desk. The small office was spartan in appearance, with only a laptop and an inch-high stack of papers on Travis's desk, and a few family photographs and citations on the walls. Brodie's own desk at CBI headquarters in Denver was crammed with so many books, files and photographs his coworkers had hinted that it might be a fire hazard. But hey, the clutter worked for him. "Emily knows Alex Woodruff and she's studied psychology," he said. "She can give us insights into his character and what he's likely to do next."

"She's an economics major—not a profiler."

"We'll still consult the CBI profiler," Brodie said. "But I think Emily will come to this with fresh eyes. Besides, she knows this county almost as well as you do. She might be able to give us some new ideas about places to look for him."

Travis shook his head. "He's probably left the county by now. The highway is open, and he has to know we're on his trail. A smart man would be halfway to Mexico by now."

"You and I both know criminals rarely behave the way most people would. Alex may be smart, but he's arrogant, too. He's been taunting you, leaving those business cards, killing a woman on your family ranch, going after one of your deputies. He still thinks he can beat you."

"Maybe." Travis fixed Brodie with a stare that had probably caused more than one felon to shake in his shoes. "This isn't some scheme you've come up with in order for you to spend more time with Emily, is it?" he asked. "Because I'm not going to stand by and let that happen again."

"Let what happen?" Brodie had a strong sense of déjà vu. He recalled another conversation with Travis that had begun like this, five years ago, when his friend—only a deputy then—had accused him of trying to seduce Emily.

"Emily really hurt when the two of you broke things off," Travis said. "It took a long time for her to get over you. I don't want her to have to go through that again."

Brodie bristled. "She's the one who ended it, not me."

"You must have had something to do with it."

Brodie ground his teeth together. He did not want to argue about this with Travis. "I didn't come here to get back together with your sister," he said. "I came to help with this case. I asked Emily to consult because I think she's another resource we can draw on."

Travis uncrossed his arms, and the tension around his mouth eased. "Fair enough. I won't rule out anything that might help us catch Alex Woodruff. Speaking of that, have you had any luck tracking down Lynn Wallace's car?"

"Not yet. She drove a white Volvo." Brodie opened his phone and read the license plate number from his notes. "Nothing flashy. Fairly common. Easy to hide."

"Right. I'll put my deputies on the lookout." He turned to a map pinned to the wall of his office. Pins showed the locations where each of the Ice Cold Killer's seven victims had been found. "Alex and Tim working together concentrated the murders in three areas," he said. "Christy O'Brien and Anita Allbritton were killed within Eagle Mountain town limits. Kelly Farrow and Michaela Underwood were both murdered in the area around Dixon Pass and the national forest service land near there. Fiona Winslow, Lauren Grenado and Lynn Wallace were all killed within a couple of miles of the Walking W ranch." Travis indicated a third grouping of pins on the map.

"Does that tell us anything about where Alex might be hiding now?" Brodie asked.

Travis pointed to a red pin on County Road Five. "We know Tim and Alex were staying at Tim's aunt's cabin, here, when the first three murders took place. They spent some time in a vacation home here." He indicated another pin. "And they may have been at this summer cabin in the national forest, here, for the other murders. Now—who knows?"

A tapping on the door frame interrupted them. Both men turned to see office manager Adelaide Kinkaid, a sixtysomething woman who wore what looked like red monkeys dangling from her earlobes, and a flowing red-and-purple tunic over black slacks. "We just got word that a fresh slide on Dixon Pass sent one vehicle over the edge and buried two others," she said. "Fortunately, they were able to dig everyone out pretty quickly, but the road is closed until they can clear up the mess."

Brodie groaned. "How many delivery trucks do you suppose got caught on the wrong side of this one?" he asked.

"Probably about as many as were able to leave town when the road opened," Adelaide said. "Everyone is just trading places."

"I'll take your word for it," Brodie said. "You do seem to know everything." He leaned toward her. "Are those monkey earrings?"

"Yes." She tapped one earring with a red-painted fingernail. "Do you like them?"

"Only you could pull off a look like that, Adelaide," Brodie said, grinning.

She swatted his shoulder. "You're the kind of man I always warned my daughters about."

"What kind is that?"

"Too smart and good-looking for your own good. The kind of man who's oblivious to the broken hearts he leaves behind."

"Adelaide, Brodie is here as a fellow law enforcement officer," Travis said. "He deserves our respect."

"I'm sure he's a sterling officer," Adelaide said. "And a fine man all around. Just not marriage material—which is probably okay with him." She grinned, then turned to Travis. "And speaking of marriages, don't you have a tux fitting to see to?"

Color rose in the sheriff's cheeks. "I don't need you to keep track of my schedule, Addie," he said. "Right now I have a case to work on."

"You always have a case to work on," Adelaide said. "You only have one wedding." She whirled and stalked away.

Brodie settled back in his chair once more. "Do you have a tux fitting?" he asked.

"I canceled it."

"Unless you're going to get married in your uniform, are you sure that's a good idea?"

Travis scowled at Brodie. "They have my measurements. They don't need me." His phone rang and he answered it. "Hello?"

He listened for a moment, then said, "I've got Brodie in the office. I'm going to put you on speaker." He punched the keypad. "All right. Say that again."

"I've got what looks like another victim of the Ice Cold Killer," Deputy Dwight Prentice said. "Taped up, throat cut, left in her car near the top of Dixon Pass. Only, she's still alive. The ambulance is on its way."

Travis was already standing. "So are we," he said.

Chapter Four

The woman—a once-pretty brunette, her skin bleached of color and her hair matted with blood—stared up at them, glassy-eyed, her lips moving, but no sound coming out. "You're safe now," Brodie said, leaning over her. "We're going to take care of you." He stepped back as the EMTs moved in to transfer the woman to a waiting gurney.

"We've already called for a helicopter," the older of the two paramedics said. "I think this is more than the clinic in Eagle Mountain can handle. They've agreed to meet us at the ball fields, where it's open enough for them to land."

Brodie's gaze shifted to the woman again. She had closed her eyes and her breath came in ragged gasps. He wanted to grab her hand and encourage her to hang on, but he needed to move out of the way and let the paramedics do their job.

Travis, who had been talking to Dwight and highway patrolman Ryder Stewart, motioned for Brodie to join them. "Her name is Denise Switcher," Ryder said. "We found her driver's license in the purse on the passenger floorboard, and the registration on the car matches. Her address is in Fort Collins."

"Did she say anything about what happened?" Brodie asked.

"I don't think she can talk," Dwight said. "One of the EMTs said the vocal chords may be damaged."

Brodie winced. "How is it she's still alive?"

"I don't know," Travis said. "But I hope she stays that way." He nodded to Dwight. "You must have come along right after it happened. Did you see anything or anyone who might have been Alex?"

"No." Dwight hooked his thumbs over his utility belt and stared toward the EMTs bent over the woman. "A trucker who was pulled over taking off his tire chains flagged me down and said he spotted a car on the side of the road near the top of the pass. He didn't see anyone in it, but thought maybe I'd want to check." Dwight pulled a notebook from inside his leather coat. "Gary Ellicott. He was delivering groceries to Eagle Mountain and somehow missed that the road had been closed again. When he got to the barricades, he had to back down a ways before he could turn around. He thinks about fifteen minutes had passed between the time he spotted the car and when he talked to me."

"I don't think she was lying there very long," Brodie said. "A wound like that bleeds fast." If much more time had passed, she would have bled to death.

"The road closed seventy-five minutes ago," Ryder said. "There was a lot of traffic up here and it took maybe half an hour to clear out. If the killer was cutting her throat then, someone would have seen."

"So this most likely happened between thirty and forty-five minutes ago," Brodie said.

"But he would have had to have stopped the car before the road closed," Travis said. "The car is on the southbound side of the road, headed toward town. That seems to indicate she was arriving, not leaving."

"We'll need to find out if she was staying in town," Brodie said. "Maybe she has family in Eagle Mountain, was leaving and, like the truck driver, had to turn around because of the barricade."

"If this is Alex's work and not a copycat, that means he didn't leave town," Travis said.

The paramedics shut the door of the ambulance and hurried to the cab. Siren wailing, they pulled away, headed back toward town. "Let's take a look," Travis said, and led the way to the car, a gray Nissan sedan with Colorado plates. It was parked up against a six-foot berm of plowed snow, so close it was impossible to open the passenger side door. The snow around the vehicle had been churned by the footsteps of the paramedics and cops, to the point that no one shoe impression was discernable. "I took photographs of the scene before I approached," Dwight said. "But I can tell you there weren't any footprints. If I had to guess, I'd say the killer used a rake or shovel to literally cover his tracks."

Brodie continued to study the roadside. "I don't see any other tire impressions," he said.

"He could have parked on the pavement," Ryder said.

"Or he could have been on foot," Travis said.

"It's four miles from town up a half-dozen switchbacks," Ryder said. "That's a long way to walk. Someone would have noticed."

"Not if he stayed behind the snow." Travis kicked steps into the snowbank and scrambled to the top and looked down. "There's a kind of path stomped out over here."

Brodie climbed up beside him and stared down at the narrow trail. "It might be an animal trail."

"It might be. Or it could be how Alex made his way up to this point without being seen. Then he stepped out in the road and flagged down Denise and pretended to be a stranded motorist."

"How did he know the driver was a woman by herself?" Brodie asked.

"He could have studied approaching traffic with binoculars."

The two men descended once more to the others beside the car. "Why would any woman stop for him, knowing there's a killer on the loose?" Dwight asked.

"She was from Fort Collins," Travis said. "I don't know how much press these murders have been getting over there. It wouldn't be front-page news or the top story on a newscast."

"He's right," Brodie said. "I've seen a few articles in the Denver papers, but not much. It would be easy to miss."

"Alex is a good-looking young man," Travis said. "Clean-cut, well dressed. If he presented himself as a stranded motorist, stuck in the cold far from town, most people would be sympathetic."

"Maybe he dressed as a woman, the way Tim did when they were working together," Dwight said. "People would be even more likely to stop for a woman."

"Alex and Tim were both amateur actors, right?" Brodie asked, trying to recall information from the reports he had read.

"Yeah," Ryder said. "And we know that, at least a

few times, Tim dressed as a woman who was trying to escape an abusive boyfriend or husband. He flagged down another woman and asked for help, then Alex moved in to attack. One woman was able to escape and described the scenario for us."

Travis pulled on a pair of gloves, then opened the driver's-side door. He leaned in and came out with a woman's purse—black leather with a gold clasp. He pulled out the wallet and scanned the ID, then flipped through the credit cards until he came to a slim white card with an embossed photograph of a smiling brunette—Denise Switcher. "Looks like she worked at Colorado State University," he said.

The hair rose on the back of Brodie's neck. "Emily's school," he said. He didn't like another connection to Emily in this case.

"Alex's school." Travis slid the card back into the wallet. "I wonder if he chose her because he recognized her."

"That might have made her more likely to stop to help him out," Dwight said.

Travis returned the wallet to the purse and rifled through the rest of the contents. Expression grim, he pulled out a white business card, the words *ICE COLD* in black ink printed on one side.

The card taunted them—a reminder that, yes, they knew who attacked Denise Switcher, but they weren't any closer to catching him than they had ever been.

They were still silently contemplating the card when Travis's phone rang. He listened for a moment, then ended the call. "That was one of the paramedics," he said. "Denise Switcher coded before Flight for Life arrived. She's dead."

Brodie silently cursed the waste of a young woman's life, as well as their best chance to learn more about Alex's methods and motives. He turned to walk back toward the sheriff's department vehicle, but drew up short as a red Jeep skidded to a stop inches in front of him. The driver's door flew open and Emily stumbled out. "Is it true? Did the killer really get Denise?" she demanded, looking wildly around.

Brodie hurried to her. She wore only leggings and a thin sweater and tennis shoes, and was already shivering in the biting cold. He shrugged out of his jacket. "What are you doing here?" he asked.

She waved off his attempts to put his jacket around her. "You have to tell me. That ambulance I passed—was it Denise? Does that mean she's still alive?"

Travis joined them. "Emily, you shouldn't be here," he said.

"I was in the Cake Walk Café, waiting. Then Tammy Patterson came in and said she heard from a source at the sheriff's department that the Ice Cold Killer had attacked another woman. I had the most awful feeling it was Denise." She bit her bottom lip, her eyes fixed on Travis, her expression pleading.

He put a hand on her shoulder. "It was Denise Switcher," he said. "But how did you know?"

"Tammy said the woman was from Fort Collins. I was hoping that was just a coincidence, but…" She buried her face against Travis's shoulder.

"Emily?" Brodie approached, his voice gentle. "What was Denise doing in Eagle Mountain?"

She raised her head and wiped away tears. "I'm sorry. I thought I said. She was coming to see me."

Brodie wore what Emily thought of as his cop face—grim determination and what felt like censure, as if he suspected her of withholding important information. She refused to give in to the temptation to cower against Travis, so she straightened and wiped the tears from her eyes.

Brodie, still scowling, thrust his jacket at her once more. "Put this on. You're freezing."

She would have liked nothing better than to refuse the offer, but the truth was, she was so cold she couldn't stop shaking. She'd been so upset she had left her own coat behind at the café. She mutely accepted his jacket and slipped into it, his warmth enveloping her, along with the scent of him, clean and masculine.

"Why was Denise coming to see you?" Travis asked.

"The lead on the research project I'm involved in had some files he wanted me to review," she said. "Denise volunteered to deliver them to me."

"She drove six hours to deliver files?" Brodie asked. "Why didn't they transmit them electronically? Or ask you to make the trip?"

"These are paper surveys students filled out," she said. "And the professor had already agreed I should stay here in Eagle Mountain until after the wedding." She hugged the coat more tightly around her. "Honestly, I don't think he would have bothered, except Denise wanted to come. She said it was a great excuse to get out of the office and spend at least one night in the mountains."

"The two of you were friends?" Travis asked.

She nodded, and bit the inside of her cheek to stave off the fresh wave of tears that threatened with that one change of verb tense—*were*. "She's the administrative assistant in the economics department and she and I really hit it off. I'd told her so much about Eagle Mountain and the ranch that she was anxious to see it." She swallowed hard. If Denise had stayed in Fort Collins, she'd be alive now.

"When did you talk to her last?" Travis asked.

"She called me when she stopped for gas in Gunnison, and we agreed to meet at the Cake Walk for lunch."

"What time was that?" Brodie asked.

"About ten thirty."

"Did Alex Woodruff know her?" Brodie asked.

Had Denise known her killer? Emily shuddered at the thought, then forced herself to focus on the question. "Maybe," she said. "Students can register online to participate in various research studies, but they can also come into the office and fill out the paperwork there. If Alex did that, he would have met Denise. And a couple of times she's helped check people in for studies."

"So there's a good chance he did know her," Brodie said.

"Yes." She glanced toward the gray Nissan. "What happened to her? I mean, I know she was killed, but why up here?"

"It's possible Alex posed as a stranded motorist in need of a ride," Travis said. "If your friend recognized him from school, do you think she would have stopped?"

Emily nodded. "Yes. Denise was always pitching in to help with fund-raisers or any extra work that needed to be done. She would have stopped to help someone, especially someone she knew." Again, she struggled for composure. "I'm sure she has family in Denver. Someone will have to tell them."

"I'll take care of that," Travis said.

She wanted to hug her brother. He had had to break the awful news to too many parents and spouses and siblings since the killings had begun. "Why is Alex doing this?" she asked.

"We're hoping you can give us some insight into that," Brodie said. "You might talk to some of the professors who knew him. We could call them, but they might be more inclined to open up to you. You're one of them."

"What is that supposed to mean?" she asked.

"You're an academic," he said. "You speak their language. I'm just a dumb cop."

Under other circumstances, she might have laughed. Brodie was anything but dumb. But there was nothing funny about what had happened here today. "I'll see what I can find out," she said. "But I'm not promising I can help you."

"We'd appreciate it if you'd try." Travis patted her shoulder. "I'm sorry about your friend, but I think you'd better go home now. There's nothing you can do here."

She nodded, and slipped off the jacket and held it out to Brodie. "You keep it," he said. "I can get it tonight."

"Don't be silly," she said. "I'm getting back in my warm car, so I don't need it." And she didn't want to give him an excuse for looking her up again later.

He took the jacket, then turned toward her Jeep, frowning. "You drove up here by yourself?" he said.

"Yes."

"You shouldn't be out driving by yourself," he said. "Alex Woodruff targets women who are in their cars alone."

"I'm not going to stop if he tries to flag me down," she said. "I'm not stupid."

"He knows that," Brodie said. "He would use some subterfuge. He's done it before."

"Brodie's right," Travis said. "From now on, when you have to come to town, take someone else with you. And don't pull over for anyone—no matter what."

She stared at them, fear tightening her throat and making it hard to breathe. Of course she knew there was a killer preying on women. But it was hard to believe she was really in danger. That was probably what those other women had thought, too. She nodded. "All right," she said. "I won't go out alone, and I'll be careful."

Brodie followed her to the Jeep and waited while she climbed in. "I know you think Travis and I are overreacting," he said. "But until this man is caught, you're not going to be truly safe."

"I know." She didn't like knowing it, but there was no use denying facts. For whatever reason, Alex Woodruff was targeting women who were alone—women in her age group. "I do take this very seriously," she said. Having a brother who was sheriff and another brother who was a deputy didn't make her immune from the danger.

Chapter Five

Emily couldn't shake a sense of guilt over Denise's death. She could have refused her friend's offer to bring the student surveys to her. She could have at least warned Denise to be careful, and made sure she knew about the serial killer who had been targeting women in the area. But she couldn't change the past, and guilt wouldn't bring Denise back to her. All Emily could do was to try to help Travis and his officers find Alex and stop him before he killed again.

With this in mind, she called the professor who had taught several of the undergrad psychology courses she had taken at the university. "It's always wonderful to hear from a former student," Professor Brandt said, after Emily had introduced herself. "Even if you did forsake psychology for economics."

"I still have one foot in the psychology camp," she said. "And I use things you taught me almost every day."

Professor Brandt laughed. "You must want a big favor indeed if you're ladling out flattery like that," he said. "What can I do for you?"

"I'm calling about an undergrad, a psychology major who participated in some research I'm conducting," she said. "I need to get in touch with him, but I'm not having any luck. I'm wondering if you know how to reach him. His name is Alex Woodruff."

"Yes, I have had Alex in several classes," the professor said. "He was enrolled in my experimental psychology course this semester, but my understanding is that he never reported for classes."

"Do you know why?" she asked. "Has he been in touch with you?"

"No. There are always a number of students who drop out each semester for various reasons."

"Do you have any idea where he might be? Did he mention moving or anything like that?"

"No. But then, I doubt he would have confided in me. He wasn't the type to seek out faculty for conversation."

"What type was he?" Emily asked. "What were your impressions of him?"

"He was intelligent, good-looking. A bit arrogant. The type of student who doesn't have to work very hard or put forth much effort to get good grades. If I had to describe him in one word, I'd say he was superficial."

"Superficial?" she repeated. "What do you mean?"

"He was chameleonlike, adjusting himself to his circumstances. He could play the part of the studious scholar or the popular jock, but I always had the impression they were all just roles for him. Watching him was like watching an actor in a play. I never had a sense that he ever really revealed anything about himself."

"Yes, I saw that, too," Emily said, a chill shuddering up her spine. When she had met Alex, he had played the role of the eager research participant, an average student earning a little pocket change, no different from the majority of other students who filled out her questionnaires. But chances were his fantasies of murdering women had been well formed by then. The literature she had read about serial killers pointed to their compulsions building from a young age.

"I do remember one time the subject of future professions came up in class, and Alex said he wanted to go into law enforcement. He specifically mentioned becoming a profiler."

Another shudder went through her. "Did that strike you as odd?" she asked.

"Not really. Television has made the profession glamorous. I always point out to students that they'll need experience in some other branch of psychology before they can make the leap to criminal profiling."

"Did Alex have any particular friends at the university?" she asked. "A girlfriend?"

"I don't know," the professor said. "Why your interest in Alex? If you're unable to follow up with him, you can always discard his responses from your research."

"It seems odd to me that such a promising student would suddenly drop out of school," she said, grappling for some plausible explanation for her interest. "I know it's none of my business, but someone must know something. I guess I hate leaving a mystery unsolved."

"Now you've got me curious," he said. "I tell you what—I'll ask around a little and see what I can find out. Is this a good number for you?"

"Yes. I'm staying with my parents for my brother's wedding this weekend. I appreciate anything you can find out."

"I'll talk to you soon, then."

She ended the call and stared out the window at the snow-covered landscape. What role was Alex playing today? Was he safe and warm in the home of an unsuspecting friend, or hunkered down in a cave or a remote cabin, preparing to kill again? Why hadn't she—or the other people who knew him—seen in him the capacity to murder? Was it because he hid that side of himself so well—or because as humans they shied away from admitting the possibility that such evil lay in someone who was, after all, so very much like themselves?

BRODIE HAD NEVER thought of Emily as a serious person. He had a fixed image of her as young, fun and carefree. But maybe that was only because they had been like that when they had been a couple five years before. Time and the job had made him more somber, and he could see that in her also. He stood in the doorway of the sunroom that evening, studying her as she sat on a love seat across the room: legs curled under her, head bent over a thick textbook, dark hair in a knot on top of her head, brows drawn together in concentration. Travis's words to him earlier still stung—had she really been so hurt by their breakup? It had been what she wanted, wasn't it—to be rid of a man she couldn't see herself with permanently?

She looked up from the book and noticed him. "How long have you been standing there?" she asked.

"Not long." He moved into the room and held out the stack of file folders he had tucked under his arm. "I retrieved these from Denise Switcher's car. I think they're the files you said she was bringing to you." The box the files had been packed in had been spattered with blood, so he had removed them. No need to remind Emily of the violent way her friend had died.

She hesitated, then reached up to take the folders. "Thank you."

When he didn't leave, but stood in front of her, hands tucked in the pockets of his jeans, she motioned to the love seat across from her. "Do you want to sit down?"

He sat. "Are you okay?" he asked.

"Why wouldn't I be okay?" She pulled a pencil from the back of her head and her hair tumbled down around her shoulders. He'd always wondered how women did that—styled their hair with a pencil or a chopstick or whatever was handy.

"It's hard, losing a friend to murder," he said.

She nodded. "It's worse knowing someone you knew killed her." She shifted, planting her feet on the floor. "Did you have something to eat? I think Rainey kept back some dinner for you and Travis."

"I'll get it in a minute."

He let the silence stretch. It was a good technique for getting people to open up. He used it in interrogating suspects—though he wasn't interrogating Emily, and he didn't suspect her of anything more than being uncomfortable around him. He'd like to change that.

"I talked to one of Alex's professors," she said after a moment. She glanced at him through a veil of dark lashes—a look that might have been coy but wasn't. "I wasn't sure if I should let on that he's a murder suspect, so I pretended I was doing follow-up for the research he participated in for our department. I told the professor I hadn't been able to get hold of him—which isn't a lie. He confirmed that Alex didn't return to classes this semester."

"We already knew that. Did you find out anything else?"

"I'm getting to that."

"Sorry. Go on."

She sat up straighter, prepared to give a report. He

imagined her in the classroom, making a presentation. She was probably a good teacher—well-spoken and direct. Pleasant to listen to, which probably wasn't a requirement, but he was sure it helped. He liked listening to her, and he liked sitting across from her like this, breathing in the faint floral scent of her soap and enjoying the way the light of the lamp beside her illuminated her skin. "Alex is studying psychology," she said. "So I asked the professor what kind of person he thought Alex was. He said he was superficial."

Brodie considered the word. An unusual choice. "What do you think he meant?"

"He said Alex struck him as someone playing a part. He knew how to act like a serious student or a popular friend, but the professor always had the sense that beneath the surface, there wasn't much there. Or maybe, that there was something darker there that Alex didn't want to show to anyone else."

"Did you ask the professor if he thought Alex was a sociopath?"

"No. And I don't think he'd make that kind of diagnosis on the basis of their relationship. It wouldn't be professional."

"I'm no psychologist, but I'd say a man who kills eight women in cold blood doesn't have normal emotions or reactions."

"I wouldn't disagree." She met his gaze and he felt the zing of attraction. However else they had both changed in the past five years, they hadn't lost this sense of physical connection. He had always believed the physical side of a relationship was the most superficial, based on hormones and basic drives. With Emily, even this felt different.

"Did the professor say anything else?" he asked, determined to keep things loose and professional. He had meant what he said to Travis about coming here to do a job, not to resume a relationship with Emily. After all, she had made it clear when she had refused his proposal that she didn't see him as the kind of man she wanted to spend her life with.

"Only that Alex was very intelligent, made good grades when he applied himself and had expressed an interest in going into law enforcement work," she said. "Specifically, he mentioned he wanted to be a criminal profiler."

Another surprise. "That's interesting. And a little unnerving. I hate to think law enforcement would be attractive to someone like that."

"I don't know—if you wanted to commit crimes, doing it as a cop, where you would be privy to all the information about the investigation, would allow you to stay one step ahead of the people looking for you. You might even be able to guide them to look in the wrong direction."

"Now I'm a little unnerved that you've put so much thought into this." He tried for a teasing tone, letting her know he wasn't serious.

"You asked me to get inside Alex's head." She shifted position on the sofa. "Though I have to admit, it's not the most comfortable place to be."

"Do you have any ideas where he might be hiding out, or what his next move might be?" Brodie asked.

"I'm a researcher, not a clairvoyant," she said. "But I am working on it. The case feels really personal now, with Denise's death. I mean, I knew a lot of the women he's killed, but this hits a little close to home."

He nodded, but said nothing, debating whether he should mention his concerns about a connection to her.

She must have sensed his hesitation. She leaned toward him, her gaze searching. "What aren't you telling me?" she asked.

"I don't want to alarm you."

"I'm already alarmed."

He blew out a breath. Maybe if he shared his theories, she'd help blow them out of the water. "I'm wondering if you might be on Alex's radar as a possible target," he said. "If, in fact, you're what brought him to Eagle Mountain to begin with."

"Why would you think that?"

"Maybe he fixated on you."

"He's killed eight other women and hasn't even threatened me."

"Maybe he's biding his time, waiting for the right opportunity."

She didn't look frightened—only skeptical. "And the other women were what—practice?"

"The first one might have been. Then he discovered he liked killing. Or maybe he's done this before, someplace else."

"I'm sure Travis has already thought of that," she said. "I don't think he found any like crimes."

"You're right. And Alex is young. His first murder may very well have been Kelly Farrow."

"I think it's just a coincidence that he ended up here," she said. "He came here to ice climb with his friend, they got stranded by the snow and he killed Kelly—maybe he'd always had a sick fantasy about killing a woman and he thought doing so in this out-of-the-way place, with a small sheriff's department, would be easier."

Brodie nodded. "And once he started, he felt compelled to continue."

"From what I've read, that's how it works with many serial killers—they're fulfilling an elaborate, engrossing fantasy."

Brodie hoped she wasn't part of that fantasy, but decided not to share that with her. He didn't want to frighten her—only make her more aware of possible danger. "I told Travis I'd asked you to help with the case," he said.

"What did he say about that?"

"He reluctantly agreed to let you help, but I don't think he was too happy about getting his little sister involved." Or about any possible involvement between Brodie and Emily.

"He and Gage both tend to be overprotective. I've learned to humor them and do what I want, anyway."

"They have a right to be concerned. I hope you took what we said this afternoon—about not going anywhere alone—seriously."

"I did."

"It applies to all the women here at the ranch, and all the women you know."

"We do talk about this, you know? I don't know any woman who goes anywhere by herself without being alert to her surroundings."

"When you live in a peaceful place like Eagle Mountain, I can see how it would be easy to get complacent."

"But I don't live in Eagle Mountain," she said. "I live in Fort Collins. And I have two brothers who are cops. I know more than I want to about how dangerous it can be out there."

"Point taken," he said. And maybe it was time to shift the conversation to something more mundane and less stressful. "How do you like living in the big city? It's a lot different from life here on the ranch."

"I love it," she said. "I really enjoy my work, and I like all the opportunities and conveniences of a bigger city."

Footsteps approached and they both turned toward the door as Travis entered. He stopped short. "Brodie, what are you doing here?"

"I dropped off the files from Denise Switcher's car," Brodie said. "The ones she was bringing to Emily."

"I could have brought them," Travis said. He was studying Brodie as if he was a perp he suspected of a crime.

"I'm sure Brodie didn't want to bother you with such a little errand," Emily said. She turned to Brodie. "Thanks again for bringing them to me."

"It's been a long day," Travis said. "I'm sure Brodie wants to get to his cabin."

Brodie resisted the urge to needle Travis by protesting that he wasn't tired in the least and had been enjoying his visit with Emily. But the sheriff looked in no mood for teasing. For whatever reason, Travis still harbored hard feelings about Brodie and Emily's breakup. At times, the sheriff seemed more upset with Brodie than Emily did. Brodie stood. "Travis is right," he said. "And I've kept you long enough."

"I enjoyed your visit," Emily said. Brodie wondered if she was saying so to goad her overprotective brother, but she sounded as if she meant it.

"Yeah, we'll have to do it again sometime." He didn't miss the dark look Travis sent him, but sauntered past the sheriff, head up. Brodie hadn't come here intending to renew his relationship with Emily. But if that did end up happening, maybe it wouldn't be such a bad thing.

As long as the sheriff didn't decide to run him out of town first.

Chapter Six

Reviewing the student surveys would have to wait until after Wednesday's barbecue and bonfire, the latest in a series of events at the ranch that Emily was hosting in an attempt to entertain friends and family trapped in town by the weather. Wednesday morning found Emily in the kitchen with Bette and Rainey, reviewing the menu for the evening. "Good plain food to help warm folks up in the cold," Rainey declared after describing the chili she would make and the kabobs Bette would assemble. "The kind of food I've been making all my life."

The ranch cook was an angular woman in her late forties or early fifties, who had reigned over the Walker kitchen for the past decade. Though she shooed Emily and her friends out of the kitchen whenever they invaded that sacred territory, she had also been known to spoil the youngest Walker sibling with homemade cookies and grilled pimento cheese sandwiches at every opportunity. Rainey's son's recent incarceration had subdued the cook a little, but she had also confided to Emily's mother that she felt less stressed, since at least now she knew her son was somewhere safe, and not causing trouble for anyone else.

"Everything will be delicious," Emily said, and handed the menu back to Bette. "And I definitely want to keep this simple. This close to the wedding, I don't want to burden either one of you."

"She's got this, and the wedding, taken care of," Rainey said.

"Rainey has been a big help with the reception preparations," Bette said, quick to praise the woman who, on her initial arrival at the ranch, had been her biggest foe.

Emily's cell phone rang. She fished it from the back pocket of her jeans and her heart sped up when she saw Professor Brandt's number. "I have to take this," she said, and hurried from the room.

Alone in the sunroom, she answered the call. "Hello, Professor."

"Hello, Emily. I asked around about Alex Woodruff and I found out a few things, though I don't know if they'll help you much."

Emily grabbed a notebook and pen from the table and sat on the sofa. "I'm all ears."

"This is an odd situation," he said. "And I'll admit, I'm curious now, too. Alex doesn't have any close friends that I could find, though he spent more time with Tim Dawson than anyone else. Do you know him?"

"Yes."

"Oddly enough, Tim failed to return to school also," the professor said. "I wasn't able to learn anything about him. When I contacted his family, they didn't want to talk to me about him. His father hung up on me."

Maybe the Dawsons didn't want to reveal that their

son had been killed while committing a crime, or that he was a suspect in a series of murders. Emily was pretty sure Travis had talked to Tim's parents, but she had no idea what had come of that conversation. "What about Alex's family?" she asked.

"He's apparently estranged from them, though he has a trust fund that pays for his schooling and living expenses, and from what I gather, anything else he wants."

"Oh." That explained how he was able to spend a month in Eagle Mountain with no worries about money.

"I have a name for you, of a young woman he apparently dated for a while. Grace Anders. She's a student here. You understand I can't give you her contact information."

"I understand." If she couldn't figure out how to get hold of Grace on her own, Brodie or Travis could help her.

"When you return to school, you shouldn't have much trouble finding her here on campus, if you want to talk to her."

"Okay, thank you. Anything else?"

"No, that's all. But do me a favor and let me know what you find out. Like I said, I'm curious now."

"I'll do that." Though if things went well, Professor Brandt would be able to read about Alex and his arrest for murder in the Denver papers.

She hung up the phone and stared at the name she had written on her pad. Grace Anders. She could give the name to Travis and have him or Gage or one of his officers contact the young woman. They were trained to elicit information from witnesses. But would Grace really confide in them? Wouldn't she be more likely to open up to another woman at the university, someone close to her own age?

She picked up her phone again and punched in the number for the sheriff's department. Adelaide answered, all crisp professionalism. "The sheriff is out at the moment," she said, after Emily identified herself.

"It's really you I want to talk to," Emily said. "I'm doing a little job for Travis and I need help finding a phone number for a friend of Alex Woodruff. Grace Anders, in Fort Collins."

"Travis did mention something about you helping with the case," Adelaide said. "He wasn't too happy about the idea, if I recall."

"I'm staying safe, just making a few phone calls for him," she said. "Can you find Grace Anders's number for me?"

"Hold on a minute."

Emily doodled in her notebook while she waited for Adelaide. She was coloring in circles around the word *trust fund* when the older woman came back on the line and rattled off a phone number. "Thanks, Adelaide," Emily said, and hung up before the office manager could question her further.

Before she could lose courage, Emily dialed the number Adelaide had given her. On the third ring a young woman answered. "If you're trying to sell something, I'm not interested," she said.

"I'm not selling anything, I promise," Emily said. "I'm calling about Alex Woodruff."

The silence on the other end of the line was so complete, Emily feared Grace had hung up. "What about him?" she asked after a minute.

"My name is Emily Walker. I'm a grad student at the university. Is this Grace Anders?"

"Why are you calling me? What has Alex done?"

Emily thought it was interesting that Grace assumed Alex had done something. Something wrong? "I understand you dated him at one time."

"Not for months. I haven't had anything to do with him for months and I'd just as soon keep it that way."

No love lost in her tone, Emily decided. "I'm trying to help a friend who had a rather unpleasant encounter with Alex," she said. That wasn't a complete lie—Denise was her friend, and Alex had killed her. Emily was trying to help find him and see that he was punished for the crime.

"Sorry about your friend," Grace said. "Alex is a creep."

"But you went out with him."

"Because I didn't know he was a creep at first," Grace said. "He was good-looking and he could be charming. We had a good time, at first."

"But something happened to change that?" Emily prompted.

"What did he do to your friend? I mean, did he steal money from her or something?"

"Did he steal money from you?"

"No. He had plenty of money of his own. I just wondered."

"He didn't steal from my friend." How much should Emily say? She wanted Grace to feel comfortable confiding in her, but she couldn't say anything that might jeopardize Travis's case against Alex.

"Did he assault her?" Grace blurted. "I mean, rape her or something?"

"Or something."

Grace swore. "I knew it. I should have said something before, but what would I have said?"

"Did Alex rape you?" Emily asked, as gently as possible.

"No! Nothing like that. It was just… I got really bad vibes from him."

"What kind of vibes?" Emily asked. "I know that's a really personal question, but it could really help."

Grace sighed dramatically. "We had sex a couple of times and it was fine, and then he wanted to do things different." She paused, then continued, "It feels so icky even talking about it, but he wanted to choke me."

Emily gasped. "Choke you?"

"Yeah, you know that autoerotic thing some people do where they choke themselves while they're getting off. It's supposed to give you some super orgasm or something, but it's crazy. People have died like that."

"But he didn't want to choke himself—he wanted to choke you."

"You get how creepy that is, right? I told him no way. I was really freaked out."

"How did he react when you refused him?"

"He got all huffy. He really pressured me, and that made me freak out even more."

"Because you had a really bad vibe."

"Yeah. I guess. It just seemed to me that it wasn't the sex he was so into, but the choking. I was worried he might like it so much he wouldn't stop. Is that what happened to your friend?"

"Something like that. You've been really helpful. If the police were to contact you about this, would you be willing to talk to them?"

"I guess. I'm sorry about your friend."

"Do you know of any other women he dated?" she asked.

"No. Like I said, I've stayed as far away from him as I could. Somebody told me he didn't come back to school this semester. I was relieved to hear it."

"Did Alex ever threaten you?" Emily asked.

"No. I just never felt comfortable around him after the choking thing came up."

"You were smart to turn him down. You have good instincts."

"Maybe I've had too much practice dating creeps. I just want to meet a good guy, you know?"

They said goodbye and Emily reviewed the conversation, organizing her thoughts to present to Travis. Maybe Alex had merely been interested in experimenting sexually, but her instincts told her Grace had read him correctly—he wasn't so much interested in the sexual experience as he was in choking a woman and knowing what that felt like.

He hadn't choked his victims, but maybe he had ruled out that method after being turned down by Grace. Or maybe he had intended her to be his first victim. He could murder her, and if anyone found out, he could claim she had died accidentally while they were experimenting. He might even have been able to get away with it.

Maybe he *had* gotten away with it. Maybe somewhere in Denver was a young woman who had died at Alex's hands, though he hadn't yet been charged with the crime.

With trembling hands, Emily punched in Travis's

number. "Are you calling to tell me you've decided to cancel the bonfire tonight?" he asked.

"No! Why would I do that?"

"I told Lacy I thought you should. I'm concerned Alex will try to repeat his performance at the scavenger hunt."

"Alex is not invited to this party."

"That might not stop him."

"It's too late to cancel the bonfire," she said, trying to quell her annoyance and not succeeding. "All the invitations have already gone out, and the ranch hands have been accumulating a mountain of scrap wood and brush that needs to be burned. Not to mention Rainey and Bette have been cooking party food for days. I'm certainly not going to tell them their extra work will be wasted."

"Which is pretty much what Lacy said. But she agreed that I could station a deputy and one of the ranch hands at the gate to check the ID of every person who enters against your guest list. So I'll need a copy of the list, first chance you get."

"All right." Part of her thought this was overkill, but the rest of her was grateful for this extra measure of safety.

"If you didn't call about the party, why did you call?" Travis asked.

"I talked to a woman Alex used to date," she said. "She said they broke up when he tried to talk her into letting him strangle her while they had sex."

"That's interesting. Does she have any idea where he is right now?"

"No. She hasn't had anything to do with him for a couple of months. But do you think this is how he started? What if some other woman agreed to his proposal and she died and everyone thought it was an accident, when really it was murder?"

"I haven't found anything like that in my research, but I can add it to his file."

"You could call someone in Fort Collins and Denver and try to find out."

"I could. But that won't help us discover where Alex is right now, and that's what I need to know if I'm going to stop him."

"No one in Fort Collins knows where he is," she said. "His professor told me he didn't have any friends but Tim, and he's estranged from his parents. Oh, and he has a big trust fund that pays for everything."

"Yes, we knew that."

"Then why did you even ask me to try to find out about him?"

"You've learned useful information," Travis said. "I don't want you to think I don't appreciate your help. But we really need to focus on where Alex might be hiding right now. Did he know anyone in Eagle Mountain before he arrived here? Does he have any relatives who live here? Did he ever complete an outdoor survival course or express an interest in winter camping?"

If Travis wanted her to ask questions like that, why hadn't he given her a list? "I don't think any of the people I talked to know those things," she said.

"Maybe no one does," Travis said. "But it's important to try everything we can think of. Is there anything else you need to tell me?"

"No."

"Then I have to go."

He ended the call and Emily frowned at her phone,

fighting frustration. She felt like she had learned something important about Alex, but Travis was right—it wasn't going to help them find him and stop him. The longer it took to locate him, the more time he had to attack and kill another woman.

She studied her notebook, hoping for inspiration that didn't come. "Emily?"

She turned toward the door, where Lacy stood. "The ranch hands brought up that load of hay bales you asked for," she said. "They want to know what to do with them."

"Sure thing." She jumped up, pushing aside thoughts of Alex for now. Time to distract everyone else—and herself—from the danger lurking just outside their doors.

FOR THE REST of the day, Emily focused on making sure the party was a success, and counted it a good sign that, though the highway was still closed due to multiple avalanches, no new snow had fallen in a couple of days, and clouds had receded to reveal a star-spangled night sky and an almost-full moon like a shining silver button overhead.

As an added bonus, though the wedding favors and guest book hadn't been delivered before the road closed again, Paige Riddell and her significant other, DEA agent Rob Allerton, had arrived and moved into the last empty guest cabin. Lacy was thrilled her friend had made it and had thanked Emily half a dozen times today for arranging the bonfire.

All the guests seemed happy to be here, gathering in a semicircle as Travis, Gage and Emily's father lit the bonfire, then cheering as it caught and blazed to life. Even before the blaze gave off much warmth, the sight of it made everyone more animated. The flames popped and crackled as they climbed the tower of old pallets, scrap wood and brush the ranch hands had spent days assembling; the sparks rose like glitter floating up into the black sky, the scent of wood smoke mingling with the aroma of barbecue and mulled cider.

From the fire, guests gravitated to a buffet set up under tents. Rainey and Bette had prepared big vats of chili, pans of corn bread and half a dozen different salads. They had also arranged skewers of kabobs and sausages guests could toast over the fire. Guests could opt for cookies for dessert, or create their own s'mores.

Seating was provided by hay bales draped in blankets and buffalo robes, shaped into surprisingly comfortable couches—some long enough for half a dozen people, others just the right size for cuddling for two. Two of the ranch hands played guitar and sang for the appreciative crowd. Alcoholic and nonalcoholic beverages added to the festivities.

"Travis tells me you're the genius behind all this." Brodie's voice, low and velvety, pulled Emily's attention from the music. She hoped the dim lighting hid the warm flush that seemed to engulf her body at his approach. He indicated the crowd around the bonfire. "It's a great party."

"Travis wanted to cancel the whole thing, but I had Lacy in my corner," she said.

"He doesn't look too upset right now." Brodie nodded toward the sheriff, who was slow dancing with Lacy on the edge of the firelight, her head on his shoulder, both dancers' eyes half-closed.

Emily couldn't help but smile at the lovebirds.

"They're so good together," she said. "It's great to see Travis so happy."

"Gage has found his match, too," Brodie said.

Emily shifted her attention from Travis to her other brother, who sat on a hay bale with his wife, Maya. The two were feeding each other toasted marshmallows and laughing, eyes shining as they gazed at one another. Emily sighed. "I never would have guessed my two brothers could be such romantics," she said.

"Are you kidding? When it comes to love, most men are completely at a woman's mercy. We may not always show our romantic side, but it's definitely there."

"I'm not talking about buying a woman flowers and delivering a convincing line to get her to go out with you—or to go to bed with you," Emily said.

"Neither am I. I think most people want to be in relationships, to love and be loved. Maybe one of the reasons a lot of men—and maybe women, too—have a hard time expressing that desire is that they know it's so important. They're really afraid of messing things up and getting it wrong."

Brodie was the last person in the world she had ever expected she'd have a philosophical conversation about love with. "Excuse me?" she asked. "Are you sure you're really Brodie Langtry? Mr. Heartbreaker?" He certainly hadn't hinted that he was so keen on that kind of deep relationship when the two of them had been together. And she still wasn't sure she believed he had never received the letter she had sent to him after their breakup. Pretending he'd never seen it made him look much better than if he had read the letter and decided to blow her off—which was what she had always believed.

"I grew up," he said, her own image shining back at her in the reflection of the firelight in his eyes. "We all do. Besides, I was never as shallow as you thought I was. When someone is important to me, I will do anything to protect them and support them."

Now he was getting really hard for her to believe. "Have you ever had a serious relationship with a woman in your life?" she asked.

"Once."

A sharp pain pinched her chest. Who was this woman who had captured his heart? And why did it hurt to hear about her? Emily wet her lips. "When was that?"

"A long time ago."

She thought she heard real regret in his voice, but why was she feeling sorry for him? "I don't believe you," she said. "You can have any woman you want. If you commit to one, you have to give up all the others, so why should you?"

"What about you?" he asked. "Are you serious about someone? Or have you ever been?"

He was the only man she'd made the mistake of falling for. "I'm getting my degree and focusing on my career. I don't have time for a relationship."

He moved closer, blocking the firelight, the sheepskin collar of his heavy leather coat brushing against the nylon of her down-filled parka. Layers of fabric separated them, yet she felt the contact, like current flowing through an electrical cord once it was plugged in. She couldn't make out his features in the darkness, but was sure he was watching her. "Now who's avoiding commitment?" he asked.

She told herself she should move away, but couldn't

make her feet obey the command. "I'm not avoiding anything," she said.

"Except me. You don't have to run from me, Emily. I would never hurt you."

Hurt wasn't always a matter of intent—maturity had taught her that, at least. This knowledge made it easier for her to forgive him, but she wasn't going to forget anytime soon how easily he had wounded her. She would have told anyone that she had gotten over him long ago, then he showed up here at the ranch and all the old feelings came surging back like the tide rushing in. No good would come of revisiting all that.

"I have to go check on the food," she said, finally forcing herself to take a step back, and then another.

He didn't come after her, just stood and watched her run away. Maybe he didn't pursue her because he didn't really want her, she told herself as she hurried toward the buffet table.

Or maybe he didn't chase her because he was so sure that if he bided his time, he could have her, anyway. That, on some level, she had never really stopped being his.

BRODIE LET EMILY walk away. Maybe what they both needed right now was space. He had never expected to be so drawn to her. He had thought he was over her years ago. He'd been angry and hurt when she turned down his marriage proposal, and had spent more than a few months nursing his hurt feelings and wounded pride.

And now that he was back in town, Emily's family acted as if he was the villain in the whole bad scene. Had Emily made up some story about him dumping her, instead of admitting that she'd turned him down? She didn't strike him as the type to lie about something like that, but as he had told her, they had both done a lot of growing up in the past five years.

He helped himself to a kabob from the buffet table and tried his hand grilling it over the fire. Gage, a skewered sausage in hand, joined him. Of the two brothers, Gage had been the friendliest since Brodie's return to Eagle Mountain. "How's it going?" Gage asked.

"Okay." Brodie glanced around to make sure no one could overhear. "I'm trying to figure out why your family is giving me the cold shoulder. I mean, they're all polite, but not exactly welcoming."

Gage slanted a look at him. "You dated Emily for a while, right?"

"Yes. Five years ago. And then we broke up. It happens. That doesn't make me the bad guy."

Gage rotated the sausage and moved it closer to the flames. "I was away at school when that all went down, so I don't know much about it," he said. "I do know when I asked about it when I came home for the holidays, everybody clammed up about it. I got the impression you dumped Emily and broke her heart. You were one of Travis's best friends, so I guess he saw it as some kind of betrayal."

"I asked your sister to marry me and she turned me down," Brodie said. "That's not exactly dumping her."

"Does Travis know that?"

"I'm sure he does. Emily didn't have any reason to lie about it."

Gage shook his head. "Then maybe you'd better ask Travis what's on his mind. You know him—he keeps his feelings to himself, most of the time."

"Maybe I will." But not tonight. Brodie looked across the fire to where Travis sat with Lacy in the golden glow of the fire, their heads together, whispering. The sheriff looked happier and more relaxed than he had since Brodie had arrived. Amazing what love could do for a person.

Someone shouting made him tense, and he turned to see Dwight helping Rob Allerton into the circle of firelight. Rob dropped onto a hay bale and pushed Dwight away, as Paige rushed to him. "What happened?" she asked, gingerly touching a darkening bruise on his forehead.

"I left my phone back in our cabin and decided to go get it so I could show someone some pictures I have on it," Rob said. "As I neared the ranch house, I noticed someone moving around by the cars. At first I thought it was someone leaving the party early, but as I drew nearer, the guy bolted and ran straight at me. He had a tire iron or a club or something like that in his hand." Rob touched the bruise and winced. "I guess I'm lucky he only struck me a glancing blow, but I fell, and by the time I got to my feet and went looking for him, he had vanished." He looked up and found Travis in the crowd gathered around him. "I think he did something to your sheriff's department SUV."

Brodie followed Travis, Gage and most of the rest of the guests over to the parking area in front of the house. Travis's SUV was parked in the shadows at the far end of a line of cars and trucks. The sheriff played the beam of a flashlight over the vehicle, coming to rest on the driver's-side door. Someone had spray-painted a message in foot-high, bright red letters: *ICE COLD.*

Chapter Seven

Emily dragged herself into the sheriff's department the next morning, the two cups of coffee she had forced down with breakfast having done little to put her in a better mood. She hadn't slept much after the party broke up last night—something she probably shared in common with everyone else in attendance at this meeting the sheriff had called. Most of the law enforcement personnel who gathered in the conference room had searched the ranch and surrounding area for Alex Woodruff late into the previous night. Once again, after leaving his blood-red taunt on Travis's SUV, he had disappeared into the darkness.

She took her place to Travis's left at the conference table, nodding in greeting at the others around the table and avoiding lingering too long when her gaze fell on Brodie. She had missed him at breakfast this morning. Her mother had mentioned that he'd left early with Travis. Though the two men hadn't been friendly since Brodie's arrival at the ranch, they did seem to work together well.

Her feelings for Brodie seemed to fluctuate between regret and relief. Regret that they couldn't pick up the easy exchange they had enjoyed Tuesday evening in the sunroom. Relief that she didn't have to revisit the tension between them beside the bonfire last night. Other people got through situations like this and were able to put the past behind them. She and Brodie would learn to do that, too.

Travis stood and everyone fell silent. "I think you all know my sister, Emily," he said. "She is acquainted with Alex Woodruff and is completing her master's degree in behavioral economics. I've asked her to sit in on some meetings, to help us try to get into Alex's mind in hopes of anticipating his next move."

"I pity you, being in that guy's mind," someone—she thought it might be Ryder Stewart—said from the other end of the table.

Travis ignored the comment and projected a map of Rayford County onto a wall screen. "As I believe all of you know, someone—we're operating on the assumption that it was Alex—vandalized my department SUV last night at my family's ranch during a party."

"How did he get by the security you had set up?" wildlife officer Nate Harris asked.

"He parked around a curve, out of sight of the guards," Travis said. "He approached the ranch house on foot, and circled around through the trees. We were able to trace his movements that far at first light."

"He must have run track." Rob Allerton had joined them this morning, the bruise on his forehead an angry purple, matching the half-moons under his eyes. "He raced out of there like a gazelle."

Travis projected a color photo of his SUV onto the wall screen. The large red letters stood out against the Rayford County Sheriff's logo. "He's always enjoyed taunting us. This seems to represent an acceleration of that."

"He knows we know who he is and he doesn't care," Ryder Stewart declared.

"He thinks he's better than all of us," Brodie said.

"We're looking for anywhere Alex might be hiding," Travis said. "We've ruled out the two sets of forest service summer cabins where we know he and Tim Dawson spent time before." He circled these sites in red on the image. "We know Alex and Tim used an unoccupied vacation home as a hideout previously, so we're working our way through unoccupied homes but we haven't hit anything there, either. We've also published Alex's picture in the paper, on posters around town and on all the social media outlets. We've alerted people to let us know if they spot him."

"If he's using someone's vacation home, the neighbors are bound to see him," Dwight said.

"Maybe he's using a disguise," Deputy Jamie Douglas said.

"Alex was in the drama club at the university," Emily said. "But I don't think he would hide in a place with a lot of people—not now when he knows you've identified him. He takes risks, but they're calculated risks." She had lain awake for a long time last night thinking about this, and searched for the right words to share her conclusions. "He knows you're looking for him, and he wants to be free to come and go as he pleases. That freedom is important to him—he has to be in charge, not allowing you to dictate his movements. Showing up at the ranch last night and vandalizing your vehicle is another way of asserting that freedom."

"He could have moved into an abandoned mine," Nate said from his seat beside Jamie. "There are plenty of those around."

Travis nodded. "We'll check those out."

"He could be in a cave," Dwight said.

"He could be," Travis said. "But remember—wherever he is has to be accessible by a road."

Emily leaned forward, trying to get a better look at the map. "What's that symbol on the map, near Dixon Pass?" she asked.

Travis studied the image, then rested the pointer on a stick figure facing downhill. "Do you mean this? I think it's the symbol for an old ski area."

"Dixon Downhill," Gage said. "I think it's been closed since the eighties. When they widened the highway in the nineties, they covered over the old access road into the place."

"I think part of the old ski lift is still there," Dwight said. "But I'm pretty sure they bulldozed all the buildings."

"Gage, you and Dwight check it out," Travis said. "See if there are any habitable buildings there where Alex might be holed up."

"I'd like to go with them," Brodie said.

"All right," Travis agreed. "Dwight, you and Nate can work on the mines." He gave out assignments to the others on the team.

"What would you like me to do?" Emily asked, as the others gathered up their paperwork and prepared to depart.

"You can go home and write up your thoughts on Alex," Travis said.

A report he would dutifully read, file away and consider his obligation to her met. Her brother might have agreed to let Brodie ask for her help, but that didn't mean he was going to let her get very involved. "I'd like to talk to Jamie," she said. "She spent time with Alex's partner, Tim, when the two kidnapped her and her sister."

"Her statement is in the file I gave you," Travis said.

"I want to talk to her," she said, with more force behind the words.

Travis gave her a hard look, but she looked him in the eye and didn't back down. "All right," he said. "Set it up with her."

"I'll see if she can meet me for lunch." She started to leave, but he stopped her.

"Emily?"

She turned toward him again. "Yes?"

"Alex Woodruff is very dangerous. Don't get any ideas about trying to get close to him on your own."

A shudder went through her. "Why would I want to get close to a man who's murdered eight women? Travis, do you really think I'm that stupid?"

"You're not stupid," he said. "But you tend to always think the best of people."

She wondered if he was talking about more than Alex now. Was he also warning her away from Brodie?

"I'll be careful," she said. "And I won't do anything foolish." Not when it came to either man.

TO REACH WHAT was left of the Dixon Downhill ski area, Brodie and Gage had to park at the barricades closing off the highway, strap on snowshoes and walk up the snow-covered pavement to a break in a concrete berm on the side of the road, where an old emergency access road lay buried under snow. Reflectors on trees defined the route. The two men followed the reflectors to a bench that was the remains of the road that had once led to the resort.

The resort itself had been situated in a valley below the pass, with lift-accessed skiing on both sides. "You can still see the cuts for the old ski runs from here." Gage pointed out the wide path cut through stands of tall spruce and fir.

"Is that the lift line there?" Brodie indicated a cable running through the trees to their right. A couple of rusting metal chairs dangled crookedly from the braided line.

"I think so. There's the lift shack, at the top."

The small building that housed the engine that ran the old rope-tow lift really was a shack, cobbled together from rough lumber and tin, a rusting pipe jutting from the roof that was probably the engine exhaust. Brodie took out a pair of binoculars and glassed the area. From this angle, at least, it didn't look as if anyone had been down there in a long time.

"They used old car motors to power some of these things," Gage said. "I'd like to get a look at this one."

"Does the lift still run?" Brodie asked.

"I don't think so," Gage said. "Though if a mechanic messed with it, he might be able to get it going again. Those old motors weren't that sophisticated, and it's been out of the weather."

Gage led the way as they descended into the valley. With no traffic on the closed highway above, and thick snow muffling their steps, the only sounds were the occasional click of the ski poles they were using against a chunk of ice, and their labored breathing on the ascent.

Brodie tried not to think of the mountain of snow on either side of them. "Did you check with the avalanche center before we came down here?" he asked.

"No," Gage said. "We probably should have, but I was too eager to get down here and see what we could see." He stopped and glanced up toward the highway. "We'll be all right as long as he doesn't try to climb up and disturb the snowpack up there."

Brodie hoped Gage was right. After ten minutes of walking, they were forced to stop, the old road completely blocked by a snowslide, the wall of snow rising ten feet over their heads. "I think it's safe to say no one has been down here in a while," Gage said. "This didn't just happen." Dirt and debris dusted the top of the slide, and the ends of tree branches jutting out of the snow were dry and brown.

"At least now we know no one has been here," Gage said.

"Is this road the only way in?" Brodie asked.

"In summer, it might be possible to climb down the rock face from the highway," Gage said. "Though I wouldn't want to try it." He shook his head. "Even if Alex could get here, there's no place for him to stay. That lift shack isn't going to offer much shelter. At this elevation nighttime temperatures would be brutal. And the only way in and out is to go up this road—which is blocked—or scramble straight up."

"Wherever he is, it's somewhere he can go with ease," Brodie said. "This isn't it."

Gage clapped him on the back. "Come on. Let's go back."

The trip up was slower going, in deep snow up a steep grade. "We should have thought to bring a snowmobile," Gage said when they paused halfway up to rest.

Brodie took a bottle of water from his pack and drank deeply. "And then if Alex had been down there, he would have heard us coming miles away."

"He's not down there." Gage looked around at the world of white. "I wish I knew where he is."

Brodie started to replace the water bottle in his pack when a loud report made him freeze. "What was that?" he asked.

"It sounded like a gunshot." Gage put a hand on his weapon.

"Not close," Brodie said. "Maybe someone target shooting?"

"It sounded like it's up on the highway," Gage said. "Maybe a blowout on one of the road machines?"

"Let's get out of here," Brodie said. They started walking again, but had gone only a few steps when an ominous rumble sent his heart into his throat. He took off running, even as a wave of snow and debris flowed down the slope toward them.

Chapter Eight

Emily arranged to meet Deputy Jamie Douglas for lunch at a new taco place on the south end of town. The former gas station had half a dozen tables inside, and a busy drive-up window. Jamie, her dark hair in a neat twist at the nape of her neck, waved to Emily from one of the tables. "Thanks for agreeing to talk to me," Emily said, joining the deputy at the table.

"Sure. What can I do for you?"

"Let's order lunch and I'll fill you in."

They ordered at a window at the back of the room, then collected their food and returned to the table. "Travis asked me to put together a kind of profile of Alex Woodruff," Emily said when they were situated. "Not as an official profiler, but because I knew him slightly from the university and he hoped I'd have some insights. You probably spent more time with his partner, Tim, than anyone else, so I thought you might have some thoughts I could add to my assessment."

Jamie spooned salsa over her tacos. "I never even met Alex," she said.

"I know. But I think more information about Tim would help me clarify some things about their relationship."

"Sure. I'll try. What do you need to know?"

"I read your report, so I know the facts about what happened when Tim and Alex kidnapped you, but I'm more interested in other behavioral things."

"Like what?"

"When you came to, you and your sister were alone in the cabin with Tim?"

"Yes."

"And he told you he was waiting for Alex to return?"

"That's right. Well, he never named him, but we knew his partner was Alex."

"Did you get the impression that Alex was the leader—that Tim was looking to him to make the decisions?"

"Yes. Tim got a phone call from his partner—from Alex—who apparently told him he had to kill us by himself. Tim didn't like this, so then they agreed that Tim would bring us to wherever Alex was waiting, and they would kill us together."

"Do you think the idea of the killings started with Alex, or was it Tim's idea?"

"Definitely Alex. Tim said the first killing freaked him out, but then he started to like it. Or, at least, he liked getting away with the crimes."

"Alex must have recognized a similar personality to his own," Emily said.

Jamie nodded. "I guess it's like they say—birds of a feather flock together."

"My understanding is that Tim acted as the decoy, dressed as a woman, while Alex came up out of the woods and attacked women?" Emily asked.

"Yes. And Tammy Patterson's description of her ordeal confirms that." Tammy was a reporter for the *Eagle Mountain Examiner* who had managed to get away from Alex and Tim after they waylaid her one snowy afternoon.

"I don't think the two were equal partners," Emily said. "Alex was dominant. He's the man who chose the targets, and probably the one who did the actual killing. Tim was his helper. I wonder if Tim would have eventually killed on his own, without Alex around to goad him into doing it."

"I don't know," Jamie said. "But I believe Tim was prepared to kill me and Donna on his own. At least, that's what he told Alex."

"How is your sister doing after this ordeal?" Emily asked. Donna was a pleasant young woman with developmental disabilities who worked at Eagle Mountain Grocery.

"She's doing good." Jamie's smile at the mention of her sister was gentle. "She had some nightmares, but Nate has moved in with us and that's helped. She gets along really great with him, and she says having him in the house at night makes her feel safer." She blushed. "He makes me feel safer, too."

Emily hadn't missed that Jamie had been sitting next to Nate Harris at the meeting this morning. "It's great that the two of you got together," she said.

Jamie rotated the small diamond solitaire on the third finger of her left hand. "We're going to be married in the spring and Donna is almost more excited than I am."

"Congratulations." Emily couldn't quite hide her surprise. The last she had heard, Jamie and Nate had only recently started dating. "You obviously don't believe in long engagements."

"We were high school sweethearts, you know,"

Jamie said. "We broke up when he went away to college. I thought it was because he was eager to be free of me and date other people. He thought he was doing me a favor, not leaving me tied down to a man who wasn't around. Anyway, I guess we needed that time apart to really appreciate each other."

Emily nodded. So Jamie and Nate weren't strangers who just got together. They had dated and split up before—like her and Brodie. Except the situation with Brodie was entirely different. The circumstances of their split, and everything that had happened afterward, made things so much more awkward between them now.

Jamie's radio crackled with words that were, to Emily, unintelligible, but Jamie set down the glass of tea she had been sipping and jumped to her feet, her face pale. "I have to go," she said.

"What is it?" Emily asked, as the alarm from the fire station down the street filled the air. "What's happened?"

"An avalanche on Dixon Pass," Jamie said, already moving toward the door. "Gage and Brodie may be caught in it!"

As the wave of white moved down the hill toward him, Brodie tried to think what he was supposed to do. He had taken a backcountry rescue course once, and he struggled to recall what the instructor had said.

Then the avalanche of snow was on him, hitting him with the force of a truck, sending him sprawling, struggling for breath. Instinct took over and he began swimming in the snow, fighting to reach the surface before it hardened around him like concrete.

He fought hard for each stroke, his thoughts a jumble of images—of Gage's startled face just before the snow hit, of his mother the last time he had seen her and finally of Emily.

Emily, the hardness gone out of her eyes when she looked at him, head tilted to look up at him, lips slightly parted in a silent invitation for a kiss…

Then he popped to the surface of the snowslide, like a surfer thrust forward by the momentum of a wave, gasping in the achingly cold air. A tree branch glanced off his shoulder with a painful blow, then a rock bounced off his head, making him cry out.

Wrenching his head around, he saw that he was on the very edge of the slide, which had probably saved him. He struggled his way out of the snow's grip, like a man floundering out of quicksand. "Gage!" he screamed, then louder, "Gage!"

Relief surged through him as a faint cry greeted him. He fought his way toward it, clawing at the snow with numbed and aching hands, repeatedly calling, then waiting for the response to guide him in the right direction. "Gage! Gage!"

At last he located the source of the cries, and dug into the snow, first with his hands, then with a tree branch. He uncovered Gage's leg, the familiar khaki uniform twisted around his calf, then he dug his way up to Gage's head. When he had cleared away enough snow, he helped Gage sit up. They slumped together in the snow, gasping for air. A thin line of blood trickled from a cut on Gage's forehead, eventually clotting in the cold.

"We need to get out of here," Gage said after many minutes.

"We need help," Brodie countered, and shifted to

reach his cell phone. The signal wasn't good, but it might be enough. He dialed 911 and said the words most likely to rush help their way without long explanations. "Officer needs assistance, top of Dixon Pass."

The phone slipped from his numb grasp and he watched with an air of detachment as it skidded down the slope. Gage struggled to extract his own phone, then stared at the shattered screen. "They'll find us," he said, and lay back on the snow and closed his eyes.

Brodie wanted to join his friend in lying down for a nap. Fatigue dragged at him like a concrete blanket. He couldn't remember when he'd been so exhausted. But the danger of freezing out here in the snow was real. "Wake up, Gage," he said, trying to put some force behind the words. "You don't want to survive an avalanche only to die of hypothermia."

"There are worse ways to go," Gage said. But he sat up and looked up the slope, to the scarred area that showed the path of the avalanche.

"What do you think set it off?" Brodie asked.

"I don't know. Maybe that sound we heard earlier. That engine backfiring."

"Or the gunshot." The more Brodie thought about that report, the more it sounded to him like a gunshot.

"Somebody target shooting in the national forest?" Gage suggested. "Sound carries funny in the canyons."

"Maybe," Brodie said. "But what if someone set off the snowslide deliberately?"

"Why would they do that?"

"Because they didn't like us taking a look at the old ski resort?"

"I don't know who would object. And you saw yourself—no one has been down there in weeks. Since before that older snowslide."

"Can we find out when that snowslide happened?" Brodie asked.

"Probably," Gage said. "Maybe. I don't really know." He tilted his head. "Does that sound like a siren to you?"

It did, and half an hour later a search-and-rescue team had descended and was helping them back up the slope. The SAR director had wanted to strap Brodie and Gage into Stokes baskets and winch them up the slope, but the two victims had persuaded him they were capable of standing and walking out under their own power, with only a little help from the SAR volunteers.

An hour after that, Brodie was in his guest cabin on the Walker ranch, fortified with a sandwich and coffee, fresh from a hot shower and contemplating a nap.

A knock on the door interrupted those plans, however. He glanced through the peephole, then jerked open the door. "Emily, what are you doing here?" he asked.

She moved past him into the room, her face pale against her dark hair. "I wanted to make sure you were all right," she said.

"I'm fine." He rolled his shoulders, testing the statement. "A little bruised and tired, but okay."

She touched his arm, and the purpling bruise where he had collided with a tree branch or boulder in his frantic effort to escape the snowslide. That light, silken touch against his bare skin sent a current of heat through him.

He moved toward her, drawn by the scent of her mingling in the lingering steam from his shower. Her eyes widened, as if she was only just now seeing him—all of him, naked except for a pair of jeans, his skin still damp, droplets lingering in the hair on his chest.

She jerked her gaze back to his bruised arm. "You should put something on this," she said, her voice husky.

"Would you do it for me?"

"All right."

He retreated to the bathroom and fetched the ointment from his first-aid kit. Did he imagine her hand trembled when he handed it to her? Her touch was steady enough as she smoothed the ointment on, so careful and caring, and so incredibly sensuous, as if she was caressing not only his wound, but the invisible hurts inside of him.

She capped the tube of ointment and raised her eyes to meet his. Time stopped in that moment, and he had the sensation of being in a dream as he slid his arm around her waist and she leaned into him, reaching up to rest her fingers against the side of his neck, rising on her toes to press her lips to his.

He had a memory of kissing her when she had been a girl, but she kissed like a woman now, sure and wanting, telling him what she desired without the need for words. When she pressed her body to his, he pulled her more tightly against him, and when she parted her lips, he met the thrust of her tongue with his own. He willingly drowned in that kiss, losing himself until he had to break free, gasping, his heart pounding.

She opened her eyes and stared up at him with a dreamy, dazed expression. Then her vision cleared, eyes opening wider. She let out a gasp and pulled away.

"I can't do this," she said, and fled, out of his arms and out the door before he had time to react.

He wanted to go after her but didn't. He lay back on the bed and stared up at the ceiling, marveling at the twisted turn his life had taken, bringing him back here, to this woman, after so long.

And wondering where it all might lead.

Chapter Nine

Emily read through the first of the surveys her professor had sent for her to review—then read through it again, nothing having registered on the first pass. Her head was too full of Brodie—of the pressure of his lips on hers, the strength of his arms around her, the taste of his kisses. For all she had been enthralled by him five years ago, she had never felt such passion back then. The Brodie she had faced in his cabin yesterday had been more serious, with a depth she hadn't recognized before. He was stronger—and far more dangerous to her peace.

At this point in her life, she thought she could have handled a merely physical fling with a fun, hot guy. But she could never think of Brodie as merely a fling. And she didn't know if she would ever be able to completely trust him with her feelings. Even five years before, as crazy as she was about him, she had never been able to fully believe that his feelings for her were more than superficial. She was another conquest, another victim of his charm. He hadn't acted particularly torn up when she had turned down his marriage proposal, and he hadn't made any effort to persuade her to change her mind.

Even if he hadn't received the letter she had sent to him later, if he had really loved her, wouldn't he have kept in touch? He could have used his friendship with Travis as an excuse to at least check on her. But he had simply vanished from her life. That knowledge didn't leave a good feeling behind, and it made getting involved with him again far too risky.

But she wasn't going to think about him now. She had work to do. Determined to focus, she started reading through the survey once more. She had just finished her read-through and was starting to make notes when her cell phone buzzed, startling her.

Half afraid it might be Brodie, she swiped open the screen, then sagged with relief when she read her brother's name. "Hi, Travis," she answered.

"There's someone here at the station I think you should talk to," he said.

"Who is it?"

"Ruth Schultz. She says she knows you."

Emily searched her memory for the name, but came up blank. "I don't think—"

"Hang on a minute… She says you knew her as Ruth Parmenter."

"Ruthie!" Emily smiled. They had been classmates in high school. "Why does she want to see me?"

"It has to do with the case. Could you come down and talk to her?"

Puzzled, but intrigued, Emily glanced at the folder full of surveys. Not exactly scintillating reading. And not all that pressing, either, not with a murderer on the loose. "Sure. Tell her I'll be there in half an hour."

Twenty-five minutes later, Adelaide looked up from her desk when Emily entered the sheriff's department.

"Mrs. Schultz is in interview room one." Adelaide pointed down the hall. "She said she can stay until twelve thirty. That's when her youngest gets out of half-day kindergarten."

"All right." Emily headed past the desk, intending to stop by Travis's office first to ask what exactly she was supposed to be talking about with Ruthie, but before she could reach the sheriff's door, Brodie stepped out and intercepted her. "Travis had to leave, so he asked me to sit in with you and Mrs. Schultz," he said.

Running into him this way, when she hadn't had time to prepare, unsettled her. She took a deep, steadying breath, but that was a mistake, since all it did was fill her head with the masculine scent of him—leather and starch and the herbal soap that had surrounded them last night. She stared over his left shoulder and managed to keep her voice steady. "What is this all about?"

"She says her younger sister, Renee, is missing."

Emily had a vague memory of a girl who had been three years behind her in school—a pretty, sandy-haired flirt who had been popular with the older boys, and thus, unpopular with the older girls. "How long has she been missing?"

"Four days. At first Mrs. Schultz thought she had left town when the road opened and got caught when the road closed again. But she hasn't answered any calls or texts and that's not like her."

"Maybe her phone lost its charge or broke," Emily said. "Or maybe she's somewhere she doesn't want her sister to know about."

Brodie frowned. "Maybe. But Mrs. Schultz is worried because she said Renee knew Alex. She went out with him at least once."

Emily sucked in her breath. "That is a frightening thought. But why does she want to talk to me?"

"Because you knew Renee, and you know Alex. Travis explained you were helping us put together a profile of Alex and he thought the information she had might help. But most of all, I think she's looking for some reassurance from you that her sister is all right."

"I don't think I can give her that," Emily said.

"Probably not. But maybe telling her story to a friendly face—someone who isn't a cop—may help her."

"Then of course I'll talk to her."

Emily remembered Ruthie Parmenter as an elfin figure with a mop of curly brown hair and freckles, a star on the school track team, president of the debate club and senior class president. She had talked about going to college on the East Coast, then taking off for Europe with a camera, maybe becoming a war correspondent or a travel journalist or something equally exciting and adventurous.

The woman who looked up when Emily and Brodie entered the interview room was still lithe and freckle-faced, though her hair had been straightened and pulled back from her face by a silver clip. She wore a tailored blouse and jeans, and an anxious expression. "Emily, it's so good to see you," she said, standing and leaning over the table to give Emily a hug. "You still look just the same. I'd have recognized you anywhere."

Emily wasn't so sure she would have recognized Ruthie. Her former classmate looked older and more careworn, though maybe that was only from worrying about her sister. She indicated Brodie. "This is Agent Brodie Langtry, with the Colorado Bureau of Investigation."

"Yes, Brodie and I have met." The smile she gave him held an extra warmth, and Emily inwardly recoiled at a sudden pinch of jealousy. Seriously? Was she going to turn into that kind of cliché?

"Why don't we have a seat?" she said, pulling out a chair.

They sat, Brodie at the end of the table and the two women facing each other. "Brodie said you haven't been able to get in touch with your sister," Emily began.

"Yes. Not since Monday afternoon, when the road opened again for what was it—less than a day? I wasn't worried at first. I assumed she'd gone to Junction to shop and maybe take in a movie. But when I called the next day and she didn't answer, I was a little concerned. And when she didn't come to dinner last night, I knew something was wrong. It was my son's birthday—he just turned six. Renee would never have missed Ian's birthday."

"Was your sister dating anyone in particular?"

"No." She waved her hand, as if brushing aside the suggestion. "You know Renee—she always liked men, but she was never ready to settle down with anyone. She hasn't changed in that respect."

"But she had dated Alex Woodruff?" Emily asked.

"Yes." The faint lines on either side of her mouth deepened. "When I saw his picture in the paper and read that he was a person of interest in the Ice Cold Killer murders, my legs gave out and I had to sit down. And I knew I had to contact the sheriff. In case..." She paused and swallowed, then forced out the next words. "In case he's the reason Renee is missing."

Emily reached across and took Ruthie's hand and squeezed it. She could only imagine how worried Ruthie must be, but she wasn't going to offer hollow words of comfort. "When did Renee last go out with Alex?" she asked.

"I'm not positive, but I think they only had the one date. I think she would have told me if there was more than one—that was back on New Year's Eve. She went with him to the Elks' New Year's dance. My husband and I met them there."

"Was that their first date?" Emily asked.

"Yeah. She told me she met him at Mo's Pub a couple of nights before. He and a friend were there, playing pool, and she thought he was cute, so she asked him to the dance."

"She asked him?" Brodie asked. "He didn't approach her?"

"Not the way she told it." Ruthie shrugged. "That was Renee—she liked calling the shots in a relationship and wasn't afraid to make the first move."

"What did you think of him?" Emily asked.

Ruthie made a face. "I didn't like him. He struck me as too full of himself, and a phony. I told Renee that, too, and she said they had a lot of fun, but she didn't think she'd go out with him again—he wasn't her type. To tell you the truth, it surprised me she went out with him that one time. She generally likes older men who are a little rougher around the edges, you know? Outdoorsmen and daredevils. Alex was close to her age, and far too smooth."

"Did Renee mention anything that might have

happened later that night, maybe when Alex took her home—anything that seemed off or upsetting?" Emily asked.

"No. Nothing like that. She just said he wasn't her type. My husband didn't like Alex, either. In fact, he and I left the dance early. I was afraid if Bob had one too many drinks he might end up punching Alex. Alex kept popping off like he was an authority on everything and I could tell it was getting to Bob."

"You married Bob Schultz?" Emily asked, picturing the rancher's son who had never really been part of their group.

Ruthie smiled, her expression softening. "Yeah. I came home for Christmas after my first semester at Brown and he and I met up at a skating party my church had organized for the youth. We just really hit it off. I ended up transferring to Junction to finish my degree and we got married my sophomore year. We have two kids—Ian is six and Sophia is five."

"Wow," Emily said, trying—and failing—to hide her surprise.

Ruthie laughed. "I know! I was going to save the world and have all these adventures. But marriage and motherhood and running our ranch is adventure enough for me."

"You sound really happy."

"That's because I am." Her expression sobered once more. "Except, of course, I'm worried about Renee."

"Now that we know she's missing, we'll be looking for her," Brodie said. "You gave Travis a description of her vehicle, right?"

Ruthie nodded. "She drives a silver RAV4. Travis said he would put out a bulletin to let law enforcement all over the state know to be on the lookout for her. Maybe they will find her in Junction with some new guy she met." She smiled, but the expression didn't reach her eyes. "That would be just like Renee."

Brodie rose, and the women stood also. "Thank you for talking to me," Emily said.

Ruthie reached out and gripped Emily's wrist. "Be honest with me. Do you think this guy went after Renee?"

"I don't know," Emily said. "He hasn't had a previous relationship with any of the other women he's killed—at least not as far as we know. And all of them have been found very shortly after they were killed—within minutes, even." She gently extricated herself from Ruthie's grasp. "But people aren't always predictable. All I can tell you is that this doesn't follow his pattern so far."

Ruthie nodded. "I know you can't make any promises, but I'm holding out hope that it's just a sick coincidence that she knew this man." She shuddered. "I can't believe we spent a whole evening with him. I thought he was a bit of a jerk, but I never in a million years would have pegged him as a killer."

"If we could do that, we could prevent crimes before they happened," Brodie said. "But we can't."

They walked with Ruthie to the front door, where she offered Emily another hug. "We'll have to get together after this is all over," Ruthie said. "I'd like you to meet my family."

"I'd like that, too," Emily said.

Brodie waited until Ruthie was gone before he spoke. "What do you think?" he asked.

Emily worried her lower lip between her teeth.

"Alex went out with Michaela Underwood, too," she said. "So we know he has used asking women out as a way to get to them."

"But he killed Michaela on that first date. Renee Parmenter went out with him at least once and lived to tell the tale."

"That was about a week before he and Tim killed Kelly Farrow and Christy O'Brien," Emily said. "Maybe Alex was still working on his plan, or maybe killing women was still a fantasy for him then."

"She didn't tell her sister about anything unusual happening on the date, but that doesn't mean nothing did," Brodie said. "She might not have wanted to worry her sister."

"If Renee was wary of Alex, she probably wouldn't have gone out with him again," Emily said.

"So you don't think he used a second date as a way to get to her so he could kill her?" Brodie asked.

"I don't know," Emily said. "Maybe he charmed her. Or she was physically attracted to him in spite of her misgivings. Attraction can make people do things they know they shouldn't."

Her eyes met his, hoping he'd get the message that what had happened between them in his cabin yesterday was not going to be repeated. Brodie wasn't a bad person—far from it. But she didn't like the way he made her feel so out of control and not in charge of her decisions.

His gaze slid away from hers. "I hope Alex didn't murder Renee Parmenter. But I can't say I've got a good feeling about this."

"No, I don't, either," she admitted.

"Have you come up with any ideas about where he might be hiding—or what he intends to do next?"

"No, I haven't."

He clapped her on the back. "Then you'd better get to work. I still think you can give us something useful if you put your mind to it."

"Because of course you're always right."

"I've got good instincts. And so do you, if you'd pay attention to them."

He strode away, leaving her to wonder at his words—and at the look that accompanied them. She and Brodie seemed to specialize in nonverbal communication and mixed messages. It was probably time they cleared the air between them, but coming right out and saying what she felt wasn't something she had had much practice at. Like most people, she liked to protect her feelings. She had allowed herself to be vulnerable to a man exactly once, and the ending made her unwilling to do so again.

Brodie had claimed a desk in the corner of the sheriff's department conference room that had been turned into a situation room. The faces of the victims of the Ice Cold Killer surrounded him as he worked, and the scant evidence collected in the case crowded a row of folding tables against one wall. He hunched over his laptop, scanning databases, trying to trace Renee Parmenter's movements since her disappearance.

Travis had asked Ruth to run a notice in the paper, asking anyone who had any knowledge of Renee's whereabouts to contact the sheriff's department, but that wouldn't appear until tomorrow. As it was, Renee had been missing four days. Brodie feared they might already be too late.

The door to the room opened and Travis entered. He scanned the room, his gaze lingering a moment on the faces of the dead before he shifted his attention to Brodie. "Are you coming up with anything?"

Brodie pushed his chair back from the table that served as his desk. "The report from the CBI profiler came in a few minutes ago," he said.

"And?" Travis asked.

Brodie turned back to the computer, found the file and opened it. "I forwarded the whole thing to you, but the gist of it is, she thinks now that Alex is working alone, and he knows we know his identity, that's increasing the pressure on him. He's likely to kill more often and perhaps take more risks. He's trying to relieve the pressure and attempting to prove to us and to himself that we can't stop him."

"We have to find him in order to stop him," Travis said. "Does the profiler have any idea where he's likely to be hiding?"

"She doesn't mention that," Brodie said. "I'm still hoping Emily will come up with some ideas."

Travis shook his head. "I don't think my sister can help us with this one. We're going to have to keep looking and hope we catch a break."

"I've been working on trying to track Renee Parmenter," Brodie said. "It looks like she bought gas here in town, charging it to her credit card, the afternoon she disappeared. After that, there's nothing."

"Maybe she ran into Alex at the gas station, or he flagged down her car on the side of the road and she stopped because she recognized him," Travis said. "He asked her to give him a lift and he killed her."

"And then what?" Brodie asked. "Did he hide her car with the body? He's never done that before."

Travis rubbed his chin. "Hiding her doesn't fit with what we know about him, either," he said. "Alex wants us to know he's killed these women—that he got away with another murder. He wants to rub it in our faces that we aren't even slowing him down."

"He and Tim kidnapped Jamie and her sister and planned to kill them later," Brodie said. "Maybe that's a new MO for him."

"They kidnapped Jamie's sister in order to lure Jamie to them," Travis said. "Tim told her they wanted to kill a deputy as a way of getting to me. Fortunately, she was able to fight off Tim until we got to her."

"If Alex did kidnap Renee, he'd have to keep her somewhere," Brodie said. "We should consider that when we're focusing on places he might be hiding."

The phone on Brodie's desk beeped. He picked it up and Adelaide said, "Is the sheriff in there with you?"

"Yes."

"I've got a caller on the line who wants to talk to him. They were pretty insistent that I had to put them through to Travis. They won't give a name and I can't tell if it's a man or a woman."

"You record the incoming calls, right?" Brodie asked.

"Of course."

"Travis is right here." Brodie hit the button to put the call on speaker and handed the handset to Travis.

"Hello? This is Sheriff Walker."

After a second's pause, a wavery voice came on

the line. "I saw that girl you're looking for. She was hitchhiking on Dixon Pass. That's a dangerous thing to do, hitchhiking."

Travis's eyes met Brodie's. He could tell the sheriff was thinking the same thing he was—how did the caller know about Renee when the story hadn't even come out yet in the paper? "Who is calling?" Travis asked. "When did you see this hitchhiker?"

"Oh, it was a couple of days ago." The man… woman…sounded frail and uncertain. "I just wanted you to know."

"Could you describe her for me, please?" Travis asked. "And tell me exactly where you saw her."

But the call had already ended. Brodie took the handset and replaced it. "I'll contact the phone company and see if they can tell us anything about who made the call," he said.

Travis nodded. "I'd bet my next paycheck they don't find anything," he said. "I don't think that was a random Good Samaritan."

"Me, either," Brodie agreed. "Alex Woodruff is used to acting. It might not be too difficult for him to disguise his voice."

"Yes. Maybe he's annoyed that we haven't found Renee's body yet and decided to give us a hint."

"Or maybe he's set a trap."

"Come on," Travis said. "Let's go up to Dixon Pass and find out."

Chapter Ten

On the way up to the pass, Travis called Gage and let him know where they were headed and why. "I don't want the whole department up there in case this is a false alarm," Travis told his brother. "And I also don't put it past Alex to do something like this to draw us away from town. Just be alert if you don't hear from us in twenty minutes or so."

"Will do," Gage said. "But if that was Alex calling to give you a clue as to where to find Renee's body, it was a pretty vague one. Where are you going to look?"

"I have some ideas."

They parked Travis's sheriff's department SUV, which still bore faint traces of Alex's graffiti on the driver's side, at the barricades two-thirds of the way up the pass. They walked the rest of the way, past two dump trucks waiting to carry away loads of snow and an idling front-end loader. Travis stopped at the post that indicated the turnoff to the former ski area, most of the old road now buried under the avalanche that had almost killed Brodie and Gage. "The highway crews were able to clear this section of road pretty quickly," he said. "Apparently, most of the snow that came down was below this point."

"I still wonder what set off the slide," Brodie said. "Gage and I thought we heard a gunshot right before it came down."

"The road crew swears they had nothing to do with it," Travis said. "They were on a break when the avalanche happened. They don't remember seeing anyone around the road who wasn't supposed to be here, either."

Brodie continued to stare down at the river of snow. Sometimes things happened for no discernable reason, but the investigator in him didn't easily accept that.

"Gage said you didn't see anything suspicious down there before the slide," Travis said.

"No. It didn't look like anyone had been around for a while. I didn't see anywhere Alex might have been hiding—though we weren't able to get down there to take a closer look at the buildings. But if we couldn't get down there, neither could Alex, so I'd rule him out."

"Let's find someone to talk to about Renee Parmenter." They set out walking again. When they rounded the next curve, they could see a wall of blinding white, easily fifteen feet high, obliterating the roadway. A massive rotary snowblower was slowly chewing its way through the wall, sending a great plume of snow into the canyon below.

A man in a hard hat, blaze-orange vest over his parka, approached. "What can I do for you officers?" he asked.

"We're looking for a missing woman," Travis said.

The man scratched his head under the hard hat. "We haven't seen any women around here."

"What about cars?" Brodie asked. "Do you ever come across cars buried under these avalanches?"

"Sometimes. But we usually know they're there going in because someone reports it. If there was a driver or passenger in the vehicle, emergency services would have already worked to dig them out, and they usually flag the car for us so we can work around it. Hitting one could wreck a plow, but our guys watch out. There are all kinds of hazards that come down with the slides—rocks, trees. Once we found a dead elk."

"You might want to keep an eye out for a car up here," Travis said.

"What makes you think your missing woman is up here?" the man asked.

"We got a call," Travis said. "She's been missing since Monday—before the slide."

The man nodded. "Okay. We'll keep our eyes open."

He walked away and Travis and Brodie stood for a few minutes longer, watching the steady progress of the blower, until Brodie's ears rang with the sounds of the machinery. "Let's get out of here!" he shouted to be heard above the din. The noise, the endless snow and the eeriness of a highway with no traffic were beginning to get to him. Or maybe he was just twitchy after almost being buried alive in an avalanche.

Back in Travis's SUV, the sheriff didn't immediately start the vehicle. "If Alex killed Renee Parmenter, I have to believe he chose her because she knew him and was inclined to trust him," he said. "He took advantage of their previous relationship."

"Same with Denise Switcher," Brodie said. "She knew him from the university, so was more likely to stop when he flagged her down. He doesn't have Tim to help him lure and subdue his victims, so he's searching for easier prey—women who are more inclined to trust him."

Travis turned to Brodie. "Who else does he know who might trust him?" he asked. "Answer that question and we might be able to figure out who his next victim will be."

"We could start by interviewing single women in town, find out who else he—or Tim—might have dated in the weeks they've been here," Brodie said.

"Emily mentioned a woman he dated in Fort Collins," Travis said. "She dropped him because he wanted to strangle her while they were having sex."

Brodie scowled. "Maybe he planned to keep on choking her until she was dead." The more he learned about Alex, the greater his urgency to stop him.

"I'll ask to dig a little deeper. Maybe he had another girlfriend who came here for a visit and we haven't heard about her yet." He started the SUV and pulled out to turn around. But before he could make the turn, the man in the hard hat and orange vest ran toward them, waving his arms. Travis stopped and rolled down his window. "What is it?" he asked.

The man stopped beside the SUV, hands on his knees, panting. "We…found something," he gasped. "A car. And there's a woman inside."

"POOR RUTH." EMILY'S first thought on hearing of Renee Parmenter's death was of her sister. Yes, Renee had suffered at the hands of a murderer, but Ruth had to live with the knowledge that the person she loved had been taken so brutally. "I guess there's no doubt Renee was murdered?"

"No," Travis said. "She was killed just like the others."

"Alex even left his Ice Cold calling card," Brodie said. He and Travis flanked Emily on the living room sofa. A fire crackled in the woodstove across from them and a pile of wedding gifts that had been delivered when the road reopened waited on a table against the wall. Everything looked so ordinary and peaceful, which made the news of Renee's murder all the more disorienting.

"Have you told Ruth yet?" Emily asked.

"No," Travis said. "I was on my way there after I talked to you."

"I want to go with you," she said. "Maybe it will make it a little easier on her if she has a friend there."

"I was hoping you'd say that," Travis said. He stood. "Let's go see Ruth. If we wait too long, she might hear about this from someone else, and we don't want that."

By the time Ruth answered Travis's knock, Emily could see she had prepared herself for the worst. Her gaze slid past Emily and fixed on Travis. "Have you found her?" she asked, her voice tight, as if she had to force the words out.

"May we come in?" he asked.

She stepped back to let them pass. The house was an older one, with nineties-era blond wood and brass fixtures, the room cluttered with toys and shoes and a pile of laundry on one end of the sofa. A large window looked out onto pastures and hayfields, now covered with snow. "The kids are in school and my husband is out checking fences," Ruth said as she led the way to the sofa. She moved a child's book off the sofa and picked up a pillow from the floor, then sat, holding the pillow in her lap. "Tell me what you've found. It can't be anything worse than I've already imagined."

Travis removed his hat and sat across from Ruth while Emily settled in next to her. "We found your sister's body at the top of Dixon Pass, in her car," Travis said. "She was murdered—probably by Alex Woodruff."

Ruth made a short, sharp sound and covered her mouth with her hand. Emily took her other hand and squeezed it. Ruth held on tightly and uncovered her mouth. "When?" she asked.

"The car was buried by the avalanche that closed the road on Tuesday morning," Travis said. "She was killed before then."

Ruth closed her eyes, visibly pulling herself together. "Is there someone you'd like me to call?" Emily asked. "Your husband, or a friend?"

"Bob will be in soon." She opened her eyes, which shone with unshed tears. "If you know who did this, why don't you arrest him and stop him?" she asked.

"When we find Alex, we'll arrest him," Travis said. "Do you have any idea where he might be hiding? That night you and your husband met him, did he say anything at all that might give us a clue?"

She shook her head. "I'm sorry. We talked about school and the dance and the weather—just ordinary small talk among people who didn't know each other well."

"And you're sure Renee never mentioned seeing or talking to him after that night?" Travis asked.

"No. I really don't think she heard from him or saw him after that one date," Ruth said.

"You said you didn't like him," Travis said. "Maybe knowing that, she decided not to talk about him."

"Renee wasn't like that," Ruth said. "If she liked

someone and I didn't, she would have made a point of mentioning him, just to give me a hard time." She shook her head. "She was really definite about not wanting to see him again. If he had called and asked her out again, she would have been on the phone to me as soon as she hung up with him." Her breath caught, and she swallowed, then added, her voice fainter, "That's how we were. We talked about everything."

"I'm very sorry for your loss," Travis said. He stood, hat in hand. "Once the medical examiner has completed his autopsy, we'll release the body to the funeral home of your choice. Call my office if you have any questions."

Ruth stood and walked with them to the door. "Are you sure you don't want me to stay until your husband gets here?" Emily asked.

"I'll be okay." She took a shuddering breath. "I do better with this kind of stuff on my own—but thank you."

Emily squeezed her arm. "Call me if you need anything. Or if you just want to talk."

Ruth nodded, then looked at Travis again. "You'll find him and stop him, won't you?" she asked, the words more plea than query.

"Yes," he said.

He and Emily didn't say anything until they were almost back to the sheriff's department. "Denise was killed the same day," Emily said. "Right before the avalanche. And her car was found at the top of the pass."

"The first two murders—Kelly Farrow and Christy O'Brien—happened within hours of each other," Travis said.

"I think he gets a charge out of getting away with not one, but two killings," Emily said.

"The profiler from the Colorado Bureau of Investigation said he's feeling more pressure from us now that we know his identity," Travis said. "She believes he'll continue to kill, as a way to relieve the pressure."

Emily nodded. "Yes, that sounds right. And he wants to prove that he can still get away with the crimes—that you'll never catch him."

"He's by himself," Travis said. "Wherever he's hiding can't be that comfortable. We're doing everything we can to alert other people that he's dangerous, so he can't move safely around town, or rely on others for help. He's going to run out of victims he can fool also. We're going to run him to ground."

"I've been thinking," Emily said. "Maybe I can help you find him."

"Have you thought of someplace he might be hiding?"

"No. But he knows me. Maybe I could lure him out of hiding by agreeing to meet him."

"No." Travis didn't look at her, but the muscles along his jaw tightened.

"I'm serious," she said. Her brother wasn't the only stubborn member of this family. "I've lost too many friends to this man. I'll do whatever I can to stop him." Alex was a killer, but she knew him. Maybe she could get to him when no one else could.

Chapter Eleven

"Over my dead body."

So what if it was a cliché? Brodie thought, as soon as he had uttered those words. Travis's announcement that Emily wanted to try to lure Alex to her had prompted a visceral reaction that went beyond coherent speech. The thought of her anywhere near that monster made his blood freeze.

"I already told her the idea was out of the question," Travis said.

"It's a stupid idea." Brodie dropped into the chair across from Travis's desk at the sheriff's department, not sure if his legs were steady enough yet for him to remain standing. "What makes her think he'd come anywhere near her?"

"She fits the profile of the other women he's murdered," Travis said. "Alex knows her. And she's my sister. He's made it clear he enjoys getting back at me and my department—it's why he went after Jamie."

"How can you even look at this logically?" Brodie groused. "She's your sister."

"I made it clear it wasn't going to happen," he said.

"We don't even know where he is," Brodie said.

"What was she going to do—put an ad in the paper asking him to meet her? He'd see that as a trap right away."

"Maybe. Or maybe he'd be too tempted by the chance to get at her."

Brodie glared at the sheriff. "You've actually considered this, haven't you? You've run all the possibilities through your head."

Travis shifted in his chair. "It's not going to happen," he said again. "But if anyone is to blame for her coming up with the idea, it's you."

"Me?"

"You're the one who asked her to help with the case. You gave her the idea that she knows Alex better than anyone, and that her insight could help."

"Insight. Her thoughts. I never meant for her to put her life on the line—or anything close to it."

"I know. And I know she really wants to help. But this isn't the way to do it."

Brodie slid down farther in his chair. "I think this case is getting to us all."

Deputy Dwight Prentice stopped in the doorway to the office. "Abel Crutchfield just called in with a tip we ought to check out," he said.

"Who is Abel Crutchfield?" Brodie asked.

"He's a retired guy, spends a lot of time ice fishing in the area," Travis said. "He was the first one to report a blonde woman hanging around near where Michaela Underwood was murdered. That woman turned out to be Tim Dawson in disguise."

Brodie nodded and sat up straighter. "What's the tip?"

"He says he saw smoke coming from some caves over by Eagle Creek," Dwight said. "Like someone was camping up there. He figured we might want to check it out."

"Take Brodie over there with you and have a look," Travis said. "But call for backup if it looks like anyone is up there."

"Right." Brodie rose. "Much as I'd like to get hold of this guy, better not try to do it by ourselves."

"We should be able to get a good look from across the way," Dwight said. "Enough to see if it's worth going in. Maybe Abel just saw snow blowing off trees and mistook it for smoke."

The drive to Eagle Creek took twenty minutes, most of it on narrow, snow-packed forest service roads. "It doesn't look as if anyone lives out here," Brodie said, staring out at the landscape of snowy woodland.

"They don't," Dwight said. "This is all forest service land. A few snowmobilers or cross-country skiers use the road, and ice fishermen like Abel."

"Sounds like a good place for someone to hide out if he didn't want to be seen," Brodie said.

The caves themselves sat above the river in a limestone formation, centuries of dripping water having hollowed out the rock to form the openings. "Most of these caves are pretty shallow," Dwight said as he led the way through the snow along the riverbank. "There are only a couple that are deep enough to provide any real shelter."

"Deep enough to live in?" Brodie asked.

"Maybe. It wouldn't be very comfortable. You'd have to have a fire to keep from freezing to death, and there would be a lot of smoke and dampness. Not to mention bats, bugs and wild animals."

"It doesn't sound like Alex Woodruff's kind of

place," Brodie said. "He struck me as someone who likes his creature comforts."

"Yeah, but he's desperate now. He can't be as choosy."

They halted on a bench of land across the river from the largest opening. Dwight dug out a pair of binoculars and trained them on the cave. "The snow around the opening is churned up," he said. "Someone—or something—has been going in and out of there." He shifted the binoculars. "And there's a definite path leading up there."

Brodie sniffed the air. "I can smell smoke—like a campfire."

Dwight handed him the binoculars. "There's no smoke coming from there right now."

Brodie focused the glasses on the cave opening. It was impossible to see into the dark space, but there was definitely no movement at the entrance. He returned the binoculars to Dwight. "What do you think we should do now?"

"I'd like to get a little closer before we call in the cavalry," Dwight said. "We can approach from below and anyone inside wouldn't be able to see us until we were almost on him."

"Sounds good to me."

It took twenty minutes to retrace their steps along the river, negotiating over icy rock and snow-covered deadfall. They had to walk farther downstream to find a place to cross—a bridge of felled trees that required stepping carefully and balancing like a tightrope walker. But when they reached the other side, they found the worn path through the snow that they had glimpsed from the other side.

Weapons drawn, they moved cautiously up the path. The rushing water tumbling over rocks and downed trees drowned out all other sound. Dwight took the lead, while Brodie covered him, staying several yards behind. They reached a series of rock steps that led up to the cave and halted. "Let me go up first, while you stay down here," Dwight whispered. "I should be able to get right up on the entrance without being seen. You come up after me and we'll flank the entrance and demand whoever is in there to come out. If we don't get an answer, we'll shine a light in, maybe try to draw his fire."

Brodie agreed and Dwight started up, keeping close to the cliff side, placing each step carefully, the rush of the water below drowning out his approach. When he was safely up the steps and stationed on the left side of the cave entrance, he motioned for Brodie to follow.

Brodie moved up more quickly and took up a position on the opposite side of the cave entrance. "Is anyone in there?" Dwight called.

The words bounced off the canyon walls and echoed back at them, but no sound came from the cave.

"This is the Rayford County Sheriff's Department!" Dwight called. "You need to come out with your hands up!"

No answer or movement. Dwight unsnapped his flashlight from his utility belt and trained the powerful beam into the cave entrance. A rock fire ring sat about two feet inside, full of dark ash and a couple of pieces of charred wood. Brodie stooped, picked up a rock and tossed it inside the cave. It bounced off the stone floor and rolled toward the back, then all was silent again.

Dwight's eyes met Brodie's. He jerked his head toward the cave and indicated he was going in. Brodie nodded. Instincts could be wrong, but it didn't feel to him as if anyone was in there. Dwight swung the flashlight in ahead of him, then entered the cave, staying close to the wall. He had to duck to enter. Weapon ready, Brodie watched him disappear from sight.

"Come on in!" Dwight called a few seconds later. "There's no one in here."

Brodie unhooked his own flashlight and followed Dwight into the cave. He swept the light over the mostly empty space, coming to rest on a pile of garbage in the corner—tin cans, beer bottles and food wrappers. He moved closer to the fire. "Someone was here for a while," he said. "And not that long ago."

"The ashes in the firepit are still warm." Dwight crouched beside the rock ring and held his hand over the charred wood.

Brodie holstered his gun and played the flashlight over the scuffed dirt on the floor of the cave. The space was maybe ten feet deep and eight feet wide, tall enough to stand up in, but barely, with a ceiling of smoke-blackened rock and a dirt floor. It smelled of smoke, stale food and animal droppings. "Not exactly the Ritz," he said.

"No one would be camping here in the middle of winter unless he had to," Dwight said. "It has to be Alex."

Brodie trained his light on the garbage pile again. "He's buying food somewhere." He nudged a beer bottle with his toe. "Lots of craft beer, chips and canned pasta."

"That sounds like a college guy's diet," Dwight said.

"If he's shopping, someone in Eagle Mountain must

have seen him," Brodie said. "Why haven't they reported him to the sheriff's department?"

"He could be breaking into summer cabins," Dwight said. "Or shopping at the grocery store wearing a disguise."

"If he was here this morning, it doesn't look as if he intends to return," Brodie said. "There's no sleeping bag, no stash of food—not even any firewood."

"We'll watch the place for a couple of days, see if he comes back," Dwight said. "But I agree—it looks like he's cleared out. Maybe he saw Abel looking up this way and decided to leave."

"There's not much here, but we'd better look through it, see if we can find anything significant," Brodie said. He smoothed on a pair of gloves and began sifting through the garbage, while Dwight examined the firepit. He combed through half a dozen beer bottles, two empty ravioli cans, several candy bar wrappers and two chip bags, but found nothing that told them where Alex might be now. They took photographs and bagged everything as evidence. They might be able to get DNA off the beer bottles that would prove Alex was the person who had hidden in this cave, but Brodie didn't see how that would be useful in their case against him.

"I may have found something," Dwight said. He used a pen to lift something from the ashes and held it aloft. Brodie recognized the coiled binding of a pocket-size notebook. "The cover is gone, and the edge of the pages are charred, but most of it's intact," Dwight said. He spread the notebook on the ground and Brodie joined him in leaning over it. Dwight flipped through the pages, which appeared to contain everything from grocery lists—*chips, lunch meat, cookies, soda, razor*—to cryptic numbers and calculations. Most of the pages were blank.

"We'll have to go through this at the office and see if there's anything significant," Dwight said. He reached into his coat and pulled out a plastic evidence bag.

Brodie continued to flip through the pages. He found what looked like phone numbers, notes on what might have been climbing routes, then stopped on a page that was simply a column of letters—*KF, CO, FW, LG, AA, MU, TP, DD, JD, LW, RP, DS, EW.*

"What have you got there?" Dwight asked. "Are they some kind of abbreviations? For what?"

Brodie repeated the letters under his breath, then stopped in mid-syllable as the realization of what they represented hit him. "They're initials," he said. "Of all the women he's killed."

"Kelly Farrow, Christy O'Brien, Fiona Winslow, Lauren Grenado, Anita Allbritton, Michaela Underwood, Lynn Wallace, Renee Parmenter and Denise Switcher," Dwight said. "There's a line through *TP*—Tammy Patterson. She got away from him. Another line through *DD* and *JD*—Donna and Jamie Douglas. They escaped, too."

"They're in order of the attacks," Brodie said. "He must have killed Renee before Denise." He frowned at the last letters on the page. "Who is *EW*?"

"Is there a victim we haven't found yet?" Dwight asked. "Or someone he's gone after today?"

Brodie stood, his stomach heaving and a chill sweeping through him. "*EW* could be Emily Walker."

He clapped Dwight on the shoulder and shoved the notebook toward him. “Bag that and let’s get out of here. We have to make sure Emily is all right.”

Chapter Twelve

"I'm fine, and I think you're both overreacting." Emily had been up to her eyeballs in surveys to review when Brodie and Travis had burst in on her late Friday afternoon, demanding to know what she was doing and if she had talked to or seen Alex Woodruff. "Alex hasn't been anywhere near here, and as for what I'm doing, I'm working. And I don't need you interrupting."

"You could be in danger," Brodie said. "Promise me you won't go anywhere without me or Travis or Gage with you."

"What are you talking about?" She turned to Travis. "Why are you both here this time of day? What's happened?"

Travis pulled a plastic evidence envelope from his coat and held it out to her. "Brodie and Dwight found this in a cave over by Eagle Creek," he said. "We think it belongs to Alex."

She studied the half-charred notebook, and the list of letters inscribed on the page in front of her. "What does this have to do with me?"

"The letters on that page are the initials of the women Alex killed," he said. His face was pale and drawn, like a man in pain. "The crossed-out letters are the three women who got away."

She read through the list again and nodded. "All right. I can see that."

"The last letters are *EW*," Brodie said. He put a hand on her shoulder. "Emily Walker."

This announcement elicited an astonished laugh from her. "*EW* could stand for anything," she said. "Ellen White. Elaine Wilson—there are a lot of women with those initials."

"What were those names again?" Brodie had pulled out a notebook and pen and was poised to write. "We'll need to check on those women, as well."

She shifted in her seat. "I don't actually know any women with those names," Emily said. "I was just giving you examples of women's names with those initials."

"We'll research tax rolls and any other records we can find for women with the initials *EW*," Travis said. "But we wanted to be sure you're all right."

"I'm fine." Some of her annoyance receded, replaced by a cold undercurrent of fear. She thought Brodie and Travis were overreacting—but what if they weren't? "I'm smart enough to stay far away from Alex Woodruff," she said.

"Last I heard, you were volunteering to lure him to you," Brodie said.

"I did. But Travis persuaded me that was a bad idea." She shrugged. "It wouldn't work without the sheriff's department's cooperation. I mean, I'm not misguided enough to try to do something like that without a whole bunch of law enforcement watching my back."

Some of the tension went out of his shoulders. "I'm relieved you're all right," he said.

His real concern for her touched her, so that she had to look away. She focused on Travis. "I'm fine. It was sweet of you to worry, but don't."

"What are you doing the rest of the day?" Brodie asked.

She really wanted to tell him that was none of his business, but that would only lead to another argument. The man never took no for an answer. "Since the favors for the wedding didn't get here while the highway was open, a bunch of us are getting together with Lacy in a little while to make everything she needs. We're going to do crafts, drink wine, eat a lot of good things and stay right here on the ranch."

"Good." Travis tucked the evidence bag back into his pocket. "Don't say anything about this to anyone."

She shook her head. "Of course not."

"Come on, Brodie. Let's see about those other women."

They turned to leave, but she stopped them. "Did you say you found that in a cave?" she asked.

Travis nodded. "It looked like Alex had spent at least a couple of nights there, though he isn't there now. We've got a reserve deputy watching the place, in case he returns."

She wrinkled her nose. "That doesn't sound very comfortable—not like Alex."

"We agree," Brodie said. "It shows how desperate he's getting. The pressure on him is increasing."

"Then he's liable to become even more violent and unpredictable," she said.

"He's more likely to make mistakes," Travis said. "We're going to take advantage of that."

"Be careful," she said, but the two men were already turning away again.

She tried to put their visit, and the disturbing news about the list of initials, out of her mind and return her focus to the student surveys. But that proved impossible. She kept repeating the names of the murdered women, and picturing that *EW* at the bottom of the list. Surely that didn't stand for Emily Walker, but the idea that it *might* definitely shook her.

Travis and Brodie and Gage and her family and friends and everyone else she knew would protect her. They formed a living barricade between her body and anyone who might try to harm her. But could they really keep Alex away? He had proved so sly and elusive, slipping in and out of crime scenes unseen, leaving scarcely a trace of evidence. Every law enforcement officer in the county had been tracking him for weeks, yet they hadn't even touched him. Could he somehow get past all her defenses and take her down when she least expected it?

She shuddered and pushed the thought away. Alex wasn't a mythical boogeyman who could walk through walls. He was flesh and blood and as vulnerable as anyone. And she was safe. She was smart and wary and protected by all those who loved her.

She didn't believe Brodie loved her—not in the way she had once wanted him to. But she believed he would protect her. He might be glibly charming and socially superficial at times, but he took his duty as an officer of the law seriously. She tried to take comfort from that.

She was grateful when Lacy came to her and asked

for help setting up for their get-together with the other women in the wedding party. "This is so nice of everyone to help," Lacy said as she and Emily and Bette set out craft supplies and readied the refreshments.

"You deserve every bit of help we can give," Bette said, arranging paintbrushes at each place setting down the long dining room table, which had been spread with brown paper to protect its polished wood surface. "Besides, this is going to be fun."

At six o'clock, the other women began arriving: Lacy's mother and all the bridesmaids—Brenda Prentice, Gage's wife, Maya Renfro, and Paige Riddell—as well as wedding guests veterinarian Darcy Marsh, Deputy Jamie Douglas and her sister, Donna. Along with Emily, Travis's mom and Bette, they made a lively party. "We're going to be decorating fancy sugar cookies," Bette explained, passing a plate of cookies shaped liked butterflies and birds. "We're using colored frosting that's the consistency of paint. Use your paintbrushes to decorate the cookies however you wish. When the cookies are dry, we'll package them up with fancy wrappings."

"I'm not very artistic," Jamie said, looking doubtful. "What if my cookies turn out ugly?"

"Then we can eat them," Donna said, sending a ripple of laughter around the table.

"I don't know," Maya said. "That might be an incentive to mess up."

"They'll turn out great," Bette said. "And when we're done, we have more cookies and plenty of other yummy party food."

Emily dipped her paintbrush in a small pot of yellow icing and began to decorate a butterfly. Though she had never considered herself an artist, the results of her efforts pleased her. "Everyone is going to love these," she said.

"Probably more than the drink cozies and pens I ordered," Lacy said. She held up a purple hummingbird. "I kind of like the reminder of spring amid all this snow."

"The weather is breaking all kinds of records this year," Darcy said. "Ryder says no one he works with can remember the highway closing so often and for so long due to avalanches and the sheer volume of snow."

"The science classes have been measuring snow amounts and tracking the weather data," Maya, a high school teacher, said. "Word is forecasts look promising for a shift in the weather to a drier pattern. That will give the snow time to settle and the highway department to get the roads in good shape to stay open."

"That's good news." Emily turned to Lacy. "You shouldn't have any trouble getting away for your honeymoon."

"Travis has to catch the Ice Cold Killer first," Lacy said. "He'll never leave town with the case still open. I'll be lucky to drag him to the altar for a few hours."

"We're getting close," Jamie said. "Now that we have a good idea who the killer is, we have everyone in the county looking for him. Someone is going to see Alex and tip us off in time to arrest him."

"I just pray they find him before he kills someone else," Bette said. The others murmured agreement.

"Do any of you know a woman in town with the initials *EW*?" Emily asked. She had promised not to tell anyone about the notebook with Alex's supposed list—but that didn't mean she couldn't do a little digging of her own.

"You mean besides you?" Lacy asked. "Why?"

She shrugged. "No reason. Just wondering."

"That's not the kind of question a person asks for no reason," Brenda said. "What's going on? Does this have something to do with Alex?"

Emily grappled for some plausible story. "I, um, saw the initials in graffiti on the bathroom stall at Mo's Pub," she said. "I was just curious." She hoped the others didn't think the story was as lame as it sounded to her.

"There's Ellie Watkins," Maya said. "But she's only six—a classmate of my niece, Casey. So I don't think anyone would be writing about her on bathroom walls."

"Elaine Wulf is one of the museum volunteers," said Brenda, who managed the local history museum. "But she's at least eighty and I can't think she'd have been up to anything that would warrant writing about it on a bathroom wall."

The others laughed and Emily forced a weak smile. "It was probably only a tourist, then. Never mind."

"What did the message say?" Lacy asked. "It must have been pretty juicy if you're asking about it now."

"Oh, it was nothing." She held up her finished butterfly. "What do you think?"

They all complimented her and began showing off their own work, but Emily was aware of Lacy eyeing her closely.

When the women took a break to eat, Lacy pulled Emily aside. "What is going on?" she asked. "What was all that about a woman with the initials *EW*? And don't give me that lame story about graffiti in the restroom at Mo's Pub. There is no graffiti there. Mo wouldn't allow it."

Emily chewed her lip. "You have to promise not to let Travis know I told you this," she said.

"I can keep a secret—within reason."

"Dwight and Brodie checked out a cave where Alex might have been camping. They found a half-burned notebook in the fire ring. In it was a list of initials that matched the initials of all the women he's killed—or attempted to kill. The last set of initials on the list was *EW*."

Lacy's face paled. "Emily Walker—you!"

"It's not me!" Emily protested. "I mean, I'm not dead, and Alex hasn't tried to get to me, so it must be someone else. I was trying to figure out who it might be."

"I'm sure Travis is looking for her, too."

"Of course he is. I just thought with a room full of women here, someone might know a woman with those initials that Travis could check on—just to make sure she's all right."

Lacy rubbed her hands up and down her arms. "I hate to think the killer is out there stalking another woman."

"And I hate that I've upset you." Emily put her arm around her friend. "Come on. Let's go back to the others and do our best not to think about this anymore. Think about your wedding and how wonderful it's going to be when you and Travis are married."

For the rest of the evening, Emily did her best to put Alex out of her mind. She ate and drank, and listened as the married women in the group told stories of their own weddings—Travis's father had apparently been late to the altar because he got lost on the way to the church, and Lacy's father had proposed by hiding an engagement ring in a piece of cheesecake…and her mother had almost swallowed it.

After they ate, Bette led them in making wedding-themed wreaths to hang on all the outside doors of the ranch house, as well as the doors of the four guest cabins. They wrapped grapevine wreaths in white tulle and silver ribbon and added glittered snowflakes and feathers. The end result was surprisingly delicate and beautiful.

They wrapped the cookies and placed them in baskets, to be handed out at the wedding in two days. "They look like little works of art," Maya said.

"Definitely too pretty to eat," Brenda said.

"You have to eat them," Bette said. "They're delicious."

"They were!" Donna said. She, like everyone else, had eaten her share of "mistakes."

After everyone had left, Emily volunteered to help Bette hang the wreaths. "I'll get the cabins, if you'll do the doors in the house," she said, draping four of the wreaths over one arm.

The four guest cabins sat between the house and the barn, along a stone path through the snow. The porch lights of each cabin cast golden pools across the drifted snow, islands in the darkness that she headed for, the chill night air stinging her cheeks and turning her breath into frosty clouds around her head. Emily hung a wreath on each door, smiling at how festive each one looked. The last cabin in the row—the one farthest from the house—was where Brodie was staying. Emily approached it quietly, not anxious to disturb him. He'd been hovering over her even more than her brothers and all the attention made her uncomfortable. The sooner the case was solved and the wedding was over, the better for all of them. Brodie could go back to Denver, she'd return to Fort Collins and everyone could go about life as it had been before.

She hooked the wreath on the nail in the cabin's door and stepped back to make sure it wasn't crooked. Satisfied, she started to turn away, but the door opened and Brodie reached out and took hold of her arm. "Come inside," he said. "We need to talk."

She could have argued that she didn't want to talk to him, but arguing with Brodie never went well. He was too stubborn and determined to be right. If he had something he wanted to say to her, she might as well hear him out now. And then she'd make him listen to a few things she needed to say, too.

Once inside, he released his hold on her and she sat in the room's single chair, while he settled on the side of the bed. He didn't say anything right away, merely looked at her—or rather, looked through her, as if he was searching for some unspoken message in her face. "What did you want to talk about?" she asked, forcing herself to sit still and not fidget.

"Why did you turn down my proposal?" he asked.

She frowned. "Your proposal?"

"I asked you to marry me and you said no."

She couldn't have been more stunned if he had slapped her. "Brodie, that was five years ago."

"Yes, and it's been eating at me ever since. I figured it was past time we cleared the air between us."

Maybe he thought that was a good idea, but did she? Was she ready to share with Brodie all she'd been through—and maybe find out he'd known about her troubles all along? That he had received the letter she had sent to him, and chosen not to get involved? She pressed her lips together, searching for the right words. "I turned you down because I wasn't ready to get married yet—and neither were you."

"You said you loved me."

"I did! But marriage takes more than love. I was only nineteen—I had so many other things I needed to do first."

"What other things?"

Maybe he should have asked these questions five years ago, but he was asking them now, and maybe answering them would help her put herself back in that time and her mind-set then. "I was only a sophomore in college. I knew I needed to finish my education and get established in my career before I married."

"Why? Lots of people get married while they're still in school. I wouldn't have held you back."

"You would have, even if you didn't intend to." She shifted in her chair, trying to find the words to make him see. "You know my family places a lot of value on education and being successful in whatever you choose to do," she said.

"I think most families are like that," he said.

"Yes, but mine especially so. My mother has a PhD, did you know that? In entomology. And my father has built the Walking W into one of the largest and most successful ranches in the state. Travis is the youngest sheriff our county has ever had, and Gage is a decorated officer with a wall full of commendations."

"I wouldn't have held you back," he said again.

"You were established in a job that could require

you to move across the state at any time," she said. "In fact, you did move, right after we broke up."

"The department takes spouse's jobs into consideration," he said, for all the world as if he was making an argument all over again for her to marry him.

"You weren't ready to settle down," she said. "Not really."

"How do you know?" he asked.

She straightened. Why not come out and say what she had been thinking? "If you really loved me so much, you would have tried harder to persuade me to accept your proposal. Instead, after I said no, you simply walked away."

He stood and began to pace, his boot heels striking hard on the wood floor. "Did you really expect me to browbeat you into changing your decision—or worse, to beg?" He raked a hand through his hair and whirled to face her. "Did you ever think that I didn't walk away because I didn't love you, but because I respected you enough to know your own mind?"

His words—and the emotion behind them—hit her like a blow, knocking the breath from her. "I… I still don't think we were ready to marry," she managed to stammer. "So many other things could have happened to tear us apart."

"Like what?" His gaze burned into her, daring her to look away. "What would be so bad our love wouldn't have been enough to overcome it?"

She wet her lips and pushed on. "What if I'd gotten pregnant?"

"We'd have been careful, taken precautions."

"We didn't always do that before, did we?"

He stared at her, and she saw doubt crowd out defiance. He studied her, eyes full of questions. “Emily, is there something you’re not telling me?” he asked, his voice so low she had to lean forward to catch all his words.

She was not going to cry. If she started, she might never stop. “I told you I wrote to you after you moved,” she said, speaking slowly and carefully.

“And I told you, I never received your letter.” He sank onto the edge of the bed once more, as if his legs would no longer support him. “Did you really think I would ignore you?”

“I didn’t know. I didn’t know what to think.”

“What did the letter say?”

She sighed. Did this really matter now? It did to her—but would it to him? “After you left, I found out I was pregnant,” she said.

“Emily.” Just her name, said so softly, with such tenderness and sorrow the sound almost broke her. She blinked furiously, but couldn’t hold back the tears. “My parents, of course, were very upset. Travis was furious. He’s the one who insisted I contact you, though at first I refused.”

“Why didn’t you want me to know?” he asked. “I would have done the right thing. I already wanted to marry you.”

“That’s exactly why I didn’t want you to know,” she said. “I was going to have a baby, but I still didn’t want to be married. And I didn’t want you to marry me because you had to. It felt like I was trapping you into something I couldn’t believe was right for either one of us.”

He leaned forward and took her hand, his fingers warm and gentle as he wrapped them around her palm.

"What happened to the baby?" He swallowed. "To our baby?"

"I'm getting to that." She took a deep breath, steadying herself, but not pulling away from him. "My father finally persuaded me that you had a right to know you were going to be a father. So I tried to call and your number had changed. I wrote and the first letter came back, so Travis got your information from the CBI. The second letter didn't come back. I thought that meant you'd received it and decided to ignore it."

"I never would have ignored it." He moved from the bed to his knees in front of her. "I wouldn't ignore you."

"I was going to try to contact you again, but then..." She swallowed again. "Then I lost the baby."

He said nothing, only squeezed her hand and put his other hand on her knee.

She closed her eyes, the sadness and confusion and, yes, relief of those days rising up in her once more like water filling a well. "The doctor said it wasn't anything I'd done—that these things just happen sometimes. I was sad, but relieved, too. I went back to school and went on with my life. We...we never talked about what had happened again."

"Did Gage know this?" he asked, thinking of his conversation with Gage at the bonfire.

She shook her head. "No. He was away at school and then summer school. He knew that something had happened with us, but he never knew about the baby. Just my parents and Travis. I— It felt easier, the fewer people who knew."

"I would have wanted to know." He stroked her arm. "I would have wanted to be there for you."

She nodded, crying quietly now, more comforted by his sympathy than she could have imagined.

"No wonder Travis insists on keeping everything strictly business between us. He thinks I deserted you and our baby when you needed me most." He looked her in the eye, his gaze searching. "I wouldn't have done that, Emily. Never in a million years. I'm sick, hearing about this now."

She put her hand on his shoulder. "I believe that now," she said. Now that she had seen the real pain in his eyes. "I'm glad you know the truth. But we can't go back and change the past. Both of us are different people now."

"Different," he said. "Yet the same." His eyes locked to hers and she felt a surge of emotion, like a wave crashing over her. Brodie still attracted her as no other man ever had. But she was no longer the naive, trusting girl she had been five years ago. She didn't believe in fairy tales, or that either she or Brodie were perfect for each other.

But she did believe in perfect moments, and seizing them. She leaned toward him, and he welcomed her into his arms. She closed her eyes and pressed her lips to his, losing herself in sensation—the scent of him, herbal soap and warm male; the reassuring strength of him, holding her so securely; the taste of him, faintly salty, as she broke the kiss to trace her tongue along his throat.

"I don't want to let you go just yet," he said.

"I'm not going anywhere." She kissed him again, arching her body to his.

"Stay with me tonight," he murmured, his lips caressing her ear.

"Yes." She began to unbutton his shirt, kissing each inch of skin as it was exposed, peeling back the fabric to expose muscular shoulders and a perfectly sculpted chest. She pressed her lips over one taut nipple and he groaned, then dragged her away and began tugging at her clothes.

She laughed as he fumbled with her bra strap. "I never could get the hang of these things," he muttered as she pushed his hands away and removed the garment herself.

Together, they finished undressing and moved to the bed, where they lay facing each other, hands and eyes exploring. "You're even more beautiful than I remember," he said as he traced the curve of her hip.

"Mmm." She kissed her way along his shoulder, smiling to herself as she thought that he was exactly as she remembered him—strong and male and exciting. He slid his hands up her thighs, calluses dragging on her smooth skin. The heat of his fingers pressed into her soft flesh, and into the wetness between her legs.

He leaned into her, the hard ridge of his erection against her stomach making her gasp. He caught the sound in his mouth, his lips closing hungrily over hers, his fingers moving higher, parting her hot folds.

She squirmed and moaned, the sound muffled by the liquid heat of his tongue tangling with her own. He dipped his head to kiss her breasts—butterfly touches of his lips over and around the swelling flesh—then latched onto her sensitive, distended nipple, sucking hard, the pulling sensation reaching all the way to her groin, where she tightened around his plunging finger.

He slid his finger out of her and gripped her thighs, spreading her wide, cool air rushing across her hot, wet flesh, sending a fresh wave of arousal through her. "What do you want?" he whispered, his voice rough, as if he was fighting for control.

"I want you."

He leaned across her and jerked open the drawer of the bedside table. When he returned, he had a condom packet in his hand. He ripped it open with his teeth and smoothed on the sheath, then pushed her gently onto her back. "Are you ready?"

She nodded. More than ready.

He drove hard, but held her so gently, his fingers stroking, caressing, even as his hips pumped. The sensation of him filling her, stretching her, moving inside her, made her dizzy. "Don't stop," she gasped. "Please don't stop."

"I won't stop. I promise I won't stop." She slid her hands around to cup his bottom, marveling at the feel of his muscles contracting and relaxing with each powerful thrust.

He slipped his hand between them and began to fondle her, each deft move sending the tension within her coiling tighter. He kissed the soft flesh at the base of her throat. "I want to make it good for you," he murmured. "So good."

She sensed him holding back, waiting for her. When her climax overtook her, he swallowed her cries, then mingled them with his own as his release shuddered through them both.

"I'm glad you stopped fighting this," he said.

"I wasn't fighting," she said.

"You kept pushing me away."

Only because he had such power over her—power to make her forget herself. She didn't trust his motives—or her own.

Chapter Thirteen

Emily woke the next morning with the sun in her eyes and a smile on her face. Last night with Brodie had been better than her best fantasies—and better than she remembered from their younger alliance. There was something to be said for a little maturity when it came to sex.

She had remembered to text Lacy before she went to sleep last night, letting her know she was tucked in safely for the night, in case her friend worried. But she hadn't mentioned she was spending the night with Brodie. For now, she wanted to keep that information to herself. But she supposed she should get back to her own cabin soon, in case someone came looking for her.

She rolled over to face Brodie, who lay asleep on his back, dark stubble emphasizing the strong line of his jaw, his sensuous lips slightly parted. She was just about to lean over and give him a big kiss when pounding on the door shook the cabin. "Brodie, wake up!" a man shouted.

Brodie sat up, instantly alert. "Who is it?" he called.

"It's Travis," Emily whispered, even as her brother identified himself.

"Quick, go in the bathroom." Brodie urged her toward the one interior door in the cabin, then swung his feet to the floor and reached for the jeans he'd discarded last night.

Emily gathered the sheet around her and shuffled to the bathroom, only partially closing the door and positioning herself so that she could see out. Brodie opened the door and Travis—scarily pressed and polished as always—said, "They've found Lynn Wallace's car."

"Where?" Brodie held the door partially closed and stepped back. Emily realized he was attempting to kick the clothing she had left on the floor under the bed.

Travis frowned and tried to move into the cabin, but Brodie blocked the move. "Never mind. You can give me all the details on the way there. Just give me a minute to get dressed."

Brodie tried to shut the door, but Travis pushed past him. "What are you trying to hide?" he asked.

"Nothing, I—" Brodie protested, but Emily had heard enough. She moved out of the bathroom, still clutching the sheet around her.

"Brodie is trying to be a gentleman and hide me," she said. "But there's no need for that. We're all adults here."

Travis's face turned white, then red. "Emily, what do you think you're doing?" he finally snapped out.

As gracefully as she could, she bent and retrieved her clothes from the floor. "I'm going to get dressed so that I can come with you to look at Lynn's car."

"You are not coming with us," Travis said.

"I'm part of the investigative team," she said. "I want to see where the car was left and what kind of condition it's in. That may help me reach some more conclusions about Alex." Plus, she knew how annoyed

Travis would be at having her push her way in like this. Her brother was a good man, but he was far too uptight, and she saw it as her duty to force him to loosen up a little.

"We don't need a civilian at a potential crime scene," Travis said.

"You can ride with me, but you have to stay in the vehicle until I clear you to get out," Brodie said.

Travis glared at him, no doubt perturbed at having Brodie overrule him. But Brodie didn't work for Travis, so Emily supposed he could make his own decisions.

"Okay." Clothes in hand, she turned back toward the bathroom.

"It is not okay," Travis said.

"Just give me a minute to get dressed," Brodie said. "I'm sure we can work this out."

Smiling to herself, Emily shut the bathroom door behind her. Later, she was sure she'd have to endure a lecture from her brother about how she was making a big mistake getting back together with Brodie. And maybe he was right. But at least this time she was going into the relationship with her eyes wide open. She would have a good time with Brodie now, and avoid thinking about forever.

TRAVIS INSISTED THE three of them travel together in his sheriff's department SUV. Brodie reluctantly agreed. He firmly believed in picking his battles, and arguing over how they were going to get to a crime scene wasn't on his list for today. Not with the promise of a bigger fight looming, judging by the icy stare Travis kept giving him. Fine. The two of them could clear the air later, preferably when Emily wasn't around.

As for the woman in question, Travis's little sister looked smug and satisfied, which should have felt more gratifying than it did. Brodie wasn't certain if she was so pleased with herself because of the fantastic sex they had enjoyed the night before—or because she'd managed to upset her usually unemotional brother.

Dwight met them at the barricade that blocked the still-closed road. He shifted the orange-and-white pylons to one side to allow Travis's vehicle to pass, then walked up to meet them after Travis had parked behind Dwight's cruiser.

Lynn Wallace's white Volvo sat crookedly across the northbound lane, both front doors open. "The crew working to clear the road found it like this when they reported for work this morning," Dwight said. "They left at about five o'clock yesterday, so someone drove it up here after that."

"Were the doors open like that, or did they open them?" Travis asked.

"They said they were open," Dwight said. "I think whoever dumped it here wanted to make sure it was noticed, and that people saw what was inside."

"What was inside?" Emily asked. She was pale and looked a little frightened, but stood her ground.

"Not another body, thank goodness," Dwight said. "Come take a look."

"Emily, you stay back here," Travis said.

"I won't compromise your crime scene," she said. "I know better than that." Not waiting for an answer, she started toward the car, so that Travis had to hurry to catch up with and pass her.

Brodie followed more slowly, so that by the time he arrived at the car, the others were gathered around, bent over and peering into the open doors. Emily took a step back and motioned for him to move in ahead of her.

The white upholstery of the Volvo, both front and back seats, had been slashed, long diagonal cuts leaving leather hanging in strips, stuffing pulled out and spilling onto the floor. Dull red liquid lay in pools on the seats and dripped onto the floor. "It's paint, not blood," Dwight said. "Regular latex. Most of it is still wet, probably from the cold. I took photos when I arrived, but the snow around the vehicle was pretty churned up. I think all the construction guys probably had a look."

The car's windshield had been smashed, the glass a spiderweb of cracks, green glass pebbles that had broken off from the cracks glittering on the dash.

Brodie rejoined Emily a short distance from the car. She stood with her arms folded across her stomach, staring at the pavement. "Are you okay?" he asked softly.

She nodded, but didn't speak until Travis joined them. "Alex is really angry," she said, looking at her brother. "Enraged. And he's coming apart."

"You think Alex did this?" Travis asked.

"Yes. I'm not an expert, but I think doing this, leaving the car up here like this, where it was sure to be found, he's sending you a message."

"What kind of message?" Brodie asked.

She glanced at him, then back at her brother. "The next woman he goes after, I think it's going to be more violent."

"And he's going to blame law enforcement for the violence," Brodie said. "We're making him do this because we won't leave him alone."

"Yes," Emily said. "I think you're right."

Travis looked back toward the Volvo, the silence stretching between them. Dwight shifted from one foot to the other. The rumble of the road machinery sounded very far away, muffled by distance and the walls of snow.

"Dwight, take Emily back to the ranch, please," Travis said. "Brodie and I will wait for the wrecker to tow the car to our garage for processing."

Emily stiffened, and Brodie expected her to argue with her brother, but she apparently saw the sense in not standing out here in the cold with nothing to do. She headed toward Dwight's cruiser, leaving the deputy to follow.

Brodie waited until Dwight had driven away and he and Travis were alone before he spoke. "If you have something to say to me, say it," he said.

Travis took a step toward Brodie, the brim of his hat shading his face, hiding his expression. Brodie braced himself for a dressing-down. Travis would tell him he had no business sleeping with Emily, that he was here to do a job and not to seduce his sister, that he had used their friendship to take advantage of Emily—nothing Brodie hadn't already told himself or heard before, five years ago, when he and Travis had also argued about Brodie's relationship with Emily. He would let Travis get out all his words and not try to defend himself. Once Travis had exhausted his anger, maybe they could have a civil discussion about Emily and Brodie's feelings for her.

But Travis didn't say anything. He reared back and belted Brodie in the chin, sending him staggering.

Brodie let out a yelp of surprise and managed to

stay upright. He rubbed his aching jaw and stared at the sheriff, who was flushed and breathing hard, hands at his sides, still balled into fists. "I reckon you think I deserve that," Brodie said.

"You don't think you do?"

"I had a long talk with your sister last night—before we went to bed together. She told me about the baby." He paused, gathering his emotions. The reality that Emily had been pregnant with his baby—that he could have been a father—was only just beginning to sink in. "I never knew, I swear. She said she wrote to me, but I never got the letter. If I had, you wouldn't have been able to keep me away from her."

Travis glared at him, wary.

"You know I asked her to marry me, right?" Brodie said.

Travis nodded.

"And she turned me down. I didn't dump her—she dumped me. But I would have come back to help her with the baby—in whatever way she wanted me to help."

He could tell the minute the fight went out of Travis. The sheriff's shoulders sagged and he bowed his head. "I'm sorry I let my temper get the best of me," he said.

Brodie rubbed his jaw again. "Maybe it was good for both of us." He offered his hand.

Travis stared at Brodie's hand. "Maybe it's none of my business, but what happens with you and Emily now?" he asked.

"I don't know. A lot of that is up to her. But it's not going to be a repeat of last time, I promise. Is that good enough for you?"

Travis grasped his hand, then pulled him close and

thumped him on the back. "You and Emily are adults, so what you do is your business," he said. He pulled away and his eyes met Brodie's—hard eyes full of meaning. "But if you hurt her again, I promise, I will hunt you down."

Brodie had no doubt of the truth behind those words. "You don't have to worry," he said. "Now come on. The killer is the only man you need to worry about hunting down right now."

"YOUR FIANCÉ ATE my prosciutto."

Saturday afternoon, Emily and Lacy looked up from the place cards they were hand-lettering for that night's wedding rehearsal dinner. The caterer, Bette, stood before them, hands on her hips and a stormy expression in her eyes. "How do you know Travis ate it?" Lacy asked.

"Because I caught him finishing off the last of it before he headed out the door this morning."

Lacy set aside the stack of place cards. "The poor man has been working so much, eating at odd hours. I hope you didn't fuss at him too much."

"I didn't. But I need that prosciutto for the dinner tonight."

"If you think the grocery in Eagle Mountain will have it, I can run and get it for you," Emily said. "I need to go to the office supply store, anyway."

"They don't have it," Bette said. "But Iris at the Cake Walk said she had some she would sell me. If you could fetch it for me, that would be a big help. I have too much to do to get ready for tonight to leave."

"Of course I'll get it." Emily looked at the place

cards spread out in front of her. "Lacy and I are almost finished here."

"Don't go to town by yourself," Lacy said. "Find one of the ranch hands to go with you."

"All right." Emily wanted to protest that she would be fine on her own, but the other women Alex had killed would have probably said the same thing. And the possibility that the *EW* on Alex's list might mean her made her even more cautious.

She and Lacy finished the place cards, each hand-lettered, with a tiny silk rose glued to the corner. "They turned out really nice," Emily said as she passed the last of the cards over to Lacy.

"They did." Lacy sighed. For a bride on the eve of her wedding day, she didn't look very happy.

"What's wrong?" Emily asked.

Lacy looked up, her eyes shiny with tears. "I'm being silly. I mean, women have died, and here I am, worrying about my wedding. It's ridiculous." She pressed her fingers to her eyes, blotting the tears.

"You're not being silly." Emily squeezed Lacy's hand. "The wedding is going to be beautiful. By tomorrow afternoon, you'll be married and it will be beautiful."

"I'm so worried something is going to happen to mess things up," she said. "Not just the wedding, but Travis—this killer hates him." She sniffed. "I know he has a dangerous job, and I told myself I could handle that, but when I think about something happening to him..." She pressed her lips together and looked away.

"Travis is smart and careful, and he loves you so much," Emily said. "Nothing is going to happen to him." She said a silent prayer that this would be true.

Lacy nodded and stood. "You're right. And my worrying won't accomplish anything." She gathered the place cards into a neat pile. "Thanks for your help with these. I think I'll go see if Bette needs me to do anything in the kitchen."

Emily wished she had had more to offer her friend than words. If only she could figure out where Alex was hiding. Finding and arresting him would allow Travis and Lacy to start their marriage off right, with a honeymoon away from all this stress and no lingering worries about local women dying.

She gathered her purse, slipped on her coat and went in search of someone to accompany her to town. She searched the barns and outbuildings, and stopped to check on Witchy, who was contentedly munching hay, her leg showing no signs of further inflammation. No one was at the bunkhouse or in the machine shed. Maybe the men had decided to make themselves scarce while the last frantic preparations for tomorrow's wedding were being completed.

On her way back from the barn she walked past the row of guest cabins. The door to Brodie's cabin opened and he stepped out onto the porch. Odd that he'd be here this time of day. "Brodie!" she called.

He turned to face her and she winced. The left side of his jaw was red and swollen. "What happened to you?" she asked, hurrying up the steps to him.

He gingerly touched his jaw. "I put ice on it, hoping to get the swelling down."

"What happened?" When she had left him and Travis on Dixon Pass, they had been waiting for the wrecker to arrive.

"It's no big deal." He took her arm and urged her

down the steps alongside him. "By tomorrow you won't even know it happened."

"You're not answering my question." She studied the injury more closely. She was no expert, but she was pretty sure someone had punched him. "Who hit you?"

"You don't want to know."

Had he tried to arrest someone and they fought back? No, he wouldn't bother hiding that information from her. In fact, she could think of only one person he might try to shield. "Did *Travis* punch you?" The last word came out as a squeak—she couldn't quite hold back her shock at the idea. Travis was so even-tempered. So aggravatingly calm almost all of the time.

But he definitely hadn't been pleased to find her and Brodie together this morning.

"It's no big deal," Brodie said again.

"Did you hit him back?" She clutched at his arm. "Lacy is going to be furious if you broke Travis's nose or something on the eve of the wedding."

"No, I didn't hit him back." He stopped walking and turned to face her. "I figured he needed the one punch to let off some of the pressure that's been building up with this case."

"Then he should go split wood or something—not punch you."

"Don't worry about it," he said. "We cleared the air, and everything is okay now."

"What did you tell him?"

He caressed her shoulders and spoke more softly. "I told him I never got your letter about the baby—that if I had, I never would have left you to deal with that alone. I still hate that you had to go through that by yourself."

The pain in his voice brought a lump to her throat.

She moved in closer and his arms went around her. They couldn't do anything to change the past, but at least now she knew he really hadn't deserted her when she needed him most. She wondered what would have happened if he had received her letter and come back to her. Would they have married, anyway? She knew she'd been right to turn down his proposal, but would knowing a child was on the way have changed her mind? She closed her eyes and pushed the thought away. The answer to that question didn't matter now.

Brodie patted her back. "What are you thinking?" he asked.

"Travis still shouldn't have hit you," she mumbled against his chest.

"It's okay," he said. "It was something we both needed, I think."

She raised her head to look at him. "Men are weird."

He laughed. "Now that that's settled, what are you up to?"

"I promised Bette I'd run to town and pick up some prosciutto for her. I was looking for someone to go with me. Want to volunteer?"

"Absolutely. What is Bette doing with prosciutto?"

"Something wonderful, I'm sure. It's for the rehearsal dinner tonight."

"I'd almost forgotten there's a wedding tomorrow."

"How could you forget? There's a big silver-and-white wreath on every door in the house—and the door of your cabin. Not to mention the wedding gifts in the hall and everyone running around like crazy people trying to get ready."

"I said almost. Besides, I've been focused on other things."

Right. Everything always came back to the killer.

Alex would probably be thrilled to know how much he was directing all their lives. She couldn't even go to the store by herself because of him. "Come on," she said. "Let's go. I have a million things to do before the dinner tonight."

On the way into town they didn't discuss Alex, or the wedding, or even the weather—all topics Emily felt had been exhausted in recent weeks. Instead, they talked about their lives on the other side of Colorado—she in Fort Collins and he in Denver. "In the spring there's a great farmers market every weekend," she told him. "I go sometimes just to hang out and people watch."

"Do you ever go hiking out around Horsetooth Falls?" he asked.

"It's been a while, but it's a great area."

"We should hike it together sometime," he said.

Her heart gave a funny little flutter. "Yeah. Yeah, we should."

He parked at the curb in front of the Cake Walk Café and followed Emily inside. The lunch crowd had dissipated, but people sat at a couple of tables, nursing cups of coffee or polishing off the last of a meal. The café's owner, Iris Desmet, waved from behind a counter at the back of the room. She disappeared into the kitchen and emerged a moment later with a paper-wrapped parcel. "I warned Bette that I've had this in my freezer for a while," she said as she punched keys on the cash register. "But she said she was desperate, so I told her she could have it for a discount."

"I'm sure it will be fine," Emily said. "Will we see you at the wedding tomorrow?"

"Of course. There's nothing like a wedding to cheer people up, and we could certainly use a little of that—

though I hear the road may open tomorrow, and the weather forecast doesn't show any more snow for a couple of weeks. Maybe the rest of the winter won't be as hard."

"I hope that's true." Emily handed over her credit card and waited while Iris swiped it, then she signed the receipt and tucked the package of prosciutto into her purse.

On the sidewalk, Dwight hailed them from across the street. "I thought you'd want to know what we found in the car once we started going through it," he said.

"Let me guess," Brodie said. "One of the Ice Cold calling cards."

Dwight nodded. "Better than that—we found some good prints in the paint. They match ones on file for Alex Woodruff."

"I don't think we had any doubt who was responsible, but it's nice to have more evidence," Brodie said. "When you get a chance, we've got a couple of questions for the CBI profiler."

Emily put a hand on Brodie's back to get his attention. "You two talk shop. I'm going to the office supply store to pick up a few things."

Brodie frowned. "I'll only be a minute."

"And the store is only two doors down." She pointed to the building with the oversize gold paperclip over the door. "You can see it from here."

He nodded, then turned back to Dwight. Smiling to herself, she hurried toward the office supply. She couldn't say why she was so happy—there was still a killer on the loose, the highway leading out of town was still closed and everyone around her was keyed up over the wedding tomorrow. And it wasn't as if she and Brodie had resolved anything. She felt closer to him now, and they'd had a night of great sex. Maybe after this was all over, they'd get together again to hike or, who knows, maybe even go out on a real date. That was still no reason for the almost giddy lightness that made her want to skip down the sidewalk and had her fighting back a goofy smile.

The bells on the door of the Paperclip jangled as she entered. The owner, Eleanor Davis, who had taught Emily when she was in third grade, waved from in front of a display of earbuds and went back to assisting an older gentleman. Emily wandered down the aisles of office supplies, admiring a beautiful pen here or an attractive notebook there. She could have spent hours in here, running her hands over the displays and breathing in the scents of ink and paper, but settled for choosing a package of colorful note cards, a sturdy wire-bound journal and a purple gel ink pen. What could she say—some women experienced euphoria when buying new shoes, while office supplies did it for her.

Outside on the sidewalk, she almost collided with an elderly man. "So sorry, miss," he said, holding out his hands defensively. He stared out at her from behind thick glasses, his expression confused and his eyes bloodshot. His gray hair hung lank to his shoulders and a wisp of a gray beard stood out against sallow skin and sagging jowls. "Clumsy of me, I…" He looked around, blinking. "I think I need some help."

The poor dear looked really out of it. Emily glanced across the street, hoping to see Dwight and Brodie and wave them over, but they must have gone back into the café—probably to get out of the biting wind. She shifted her purchases to one hand. “What can I do to help you?” she asked.

“It’s my car. There’s something wrong with it.”

“Let me call someone for you.” She fumbled in her purse for her phone.

“No.” He put out a hand to stop her. “Don’t go to so much trouble. I know what’s wrong. I just need to find the auto parts store.”

“There’s one out on the highway,” she said. “Near the motel. But it’s a little far to walk in this weather.”

“You could give me a ride,” he said. “I know it’s a lot to ask, but it would help me so much.”

She glanced toward the café again. “I’m with someone,” she said. “But I’m sure he wouldn’t mind giving you a ride—”

“No!” The man’s hand clamped around her wrist—hard. Startled, she stared at him. The confused look had vanished from his eyes, and he no longer looked so old. Something sharp pricked her side—a knife. “Come with me now, and don’t make a scene,” he said.

Chapter Fourteen

Emily opened her mouth to scream, but no sound emerged. The old man put his arm around her, pulling her close. The odors of wood smoke and sweat stung her nose, and the knife dug into her side, so that it hurt to even breathe deeply. She dropped her purse, the contents spilling out onto the sidewalk, the package of ham coming to rest in a snowbank. "That's right, come along nice and easy," the man—she was sure it was Alex—crooned.

He still looked like an innocent old man, but nothing about him was harmless. He had a grip like iron—she imagined him breaking her wrist if she tried to jerk away. And then he would slash her open with the knife before she had time to run.

"Hey!" The shout boomed out, making her jump. Alex turned, dragging her around with him, and she stared as Brodie raced toward them. She had the sensation of being somewhere outside herself, watching a slow-motion movie—Alex opening his mouth to say something, Brodie reaching into his coat and pulling out a gun—the knife pressing harder against her side.

Then everything sped up. Someone screamed, Brodie shouted, then Alex shoved her away, so hard that she fell, slamming her knees into the concrete of the walkway. Brodie's boots thundered past her, then a woman knelt beside her, trying to help her to her feet.

But Emily didn't get up until Brodie returned. He bent over her, chest heaving, the gun out of sight now. For a long moment, neither of them said a thing, their eyes locked, his expression reflecting all the terror she felt. "Are you…all right?" he managed to gasp at last.

She nodded, though she still couldn't seem to speak. By now a crowd had gathered, everyone wanting to know what had happened, and if they could help. Brodie grasped Emily's hand and pulled her to her feet. She caught her breath at the sudden sharp pain in her side, and clamped her hand over the spot. "He had a knife," she said.

Brodie pushed her hand away, then yanked down the zipper of her coat and shoved it aside. She stared at the quarter-sized blossom of red against the white of her sweater. "We need to get you to the clinic," he said, then, without waiting for a reply, scooped her into his arms and started across the street.

"Brodie, put me down. Please!" She beat her fists against his chest, but his expression never changed. People called after them, a car braked to a halt as he stepped in front of it and horns honked, but Brodie appeared to hear none of it. He burst into the Eagle Mountain medical clinic and everyone in the small waiting room stared at them.

"She's hurt," he said. "She needs to see the doctor now."

She wanted to demand once more that he put her down, but doubted he would even hear her. When the door leading to the examination rooms opened, he carried her through it and into the closest empty room. A woman with a stethoscope followed them inside. "What is the meaning—"

But she got no further. Brodie took out his badge and shoved it at her, then pulled back Emily's coat to show the spot of blood. "She's been stabbed."

The woman's eyes widened, but she recovered quickly and took charge. She pushed Brodie out of the way, then eased the coat off Emily and pulled up the sweater.

In the end, Emily needed four stitches, a tetanus shot and some antibiotics to ward off infection. Brodie sat in a chair, scowling and silent, while the nurse practitioner on duty stitched up Emily. No one talked about what had happened, and Emily didn't know if she was relieved about that or not.

The nurse had just finished administering the tetanus vaccine when someone knocked on the door. "It's the sheriff," Travis said. "May I come in?"

"You might as well," the nurse practitioner said, and shifted so that Travis could squeeze in behind her.

"I'm fine," Emily said, sliding off the exam table, wincing a little at the pain in her side. "It was just a little cut."

Travis's answer was to pull her close and squeeze her so tight she couldn't breathe. Her brother wasn't much for words, but the concern in that hug made her tear up, and she had to force herself to smile and push him away. "I'm okay," she said. "Really."

Brodie stood and Travis turned to him. "I've got everyone available out looking for this guy, but I'm afraid he's done another disappearing act."

"Let's talk about this outside," Brodie said. He

picked up Emily's coat and helped her back into it. Then, one hand on her back, he followed her into the waiting room, where, once again, everyone stared at them.

"Someone brought these for you," the receptionist said, and handed over Emily's purse, the package of office supplies and the paper-wrapped parcel of prosciutto. Emily stared at the ham, teary again. It felt like hours since she had set out to run a simple errand for Bette, yet the prosciutto was still cold.

"Let's go to my office," Travis said, and escorted them out of the clinic. The three of them piled into his cruiser, Brodie in the back seat with her. She lay her head on his shoulder, closed her eyes and tried not to think about what had happened, although she knew she would have to give a statement to Travis. All she wanted was a few more minutes to pretend she hadn't just come within seconds of death.

At the station, Adelaide clucked over her and brought her a cup of tea. "Drink that," she ordered. "And don't let these two bully you into anything." She scowled at Brodie and Travis as if she blamed them for the attack, then left, closing the door to Travis's office behind her with a solid *Click!*

"I'm not going to bully you," Travis said. "But we need to know what happened. We got a description of the man who attacked you from a few people, but about all they said was that it was an old guy with a patchy beard, and none of them remembered seeing him before."

She took a long sip of the sweet, hot tea, then set the cup on the edge of the desk and took a deep breath. She could do this. She was alive and safe and what she had to say might help Travis and Brodie stop this man. "It was Alex," she said. "I didn't recognize him because he was wearing a disguise. A good one. But I'm sure it was him."

"Start with a description," Travis said. "We'll go from there."

She described the old man who had approached her—his glasses and long hair and saggy jowls. "He looked confused and harmless," she said. "Stooped over and a little shaky. I felt sorry for him. He wanted me to feel sorry for him, to not see him as a threat. I'm sure that's what he did with the other women, too."

"He didn't run like an old man," Brodie said. "He took off like a track star. He ducked down an alley and I lost him within seconds."

"He said he was having car trouble and asked me for a ride to the auto parts store," Emily said. "When I told him I was with someone, and started toward the café, he grabbed my wrist and stuck the knife in my side. His whole demeanor changed. That's when I knew it was Alex." She swallowed hard, remembered terror making her light-headed.

"I came out of the café with Dwight and saw Emily cozied up with this old guy," Brodie said. "Even though her back was to me, something about the situation didn't look right. When I called to them, the guy swung her around toward me. He looked angry—enraged—and I could see that Emily was terrified. I drew my weapon and ordered him to stop. At first I thought he would resist, or try to use Emily as a shield. Instead, he released her and took off running." He raked a hand through his hair. "I should have insisted you stay with me. And I never should have gone into the café with Dwight."

"I was in a public place with other people all around," Emily said. "What was Alex thinking?"

"He thinks he's invincible," Travis said. "That law enforcement is stupid and we'll never catch him. But we will."

A knock on the door interrupted them. "Come in," Travis called.

Dwight entered, a bundle of cloth in his hand. "We found these in the trash bins behind Mo's Pub," he said, and laid the bundle on the desk.

Emily stared at the drab shirt, thick glasses with scratched lenses, and thin gray beard and long hair. "That was his disguise," she said.

"I figure he ditched the clothes and either put on another disguise or walked away as himself," Dwight said.

"He's good at blending in," Emily said. "He can be noticed when he wants to be, but when he doesn't, he fades into the crowd."

"I interviewed some of his professors over the phone," Travis said. "Most of them didn't even remember him."

"He's decided to go after you now," Brodie said.

"But why? Because I knew him at school?"

"Maybe," Brodie said. "Or because you're Travis's sister. He wants to prove he's better than any cop."

She welcomed the anger that surged through her at the thought. It made her feel stronger. She stood. "I'm not going to sit quietly and play victim for his sick fantasies."

"No, you're not," Brodie agreed. "And he's not going

to get close enough to hurt you again." He stood also, and took her hand in his. "Because from now on, I'm not letting you out of my sight."

THAT EVENING, BRODIE sat in the Walkers' living room as Emily descended the stairs to the strains of Pachelbel's Canon. Something tugged hard at his chest as she paused at the bottom of the stairs and met his gaze, then she ducked her head and turned away to take her place in front of the fire, where the officiant, a plump woman with auburn hair, waited for the run-through of the wedding ceremony.

The other bridesmaids followed—Gage's wife, Maya, Paige Riddell and Brenda Prentice. The music switched to the traditional bridal entrance tune and Lacy, in a blue lace dress, carrying an imaginary bouquet, appeared at the top of the stairs. Even though this was only a rehearsal, Brodie and the other observers rose as Lacy descended the stairs.

Rather than watch the bride, Brodie kept his eyes on Travis, who stood with Gage, Ryder Stewart, Nate Harris and Cody Rankin in the archway between the living and dining room. The sheriff's stance was casual: hip cocked, face impassive. But as Lacy neared, Travis straightened, then reached out his hand to her. In that moment, Brodie was sure Travis wasn't thinking about a killer or the women who had died, or about anything but this woman and their future together.

Love had the power to do that—to push aside every worry and distraction, to focus attention on what mattered most, on life and hope, even in the midst of tragedy.

Brodie shifted his gaze to Emily. She was watching her brother and Lacy, eyes shiny with unshed tears, joy radiating from her smile. Brodie's heart hammered and he had trouble catching his breath, the knowledge of how much he loved her a sucker punch to the gut.

If only she would look at him, and let him see that she felt the same—that she loved him. But her eyes remained fixed on the bride and groom as the officiant explained what would happen next.

"You may practice kissing the bride if you like," the officiant said. Everyone laughed as Travis moved in to kiss Lacy and the spell was broken.

"Now that that's over, we can eat," Gage said, ignoring the scolding look from Maya.

Brodie stood and went to Emily. Though he was not a member of the wedding party, and had not even received an invitation to the wedding, Travis had embraced the idea of Brodie as Emily's bodyguard. He had also apparently persuaded his mother and father that Brodie was not the scoundrel they had assumed and now they, too, seemed happy to have him protecting their daughter.

As for Emily, he wasn't certain what she felt about him becoming, by default, her "plus-one" for the wedding. She smiled as he held her chair for her, next to his at the table, then quickly turned her attention to the other guests. Most of the wedding party was made up of other law enforcement officers and their spouses or significant others.

Travis and the bride-to-be sat side by side in the middle of the long table, Lacy smiling and beautiful, Travis stoic and tense, his smiles doled out sparingly for his beloved. He was putting on a good show, but Brodie knew his mind was back on Alex. Like Brodie, he was probably wondering if, while they ate and drank and toasted the happy couple, the Ice Cold Killer was claiming another victim.

The officiant, Reverend Winger, sat across the table. As Bette and the ranch cook, Rainey, set salads in front of the guests, she leaned across and asked, "Are you in law enforcement, too?"

"Yes, ma'am. I'm a detective with the Colorado Bureau of Investigation."

"This must be the safest place to be in the whole county right now," Reverend Winger said.

"Reverend Winger, I understand you vacationed in Italy last year." Lacy leaned across to address the pastor. "What was your favorite thing about that trip?"

As the reverend launched into a description of her visit to Tuscany, Brodie silently applauded Lacy. Before the rehearsal began, she had laid down the law—absolutely no discussion of the case tonight. *We're going to focus on the wedding and be happy*, she had insisted.

"The prosciutto doesn't look any worse for wear," Emily leaned over and whispered to Brodie as a plate of prosciutto-wrapped asparagus and petite sirloin steaks was set before each of them.

"No one will ever know," he said, and popped a bite of the asparagus into his mouth. No one would know what Emily had been through earlier that day, either. If he detected a little more tension around her eyes, that was only because he was so focused on her.

"You know, it's hard to eat when you're staring at me like that," she said.

"Sorry." He was tempted to say something about her being so beautiful he couldn't keep his eyes off her, but he was sure such a cheesy line would only make her groan. He focused on his own food. “This is delicious,” he said. “Bette did a great job.”

“She really did,” Emily agreed. “Though in addition to the stress of my prosciutto problem, she had to deal with a no-show by the florist.” She gestured toward the center of the table, where an arrangement of greens and pine cones, tied with silver ribbon, filled a silver vase. “This was a last-minute substitution.”

“What did the florist have to say about the failed delivery?” he asked.

“By the time Bette had a chance to call, they were already closed. But she left a stern message—and she’s going to double-check with them in the morning to make sure the wedding flowers get here in time.”

“I’ll be sure and tell her everything looks—and tastes—great.”

“Speech! Speech!” Nate Harris, at one end of the table, tapped his spoon against his water glass.

Travis’s father shoved back his chair and stood as the guests fell quiet. “Thank you, everyone, for coming here this evening,” he said. “I especially want to thank Bette and Rainey for putting on such a lovely dinner.”

Cries of “hear, hear” and light applause followed this remark.

Mr. Walker turned to Travis and Lacy. “Your mother and I have looked forward to tomorrow for a long time,” he said. “We’re so happy to welcome Lacy into the family and we wish you only the best.” He raised his glass in a toast and everyone followed suit.

“Is this where everyone else in the wedding party feels compelled to also give a toast?” Emily whispered to Brodie. “If it is, I’m going to need more wine.”

But instead of toasts, Bette arrived with dessert—a

baked Alaska that Brodie, at least, would have awarded first place in any bake-off.

Half an hour later, stuffed and happy, the guests who weren't staying on the ranch made their way to the door. Brodie stood with Emily, saying goodbye. When everyone was gone, Brodie led Emily aside, where they could talk without being overheard. "About the arrangements for tonight," he said. "I meant what I said before about not letting you out of my sight."

"So you're saying we have to sleep together?" He couldn't decide if the look in her eye was teasing or not.

"I'm saying I'm going to spend the night in the same room as you—sex is optional."

"Alex isn't going to come into this house and up to my bedroom," she said. "He wouldn't dare!"

"I wouldn't put anything past him at this point." After all, Alex had tried to crash the barbecue Wednesday night. Brodie took her arm and pulled her closer. "I'm not going to give him any opportunity to get to you again." The memory of her crumpled on the sidewalk, bleeding from Alex's knife, still made it hard to breathe.

"All right." Her smile made the tight band around his chest ease. "I was planning on sneaking out to your cabin later, anyway." She snuggled against him.

"Oh, you were?" He lowered his head to kiss her, but an uproar at the front door made them pull apart and turn toward the clamor. Lacy's parents, who had been among the first to leave, stood with Travis and Lacy—Mrs. Milligan in tears, her husband white-faced. "That poor woman," Mrs. Milligan moaned.

Brodie moved toward them, Emily close behind, as

Dwight shoved through the crowd. “The florist van is blocking the end of the driveway,” he said. “The delivery driver is inside, dead.”

Chapter Fifteen

Emily urged Brodie to go with Travis and the others to investigate the crime scene, but he insisted on staying by her side as she helped her mother and Lacy soothe the Milligans. She volunteered to let Lacy's parents stay in her room that evening. Her own parents didn't ask where she planned to spend the night, though she was aware of her mother watching her and Brodie more closely as the evening progressed.

Several hours passed before the other guests could leave. While they waited for the crime scene investigators and coroner to finish their work, for the ambulance to remove the body and for the wrecker to arrive to tow the van to the sheriff's garage, Emily poured coffee and served snacks that no one ate, and tried to make small talk about anything but the murders.

It was after midnight before she was able to retrieve her clothes and toiletries, along with a change of clothes for the next day, from her room and go with Brodie to his cabin. She should have been exhausted by the strain of the day, but instead felt hyperalert and on edge. Halfway down the path to the cabins, she put her arm out to stop Brodie. "Stop just a minute," she said. "This feels like the first time things have been quiet all day and I want to take it in."

She closed her eyes and breathed in deeply of the cold, clear air, then tilted her head back and stared up at the night sky, thousands of stars glittering against the velvet blackness.

"It's beautiful," Brodie said, standing behind her and wrapping his arms around her.

"It's surreal to think of violence in the midst of such peace," she said. "Especially while we were celebrating such a happy occasion."

He kissed the top of her head—such a sweet, gentle gesture. "Come on," he said. "You're shivering. It's warm in the cabin."

The cabin was warm and neat, the bed made and clutter put away. Was this because Brodie had been expecting her to stay with him tonight, or because he was a neat and organized guy? She suspected a little of both. "I want to change out of this dress and these heels," she said, staring down at her fashionable, but definitely chilly, attire.

"Go right ahead," Brodie said.

She retreated to the bathroom, where she changed into yoga pants and a T-shirt. She studied her reflection in the mirror over the sink, hesitating, then turned on the water and washed off her makeup, then brushed out her hair. It wasn't as if Brodie hadn't seen her like this before.

"How is your side doing?" he asked when she emerged from the bathroom. He had removed his shoes and untucked his shirt, and his gun lay on the table beside the bed.

She made a face. "It hurts some," she said. She had

been mostly successful at distracting herself from the pain. "It's more annoying than anything."

"Do you mind if I have a look?" he asked.

"All right."

He crossed the room to her and carefully lifted up the T. When she had changed for dinner earlier, she had removed the dressing, so that the stitches were exposed, the skin slightly puffy around the neat row of dark thread. Brodie studied the wound for a moment, then bent and gently kissed the skin above the stitches.

She threaded her fingers through his hair and held him to her for a moment, before dragging his face up to hers and kissing him. She molded her body to his, enjoying the feel of him so close, the anticipation of spending another night getting to know him even better like a pleasant hum through her.

"I don't want to hurt you," he murmured, his mouth against her hair.

"You won't." Not physically, at least. She wouldn't think about what might happen if he left her again.

They kissed again, heat building, and were moving toward the bed when someone knocked on the door. Brodie turned toward the sound. "It's Travis. Can I come in?"

Brodie opened the door and Travis entered. He looked cold and exhausted, Emily thought. He needed a hot drink and a good night's sleep, but she doubted he would get either. He glanced at Emily, then turned to Brodie. "I wanted to update you on what we found," he said.

"Emily will have to stay and hear." Brodie sat on the side of the bed and Emily settled next to him.

"All right." Travis took the chair and sat with his elbows on his knees, head down. "The woman is Sarah Geraldi, a part-time delivery person for the florist," he said. "She was killed like the others, hands and feet bound, the Ice Cold calling card tucked into her bra." He glanced at Emily again. "You were right. There was more violence this time. He cut her up pretty badly, and there was more blood."

"He would probably have blood on him," Brodie said. "He's not being as careful."

"He knows you know who he is," Emily said. "He's not trying to hide his identity anymore. In fact, I think he likes knowing you know that he's the one who's getting the better of you. At least, I think that's how he sees it."

Travis nodded. "The medical examiner thinks she was killed much earlier today, hidden in the van, then driven here a short time ago. The delivery van's engine was still warm."

"He killed her someplace else and brought her here to taunt you," Brodie said.

Travis nodded. "It looks that way."

"If Alex drove the van here with the body in it, how did he get away?" Brodie asked. "Has he recruited another accomplice? Stashed another vehicle somewhere? It's still seven miles to town."

"Maybe he didn't leave." Travis raised his head, his gaze steady, his expression grim. "Maybe he's still here, hiding somewhere."

TRAVIS'S ANNOUNCEMENT DID nothing to help Emily or Brodie sleep. They made love tenderly, but with an air of desperation, eager to suppress, at least for a little while, thoughts of the horror that might lurk outside the door. They both woke early and dressed without saying much, then made their way up the path to the house. Brodie walked with one arm around Emily, the other hand on his gun, constantly scanning around them for any sign of an intruder.

"I'm jumpy enough without you acting as if Alex is going to leap out of the bushes and grab me," she said. "You heard Travis—he had every extra man searching around here last night. Alex isn't here."

"I don't believe in taking chances when the stakes are so high," Brodie said.

The look he gave her had a lot of heat behind it, and she had to look away. She really needed to keep her emotions in check so that she could support Lacy today. She couldn't afford to let her confusing responses to Brodie reduce her to a sodden puddle of feelings.

The wedding was scheduled to take place at five o'clock. Before then, there was still a lot to do to prepare for the ceremony. Bette appeared in the doorway to the dining room as Emily and Brodie were finishing up breakfast. "I need you two to help with the decorations," she said.

"Sure." Emily handed her dirty dishes to Brodie, who had volunteered to carry them into the kitchen. "What can we do?"

"Give me those." Bette took the dishes, then dumped them in a bus tub on the end of the sideboard. "Needless to say, things are as chaotic at the florist's this morning as they are here, and we may not be getting all the flowers we ordered, so we're making some last-minute adjustments. Come with me."

She led them through the living room, where she had assembled a pile of evergreens, silver ribbon and a mass of white silk flowers. "I raided the attic and the rest of the house for every flower arrangement on the premises," Bette explained. "Now we're going to use them to transform this room into a woodland winter wonderland."

Under Bette's direction, Emily and Brodie began cutting and wiring the greenery to make garland. Bette came along behind them and attached ribbons and flowers. "I guess the florist was pretty upset when she got the news about her employee," Emily said as she snipped a section of pine branches.

"It's even worse than you think," Bette said. "The woman who was murdered was the shop owner's daughter."

"Oh, no!" Emily's chest tightened in sympathy for the poor woman.

"Believe me, I'd gladly throttle Alex Woodruff with my bare hands if I could find him." Bette yanked hard on the end of a silver bow. "Not only am I sick over all the women he's killed, but I hate that this has cast such a pall over the wedding. Lacy, of all people, deserves to be happy on this day."

"Of course she does," Emily murmured in sympathy. Travis deserved to be happy, too—and he wouldn't be until Alex was arrested and locked behind bars, where he couldn't hurt anyone else.

"Oh, Bette, it's going to look wonderful."

The three of them turned to see Lacy, dressed in black yoga pants and a too-large sweatshirt that had *Rayford County Sheriff's Dept.* emblazoned across the front, her hair rolled up in large foam rollers, her face pale from both lack of makeup and lack of sleep, and her eyes dull with a frazzled, distracted expression. She moved into the room and fingered a white silk rose, and a single tear rolled down her cheek.

"Oh, honey, it's going to be all right." Bette enfolded her friend in a hug.

Lacy gave in and sobbed on Bette's shoulder. "This is supposed to be the happiest day of my life," she said between tears. "And I'm so worried and scared and angry. What if something happens to Travis? What if someone else gets hurt? It's just so awful." And a fresh wave of weeping engulfed her.

Bette patted her back and looked over her shoulder at Emily and Brodie. "You two can finish up here, can't you?" she asked. "The garland is mostly done—you just need to add a few more bows and then put it around the archway." She indicated the arch between the living and dining room, where Lacy and Travis would stand to recite their vows.

"Of course we can," Emily said.

Bette nodded. "Come on, Lacy, let's go fix you a cup of tea and get something to take the puffiness out of your eyes," she said, leading the distraught bride away. "Everything is going to be fine."

Emily and Brodie finished the garland. Emily didn't think her bows looked as professional as Bette's, but she told herself everyone was going to be focused on the happy couple, and not the decorations. "You'll have to start attaching this over the archway," she said, handing Brodie a length of garland. "I'm not tall enough to do it without a ladder."

"What do I attach it with?" he asked.

She searched the table and spotted a staple gun. "Use this." She handed it to him. "If Mom complains later, I'll take the blame."

He positioned the garland, pressed the staple gun against it and…*click!* He frowned. "I think it's out of staples."

"I know where they are," she said, and raced to retrieve the box. Her mother kept all her household tools in an old pie safe at one end of the front porch. She hurried to the cabinet and found the box, half full of staples, and let out a sigh of relief. One less thing to worry about.

She was halfway back to the front door when a plaintive cry stopped her. She held her breath, listening, and it came again. "Tawny?" she called, and the cat answered, sounding even more distressed than before. She must have decided to have her kittens near the house, but where?

Emily moved to the end of the porch. "Tawny?"

The cry came again. Was the cat under one of the cars? Was she hurt? Heart hammering, Emily hurried toward the sounds of distress. "Tawny!" she called again, and bent to look underneath Brodie's SUV.

Strong arms grabbed her from behind, and a hand slapped over her mouth so that she couldn't cry out, and she couldn't move. She stared up into Alex's face. "Isn't this going to be a nice surprise for the sheriff on his wedding day?" he asked.

Chapter Sixteen

Brodie was about to go after Emily when Bette called to him from the other room. "Brodie, can you come in here a minute, please?"

He looked after Emily, who was closing the front door behind her.

"Lacy wants to speak to you," Bette said.

Telling himself Emily would be fine, he followed the sound of Bette's voice to the sunporch, where she and Lacy sat with teacups in hand. Lacy beckoned him. "I have a favor to ask," she said, and patted the love seat beside her.

"Of course." He perched on the edge of the seat, anxious to get this over with so he could check on Emily.

"Promise me you'll see that Travis gets to the altar for the wedding," she said. "There are plenty of other law enforcement officers here today who can handle things for a while. All I need are a couple of hours of Travis's undivided attention so that we can get married."

He nodded. "Of course." Though the sheriff was in charge of the case, there was no reason he couldn't take a break for a few hours.

"I'm going to find Gage and make him promise the same thing," Lacy said. "And any of the other officers who are here today." She set her teacup aside and stood. "And now I'd better get upstairs and take my bath. Paige is coming by soon to do my nails."

"I've got plenty to do, too," Bette said, standing also. "Brodie, did you and Emily finish the decorations?"

"Emily went to get more staples. I'll go find her." She had been gone much too long, he thought, quickening his pace through the house.

He grabbed his jacket from the hooks by the door and pulled it on as he stepped out onto the porch. The door to a cabinet at the end of the porch stood open. The cabinet contained a hammer and other small tools, paintbrushes, some flowerpots and other items that might be useful for minor repairs or outdoor decorating. Was this where Emily had retrieved the staples? But where was she?

A gray tabby cat came around the side of the house, heavily pregnant belly swaying from side to side. She jumped up onto the porch and rubbed herself against his legs. Brodie ignored her and stepped off the porch, studying the snow. Footprints overlaid each other in the snow on the edges of the shoveled path, but none stood out as particularly fresh, and he couldn't tell if any of them were Emily's.

A sheriff's department SUV pulled up in front of the house and Travis climbed out. "Are you hiding out here from the wedding chaos?" Travis asked.

Brodie opened his mouth to share his concern about Emily, then closed it again, remembering his promise to Lacy. Travis needed to focus on the wedding today. If Brodie needed help, there were plenty of other people around here who were qualified to give it. "What are you doing in uniform today?" he asked.

"I had to get a haircut and I stopped in the office to check on a few things," Travis said. "The wedding is hours away and there's not much for the groom to do but show up and say his lines when the time comes."

"I think Lacy is upstairs getting her nails done or something," Brodie said.

"That's okay. I really came by to take another look at the crime scene." Travis scanned the area around the house. "The searchers never found any sign of Alex last night, but I can't shake the feeling that he's hiding somewhere close by."

"We're all keeping an eye out for him," Brodie said.

Travis nodded. "I think I'll go in and check in with Lacy," he said. "She's a little stressed about all of this. I think she's worried I'm going to leave her at the altar or something."

"You wouldn't do that," Brodie said.

"Of course not." Travis moved past him. "Not permanently, anyway."

Brodie headed to his cabin, telling himself Emily might have gone there in search of something she had left behind the night before, maybe. But the place was empty, though the scent of her perfume lingered in the rumpled sheets on the bed, recalling their night together and how much she had come to mean to him.

He turned on his heel and headed to the barn. Maybe she had gone to check on her horse. But Witchy was contentedly munching hay in her stall. The mare swiveled her head to look at Brodie when he leaned over the stall door. She shook her head and whinnied, as if impatient that he was invading her home. "Next time,

I'll bring you a carrot," he said, and headed back to the house.

After checking that no one was lurking around to ask him what he was up to, he made his way up the stairs to Emily's bedroom. Five years ago, he had done much the same thing, sneaking past Emily's parents to rendezvous in her room, embracing the role of the dangerous bad boy up to no good with his best friend's sister.

He was cautious this time, not because he thought he had to hide what he was doing, but because he didn't want to upset and alarm the family if there was no need. He knocked softly on the door and relief surged through him as footsteps approached from the other side.

Mrs. Milligan blinked at him, her hair in curlers and some kind of greenish cream on her face. Brodie took a step back. "Have you, um, seen Emily?" he asked.

"No, I haven't."

"Thanks." He backed away, then turned and hurried down the stairs, heart pounding. Something had happened to Emily. She was gone. Now it was time to panic.

"WHERE ARE YOU taking me?"

Alex hadn't bothered to gag Emily, though he had bound her hands and feet with tape, holding her in an iron grip that had left bruises on her upper arms. He had dragged her through the woods to a dirty white van and belted her into the back seat, her head at an uncomfortable angle, every jolt of the vehicle on the uneven ground sending pain through her bound arms.

"You'll see." Alex, his head almost completely covered by a knit cap pulled low and a scarf wound over his mouth, nearly vibrated with suppressed elation. "The sheriff and his deputies were so sure they could stop me this time," he said. "They don't realize who they're dealing with. I'm an expert who's making them look like a bunch of amateurs."

"Why would you want to be an expert at murder?" Emily asked. "You're smart enough you could have excelled at almost anything." She figured it couldn't hurt to flatter him—and as long as they were talking, she could remain alive. Brodie would have missed her by now. He and the others would be looking for her. All she had to do was stay alive until they found her.

"Murder is the ultimate crime," Alex said. "The one that captures everyone's attention and focuses all the effort and money on the killer." He pounded the steering wheel with the heel of his hand. "Talk about a rush."

"Why come to Eagle Mountain?" Emily asked. "Couldn't you have gotten away with a lot more in Denver?"

Alex laughed—a maniacal chuckle that made the hair on the back of her neck stand on end. "You don't get it, do you?" he asked. "You're as clueless as the rest of them. Honestly, I expected better of you."

"Get what?"

"I came to this 'middle of nowhere' excuse for a town because of you!"

You came here to kill me. But she couldn't say the words.

"When we first met, I was intrigued," he said. "You were pretty and smart, and you had a certain *fragile* quality I appreciated. I thought about asking you out, but as I observed you, I noticed that you didn't appear to date anyone—male or female. If I asked you out, chances were you would turn me down. And sex wasn't what I was really after. No, I wanted a much deeper connection. Do you know what that is?"

"No." She had to force the single syllable out. Alex's words terrified her even more than his actions. He had seemed so normal on the outside, yet talking with him now, she understood clearly how unhinged he had become.

"Before I kill someone, I look into her eyes and she realizes her life—her very existence—is in my hands. It is the most profound connection I could ever have with another human being. The feeling I have at that moment, the power and, yes, the love, is incredible. I wanted to experience that with you."

She said nothing, no longer wanting to encourage him.

But he didn't need her encouragement. "I decided I needed to work my way up to you," he said. "I had to experiment and perfect my methods."

"What about Tim?" she asked, hoping to change the subject.

More stomach-turning laughter. "I asked him to come with me because I thought he could be my first victim. But he turned out to be useful."

"He helped you murder the first few women."

"He did. Turns out, he had a taste for killing and I was able to exploit that. Of course, he was nowhere near my level of genius. Which is why he was caught in the end." He giggled. That was the only way Emily could think to describe the sound he made, like a little child chuckling over a silly cartoon. "Things kept getting better and better for me after I came here. The local sheriff's department was as tiny as the town, and they had tiny brains, too. And then I found out your older brother was the sheriff. Such delicious synchronicity. As if this was all meant to be."

He had turned onto the highway up Dixon Pass. Emily craned her head to see out the window. "Is the pass open now?" she asked.

"It doesn't matter if it is," Alex said. "We're not going all the way to the top."

Emily strained forward, staring down the empty road. They passed a sign warning of the road closure, then the orange barricades loomed in sight. But before they reached the barricades, Alex jerked the steering wheel to the right and the van lurched to the side. Unable to brace herself with her bound hands and feet, she jerked painfully forward against the seat belt and her head bounced against the window. Tears stung her eyes from the pain.

The van jolted to a stop, the vehicle's nose buried in a snowbank. Alex shut off the engine, then came around and slid open the side door. He leaned in to unbuckle Emily and she wondered if she could find a way to fight him off. But then he was pulling her from the vehicle. He dumped her into the snow like an old suitcase and slammed the door shut behind her.

"Come on," he said, then grabbed her by the ankles and began dragging her through the snow.

She screamed, hoping to attract the attention of one of the highway workers who were clearing the pass. "Shut up," Alex said, no heat in the words. He climbed over a snowbank and came down in a narrow alley cut through the snow. The passage was just wide enough for one person to walk. He strode down it, dragging Emily by her heels after him. The packed snow scraped her body and sent stabbing pains through her arms. The cold bit into her until her teeth were chattering, and tears streamed down her face from the pain as her head repeatedly pounded against the ground. She wanted to protest, to beg him to stop hurting her, but what difference would it make? He was going to kill her, unless Brodie and Travis and the others got here in time.

Then, as suddenly as he had started, Alex stopped. Emily lay in the snow, staring up at the blue, blue sky, wondering if this would be the last sight she would ever see. Alex came and bent over her, the scarf no longer hiding his face. "Wait for me at the bottom," he said, then gave her a hard shove.

She flew down a steep slope, over the packed snow, sliding on her back, and then she was falling, tumbling. She pressed her arms tightly to her body and tried to curl into a fetal position, sure she was going to break something. Her body turned and bounced and slid some more, until at last she came to rest in a drift of snow, so cold she could no longer shake, numb with fear and the certainty of impending death.

Then Alex was standing beside her. "Was that fun?" he asked. "It looked like it might be." He hauled her upright and tossed her over his shoulder, as if she weighed no more than a sack of flour. "One more trip and we'll be home."

She heard the sound of a motor coming to life, and the creak of turning gears. She craned her head to look and saw an old ski lift with chairs wide enough for two people. Alex shoved Emily into one of the chairs, then sat beside her, and they started up at a rapid clip. She thought of jumping from the lift, but the fall would probably hurt, and with her hands and feet still taped, she wouldn't be able to get away. "Is this where you've been living?" she asked.

"Pretty cool, huh?" he asked. "I got the old ski lift going, and I fixed up the lift shack at the top as a cozy little hideaway."

"Did you set off the avalanche the day Brodie and Gage came here?" she asked.

"They were stupid enough to come here when the avalanche danger was so high. I figure I did a public service, reminding them."

"Are you going to kill me up there?" Emily asked. Maybe it was a stupid question, but she wanted to know. If he answered yes, maybe she would risk jumping off the lift, and find a way to take him with her. With luck, he'd be the one to break a bone or hit his head when they landed.

"I'm going to kill you eventually," he said. "That's the point, isn't it? But not right away. First, we're going to wait."

"Wait for what?"

"For your brother and his men to come after you. I have a big surprise in store for them."

Chapter Seventeen

Brodie descended the stairs two at a time. He met Bette crossing the living room. "Have you seen Gage or Cody?" he asked.

"They and the other groomsmen went into town to pick up their tuxes. And I think they were all going to have lunch together. Why?"

He shook his head and went past her, back onto the porch. He could call Gage and break up the lunch—and probably end up disrupting the whole wedding. Or he could try to locate Emily and Alex on his own, and summon help then. He surveyed the empty porch again, then moved into the yard and parking area. He was staring at the ground, trying to find what might be Emily's footprints, when he spotted something he hadn't noticed before.

He picked up the box of staples, a cold piercing him that had nothing to do with the outside temperature. Something protruded from the corner of the box. He lifted the lid and shuddered as a small white card fluttered to the ground. He could read the words printed on it without bending over: *ICE COLD.*

Alex had Emily, and he wanted Brodie and the others to know he had her. Maybe he even wanted them to come after him.

Brodie picked up the card and tucked it back into the box of staples, then slipped them into his pocket. He surveyed the snow near where the card had fallen, the surface smooth and undisturbed. But a short distance away, he spotted an area of churned-up ice, with drag marks leading away from it.

He followed the marks for several hundred yards, to a wooded area on the edge of the Walker property. Someone had parked a vehicle here, the impressions from the tire tread making a distinctive pattern in the snow, dripping oil forming dark Rorschach blots between the treads. The tracks circled back to the road that led away from the ranch. When Brodie reached the road, he turned and jogged back toward the house to retrieve his truck. Travis's SUV was still parked in front of the house, but the sheriff must still be inside.

Good. Brodie would follow Alex, and once he found him, he'd call for help. And heaven help the man if he hurt one hair on Emily's head.

The oil drip made Alex's tracks relatively easy to follow. Brodie wondered once again if Alex had planned it that way. The man didn't seem to do anything by accident. Had he set up an ambush to take down any law enforcement who followed him? Did he really think he could defeat a whole phalanx of lawmen? Maybe he thought Emily would be enough of a shield to protect him.

The idea made Brodie's stomach churn, but he told himself if Alex intended to use Emily as a shield, he would keep her alive as long as she was useful to him.

And no matter what the murderer thought, he wasn't going to be able to outwit and outrun them much longer.

The oil drips turned onto the highway leading up to Dixon Pass. Brodie followed them, keeping his speed down, watching the roadsides for any sign of Alex or Emily, or anything that looked like a trap. Alex might be in disguise, or he might use other people to help him, as he had done before. But Brodie saw no other traffic or pedestrians as the road climbed toward the pass. He sped by the sign warning of the road closure, and was almost to the barricades when he spotted an old van, nose first in the snowbank that marked the site of the avalanche he and Gage had been caught in.

He pulled the truck in behind the van, blocking it, then sat for a long moment, staring at the empty vehicle, noting the puddle of oil beneath the rear axle and the opened passenger-side sliding door. The van had no license plate, and was scratched and battered, the bumper wired in place and a deep scratch running the length of the driver's side. Minutes passed, with no sign of life from the vehicle, and no sound but the ticking of the truck's cooling engine.

Weapon drawn, Brodie eased open the door and exited the truck, then approached the van. The vehicle was empty, the keys dangling in the ignition. A glance inside showed a roll of duct tape on the back floorboard, and a single long, dark hair caught in a tear in the upholstery on the back seat. Brodie stared at the hair, struggling to rein in his emotions. Emily had been in this van. So where was she now?

The deep snow made it easy to follow a set of footprints and drag marks from the van, up over a berm of snow to a perfectly carved channel, just wide enough for one man to pass through.

Brodie crept down this channel, the cold closing in around him, as if he were passing through a freezer. He kept his weapon drawn, alert for any activity over and above him. But the only sound was the heavy inhale and exhale of his own breath.

He emerged at the top of a rise and stared down at the old Dixon Downhill ski resort. As before, all was silent. A single chair dangled from the old lift and no life stirred below him.

Except… He sniffed the air. Yes, that was smoke, rising in a thin ribbon from a stovepipe on the other side of the canyon, where the old ski lift shack huddled at the top of the lift line. Brodie stared at the smoke, a vise clamped around his heart. Then he turned and walked back to his truck, where, fingers shaking so hard he could hardly make them work, he punched in Gage's number. After three rings, Gage answered. "What's up?" he asked, the sounds of laughter behind him.

"I've found Alex," Brodie said. "He's got Emily. We've got to stop him before it's too late."

ALEX FED MORE wood into the cast-iron stove that crouched at one end of the lift shack, until the flames leaped and popped, the heat almost overpowering, even though Emily was sprawled on the bench seat from an old pickup truck that had been placed in the opposite corner of the little wooden building. Alex—or someone else—had also brought in a rusting metal table, two wooden stools and a cot draped in blankets, presumably where Alex slept. "They should be able to see the smoke from the highway," he said, closing the door of the stove and standing. "I did everything I could to draw them here, but they're so dim, I need to practically lead them by the hand."

"There'll be more of them than there are you," she said. "You can't kill them all."

He turned to face her, firelight reflecting in his eyes, making him look as insane as he probably was. "But I can." He swept a hand toward the slope opposite them. "I've got explosives planted everywhere on that slope. I stole the dynamite and fuses from the highway crew. They use them to set off avalanches when the road is closed. There's enough gunpowder out there to take out half the mountain."

"If you do that, you'll be killed, too," she said.

"I'll be gone before it blows. Of course, you'll still be here." He tilted his head, studying her. "Do you think I should kill you before I go—or let you die with your brothers in the explosions?"

She closed her eyes, unwilling to look at his face any longer. The mania in his eyes frightened her. Had the insanity been there all along and she had simply failed to see it, believing he was just another undergrad, not someone she really noticed?

"They're here." She opened her eyes at his words, in time to see him pick up a rifle and carry it to the sliding window that filled half of one side of the shack. Originally, the window had allowed the lift operator a view of the lift line and the skiers unloading at the top of the lift. Now it gave Alex a view back toward the opposite slope, beyond which the van was parked. "They're really going to make this too easy for me," he said, sliding the window open a few inches.

She tried to rise up and look past him out the window, but the pain in her arms and legs made movement difficult. The best she could manage was a view of the sky and the back of his head.

Without warning, a blast echoed through the shack. Emily screamed. Alex steadied the rifle against his shoulder and fired again. The smell of gunpowder filled the air, and cold from the open window settled over her like an icy blanket. Alex straightened and laughed. “You should see them out there, running around like frightened rabbits,” he said. “I can’t believe they thought they were just going to walk up here and take me.”

Emily closed her eyes again and said a silent prayer that no one had been hurt.

A melody full of Celtic pipes and drums filled the small shack. Alex whirled to face Emily once more. “What is that?”

“I… I think it’s my phone.” How was that even possible? She’d been carrying the phone in her back pocket when she stepped out onto the porch, but she would have thought it would have either fallen out or been damaged as she was dragged, and then pushed, down the snowy road.

The music continued to play. Still clutching the rifle, Alex stalked over, shoved Emily onto her side and extracted the phone from the back pocket of her jeans. He studied the screen, then swiped to answer. “Emily can’t take your call,” he said. “She’s a bit tied up at the moment.” He laughed, and her stomach churned.

Alex moved back to the window, his back to her. “Who do you think this is? This is the Ice Cold Killer. Who is this? Wait. I’m going to put you on speaker.”

"What have you done to Emily?" Brodie's voice boomed over the phone. She choked back a sob, though whether of relief or panic, she couldn't say.

"I haven't done anything to her…yet." Alex held the phone out toward her. "Say hello to Agent Langtry," he said.

"Brodie, it's a trap," she said. "He's—" But before she could finish her warning, Alex hit her, hard, almost knocking her off the seat. She tasted blood from her split lip.

"Let her go now." Brodie's voice was louder, more urgent. "Release her and we can negotiate with you."

"You don't expect me to believe that, do you?" Alex said. "After all, you think I murdered ten women. Besides, I need her. The sheriff and his deputies won't dare hurt me if it means hurting his dear baby sister, too."

"Let her go and take me," Brodie said. "They won't hurt you with a fellow cop as a shield."

Emily held her breath, not sure she had heard correctly. Why would Brodie offer to take her place with a killer?

"Oh, you do tempt me," Alex said. "But I'm not interested in you. I came here originally to kill Emily and I believe in carrying through with my plans."

"What do you want from us?" Brodie asked.

"I want you to play a game with me. You won't win, but I'll try to make it challenging."

"What is the game?"

"Where is the sheriff?" Alex asked. "I want to talk to the sheriff."

"He isn't here."

"Why not? Does he think his wedding is more important than me? More important than his sister?"

"Tell me what you want," Brodie said.

"No. I'm done talking with you now. And I'm destroying this phone. Don't bother calling back." He hit the button to end the call, then jerked open the door to the stove and tossed the phone inside. The smell of burning plastic filled the air.

"Isn't that noble of him, wanting to take your place?" Alex said.

Emily didn't have words to explain how Brodie's offer made her feel. Was he only doing his job as an officer of the law, or did she really mean that much to him?

BRODIE, GAGE, DWIGHT, Jamie, Nate, Ryder and Marshal Cody Rankin gathered at the top of the rise looking down onto the ski lift, just out of range of Alex's rifle. Brodie punched Emily's number again and listened to it ring and ring. "He probably really did destroy the phone," Ryder, who was standing next to Brodie, said. "He doesn't strike me as one to bluff."

"Maybe we should get Travis out here to talk to him," Dwight said.

"Not yet," Gage said. "Rob is with him. His job is to keep him occupied and in the dark." DEA agent Rob Allerton was Paige Riddell's boyfriend and had the least involvement of any of them in this case.

"Alex might make a deal with Travis," Dwight said.

"He's more likely to kill him," Gage said. "I promised Lacy I'd do my best to see that she wasn't a widow before she was a wife."

"How are we going to get closer to him?" Nate asked.

"The snow down in the valley must be six feet deep," Jamie said. "You'd never get through there without a snow machine. Even if you could somehow manage on snowshoes, you'd have to climb down there first, and Alex would have plenty of time to see you and pick you off."

"How did he get up to the lift shack?" Brodie asked, studying the steep, rocky incline from the bottom of the lift to the top. "And how did he get Emily up there with him?"

"I think they rode the lift," Dwight said.

"The lift's broken," Gage said. "It hasn't worked in years."

"Maybe he figured out how to get it running," Brodie said. "Didn't you say it's powered by an old car motor?"

"That doesn't help us," Nate said. "If we try to start the lift, he'll just shoot us. He can let us get almost to him and pick us off."

"Maybe we could lure him out of the shack and pick him off with sniper fire," Ryder said.

"He'd never come out of that lift shack," Gage said. "Not without Emily as a shield. He's too smart for that."

"I still say we need to get Travis here to talk to him," Dwight said.

Brodie studied the scene below him while those around him debated the best approach. "What if instead of climbing up to him, we climb down?" he asked after a moment.

"Climb down from where?" Jamie asked.

"From above the lift shack." He indicated the cliff that rose behind the shack, part of a long ridge that formed the east side of the pass. "That may be how

Alex got down there in the first place. He's a rock climber, right?"

"How would you even get there?" Gage asked, squinting at the mountain that rose above the lift shack.

"There's an old mining road that runs along there, just above the ski area," Nate said. "See that narrow ledge." He pointed, and Brodie thought he could make out the relatively horizontal path along the cliff face. "Climbers use it in the summer. You can take a Jeep up there then, but you'd have to snowshoe in now."

"And if Alex did turn around and see someone up there, he could pick them off with that rifle." Gage shook his head. "It's too risky."

"He hasn't got a view of the slope behind him from the lift shack," Brodie said. "He'd have to step outside to see anyone up there, and we've already established he's unlikely to do that. The thing we need to do is keep him distracted."

"How?" Jamie asked.

"We could take turns approaching behind cover and taking potshots at him," Dwight said. "Or launch flares at him."

"Have to be careful with that," Nate said. "You don't want to set off another avalanche."

"Okay, so we could probably distract him," Dwight said. "But who are we going to get to make the climb? It looks pretty technical."

"I've done some climbing," Brodie said. All of it in a gym, but they didn't have to know that. He knew how to use the equipment, and he was desperate to get Emily out of there before she suffered even more than she already had.

"It's too risky." Gage shook his head.

"It's our best chance of getting to him," Brodie said. "He won't be expecting it because he sees himself as the expert and we're all the amateurs. He's probably made the climb, but he believes we'd never attempt it."

"He's right. You shouldn't attempt it," Dwight said.

"If it was Brenda trapped there, would you do it?" Brodie asked.

Dwight compressed his lips together. "I don't know," he said after a moment. "I'm just glad my wife isn't in there with him."

Emily wasn't Brodie's wife, but if things had worked out differently, she might have been. He wasn't going to let her die if he could do something—even a crazy, reckless stunt like rappelling down an icy cliff—to save her.

He turned to Gage. "Where can I get climbing gear?"

Nate clapped Brodie on the shoulder. "I've got a friend who can fix you up."

"Then let's go. We don't have any time to waste."

Chapter Eighteen

Alex paced back and forth across the floor of the lift shack, alternately cursing to himself and stopping to stare out the window. "Why aren't they doing anything?" he asked. "Nobody up there has moved for the past half an hour." He turned back to Emily. "Maybe they've decided to just let you die. What do you think about that?"

She swallowed and held her head up, though every movement sent pain shooting through her. Alex had let the fire go out and the cold made the pain worse. She couldn't stop shivering, but Alex, dressed in a fleece top and jeans, didn't seem to notice. "Maybe they went to get Travis," she said. "You burned my phone, so they don't have any way of letting you know."

"They better not be planning any tricks. They'll find out soon enough they can't trick me. Do you know why I chose this place for this standoff?" He put his face very close to hers, so that she could smell his stale body odor. It must have been a while since he had showered. How long had he been living up here in this primitive shack? "Do you know?" he demanded.

"No."

"It's because that road up there—" he gestured with

the rifle he still held "—that road is the only way in here." He laughed. "Unless they decided to try to land a helicopter down here. Not easy, and if they do, I'll just set off the explosives as soon as it touches down." He returned to watching out the window. "They can't get at me any other way."

"If they can't get in, how are you going to get out?" she asked.

He grinned, the expression in his eyes telling her he was long past any concrete grip on reality. "I'm going to climb out." He gestured behind them. "That cliff is a 5.9, maybe a 5.10 route. Expert only. But I've done it half a dozen times. I could do it with my eyes closed. By the time I make it to the top, they'll be trapped down here under tons of rock. I'll be far away from here, with a new identity, before anyone even starts to look for me."

"It sounds like you've thought of everything." She was back to flattery—anything to keep him talking and get on his good side.

"Of course I have. It's how I've been so successful so far. These country rubes aren't used to dealing with genius."

"You told them on the phone that you had a game for them to play," she said.

"For the sheriff. Of course, it's a game he can't win. I'm not stupid enough to design it any other way."

She wet her dry, cracking lips. "What is the game?"

"He has to guess the way I've planned for him to die."

"Why would he want to play a game like that?"

"If he guesses right, I'll slit your throat and you'll die quickly. If he guesses wrong..." He let the words trail away, leaving her to imagine the dozens of ways he might choose to make her suffer. She pushed the thoughts away. She wasn't dead yet. She wasn't going to give up hope. A person could live a long time on hope, or so she had read.

Hurry, she sent the thought to whatever rescuers might be mustering to help her. *Hurry, because I don't know how much longer I can hang on.*

"I'VE DONE THIS climb before, but not with the snow and ice." Nate's friend, a wiry thirtysomething who went by the single name Truman, handed Brodie a climbing helmet. "You're certifiable if you want to do it now."

"I don't have any choice." Brodie tugged the helmet on and fastened the chin strap, then reached for a pair of climbing gloves.

"We could try to bring in a helicopter," Nate said. "I bet he'd come outside when he heard that. We could probably get a good shot at him from inside the chopper."

"Or he could decide to kill Emily then and there." Brodie pulled a down jacket over his wool sweater. A Kevlar vest and thermal underwear added extra protection from the cold and gunfire, though he had doubts the vest would stop a bullet from a high-powered rifle—or prevent him from breaking every bone in his body if he fell from the cliff.

"The safety harness should protect you from a fall." Truman demonstrated hooking into the safety line. "It won't help if you bash into the rocks while you're swinging there, but if you lose contact with the cliff, we'll do our best to haul you up."

"I feel so much better now," Brodie said.

Truman made a face and ran through a checklist of the gear. None of the terms were new to Brodie, and he was beginning to feel more confident. "Come on," he said. "We need to get to the site where I'll start the downclimb." Every minute that passed was another minute that might cause Alex to lose patience and take his frustration out on Emily.

They drove as far as they could in Truman's Jeep, then strapped on snowshoes for the rest of the journey. They had to snowshoe almost two miles until they reached a point directly above the lift shack. Brodie peered down at the little tin-roofed building. "There's no smoke coming out of the stovepipe now," he said.

Nate was on the phone with Gage and relayed Brodie's observation. "Gage says Alex and Emily are still in there. He can see them through his binoculars."

"What are they doing?" Brodie asked.

"Just sitting there, he says. Waiting."

"Somebody's been climbing this route recently." Truman pulled back a tarp underneath a spindly fir to reveal a pair of snowshoes.

"Alex," Brodie said. "I figured he had to be getting to and from the shack this way, at least part of the time."

"Then you might be in luck," Truman said. "He may have set anchors in the rock that you can hook on to. Watch for areas cleared of snow—that might mark his hand-and footholds."

Brodie nodded and focused on checking and double-checking his safety harness.

"Why can't he just rappel down?" Nate asked. "It seems like that would be a lot faster."

"It would, if the cliff was straight down," Truman

said. "But it's not. There are a lot of rocks and trees and stuff that stick out. Try to rappel that and you'll just smash into stuff. No, our man is going to have to down-climb." He grinned at Brodie. "Sucks to be you, dude."

Brodie grunted and moved to the edge of the cliff. "You two just hang on if I slip."

Truman moved up beside him. "The route is hard to see from this angle," he said. "We're sort of jutting out over most of the area you'll be descending. But there's a ledge about fifteen feet down that will be a good place to stop and rest."

"If we can't see him, how are we going to know what to do to help him?" Nate asked.

"You can get a good idea of what's happening by the feel of the ropes." Truman clapped Brodie on the back. "Ready?"

Brodie nodded. His brain was telling him he was crazy to risk his life this way, but he was ignoring his brain. His heart was saying he didn't have a choice, and he was choosing to go with his heart. "Tell the others it's time to start whatever they've come up with to distract Alex."

"I've told them," Nate said. "Good luck."

The first step off the cliff, blindly groping for a foothold in the slick rock, was the worst. Relief surged through him as his foot found purchase and he was able to steady himself, but he couldn't stop to enjoy the sensation. He had to keep going. Glancing down, he could see the shallow rock ledge Truman had mentioned, and he focused on getting to it. One foot here, one hand there. Test the next foothold to see if it would support his weight. Reject another foothold as too weak or too slick. He wedged his foot into a niche in the rock. It felt secure, so he lowered himself down, searching for the next foothold.

Then the rock gave way. He flailed around, seeking purchase and finding none, swinging free against the rock face, like a pendulum in a crazy clock. Truman, very pale and very far away, looked over from the top. They had agreed that they couldn't shout to one another for fear of attracting Alex's attention. Nate also leaned out and gave him a thumbs-up. Truman pointed to the ledge and pantomimed lowering the rope. Brodie nodded. They were going to lower him to the ledge. Good idea.

Once safely on the ledge, he rested a moment, his body plastered to the rock, the cold seeping into him despite the layers of clothing. In contrast, the sun at his back burned. When he was breathing more or less regularly again, he tugged on the rope, a signal that he was ready to start down once more.

He fell three more times on the way down, each time the safety harness catching him, the rope stretching and bouncing him slightly. He learned to relax until the swaying slowed, then to find purchase in the rock once more. As Truman had guessed, Alex had hammered pitons into the rock face, allowing Brodie to clip into these as he moved down the cliff, untethering from Truman and Nate above.

About three-quarters of the way down he realized he was no longer afraid. He was actually doing this. The adrenaline rush was exhilarating, and if what awaited him at the end of the climb wasn't so important, he might have lingered to enjoy himself.

But he had no time to indulge himself. He moved

as quickly as possible. When he touched ground only a dozen feet behind the lift shack, his hand shook as he unhooked from the safety rope and climbed out of the harness. He took the time to roll up everything and stash it underneath a tree, not wanting to provide an escape route if Alex managed to make it out of the lift shack before Brodie got to him.

He straightened, drew his weapon and started toward the shack. His plan was to go in, surprise Alex and make an arrest with no one getting hurt. It was a good plan, but he had no idea if it would really work.

EMILY HAD FALLEN into a kind of stupor on the old car seat, while Alex slumped on a stool in front of the window, the rifle propped against the wall beside him. Earlier, she had spent some time groping around the seat, hoping to find a popped spring or a protruding bit of metal to cut the tape at her wrists or ankles, but no such luck. All she could do was wait and pray. She tried asking Alex questions about himself, but after a while he had stopped answering her.

Suddenly, he shoved back the stool and stood. "It's about time," he said.

Emily pushed herself up straighter. "What's happening?" she asked.

Alex gestured toward the window. "They've found a way to communicate."

By arching her back and craning her neck, Emily was able to make out someone holding what looked like a poster with writing on it. But it was too far away to read. "What does it say?" she asked.

Alex pulled out a pair of binoculars and studied the sign. "*THE SHERIFF IS READY TO TALK.*"

"Travis is there?" Emily's heart pounded. Travis shouldn't be here! He should be with Lacy, getting married.

Alex scowled. "There's someone there in a sheriff's department uniform, with a big hat and a star on his chest, but I can't tell if it's your brother." He set down the binoculars and looked around the lift shack. "I need something to write on. I need to tell him to move in closer—and to take off the stupid hat."

"You should have thought of that before you burned up my phone." Emily braced herself for another blow, but Alex only scowled at her and began digging through the debris against the walls of the shack. Amazingly, he came up with a small whiteboard, roughly two-foot square. Emily recalled seeing similar boards at lift shacks at other resorts, used to convey messages such as "Mr. Reynolds, contact child care" or "New snow overnight 4 inches!"

In a drawer, Alex found a set of dry-erase markers. He scrawled his message, *COME CLOSER AND TAKE OFF THE HAT.*

"They're not going to be able to see that from in here," Emily said. "You'll have to go outside."

"And give them a clear shot at me?" Alex shook his head. "No, you'll go out." He pulled the knife from his belt and she shrank back in fear. But he bent and cut the tape from her ankles, then did the same for her wrists.

She cried out as she brought her hands in front of her again, the stabbing pain doubling her over. Alex chafed her ankles between his hands. "You'll be fine in a minute." He straightened and thrust the sign and the marker at her. "Go out there and hold this up. And don't try anything. If you run, I'll shoot you in the back." He held up the rifle.

She gripped the board with numb, aching fingers and he tucked the marker into the pocket of her jeans and hauled her to her feet. She could barely walk, much less run. Alex took her arm and dragged her toward the door of the lift shack. "Get out there!" he called, and thrust her out the door.

She landed sprawling in the snow, the sign facedown beside her. "Get up!" Alex shouted, and she looked back to see the rifle pointed at her.

Clenching her teeth, she shoved to her knees, then slowly stood, bringing the sign with her. Holding on to the lift shack for support, she made her way around to the side facing the road, moving through snow that came past her knees. Finally she stopped and held up the sign. Seconds later, an answer appeared: *YOU OKAY?* in letters large enough to be seen clearly even at that distance.

She nodded, hoping someone was watching through binoculars. Then she scrawled *YES* beneath Alex's message. A cold wind buffeted her, and she was shaking so badly she had trouble holding on to the sign. "Get back in here!" Alex shouted.

She wanted to ignore the command, to run as fast and as far as she could. But that wouldn't be very far. The snow here was several feet deep and she could scarcely move. She would be dead before she took more than a few steps.

"Get in!" Alex shouted again.

Instead, she moved up against the lift shack once more, the thick logs providing a barrier to the wind and, she hoped, bullets from the man inside. She sank into the snow and sat, arms wrapped around her knees. Alex couldn't see her from here, and he wouldn't be able to shoot her without coming outside—something he apparently was loath to do. She would sit here until her strength returned and some of the pain in her limbs subsided. By then, maybe someone below would have come up here to her, or found a way to get to her. Having her out of the way might even help them.

Alex was screaming now, a stream of profanities aimed at her. She closed her eyes and shut him out, focusing instead on the whistle of the wind around the corner of the lift shack, and the creak of the chair on the overhead cable.

And the sound of footsteps moving through the snow.

Her eyes snapped open, fear choking her. Alex's rage at her must have overcome his fear of leaving the shack. But instead of Alex, she was amazed to see Brodie standing at the corner of the shack, one finger to his lips. "How?" She had scarcely uttered the single syllable before he shook his head. He motioned for her to stay where she was, and indicated he intended to go inside the shack.

She shook her head. If Brodie went in there, Alex would kill him. He had the rifle, and a knife, and then there were the explosives everywhere on the mountain. How could she warn Brodie without Alex overhearing? She picked up the sign and rubbed out the message there with the sleeve of her sweater, then wrote, *HE HAS EXPLOSIVES ALL OVER THE MOUNTAIN. WILL DETONATE.*

Brodie read the message and nodded. Then his eyes met hers, and the determination and, yes, love in that single glance made her almost giddy. Then he was gone, around the back of the shack once more.

Emily shoved to her feet. She couldn't sit here, not knowing what was happening with Brodie and Alex. She followed Brodie around the back of the shack, floundering through the thick snow, which covered the sound of her approach. At the door of the shack he stopped, weapon raised, then burst inside.

She braced herself for the blast of gunfire or the sounds of a struggle, but only ringing silence followed. Cautiously, she moved forward, until she was just outside the open door. "What's happening?" she called.

"He isn't here," Brodie called. He stood over the table, examining the items scattered across it. "He must have slipped out while I was with you."

"A very good deduction," Alex said as he grabbed Emily from behind and put a knife to her throat.

This can't be happening, Emily thought, as Alex crushed her against him. The knife bit into her throat, but she scarcely felt it, as if her body was becoming immune to pain.

"Let her go," Brodie said, his gun leveled at Alex.

"Drop the gun or she dies now." Alex pulled her more tightly against him, so that she could hardly breathe, her body angled so that she was between his legs, one hand almost resting on his groin.

Brodie tossed the gun aside. It sank out of sight in the snow. "What now?" he asked.

"That's right," Alex said. "I'm calling the shots."

Emily gripped the dry-erase marker in her hand. As weapons went, it was pathetic. But it was all she had. Several years before, when she was an undergrad, she had attended a presentation on self-defense.

All she could remember was the instructor's advice to use whatever was at hand as a weapon. Most of the feeling had returned to her fingers. She made a fist around the marker, then drove it as hard as she could into Alex's groin.

The knife slid across her throat, but she was able to shove out of Alex's grasp as he doubled over. Brodie jumped on him and the two grappled in the snow. Emily knelt by the shack, watching in horror as blood stippled the pristine surface of the snow with red.

The two men rolled over and over in the snow, first Brodie on top, then Alex. With a cry of rage, Alex heaved Brodie off him and jumped to his feet. Then he was running, headed for the cliff. He began to climb, clambering up the steep slope without aid of harness or ropes or even gloves.

Brodie knelt beside Emily. "It's bleeding a lot, but I don't think the cuts are too deep," he said. He stripped out of his jacket, peeled off his sweater and wrapped it around her neck.

"There's a rifle in the shack," she said through chattering teeth. "You need to get it and go after him."

"It's okay," he said, one arm wrapped around her. "Nate and another man are waiting at the top of the cliff. He won't get away from them."

They stared as Alex scaled the cliff, swarming up the rock face. Emily gasped as he slipped, then regained his foothold. "He's going too fast," Brodie said. "He's being reckless."

He was almost to the top, where the rock jutted out and he had to pull himself over it. He had almost made it when something at the top caught his attention. "It's Nate," Brodie said. "He's got him covered."

A rope dropped over the edge of the cliff and dangled beside Alex. "Nate will pull him up and arrest him," Brodie said.

But Alex didn't take the rope. Instead, he looked back over his shoulder. He took one hand from the rock and balanced for a second, before releasing the other hand and falling backward.

Emily buried her face in Brodie's shoulder. Alex's cries echoed around them, then all fell silent. "Is he dead?" she asked.

"If he isn't, he's badly hurt." He stood. "Gage is sending a couple of snowmobiles down to get us. Let's go meet them."

"Can we sit here a little bit, until they get here?" she asked.

"Are you too weak to walk?" His voice rose in alarm. "Do you want me to carry you?"

"No, I don't want you to carry me." The idea made her want to laugh.

"What's so funny?."

"I'm wondering if there's a statute of limitations on proposals."

He hesitated, then said. "What do you mean?"

She pressed her palms to his chest, over his heart, and looked into his eyes. "I mean, I don't want you to carry me. But I might want you to marry me."

"Because I scaled a cliff and faced death to save you?"

"Because you did those things. And because I love you. More than I was willing to admit before."

"Why weren't you willing to admit it?"

"Are you always so full of questions?"

"I want to be sure you're not out of your mind from loss of blood."

"I turned down your proposal before because I was afraid of what I would have to give up if we married," she said. "Now I'm old enough to see that marriage isn't about giving things up—it's about gaining a partner who can help you get even more out of life."

He gently brushed her hair back from her face and looked into her eyes. "Emily Walker, will you marry me?" he asked.

Tears—of relief, and such joy she could hardly contain it—flooded her eyes and she pressed her lips to his.

The roar of an approaching snowmobile interrupted their kiss. Two more snowmobiles followed. They stopped nearby and Gage pulled off his helmet. "Are you okay?" he asked.

"Emily's wounded," Brodie said. "I'm fine." He looked toward the cliff. "Alex is either dead or wounded."

The man on the second snowmobile collected a medical kit from the back of the machine and started through the snow toward the cliff. The driver of the third snowmobile, a woman, approached Emily. "Let's take a look," she said, and began to unwind Brodie's sweater. She surveyed the wound. "It's mostly stopped bleeding. You might need a few stitches and you might be more comfortable wearing scarves for a while, but in a year or two I'll bet the scar hardly shows."

"I'll take a scar over the alternative," she said.

"I'll just get you cleaned up a bit," the woman said, and opened her medical kit.

The other paramedic returned, shaking his head. "That one doesn't need me anymore," he said.

Emily tried to feel some sympathy or sorrow for

the man Alex might have been—handsome, smart, with every advantage. But she felt only emptiness. She didn't have it in her to hate someone so twisted, but she could admit she was relieved he would never terrorize anyone else again.

The paramedic helped her to the snowmobile and assisted her in climbing on. Brodie rode behind Gage. They were at the top again before Emily remembered one of the most important questions of the day. She looked at Gage. "Where is Travis?"

Gage checked his watch. "I hope he's getting married about now."

"But you're the best man," she said. "And I'm one of the bridesmaids."

"I think they can finish the ceremony without us," Gage said.

"He's going to be furious when he finds out what happened," Emily said.

"He is. But he'll get over it."

"Get over what?"

They turned to see Travis, a leather duster pulled on over his tux, striding toward them. Lacy, a down parka over her wedding dress, and the rest of the wedding party trailed behind. "What are you doing here?" Gage demanded.

"I came to see this case to the finish." He turned to Emily. "Are you okay?"

She nodded. "I'll be fine." At least, she would be, given time to rest and heal.

Travis nodded and turned back to Gage. "Alex?"

"He's dead."

"He jumped off the cliff, rather than face arrest," Brodie said.

"It's over," Emily said, the impact just beginning to hit her. "It's really over."

"It is." Gage put one arm around his brother. "You can leave the mop-up to us. Now you can get on with the honeymoon."

"We have to get married first," Lacy said.

"You're not married yet?" Emily asked.

"We couldn't get married with most of the wedding party—and some of the guests—up here on the pass," she said.

"You all weren't coming to the wedding, so we decided to bring the wedding to you," Bette said. She indicated everyone around them. "We're all here, but it's a little chilly, so let's get going, why don't we?"

Emily put a hand to her throat. "But I'm not dressed for a wedding."

"No one is looking at you." Bette handed her a bouquet. "Now hold this, stand over there. Lacy, you stand here."

Bette arranged everyone, and within five minutes Emily was blinking back tears as her eldest brother and her dear friend promised to love, honor and cherish each other for the rest of their lives. The officiant pronounced them husband and wife and they kissed as a tinny rendition of the Wedding March—courtesy of someone's phone—serenaded them.

"Now everyone come back to the reception," Bette said. Gage started to object, but she held up a hand. "I know what you're going to say. You have a crime scene to process. I'll send refreshments back to you."

"If it's all right with you, I'll stay with Emily," Brodie said.

"You do that," Travis said. "I think I can trust you to take good care of her this time."

"This time, and for every time to come," he said.

The others piled into their vehicles and drove away, Travis and Lacy in a white pickup truck with tin cans tied to the back and *Just Married* scrawled across the back window. Then Brodie walked Emily to the ambulance and climbed in after her. "I don't think you ever gave me an answer to my proposal," he said, taking her hand.

"Yes," she said. "Yes, I'll marry you."

He held her gaze, steady and sure. "I never want to hold you back from your dreams," he said. "I only want to be part of them."

"You are." She kissed him, a sweet meeting of their lips full of promise and hope and all things she was determined to never give up again.

* * * * *

"You all first," Travis said. "I think I can trust you to take good care of her this time."

"This time, and for every time to come," he said.

The others piled into their vehicles and drove away. Travis and Lacey in a white pickup truck with cans tied to the back and *Just Married* scrawled across the back window. Then Brodie walked Emily to the ambulance and climbed in after her. "I don't think you ever gave me an answer to my proposal," he said, taking her hand.

"Yes," she said. "Yes, I'll marry you."

He held her gaze, steady and sure. "I never want to hold you back from your dreams," he said. "I only want to be a part of them."

"You are." She kissed him, a sweet meeting of their lips, full of promise and hope and all things she was determined to never give up again.

* * * * *

WARNING SHOT

JENNA KERNAN

For Jim, always.

Chapter One

Homeland Security Agent Rylee Hockings paused on the way into the sheriff's office at the foul language booming from the side of the building. The deep baritone voice continued in a colorful string of obscenities that made her think the speaker had been in some branch of the armed services.

A military brat herself, she had heard her fair share of cussing during her formative years while being dragged from one base to another, Kyoto to Hawaii to Germany and back to Hawaii. The youngest of six, she had the distinction of being the only one of her family not to join the US Marines. Some of the military upbringing had worn off on her because she still believed that one was judged on performance. It was one of many reasons she planned to kill this assignment and show her supervisor she had what it took to be a field operative.

It was just past noon on Labor Day. Because of the federal holiday, she had not expected to find the sheriff in his office, but stopped as a courtesy. The second day of September and sunny, but the sunshine did not warm this frozen block of a county in upstate New York. Here it already felt like November. The leaves were pretty. Already at peak leaf-peeping season.

She rounded the building and found a tall man with strands of honey-blond hair falling over his flushed face as he jammed a coat hanger in the slot between the weather stripping and the driver's side window of the vehicle before him.

The vehicle was a white SUV and on the side panel in gold paint was the county seal and the word *Sheriff.*

The man had his back to her and he had not heard her approach due to the swearing and stomping of his feet on the frozen ground. His breath showed in the blast of cold air. The collar of his jacket was turned up against the chill. His distraction gave her a moment to admire an unobstructed view of one of the nicest looking butts she had seen in some time. His uniform slacks were just tight enough and his posterior just muscular enough to keep her interest for a little too long. He wore a brown nylon jacket, heavily padded and flapping at his sides as he threw the coat hanger to the ground.

"Unsat," she said, using the US Marine jargon for unsatisfactory.

He whirled and met her gaze by pinning her with eyes so blue they should have belonged to a husky. Her smile dropped with her stomach. Straight nose, square chin and a sensual mouth, the guy was the complete package, and then he opened his mouth.

"Sneaking up on a sheriff is a bad idea."

"As bad as locking your keys inside?" She squinted her eyes and dragged her sunglasses down her nose. "I could have had an entire unit with me, and you wouldn't have heard."

He stooped to retrieve his twisted coat hanger, snatching it from the ground with long elegant fingers.

"FUBAR," she said.

"You in the Corps?" he asked, referring to the US Marine Corps.

"My father, two brothers and a sister." She motioned to the sheriff's vehicle. "No spare?"

"Lost them," he admitted.

"Why not use a Slim Jim?"

He scowled and thumbed over his shoulder. "It's in the back."

She wished she'd checked into the background of the sheriff of Onutake County before this meeting, but time had been limited. Knowing what he looked like would have been helpful right about now. For all she knew, this guy was a car thief.

She made a note to do some background checking as soon as she found a moment.

"You Sheriff Trace?"

"Who's asking?"

"Rylee Hockings, Department of Homeland Security." She retrieved her business card case from her blazer and offered him a card, leaning forward instead of stepping closer. There was something other than his vocabulary that urged her to keep her distance. She listened to that voice instead of the one that wondered if he were single. But her traitorous eyes dropped to his bare hands and the left one, which held no wedding band.

He nodded, not looking at her card.

"Didn't expect to find you on the job today, Sheriff."

"More calls on weekends and holidays. Just the way of the world."

He'd have trouble responding without his car, she thought.

"What can I do you for?"

"Just an introduction. Courtesy visit."

"Uh-huh," he said, his expression turning skeptical. "So, you plan on treating me like I'm still a marine?"

"Excuse me?"

"Muscles are required, intelligence not essential," he said, choosing one of the tired jokes members of the army often leveled at the marines.

"So you were army, then." She knew that much from the jibe toward her family's branch of the military.

"Once." He smiled and her heart jumped as if hit with a jolt of electricity. The smile and those eyes and jaw and, holy smokes, she was in trouble. She forced a scowl.

"You know, you should always run a check of your equipment before you lock up."

"You a newbie, reading manuals, going by the book?"

She was and the assumption was insulting.

"Why do you ask?"

"You still have that new car smell."

Her scowl was no longer forced. What did that even mean? "I'm not the one locked out of my unit."

"It isn't even locked. The alarm is just on and I didn't want to set it off again."

Again. How often did he do this? she wondered. "I'll be doing some investigating in your county."

"What kind of investigating?"

She smiled. "Nice to meet you, Sheriff."

"You want an escort?"

"From a sheriff careless enough to leave his keys and—" she glanced through the windshield to verify her suspicion "—his phone in his unit? Thank you but I'll manage."

She turned to go. *New car smell.* She growled and marched away.

"You got a Slim Jim in your vehicle, Hockings?" he called after her.

"I do, but I wouldn't want to chance damaging yours. Maybe try Triple A."

"Where you headed?"

"Kowa Nation," she said and then wished she hadn't.

"Hey!"

Rylee turned back. Throwing her arms out in exasperation. "What?"

"They know you're coming?"

"Where's the fun in that?"

"Agent Hockings, I advise you to call the tribal leadership and make a formal request to visit."

She cast him the kind of wave that she knew was dismissive. Those damn blue eyes narrowed. They were still enthralling. As blue as the waters of the Caribbean.

Rylee straightened her shoulders and kept going. When she reached the front of the building, she heard the sheriff's car alarm blare and then cut short.

From her official vehicle, Rylee logged in to the laptop affixed to the dash and checked out the sheriff's official records. Sheriff Axel Trace had been taken into state custody at thirteen and listed as orphaned. She gazed at the entry. There was a hole there big enough to drive a truck through. No birth record or school records. His paper trail, as they used to call it, began with the entry by the sheriff of this very county when he took custody of the lad. Axel's parents were listed as deceased, but no names for her to search. No cause of their deaths or circumstances, no guardians noted, no relatives. Just record of Axel's temporary placement with Kurt Rogers, the county sheriff at the time. The placement lasted five years until Axel enlisted out of high school. Rylee scanned and clicked and scanned some more. Impressed didn't quite cover it. There were plenty of records now, and all exemplary. She'd read them more carefully later. But on a fast pass, the man had distinguished himself in the US Army as an MP and reaching the rank of captain in Iraq. She scanned his records and noted his transfer to Hanau, Germany.

"Oh, no," she said.

Captain Axel Trace had broken up a brawl in a bar that had resulted in the death of two servicemen. She would read all the details later. For now, she skimmed and noted that Trace had been attacked and engaged with appropriate use of force.

"And two months later, you chose discharge rather than reenlistment." She wondered if the incident had been the cause of his decision to leave the service and his prospects behind.

He seemed to have had a great opportunity for advancement and she wondered why he had instead elected discharge and returned to his home county to run for sheriff, replacing the man who had held the position until retirement six years ago. It seemed an odd choice.

Perhaps it was just her ambition talking, but the sheriff could have done a lot better than this frozen Klondike Bar of a county. The entire northern border was Canada and, other than the St. Lawrence River, she saw nothing but trees and more trees. She didn't understand why anyone with his training would allow himself to get stuck in a crappy, freezing county where you reached the highest possible position at thirty. Sheriff Trace had no family up here, none anywhere according to his records. And now he had nowhere to go but sideways and no increase in salary unless the good people of the county wanted their taxes raised.

Meanwhile, Rylee had nothing but advancement in her sights. Her plans included filling in that blank spot in her résumé under field experience. Eliminating the possible terrorist threats up here was a good start. She wasn't fooled that this was a great opportunity. This county had been tagged by the DHS analysts as the least likely spot for the crossing. But that didn't make it impossible. This morning she had gotten her break. Her initial assignment was to speak to four groups who might be connected with the terrorist organization calling itself Siming's Army. Just initial interviews, but it was a start. But en route, Border Patrol called her to report an illegal crossing: a single male who was carrying a canvas duffel bag. The contents of that bag were her objective. Until she knew otherwise, she'd act as if the contents of the bag was the object for which her entire department hunted. They had abandoned pursuit when the target entered onto Mohawk land. She had a chance now, a possible break in the search for the entry point of this threat.

Her attempt to reach her boss, Catherine Ohr, ended in a voice mail message, and she had yet to hear back.

She had lost the GPS signal with her directions to the Kowa Mohawk Nation just outside of town. Not that it mattered. One of the things her father had taught her was how to read a map.

Federal officers investigating leads did not need appointments to visit federal land. Sheriff Axel Trace should have known that, but it wasn't her job to tell him what he should know.

Newbie. New car smell. First field assignment.

Rylee lowered her chin and stepped on the gas.

Chapter Two

Sheriff Trace responded to the call from the Kowa Nation one hour later, passing the border patrol checkpoint just off their rez and knowing that would only further ruffle feathers. Likely, this was also the work of Rylee Hockings.

Homeland Security Agent Hockings didn't look like trouble, as she sat small and sullen in the seat beside the desk of the Kowa Mohawk Reservation's acting chief of police. But having already met her, he could not help but take in the moment. Having ignored his advice and dismissed him like the help, there was a certain satisfaction in seeing her in wrist restraints.

He didn't know the exact point when his moment to gloat changed into a completely different kind of study, but he now noticed that Rylee Hockings had a heart-shaped face, lips the color of the flesh of a ripe watermelon and large, expressive brown eyes with elegant arching brows that were the brown of dry pine needles. Her straight, fine blond hair fell forward, making her flushed cheeks seem even pinker. Their eyes met, and her brow descended. Her lids cinched as she squinted at him with open hostility.

Axel could not resist smiling. "The next time I ask you if you'd like an escort, maybe don't flip me the bird."

"I didn't flip you off." Her reply was a bark, like a dog that might be either frightened or angry but either way sent clear signs for him to back off.

"No, I believe you said that when you wanted the help of a sheriff who was dumb enough to lock his keys in his cruiser, you'd ask for it."

He glanced at her wrists, secured with a wide plastic zip tie and hammering up and down on the knees of her navy slacks as if sending him a message in Morse code. He wondered why federal agents always advertised their profession with the same outfits. A blazer, dress shirt and slacks with a practical heel was just not what folks wore up here.

"I didn't say dumb enough. I said *careless enough*."

He glanced to the acting chief of police, Sorrel Vasta, who said, "Potato, Pa-tot-o."

"I also mentioned that the Kowa tribe does not do drop-in visits," said Axel.

"Especially from feds," added Vasta. He folded his arms across his chest, which just showed off how very thin and young he really was.

"This," said Agent Hockings, "is federal land. As a federal officer, I do not need permission—"

"You are a trespasser on the Mohawk Nation. We are within our rights to—"

Whatever rights Vasta might have been about to delineate were cut short by the blast of a shotgun.

Hockings threw herself from the chair to the floor as Vasta ducked behind the metal desk. Axel dropped, landing beside Hockings, pressed shoulder to shoulder.

"Shots fired," she called, reaching for her empty holster with her joined hands and then swearing under her breath.

"Who are you yelling to exactly?" Axel asked. "We all heard it."

She pressed those pink lips together and scowled, then she scrambled along the floor, undulating in a way that made his hairs stand up and electricity shiver over his skin. He hadn't felt that drumbeat of sexual awareness since that day in high school when Tonya Sawyer wore a turquoise lace bra under a T-shirt that was as transparent as a bridal veil. She'd been sent home, of course, to change, but it hadn't mattered. Images like that stuck in the memory like a bug on a fly strip. He had a feeling that the sight of Hockings's rippling across the floor like a wave was going to stick just like that turquoise bra.

"Out of the way," Hockings said, her thigh brushing his shoulder.

The electricity now scrambled his brain as the current shot up and then down to finally settle, like a buzzing transformer, in his groin. High school all over again.

Vasta squatted at the window and peeked out. The only thing he held was the venetian blinds. His gun remained on his hip. He glanced back at Axel and cocked his head.

Axel realized his own mouth was hanging open as if Agent Hockings had slapped him, which she would have, if she knew what he had been thinking.

"They shot her car. Peppered the side," said Vasta.

Her head popped up like a carnival target from behind the desk.

"Who did?" Her perfect blond hair was now mussed. Axel resisted the urge to lay the strands back in order. Was her hair silky or soft like angora?

"I dunno, but they are long gone," said Vasta. "Even took the shell."

"How do you know that?" She reached his side.

"Shells are green and red, mostly. Easy to spot on the snow."

Agent Hockings moved to the opposite side of the window. "There is a whole group of people out there. Witnesses."

Axel's laugh gleaned another scowl from Hockings. Vasta's mouth quirked but then fell back to reveal no hint of humor when Hockings turned from Axel to him.

Now Axel was scowling. Vasta was making him look bad, or perhaps he was doing that all on his own.

Axel reached the pair who now stood flanking the window like bookends. He pressed his arm to hers, muscling her out of the way in order to get a glimpse outside. Her athletic frame brought her head to his shoulder, and he was only five foot ten. She was what Mrs. Shubert, the librarian of the Kinsley Public Library, would have called petite. Mrs. Shubert had also been petite and was as mighty as a superhero in Axel's mind. He knew not to judge ferocity in inches.

"Or," said Hockings, "you could see if any of the spectators have a shotgun in their hand or shell casing in their pocket."

"Illegal search," said Vasta. "And none of them have a shotgun any longer. So, here's what's going to happen. Sheriff Trace is going to escort you out in restraints and put you in the back of his unit. Then he's going to drive you outta here. If you are smart, you will keep your head down and look ashamed, because you should be."

"I will not."

"Then they will likely break every window in Axel's cruiser and possibly turn it over with you both inside."

Hockings stiffened as her eyes went wide with shock. The brown of her irises, he now saw, were flecked with copper. She looked to him, as if asking if Vasta were pulling her leg.

He hoped his expression said that the acting chief of police was not.

She turned back to Vasta. "You'd have to stop them."

"Listen, Agent Hockings, it's just me here. Last week, I was an officer, and now this." He motioned to his chief's badge. "Besides, I'm tempted to help them."

Hockings looked from Vasta to Trace and then back to Vasta.

"Are you pressing charges against Hockings?" Axel asked Vasta.

"Are you serious?" she asked the sheriff.

He gave her a look he hoped said that he was very serious. "They have tribal courts and you do *not* want to go there."

"They can't prosecute a federal agent."

"But can hold you until your people find out."

Her fingers went straight, flexing and then lacing together to create a weapon that he believed she was wise enough not to use.

"Fine. So contrite. That will get us out of here?"

The acting chief of police nodded.

"What about my vehicle?"

"I'll drive it to the border and leave it for you."

"The border?" To Rylee, the border was Canada. Vasta enlightened her.

"The border of our reservation."

Her gaze flicked between them and her full mouth went thin and miserly. But she thought about it. Axel just loved the way the tips of her nose and ears went pink as a rabbit's in her silent fury.

"Fine. Let's get going, if you have your keys," she said, pushing past him.

The acting chief of police was faster, beating them to the door to the main squad room. There, two officers sat on a desk and table respectively, both kicking their legs from their perches where they had been watching the drama playing out through the glass door of the chief's office.

"Josh and Noah, you two have point," said Vasta, instructing the men to lead the escort.

Both men rose, grinning. Each wore tight-fitting uniforms. Josh's hair was black and bristly short. Noah wore his brown hair in a knot at his neck.

They headed out behind the officers, with Axel holding

Hockings's taut arm as if she were his prisoner. Behind them came the acting chief of police. Trace tried and failed not to notice that he could nearly encircle Rylee's bicep with his thumb and index finger and that included her wool coat. She glared up at him and her muscle bunched beneath his grip. Hockings clearly did not like role-play.

The crowd that Hockings had insisted Vasta question were now calling rude suggestions and booing. Vasta waved and spoke to them in Kowa, a form of the Iroquoian language. The officers before them peeled away, giving Axel a view of his cruiser and the rear door. For reasons he did not completely understand, his squad car was untouched. Axel hit the fob, unlocking his unit. Noah swept the rear door open.

Axel made a show of putting his hand on Hockings's head to see that she was safely ensconced in the rear of his unit. The effect brought a cheer from the peanut gallery and allowed him to get the answer to one of his many questions about Hockings.

Her hair was soft as the ear of an Irish setter and blond right to the roots. Hockings fell to her side across the rear seat and remained on her side. *Wise beyond her years*, he thought.

The booing resumed as he climbed behind the wheel. It pleased him that Josh and Noah now stood between his unit and the gathering of pissed-off Mohawks.

And off they went. They were outside of Salmon River, the tribe's main settlement, but still on rez land before Rylee sat up and laced her fingers through the mesh guard that separated his front from the back seat. Her fingernails were shiny with clearish pink polish and neatly filed into appealing ovals. Her wrists were no longer secured.

"How did you get out of that?" he asked.

"My father says you can measure a person's IQ by whether or not they carry a pocketknife."

"With the exception being at airports?" he asked.

"You going to keep me back here the entire way?"

"Not if you want to sit beside me."

She didn't answer that, just threw herself back into the upholstery and growled. Then she looked out the side window.

"They better not damage my car," she muttered.

"More," he said.

"What?"

She wasn't looking at him. He knew because he was staring at her in the rearview until the grooves in the shoulder's pavement vibrated his attention back to the road.

"Damage your car more," he clarified. "They already shot at it. So, you find who you were looking for?"

She folded her arms over her chest. Just below her lovely small breasts, angry fists balled. She was throwing so much shade the cab went dark.

"How do you know I was looking for someone?"

"What Home Security does, isn't it, here on the border?"

"In this case, yes. We have an illegal crossing and the suspect fled onto Kowa lands."

"They have your suspect?"

"Denied any knowledge."

Homeland Security Agent Rylee Hockings was about as welcome in Salmon River as a spring snowstorm.

"Maybe Border Patrol has your guy."

"No. They lost 'em. That's why they called me. They abandoned pursuit when our suspect crossed onto Mohawk land. Both the suspect and the cargo have vanished." She glanced back the way they had come. "I need my car."

What she needed were social skills. She didn't want his help, but she might need it. And he needed to get her out of his county before she got into something way more dangerous than ruffled Mohawk regalia. Up here on the border, waving a badge at the wrong people could get you killed.

The woman might have federal authority and a mission, but she didn't know his county or the people here. Folks who lived on the border did it for one of three reasons. Either it was as far away from whatever trouble they had left as they could get, or they had business on the other side. He'd survived up here by knowing the difference, doing his job and not poking his nose into the issues that were not under his purview.

There was one other reason to be up here. If you had no other choice. Rylee had a choice. So she needed to go. Sooner was better.

He considered himself to be both brave and smart, but that would be little to no protection from Rylee's alluring brown eyes and watermelon-pink mouth. Best way he knew to keep clear of her was to get her south as soon as possible.

"The Mohawk are required to report illegal entry onto US soil," she said. "And detain if possible. They did neither."

"Maybe they aren't interested in our business or our borders."

"America's business? Is that what you mean?"

He scratched the side of his head and realized he needed a haircut. "It's just my experience that the Mohawk people consider themselves separate from the United States and Canada." He half turned to look back at her. "You know they have territory in both countries."

"Yes, I was briefed. And smuggling, human trafficking and dope running happen in your county."

She'd left out moonshining. But border security was thankfully not his job. Neither were the vices that were handled by ATF—the federal agency responsible for alcohol, tobacco, firearms and recently explosives. He was glad because enforcement was a dangerous, impossible and thankless assignment. His responsibilities, answering calls from citizens via EMS, traffic stops and accidents made up the bulk of his duties. He was occasionally involved with federal authorities, collaborating only when asked, and Agent Hockings seemed thrilled to do everything herself. He should leave it at that.

"Borders bring their own unique troubles."

"Yet, you have made limited arrests related to these activities. Mostly minor ones, at that, despite the uptick in illegal activities, especially in winter when the river freezes."

He ignored the jibe. He did his duty and that was enough to let him sleep most nights.

"It doesn't always freeze," he said.

"Hmm? What doesn't?"

"The river. Some years it doesn't freeze."

She cocked her head and gave him a look as if he puzzled her. "How long have you been sheriff?"

If she were any kind of an agent, she knew that already, but he answered anyway.

"Going on six years this January."

"You seem young."

"Old enough to know better and halfway to collecting social security."

"You grew up here, didn't you?"

"I've never lived anywhere else."

"You have family up here?"

His smile faltered, and he swerved to the shoulder. He gripped the wheel with more force than necessary and glanced back at her, his teeth snapping together with a click.

One thing he was not doing was speaking about his past. Not his time in the military, not the men he'd killed or the ones he couldn't save. And he wasn't ever speaking of the time before the sheriff got him clear of the compound. He needed to get this question machine out of his county, so he could go back to being the well-respected public servant again.

As far as he knew, only two men knew where he came from—his father and the former sheriff. And he looked nothing like that scrawny kid Sheriff Rogers had saved. So changed, in fact, he believed his own father would not know him. At least that was what he prayed for, every damn day. All he wanted in this world was to live in a place where the rules made sense, where he had some control. And where, maybe someday, he and a nice, normal woman could create a family that didn't make his stomach knot. But for now, he needed to be here, watching his father. Here to stop him if he switched from preaching his unhinged religious vision to creating it.

She opened her copper-flecked brown eyes even wider, feigning a look of innocence.

"What?" she asked.

He unlocked his teeth, grinding them, and then pivoted in his seat to stare back at her.

"Two hours ago, you showed up in the city of Kinsley at city hall, making it very clear that you did not want the assistance of the county sheriff. Now you want my résumé."

"Local law enforcement is obliged to assist in federal investigations."

"Which I will do. But you asked about my family. Like to fill in some blanks, that right? Something before I turned thirteen?" She was digging for the details that were not in public records or, perhaps, just filling time. Either way, he was not acting as the ant under her magnifying glass.

She met his stare and did not flinch or look away from the venom that must have been clear in his expression. Instead, she shrugged. "What I want is out of this back seat."

He threw open his door and then yanked open hers. She stared up at him with a contrite expression that did not match the gleam of victory shimmering in the dark waters of her eyes. *Dangerous waters*, he thought. Even through his annoyance, he could not completely squelch the visceral ache caused by her proximity.

"You prefer to drive?" he said.

She slipped out of his vehicle to stand on the road before him. "Not this time. When do I get my vehicle back?"

He drew out his phone and sent a text. By the time she had settled into the passenger side, adjusted both the seat and safety belt, he received a reply.

"It's there now," he said. The photo appeared a moment later and he plastered his hand across his mouth to keep her from seeing his grin. Axel slipped behind the wheel and performed an illegal turn on a double solid, a privilege of his position, and took them back the way they had come.

"Why are you whistling?" she asked.

Was he? Perhaps. It was just that such moments of glee were hard to contain. By the time they reached the sign indicating the border of the Mohawk rez, she caught sight of her vehicle.

Someone had poured red paint over the roof and it was dripping down over both the windows and doors on one side. There were handprints all over the front side panel.

"My car!" she cried, leaning forward for a good look. Then she pointed. "That's damaging federal property."

"Looks like a war horse," he said, admiring the paint job. It was so rare that people got exactly what they deserved.

Chapter Three

Rylee Hockings stood beside the surly sheriff with hands on hips as she regarded the gooey paint oozing from the metallic door panel of her official vehicle and onto the road. She struggled to keep her chin up. Her first field assignment had headed south the minute she headed north. When her boss, Lieutenant Catherine Ohr, saw this car, she would be livid.

Her vehicle had been towed and left just outside the reservation land and abandoned beneath the sign welcoming visitors to the Kowa Nation.

"Maybe the paint will fill in the bullet holes," offered Sheriff Trace.

His chuckle vibrated through her like a call issued into an empty cave. Something about the tenor and pitch made her stomach do a funny little tremble. She rested a hand flat against her abdomen to discourage her body from getting ideas.

"I could use those prints as evidence," she said to Sheriff Trace.

"Or you could accept the life lesson that you might be the big cheese where you come from but to the Kowa, you are an outsider. Up here, your position will get you more trouble than respect. Which is why I offered you an escort."

And she had turned him down flat. Despite his mirthful blue eyes, extremely handsome face, brown hair bleached blond from what she presumed was the summer sun, and a body that was in exceptionally good shape, something about this man rubbed her the wrong way. The sheriff seemed to think the entire county belonged to him personally.

"I need to call Border Patrol." She left him to gloat and made her call. Border Patrol had lost their suspects after they entered Mohawk territory yesterday, Sunday, at three in the afternoon and had had no further sightings. Now she understood why they ceased pursuit at their border of the reservation and called her field office. They had set up a perimeter, so the suspect was either still on Mohawk land or had slipped off and into the general population. The chances that this man was *her* man were slim, but until she had word that the package and courier had been apprehended elsewhere, she would treat each illegal border crossing as if the carrier came from Siming's Army.

Her conversation and update yielded nothing further. The perimeter remained in place. All vehicles entering or leaving the American side of the Kowa lands were being checked. They had not found their man.

She stowed her phone and returned the few steps to find her escort watching the clouds as if he had not a thing to do.

"They tell you they wouldn't go on Mohawk land?" he asked.

She didn't answer his question, for he seemed to already know their reply. "So, anyone who wants to avoid apprehension from federal authorities just has to make it onto Mohawk land as if they had reached some home-free base, like in tag."

"No, they have to reach Mohawk's sovereign land and the Mohawk have to be willing to allow them to stay. The Kowa people have rights granted to them under treaties signed by our government."

They had reached another impasse. Silence stretched, and she noticed that his eyes were really a stunning blue-gray.

"You want me to hang around?" he asked, his body language signaling his wish to leave.

"Escort me to a place that can get this paint off," she said.

He touched the paint and then rubbed it between thumb and forefinger. He wiped his finger and thumb on the hood, then tapped his finger up and down to add his fingerprints to the others.

"Stop that!"

He did, holding up his paint-stained hand in surrender. "Oil based. Can't use the car wash. Body shop, I suppose."

"You have one?"

"Not personally, but there is one in town."

"I'll follow." She used her fob to open the door and nothing happened.

He lowered his chin and lifted his brows. The corners of his mouth lifted before he twisted his lips in a poorly veiled attempt to hide his smile.

Had the vandals disconnected her battery or helped themselves to the entire thing?

"Tow truck," he said.

She faced the reservation sign, lifted a stone from the road and threw it. The rock made a satisfying *thwack* against the metal surface.

He placed the call and she checked in with her office. No messages.

"Tow truck will be here in twenty minutes. Want to wait or grab a ride with me?"

"What do I do with the keys?"

"Tow truck doesn't need those," he said.

She nodded. "I knew that."

Did she sound as green as she felt? How much more

experience in the field did Trace have? He'd been an army MP and now was a sheriff.

"How did you decide to run for sheriff?" she asked.

His mouth tipped downward. He didn't seem fond of speaking about his past. She decided to find out why that was. She'd missed something in her hasty check.

"My friend and mentor, Kurt Rogers, was retiring. He held on until I got out of the service and threw his support behind me. Been reelected once since then."

Rylee managed to retrieve her briefcase and suitcase from the trunk, half surprised to see them there and not covered with paint. They walked back to his sheriff's unit side by side.

"Must be hard to be popular in this sort of work."

He cocked his head. "I don't find it so."

He helped her place her luggage in the rear seat and then held the passenger door for her. She had her belt clipped as they pulled back on the highway.

They did not speak on the ride into town. The air in the cruiser seemed to hold an invisible charge. She shifted uncomfortably in her seat and he rubbed his neck.

"Motel or the body shop?" he asked as they hit the limits of the town of Kinsley, which was the county seat.

"Motel."

It bothered her that, of the three possible choices, he took her directly to the place where she was staying. She didn't ask how he knew.

The sheriff pulled to a stop and she retrieved her bags.

He stood on his side of the vehicle, staring across the roof at her. "You feel like telling me where you'll be next, or should I just follow the sound of gunfire?"

She refused to take the bait and only thanked him for the lift.

"Don't mention it," he said and then added, as he slipped back into his unit, "I surely wouldn't."

She stooped to glare at him through the open passenger door. "Why not?"

"You won't need to. Soon everyone in the county will know you are here and what happened on Mohawk land, because a good story spreads faster than wildfire and because you used exactly the sort of strong-arm tactics I'd expect from a rookie agent. What I can't figure is why your supervisor sent you up here without a babysitter. You that unpopular he couldn't even find you a partner? Or is he just that stupid?"

"*She* is not stupid and it's an honor to be given a solo assignment," she said, feeling her face heat. "A show of respect."

"Is that what she told you?"

She slammed the door and he laughed. Rylee stood, fuming, as he cruised out of the lot.

What did she care what he thought? She had work to do. Important work. And she didn't need the approval of the sheriff of one of the most sparsely populated counties in the state.

Kowa Mohawk people were on her watch list along with a motorcycle gang calling themselves the North Country Riders. This gang was known to smuggle marijuana across the Canadian border. Additionally, she needed to investigate a family of moonshiners. The Mondellos had for years avoided federal tax on their product by making and distributing liquor. Finally, and most troubling of all, was a survivalist compound headed by Stanley Coopersmith. Their doomsday predictions and arsenal of unknown weapons made them dangerous.

This was Rylee's first real field assignment and they had sent her solo, which was an honor, no matter what the sheriff said. She was unhappy to be given such an out-of-the-way placement because all the analysis indicated this as the least likely spot for Siming's Army to use for smuggling. Most of department had moved to the Buffalo and Niagara Falls regions where the analysis believed Siming's Army would attempt infiltration.

She let herself into her room and went to work on her laptop. She took a break at midafternoon to head out to the mini-mart across the street to buy some drinks and snacks.

Her car arrived from the body shop just after six o'clock, the telltale outline of the red paint still visible along with the outline of three handprints.

"Couldn't get those out without buffing. Best we could do," said the gaunt tow truck driver in navy blue coveralls. "Also replaced the battery."

"Dead?" she asked.

"Gone," he said.

He clutched a smoldering half-finished cigarette at his side and her invoice in the other. The edges of the brown clipboard upon which her paperwork sat were worn, rounded with age.

She offered her credit card. He copied the numbers and she signed the slip.

The tow truck operator cocked his head to study the vehicle's new look with watery eyes gone yellow with jaundice. "Almost looks intentional. Like those cave paintings in France. You know?"

Rylee flicked her gaze to the handprints and then back to the driver.

"Like a warrior car. I might try something like it with an airbrush."

Rylee her held out her hand for the receipt.

"If I were you, I'd stay off Mohawk land. Maybe stick to the casino from now on."

She accepted the paperwork without comment. The driver folded the pages and handed them to her. Rylee returned to her room and her laptop. It was too late to head out to the next group on her watch list. That would have to wait until tomorrow.

Her phone chimed, alerting her to an incoming call. The screen display read *Catherine Ohr*, and she groaned. She couldn't know about the car already.

"Did you not understand the Mohawk are a sovereign nation?" said her boss.

"On federal land."

"On Kowa Mohawk Nation land. When I asked you to speak to them, I meant you should make an appointment."

"At eight a.m., Border Patrol notified me of a runner. A single male who crossed the border on foot carrying a large navy blue duffel bag. He was believed to have been dropped off by his courier on the Canadian side. That same courier then picked him up on the US side. They were sighted on River Road. Border Patrol detained the pickup driver thirty minutes later just outside Mohawk lands. The passenger fled on foot onto the reservation, carrying the large duffel on his back."

"They questioned the driver?"

"Yes. He denies picking anyone up."

"Name?"

"Quinton Mondello. Oldest son of Hal Mondello."

"How many sons does he have?"

"Four. Quinton runs things with his father. He's the heir apparent, in my opinion."

"So, the moonshiners were carrying moonshine. Made a drop in Canada and were heading home with an empty truck."

"Then why run?"

"You believe the passenger was an illegal immigrant?"

"At the very least," said Rylee.

"You believe the Mondello family is engaged in human trafficking?"

"Or they are assisting the Siming terrorist."

"That's a stretch. Border Patrol saw the passenger flee?"

Rylee's stomach knotted. "No. They were acting on an anonymous tip who reported seeing the passenger flee prior to Border Patrol's arrival. Border Patrol stopped a truck of similar description just outside Mohawk lands."

"Could have been a Mohawk carrying cigarettes from Canada. Could have been a moonshiner. Pot grower. Poacher. And their tip could have been a rival poacher, moonshiner or pot grower. Any of those individuals would have reason to flee. Hell, they have ginseng hunters up here trespassing all the time."

"Not in the fall."

Ohr made a sound like a growl that did not bode well for Rylee's career advancement plans.

"It could also be a suspect," added Rylee, pushing her luck.

"Therefore, we don't really know if there even was a passenger."

"Quinton Mondello denies carrying a passenger."

"Of course, he does. And he may be telling the truth."

Rylee didn't believe that for a minute.

"So, you decided to follow, alone, without backup and without notifying the tribal police," said Ohr.

Rylee dropped her gaze to the neatly made bed and swallowed, knowing that speaking now would reveal an unwanted tremor in her voice.

"Hockings?"

"Border Patrol didn't pursue." There was that darn tremor.

"Because they understand the law. That is also why they had to release Quinton Mondello. No evidence of wrongdoing."

Silence stretched.

"Do I need to pull you?"

"No, ma'am."

"I do not have time to clean up your messes, Hockings."

Rylee thought of the handprints on her federal vehicle and her head hung in shame.

"Do not go on Mohawk land again for any reason."

"Yes, ma'am."

Ohr hung up on her.

Rylee needed some air. She gathered her personal weapon, wallet, shield and keys before heading out. The September night had turned cooler than she realized, and she ducked inside to grab a lined jacket. She stepped outside again and glanced about. The night had fallen like a curtain, so much blacker than her suburban neighborhood with the streetlights lining every road. Here, only the parking lot and the mini-mart across the road glowed against the consuming dark. She'd seen an ice-cream place, the kind that had a grill, on their arrival. A burger and fries with a shake would hit the spot. It wasn't until she was driving toward her destination that she realized she had snatched the blue windbreaker that had bold white letters across the back, announcing that she was Homeland Security.

The dash clock told her it was nearly 8:00 p.m. and she wondered how long the ice-cream joint might stay open. The answer turned out to be eight o'clock. She arrived to see the lot empty except for one familiar sheriff's vehicle and a clear view of the solitary worker inside, cleaning the grill. Out front, sitting on the picnic table surface with his feet on the bench, was Sheriff Trace and a very young man.

She ignored them, which wasn't easy, as she had to walk from her vehicle to the order window.

"Ms. Hockings," said the sheriff.

She nodded and glanced at the pair.

"Who's that?" asked the young man. The sheriff's companion had peach fuzz on his jaw and hair shaved so short that it was impossible to know if his hair was blond or light brown and a stunned expression. There was an old crescent scar on his scalp where the hair did not grow.

The sheriff mumbled something as she reached the order window and was greeted by a red-faced woman who said, "Just cleaned the grill. You want something to eat, have to be the fryer."

"All right. So…what are my choices?"

"Fried shrimp, mozzarella sticks or French fries."

"Ice cream?"

"Yup." She motioned a damp rag at the menu board behind her. "Ain't cleaned that yet."

Rylee ordered the shrimp and fries with a vanilla shake. The woman had the order up in less than four minutes and the counter light flicked off as Rylee retreated with her dinner in a box lined with a red-and-white-checked paper already turning transparent in the grease.

The sheriff called to her before she could reach her car.

"Agent Hockings. Join us?" he asked.

She let her shoulders deflate. Rylee wanted only to eat and have a shower. But she forced a smile. Establishing working relationships with local law enforcement was part of the job. Unfortunately, this local made her skin tingle when she got too close. She hated knowing from the heat of her face that she was blushing. He returned her smile and her mind wandered to questions that were none of her business, like what Axel Trace's chest looked like beneath that uniform.

Two months ago, Rylee had had a steady boyfriend but that ended when she got promoted and he didn't. The help she'd given him on course work might have worked against him in the written testing when he didn't know the information required. In any case, he blamed her, and she'd broken things off. Showing his true colors made getting over him easy. Except at night. She missed the feel of him in her bed; that had been the only place they had gotten along just fine. Now she knew that attraction was not enough of a foundation for a relationship. So why was she staring at the sheriff's jawline and admiring the gap between his throat and the white undershirt that edged his uniform?

Because, Rylee, you haven't been with a man in a long time. She swept him with a gaze and dismissed this attraction as the second worst idea of the day. The first being pursuit onto Mohawk land.

Rylee sat across from the pair, who slipped from the surface of the picnic table and onto the opposite bench, staring at her in silence as she ate the curling brown breading that must have had a shrimp in there somewhere. The second bite told her the shellfish was still frozen in the center. She pushed it aside.

"Want my second burger?" asked Axel.

"You have a spare?"

"Bought it for Morris, here. But two ought to do him."

Morris gave the burger in the sheriff's hands a look of regret before dipping the last of his fries into his ice-cream sundae.

"This is Morris Coopersmith," said Trace. "Morris, this is Rylee Hockings. She's with Homeland Security."

Stanley Coopersmith was one of the persons of interest.

Morris's brows lifted, and his hand stilled. When he spoke, his voice broke. "Nice to meet you."

"Likewise." Rylee accepted the wrapped burger Sheriff Trace extended. "Any relationship to Stanley Coopersmith?"

Morris grinned and nodded. "That's my dad." Then the smile waned. "He doesn't like comics."

Morris's dad was on her watch list. He led a colony of like-minded doomsday survivalists, who had their camp right on the New York side of the border. It would be simple for such a group to transport anything or anyone they liked through the woods and over the border in either direction.

"Want some pickles?" asked Morris, offering the ones he had plucked from his burgers.

"No, thank you," she said to Morris. Her phone chimed and she checked to see the incoming text was unimportant.

Morris pointed. "Do you have a camera on that?"

Rylee nodded.

"Take our picture," he insisted and moved closer to the sheriff.

Rylee gave the sheriff a questioning look and received a shrug in response, so she opened the camera app and took a photo.

Morris reached for her phone and she allowed him to take it and watched closely as he admired the shot. At last, he handed her back her phone.

She asked the sheriff, "Are you two related?"

It was a blind guess. Morris was pink and lanky; his body type more like a basketball player. Axel's blond hair, sun-kissed skin and muscular physique seemed nearly opposite to the boy's.

She wasn't sure why she didn't delete the photo, but she left it and tucked her phone away. Then she turned her attention to her meal. She had a mouthful of burger when the sheriff dispelled her first guess.

"I'm transporting Morris from his home to the jail in Kinsley due to failure to report to his last hearing. He's got to be in court in the morning."

"Oh," she said, forcing the word past the mouthful of food. She knew the shock was clear on her face. Did he usually stop to buy suspects dinner? She had so many questions but turned to Morris. "I'm sorry for your trouble. I hope the hearing goes well."

"Doubtful. Not the first time I got picked up."

"Oh, I see." The investigator portion of her was dying to ask what exactly he had repeatedly been picked up for.

"I steal things," said Morris and grinned.

"Morris," said the sheriff, his tone an admonition. "What did I say?"

"Let my lawyer do the talking?" said the boy.

"And?"

"Don't discuss the case."

Axel Trace nodded solemnly.

Morris turned to Rylee. "But I wasn't stealing for me this time. So that will be all right." He glanced to the sheriff for reassurance and received none.

Axel Trace looked as if he were taking his dog to the vet to be put down. His mouth tugged tight and his eyes… Were they glistening? His repeat blinking and the large swallow of soda he took seemed answer enough. Sheriff Trace cared for this boy.

Rylee choked down the rest of the burger in haste. Morris finished his sundae and grinned, smacking his lips in satisfaction. On closer inspection, he did not seem quite a boy but a man acting like a boy. He certainly didn't have a grip on the seriousness of his position. Why hadn't the information on Stanley Coopersmith included that he had a boy with special needs?

"How old are you, Morris?" she asked.

"Twenty." He showed a gap-toothed smile.

That was bad news. "I see."

She glanced to Trace, whose mouth went tight. Then she looked back to Morris. Her gaze slid to the sheriff.

He motioned to Morris with two fingers. "Come on, sport. Time to go."

Morris stood, towering over the sheriff by six inches. He was painfully thin. He wore neither handcuffs nor zip ties on his wrists. Trace pointed at his unit. Morris wadded up his paper wrappers and shot them basketball-style, as if hitting a foul shot. Then he cheered for his success and finally slipped into the passenger side of the sheriff's car.

"Is that wise? Having him up front with you?" she asked.

"Morris and I have an agreement."

Morris called from inside the cruiser. "Coke and comic for good behavior."

She stared at the young man and staunched the urge to open the door and release him.

"You have a good evening, Rylee."

"Thank you for the burger, Axel." The intentional use of his first name seemed all right. He'd used her given name first. But he just stood there, staring at her. And her breath was coming in short staccato bursts; she regretted dropping the distance of formality.

He gave her the kind of smile that twisted her heart and then returned to his duty, delivering a boy who should be entering a group home to the court systems.

Rylee headed back to her motel but then veered instead into the Walmart parking lot. It wasn't until she found herself in the books section that she realized she was looking at comics. The boy was spending the night in jail; he could at least have another superhero to keep him company.

Rylee made her purchase and used the GPS to find the jail in Kinsley. There, she was buzzed in and escorted back by a patrolman who allowed her to give Morris the graphic novel.

"You are a nice lady." Morris beamed. Then his voice held a note of chastisement. "Did you pay for this?"

She would have laughed if not faced with a boy who should not have been there in the first place.

Chapter Four

Observe and report. Rylee took her chief's directive to heart as she set off the next morning, the first Tuesday of September, to observe the next group on the watch list. The survivalists headed by Stanley Coopersmith. The group's rhetoric centered around surviving the apocalypse triggered by foreign terrorists. Ironic, as that scenario might turn out much more plausible than anyone in federal law enforcement had thought until a few months ago and the very reason she was here today.

It was hard to believe that such a group might aid foreign terrorists until you recalled your history and cult leader Charles Manson's attempts to begin a race war by murdering innocent affluent white victims, including Sharon Tate. It was terrifying, the lengths individuals might go to bring about their worldview.

At 7:00 a.m., Rylee left her car on the shoulder and hiked through the woods to a place where she could observe the central compound. Even though she was dressed all in earth colors for camouflage and was wearing a forest green wool sweater and a brown leather jacket atop her gray jeans and brown work boots with thick socks, she had underestimated the chill in the morning air. She had plenty of time to think about her inadequate wardrobe, among other things, as she lay on her belly in the pale green ferns.

A cool September breeze shook the leaves overhead, sending down a cascade of yellow leaves through the fog.

"Should have worn a wool cap," she muttered to herself.

Maple leaves fluttered through the shafts of sunlight, giving hope that the fog would lift, as she watched the compound through binoculars. From this position, she had a clear line of sight to a large crumbling former dairy barn that might have once been yellow, two new prefab outbuildings with metal exteriors and roofs and a weathered farmhouse, looking patchy with the graying wood peeking out beneath flaking white paint.

One of the newer structures was a dock with a covered large boathouse on the St. Regis River that flowed into the St. Lawrence. That structure meant that it was reasonable to assume that the survivalists did leave their land. Did they use their boats to traffic in illegal drugs or human beings? Operations needed funding and she had yet to discover theirs. They were no longer farmers. That much was certain.

Had Stanley Coopersmith headed to court to defend his son?

Her reports on this group said that their leader never left the facility and his younger brothers, Joseph and Daniel, both married with children, rarely left their land. Stanley, who was married to Judy Coopersmith, had two grown boys—Edward, who they called "Eddie," and Morris, whom she had met on the night of her arrival.

She shivered with the cold as she counted occupants, noted physical descriptions into a digital recorder and snapped shots through her telephoto lens. As the morning stretched on and the sunlight finally reached her, she daydreamed about making a major arrest. Was it possible her runner had left Mohawk land? The Mohawk reservation land ended at the St. Regis River, just a short distance from Coopersmith's property. Had this been the runner's destination? The journey along would have been easy overland, or on the St. Lawrence River, with an escort of survivalists.

If she intercepted the shipment from Siming's Army, her boss would have to promote her. Then Rylee might ask for an assignment in New York City. What would her father think of that?

She sighed. Would he be proud?

The sound of a trigger's click dropped her from her daydreams like an acorn from an oak and made her stiffen. Her skin flushed hot and her fingers tingled. She held the binoculars; making a grab for her weapon seemed like suicide. Why hadn't she placed her weapon nearer to hand?

"Lace your fingers behind your head," came the order from a male voice behind her. The smell of the earth beneath her now turned her stomach and the ground seemed to churn as if heaved by an earthquake.

"Roll over," ordered her captor.

"I'm a federal agent. Homeland Security." For once, her voice did not shake.

There was a pause and then the command to roll over again.

She pushed off and rolled, coming to her seat. The man holding a rifle was the brother of the family's leader—Daniel Coopersmith. She recognized him by his ginger beard and the scar across the bridge of his nose. He held the rifle stock pressed to his cheek and the barrel aimed at her chest.

"Stand up."

She released her laced fingers as she did so. The blood pounding through her veins made her skin itch. This might be her only chance to reach her weapon. Her only chance to avoid capture.

"Don't," he advised.

The roar in her ears nearly deafened her.

He wasn't taking her. That much she knew, because she was not creating a hostage situation on her first assignment. As she came upright, she swept her leg behind his and knocked him from his feet. As his arms jerked outward in reflex, she seized the barrel of the rifle and yanked. By the time Daniel recovered enough to scramble backward, she had his rifle pointed at him.

"It ain't loaded," he said.

She felt the weight of the firearm and gave him a look of disappointment.

"Daniel, have you had any visitors, other than me, recently?"

"What kind of visitors?"

"Smugglers."

"Anyone crosses our land we know it. Got cameras everywhere. How we spotted you."

"Your family likes their privacy?"

"We don't assist illegals if that's what you mean."

"Why is that?"

"They're carriers. Part of the scourge to come."

She knew the dogma.

"You know your nephew is in court this morning?" she asked.

Daniel curled his fingers around his beard and tugged. "I knew he run off again. He get arrested?"

"Shoplifting."

"Comics again?"

She shrugged.

"Stan is gonna tan his hide."

"Not if he's in prison. Second offense."

Daniel seemed to forget she was pointing his rifle at him as he turned to go.

"I gotta go tell Judy." He glanced at her over his shoulder. "You best git. Leave my rifle on the road by your vehicle. That is if Stan don't already got your car."

"Stop." She had her weapon out and it *was* loaded.

He stopped and glanced back at her.

"You threatened a federal agent," she said to her retreating would-be opponent.

"I threatened a trespasser who's also an agent. We got constitutional rights. Illegal search. Illegal surveillance. Just cause. Illegal seizure." He continued speaking about rights and threats as he wound through the trees and out of sight.

She watched him go.

As it happened, when she reached her vehicle, she found Stanley Coopersmith waiting with his wife, Judy. Coopersmith was a man in his sixties, silver-haired, slim and muscular with a mustache that would have made any rodeo cowboy proud. His wife's hair was short and streaked with silver. She had the body of a woman accustomed to physical work and the lined face of a smoker.

Coopersmith did not move the rifle he held resting over his shoulder at her approach. She kept her personal weapon drawn but lowered.

"You holding my boy?"

"Sir, I'm Homeland Security—"

"We know who you are," said Judy Coopersmith, her chin now aimed at Rylee like a knife. "You holding my boy?"

"No, ma'am. Morris was arrested for shoplifting by local law enforcement. He has a hearing scheduled for this morning."

"You come here to tell us this?" said Coopersmith.

"No. I'm here investigating a case."

"You here to shut us down?"

Visions of Waco, Texas, flared like a dumpster fire in her mind.

"I am not. My job is to secure our borders."

"Well, we can assure you that this border is secure.

Nobody sneaks through this patch of ground without us knowing. Yourself included."

"That's reassuring," said Rylee. "Has anyone tried recently?"

The two exchanged a look but did not reply. *No answer is still an answer*, she thought.

She took a leap of faith that their mutual threat made her, if not an ally, at least not an enemy. "We have intelligence that indicates something dangerous might be coming over from Canada. I'd ask you to be extra vigilant and hope that you will alert me if there is anything that threatens our national security."

Another long look blazed between the two.

"Why do you think we're up here?" asked Coopersmith. "Just a bunch of crazies playing war games in the woods? We know what's coming."

"And you do not think the federal government is capable of stopping threats from foreigners."

"If I did, why would I build a bunker?"

Rylee glanced toward her vehicle. "I'd best get back."

It was a long, long walk…to her vehicle. She did not draw an easy breath until she was safely behind the wheel. However, when she pressed the starter, her vehicle gave only an impotent click. The engine did not turn over on any of her next three attempts. There was no motor sound. In fact, the only sound was the thumping drumbeat of her heart.

THE FOG HAD settled into a steady drizzle by midday. Axel reached the stretch of old timber bordering Coopersmith land. He'd received a tip from Hal Mondello, who knew how to spot a fed's car if anyone alive did, that Rylee had headed past his place. Beyond Mondello land was the cult that called itself the Congregation of Eternal Wisdom. Beyond that was Hal Coopersmith's spread and his survivalist family. He didn't know which was a worse place for Rylee. For personal reasons, he decided to try Coopersmith's first and backtrack if necessary.

Hal Mondello was not a friend, but he protected his self-interest. Having the sheriff rein in a fed nosing around would be to his benefit. Hence, the call.

Mondello called himself a farmer, but everything he raised went into his cash crop, moonshine. Hal supplied most of the entire region with hard liquor. His brew was popular for its potency and the fact that it was cheap, due to Hal's complete avoidance of paying any federal tax. That made his moonshine a working man's favorite. Thankfully, that sort of violation fell under the auspices of the ATF, who had found his operation too small to be bothered with.

Axel raced out to the Coopersmiths' main gate, running silent, but exceeding the speed limit the entire way. He understood the Coopersmiths' desire to live off the grid, be largely self-sufficient, but he didn't understand living in a constant state of fear of some upcoming disaster from which only you and yours would survive. What kind of a world would that be, anyway? The thought of only Axel and his family surviving such a calamity gave him a shudder.

On the other hand, he did admire the Coopersmith family. Before they'd taken to their compound and ceased interacting with the outside world, Axel had been to their farm and respected the close-knit group. Anything could be taken too far. Religion came to his mind and he shuddered again.

He'd just be happy to have a family that didn't scare him so much that he didn't dare leave them out of his sight. And he owed Stanley Coopersmith for getting him out of his abysmal situation and helping him take his GED. Without him and Kurt Rogers, Axel didn't know where he might be now.

Axel was pleased to find Stanley's oldest son, Edward Coopersmith, minding the gate when he roared up. He and Eddie had enlisted in the army together and the two had been friends up until a year ago when his father had shut the family up on their land.

By the time Axel had left his sheriff's unit, the dust he'd raised was falling about them in a fine mist, settling on his hat and the hood of his car. Here, beneath the cover of trees, the drizzle had not succeeded in reaching.

He and his former comrade stood on opposite sides of a closed metal gate.

"Where is she, Eddie?"

"Who?"

"The homeland security agent your family is detaining."

Eddie could not meet his gaze.

"No concern of yours, I reckon."

"Eddie!"

His friend gripped the shoulder strap of the rifle slung over his shoulder so tightly his knuckles went bloodless.

"She's up at the farm," Eddie admitted.

"Under duress?"

"Not that I could see. But they was armed. So was she, come to that."

"Trespassing?"

"Well, she was."

"Eddie, she's a federal agent. You do not want her harmed."

His friend offered no reassurance.

"Bring me up."

"No outsiders."

"I'm not an outsider. I've eaten at your table. Your ma taught me algebra."

"Still…she ain't your concern."

Axel imagined the news crews and federal helicopters circling the compound. He had to stop this right now.

Looking back, he didn't know why he did it. Perhaps because it was the only idea that popped into his head.

"She's my girl," said Axel.

"She's what now?" Eddie cocked his head.

Axel doubled down. "That's why she's up here, berry picking."

"With binoculars?"

"She's my fiancée and I won't have her touched."

"If she's your girl, why she up here alone?"

"Rylee is deciding if she wants to live up this way. I imagine she got...confused. Turned around."

"She was armed."

"Everyone up here is armed. We got bear and moose and elk." *And survivalists with semi-automatic assault rifles*, he finished silently.

Eddie released his grip on the rifle strap to scratch under his jaw at the coarse black beard. He looked so much different than from just a few years back when he was muscular and fit. Now his body looked undernourished and his face gaunt.

Axel watched Eddie as the man considered his options in silence.

After a long silent stretch, Axel had had about enough. "Open the gate or I'm ramming it."

"You can't do that." Their eyes met.

"I'm getting my girl so open up or stand aside."

Chapter Five

"Your girl, huh?" His old friend did little to hide his disappointment and Axel wondered if perhaps Eddie was attracted to Rylee. His answer came a moment later.

"She's very pretty. Kind of prickly, though."

"True on both accounts."

He realized that here on the compound, Eddie had little opportunity to meet eligible women. Rylee was a beauty and smart and he was certain she would have zero interest in locking herself up on nine hundred acres to wait for disaster.

Rylee was here to stop that impending doom from arriving. He admired her for that.

"Eddie, I'm getting in my vehicle. That gate best be open before I get there."

It wasn't a bluff. He knew that his modest yearly budget did not include major damage to his vehicle, but he was getting up to the farm. By the time he had his unit in drive, Eddie was swinging back the gate.

Axel paused just inside to speak to Eddie. "Why don't you come to my place for dinner one day?"

"Can't." Eddie made a face.

"Open invitation," he said and headed off. Axel bounced along the twin groves that served as the access road to the compound, his windshield wipers screeching over the glass as he tried to clear the mist and mud.

RYLEE HAD BEEN stripped of her weapons and now accepted escort to one of the outbuildings. Judy Coopersmith had left her to see to her youngest son, Morris, who was heading to court today. Before leaving, she warned her husband, Stanley, that *this little gal is a guest and is to be treated like one.*

Stanley Coopersmith had his brother Joseph working on her car that had either a bad starter or a bad battery. Stanley thought Rylee should see something in his garage before leaving. She had time on her hands and so if Mr. Coopersmith wanted to give her a tour, she was happy to take it.

The garage turned out to be a huge prefab carport of aluminum, with a vertical roof that looked wide enough to park two tractor trailers in.

"We use it to repair our vehicles and construction. It's right in here."

The odor of motor oil, mildew and rust assaulted her before they'd cleared the single door that stood beside the huge twin garage doors. Inside, two pickup trucks stood end to end, one on blocks and the other with the hood open and a greasy tarp draped over one side.

Beside these casualties sat a backhoe with the bucket removed and showing one broken tooth. Along the back was a long tool bench. She picked her way past various replacement parts that littered the grease-stained concrete. On the cluttered surface of the tool bench sat one pristine device. It was a drone—white, approximately thirty-four inches with eight rotors, one of which had been damaged. She glanced at Coopersmith, who motioned her forward.

"Go on," he said.

"Where did this come from?"

"Darned if I know, but I took that shot. It was carrying something, like a duffel bag. It dropped it across the river before I made that shot. Crashed out back and we scooped it up."

"What's across the river?" she asked.

He looked startled. "That's the Mohawk Nation."

"Do you believe that it is theirs?"

"No saying. I didn't shoot it until it was over my place."

"And its cargo?"

"Dropped on the Kowa side of the river."

"Did they retrieve what the drone was carrying?"

"Can't say. But I know someone has been trying to activate that drone remotely."

"How do you know that?"

"Because the damn thing keeps moving around the garage. It's why I chained her down."

Rylee used a cloth to lift the drone. "Heavy."

"Thirty pounds and no serial number. No markings at all that I can see."

"When did you find it?"

"Yesterday."

Monday, she realized, and the same day that Border Patrol followed a small man dropped off on the Canadian side, who crossed the border through a wooded area and then fled onto Mohawk land carrying a duffel bag. Had their suspect had the drone to carry out the cargo or did he have outside help?

"Were you planning to report it?"

"No. I was planning to take it apart and keep it. But if you want it, I'll accept offers."

"Offers?" She did a poor job holding back her surprise. "How much?"

"Take five hundred for it."

"Done."

She reached for her wallet, zipped in her blazer.

"You carry that much?"

She nodded, opening the billfold.

"Should have asked for six," he said.

"I'll give you seven." And she did.

Stanley accepted the cash.

"Has this happened before?"

"Trespassers? Sure. Just today, for instance." He gave her a pointed look and she flushed as he continued on. "But drones. That's a new one for me."

A voice came from behind the pickup.

"Pop?"

"Back here."

Edward Coopersmith appeared, red-faced and unable to make eye contact with her. Behind him came Sheriff Trace. He had no trouble making eye contact and the result was an instant acceleration of her heartbeat. The physical reaction to this man was getting bothersome. She scowled at the pair as they continued toward them.

"Axel, what a surprise." Stanley offered his hand to Trace and cast a scowl at his son.

"I wouldn't have brung him, but this here is his gal and he's worried."

Stanley looked from Axel, whose jaw was locked tight, to Rylee, whose mouth swung open.

"Interesting news, seeing she's only been here a day and a half."

Edward glared at Axel, who shrugged.

Stanley Coopersmith spoke again. "We aren't detaining her, Axel. Fact, she's leaving anytime. You want to give her a lift?"

"I'll need my weapons," said Rylee.

"'Fraid our policy is to confiscate the firearms of trespassers."

"And my vehicle?"

"Also confiscated."

"It was on a county road."

"The road belongs to the county. The land is ours. You left the government land when you left the road."

"Taking a federal vehicle might be a problem for you," said Rylee.

Coopersmith did not blink. She looked to the damaged drone, itching to get it to her people. A glance at Trace told her he was worried. He motioned with his head toward the exit.

Rylee looked to Coopersmith. "What do you want for them?"

"Money is good."

"What about shotgun shells? I have ten boxes in my trunk."

"You don't anymore."

Here, Axel stepped in, looping an arm around her waist and cinching her tight. Her side pressed against his and even though their skin never touched, her body tingled with awareness and she temporarily lost the ability to speak. His scent enveloped her. He smelled of pine soap and leather.

"I appreciate you looking out for my girl, Mr. Coopersmith. And for all you did for me when I was a boy. I'd appreciate you allowing us safe passage through your land."

"Very fact she's up here shows I'm right. It's coming. I feel it in my bones."

Rylee glanced to Trace to see what *it* might be. His hand rested familiarly on her hip and she found it harder to think as her body pressed to his.

"What about two cases of MREs for your trouble?" he offered, referring to the military Meals Ready to Eat. The food staple stored for years and he thought might just appeal to a man ready to hide in a bunker.

"I'll take six for the drone and safe passage off our lands."

"And her vehicle, weapons and anything else you took from her car."

"Done."

Axel released her to shake on the deal. Rylee stepped away from both men and headed toward the door.

She resented being bargained for like a milk cow. But she said nothing. Safely clear of Axel's embrace, her mind began functioning again. She retrieved the drone and carried it with her as they left the garage.

Edward hovered by her opposite side. "If things don't work out for you two, you could give me a call."

She blinked at the strange offer. "You have phones out here?"

"No, but Axel can get a message to me."

Axel chose this moment to press a hand to her lower back. The gesture was intimate. "We best be on our way, sweetheart."

The endearment sounded forced but made Edward flinch. Inexplicably, she felt a tightening in her throat and her breath came in tiny gasps. She forced her mouth closed and breathed through her nose all the way to her vehicle, parked before the main house.

There, she watched her weapons loaded back in her trunk. Everything went back in place except the shotgun shells. She placed the drone on top and accepted the keys from Stanley.

"You understand this is a one-time deal on account of my wife saying you was to be treated as a guest."

"Do you always ransom your guest's belongings?"

Stanley Coopersmith's smile was wily. "Generally, I just keep them."

"You will have to notify me if you apprehend or spot any more trespassers or see any unusual activity."

"Actually, I don't have to." Stanley accepted her card.

Axel held open her door and cast her an impatient look. Those gray-blue eyes relayed messages that she could not decipher other than his impatience and a possible brewing storm.

Rylee allowed Axel to walk her alongside of the sedan and tuck her into her seat as if she were a child unable to successfully open or close a car door. Then she followed his vehicle off the property and out of a gate that was the only gap in a perimeter fence that stretched into the woods in either direction.

A chill now lifted the hairs on her arms and neck. Had Stanley actually been considering ransoming her? She was a federal agent and taking her hostage would have brought the FBI straight to his property line. There, federal authorities would have waited during negotiations that she realized might have stretched on and on. For the first time, her annoyance with Axel turned to the realization that she might just owe him her thanks. If that situation had escalated, the ramifications could have been disastrous for all parties.

Axel had gotten her out of a survivalist camp without bloodshed, quickly and with only the merest gesture of a bargain. Just the dashboard computer was worth far more than a few cases of prepackaged food and shotgun shells.

That was twice now he'd pulled her fanny from the fire. Rylee gripped the wheel as she followed Axel onto the highway and back toward Kinsley. Perhaps a collaboration with the locals was not just some empty gesture and words from her department. She might get farther with his help if she included him in her investigation and, perhaps, keep custody of her car.

Trouble was she didn't trust him. All she really knew was that he was a local guy, generally liked, with an impressive military career that he had left to come here. His background information was general at best. But where had he been before he was fostered to Kurt Rogers at age thirteen? And what had happened to make him leave the army shortly after his fatal shooting of fellow servicemen?

As an army brat, she didn't approve of his taking the

early discharge option. Her father, sister and brothers were all career Marine Corp so she shared her father's aversion for the army.

"One way to get to know someone is to speak to them," she said to the car's interior.

Rylee was not a joiner. An introvert by nature, she was comfortable only with her siblings, and some more than others. They were nearly back to Kinsley before her phone picked up cellular service. She used the vehicle's communication system to call her boss.

Someone from the Glens Falls office would pick up the drone. Hopefully, they could glean some information from the navigation system. She'd seen her share of drones during professional training and recognized this one was not the garden-variety hobbyist craft. Too sophisticated and too expensive for the average operator.

By the time she reached her motel, she realized she had missed lunch and was starving. In the motel lot, the sheriff peeled off to park in the guest area. She checked the drone in the trunk. It was not in the spot she had placed it and there were scrape marks on the inner surface of the trunk. The blades began to whir, and she slammed the trunk closed.

This was a safer spot to hold the device than the motel room and she wasn't sure she could get it in there without it getting away. She glanced around. You usually had to be within sight of a drone to effectively operate it. This sort might have a longer range and all sorts of navigational upgrades.

Axel was beside her car as she locked the vehicle.

"You know, I do have other things to do besides collect you from private property."

She turned and met him with a bright smile. "And I appreciate your efforts and I'd like to take you out to lunch as a thank-you."

It was as if she'd frozen him in some tractor beam. He stood with his mouth half open, a finger raised to continue his lecture, and now seemed unsure how to proceed.

She closed her hand around his extended index finger and lowered his hand to his waist. He frowned before drawing his hand back. She doubted he intended the action of gliding his digit from her closed palm to be sexual, but from the startled gaze and the drop of her stomach, the friction had done just that.

He stood speechless, and she was finding a lack of oxygen in this corner of the parking lot. *Oh, no*, she thought. Not this one. He's overbearing and judgmental. He's in a dead-end career at the top of the world. She had the impression he played fast and loose with the law and enforced only the regulations that fell under his auspices. But those blue-gray eyes. They reminded her of a winter sky. Axel lifted his hands and for a moment she thought he would hold her again. The little show for Coopersmith replayed in her mind with the firm feel of his fit body.

She stepped closer. He grasped her shoulders and for just a second he seemed unsure if he should push or pull. Rylee leaned toward him and he extended his arms, sending her back a step.

"Separate cars. You follow me," he said and whirled away. His retreat came as close to a jog as a man could manage and still be walking. She'd never seen someone in such a hurry to be rid of her.

It only then occurred to her that the sheriff might be as hesitant of her as she was of him.

Her hands went to her hips. "We'll see about that."

Chapter Six

Axel checked the rearview every ten seconds to be sure that Rylee was following him. His heart was thumping as if he had run all the way to Bear Creek Café. He tried and failed to convince himself he was just anxious that she not veer off to find herself in another jam that required an extraction.

But it was a lie. He wanted her in his arms again. That little stunt for the benefit of the Coopersmiths had been a mistake. He'd been close enough to smell the light floral scent of her hair and feel the fit of her body against his. Both made him hungry for far more than lunch.

He realized, with a sinking feeling, that he was spending so much time minding her business because she was so appealing. Even her false bravado came across as charming. He groaned aloud as he set his blinker tapping and made a slow turn into the lot. Rylee was parked and out of her car before he even had his turned off.

"Fast woman," he muttered.

He tried to hold the door for her, but she made it inside unassisted and told Bonnie they'd prefer a booth. Then she took the one farthest from the counter.

"Waitresses have ears like elephants," she told him as she slid into her side and used a napkin from the metal dispenser to send the crumbs from the last patron's meal onto the floor.

She sat to give herself a clear view of her vehicle out the window.

Smart, he thought. *Keep an eye on that drone.*

Bonnie followed them back with menus and a wet cloth to finish the job Rylee had started.

"Drinks?" Bonnie said, grinning broadly at Axel as she wiggled her eyebrows at him.

His scowl only made her smile broaden. Bonnie was short and round and the pink apples of her cheeks seemed more responsible than her nose for keeping her owlish glasses in place. Her hair was blond, short and starched straight as the rails on a fence. She stood on tiny feet, balancing her girth with the skill of an acrobat.

"Iced tea," said Rylee, flipping the laminated menu over and over as if something new might appear.

Bonnie didn't ask Axel what he wanted but did pause to give him a "what's her deal?" look before departing. She returned a moment later with black coffee and Rylee's iced tea.

Axel removed his jacket and set it beside him in the booth. They ordered—a burger with fries for her, an egg salad sandwich with fresh fruit for him. She lifted her brow at his choice but said nothing.

"Any news from your home office?" he asked.

"None that I can discuss."

"They coming for the drone?"

"Of course."

She glanced out the window as a line of bikers roared past, rattling the window.

"They part of the North Country Riders group?" she asked, making the question seem casual.

The fact that she knew not only that they had a motorcycle gang—or "club," as they self-identified—up here but also their name did not bode well.

"How you know of them?"

"Briefings. They bring weed over the border. How is up for debate. You made any arrests in that department?" She sounded as if she already knew the answer and did not approve. He switched from wanting to kiss her to wanting to ditch her.

"Smuggling is your department. Best leave the borders to BP boys and ICE, right?" he said, referring to Border Patrol and Immigration and Customs Enforcement, the two branches of Homeland Security working on drug enforcement up here.

"Not if they sell it in your county," she countered.

"They don't."

"So it just passes through here like the water through the aquifer?"

"More like the St. Lawrence. What travels past us and down state isn't my concern."

"Maybe it should be."

"You have no idea what I do up here all day. Do you?"

"Eat barbecue and gamble at the casino?" she guessed.

"I cover up to thirty calls a day. Mostly folks who smeared themselves and their vehicles all over our roads. Drunk drivers, texting drivers, sleepy and distracted drivers and then we have the domestic violence calls, drunk and disorderly, and you might not be surprised to hear that most of those last ones are guests on vacay. But the winters up here are hard, lonely, and we have suicides. I also accompany Child Protective Services and they are way too busy here." He took a sip of coffee, burned his tongue and quickly chased the brew with ice water.

"You okay?"

"I will be when you head back down to Glens Falls."

"You got a particular reason you want me gone?" That one sounded like an accusation.

"You insinuating I'm dirty?"

"Just that you work up here without much supervision."

"I'm supervised by the town council and elected by the citizens I serve."

"Eloquent." She pursed her lips and his blood surged in all the wrong places.

Truth was, just sitting this close made his nerves jangle like a jar full of quarters rolling along the floor.

"Anything else?" she asked.

"I don't like your brand of cooperation."

"How's that?"

"The kind where you expect me to assist in an investigation of which I have no information."

She sat back and folded her arms. Her posture said that she wasn't interested in any sort of cooperation. Then, unexpectedly, her arms dropped to her sides and she leaned in until her torso pressed to the edge of the table. He leaned in as well, close enough to smell her skin and the spicy, earthy scent of something that seemed wildly erotic. His fingers, resting on his knees, curled, wadding the fabric of his trousers in his fists, and he told himself to sit back. But he didn't.

"All you need to know is that I am searching for illegal border crossings."

"You looking for a person or what they carry?"

"Both."

The lines on her face told him the rest.

"It's soon?"

"Any time."

"So why you?"

"Why not me?"

"You clearly don't have experience in the field. Either that or your method of investigation is to piss everyone off. Are you trying to rattle them into doing something stupid?"

Her chin lifted and she said nothing. But her cheeks blazed, indicating to him that her technique was no ploy.

The high color bloomed on her throat and the vee of skin visible above her buttoned-up blouse. His blood sizzled and turned to ash.

"I volunteered." She clasped her drink between both hands, lacing her fingers around the glass. "Most of my department is assigned elsewhere."

He pictured the briefing and this county being mentioned and her hand shooting in the air. She wasn't up to it. Now he felt irritated at her supervisors for sending her and annoyed that he'd have to babysit her during her little field trip.

"Were you that kid with her hand in the air, asking if there was homework?"

The flush bloomed brighter. "Homework is important." She cleared her throat. "This assignment is important."

"If that's true, why send you up here all alone?"

"Who said I'm alone?"

Did she have contacts, informants or undercover agents up here? He tried to think of any new arrivals. But the fall season brought many visitors to watch the leaves turn and boat on the St. Lawrence.

"Still, if this were a likely place for your illegal border jumpers, I'd expect a higher presence."

She conceded the point with a slight incline of her head. "Intel indicates that this crossing will be at the other end of the state."

"Buffalo?"

"Most likely. But this area is still a possibility."

"How possible?"

"Least likely, according to the analysts' report."

"So they sent you in the opposite direction of trouble. That about it?" In other words, her department was trying to get rid of her. He had a few thoughts of his own on why. Where he came from they called that a snipe hunt.

He waited for an answer.

She glanced away.

"I see." He hadn't meant that to sound so insulting. But it had.

Rylee sat back as if she'd slapped him. The arms came up and around her chest again. Her face hardened, and her eyes went cold as frozen ground.

"I know it can be difficult, having federal involvement in your county."

No use holding back. He laid it out there. "You're what's difficult. And I'm guessing that is exactly why they sent you up here. Not the most popular agent down there in Glens Falls. Am I right?"

"From my perspective, I'm thorough."

He continued to stare, and she glanced away.

"You can rub folks wrong."

She nodded, forcing a smile that struck him as sad. She was the know-it-all in the office. Least popular because she was often right. And she had the social skills of a bull shark.

So why did he feel the need to help her?

"You could get better cooperation if you turned down the aggression a notch."

The arms slid back to her sides and she clasped her hands before her on the table. Her perfectly shaped pink nails with the white French tips tapped restlessly. She eased back into the vinyl seat. Their eyes met and a chill danced over his skin.

"I wanted a field assignment and I got one. I'll admit that I don't play well with others. Abrasive and dictatorial were the words my supervisor used just before shipping me up here."

"I can see that. I might have said headstrong." He sipped his coffee, now just the right temperature to scald his throat without leaving any permanent damage. "Thank you for telling me all that."

"I'm sure you are even more anxious to see my back than she was."

He lowered his chin. "No, I think your analysis might be wrong."

Her eyes lit up and looked at him as if for the first time.

"Were you sent here, or did you choose to come here?" he asked.

"I chose because I think the analysis is wrong. This border is a strong possibility."

"But the boss went with the numbers and was happy to let you take a field trip."

She puffed out her cheeks and blew away a breath. He waited and at last she said, "Yes."

"How big a load?"

Her brows rose and studied him. Judged him, he thought. Then she shook her head.

No details for the sheriff, he realized.

"I'd like to ask you about some of the organizations in your county."

The path between them was back to a one-way road, he realized. She didn't trust him, and he wasn't sure if that was standard or if she had something on him. The obvious reared up inside him like a jab to his belly. How thorough had her research been before her arrival?

He studied her and decided she likely knew it all. He sank down in the booth seat, bracing his hands on either side of him so they acted like flying buttresses to the cathedral.

She continued, all business again, "The Kowa Mohawks are on my watch list because of their known smuggling activities."

"Cigarettes."

"What?"

"They buy in Canada and sell on their reservation and skip the federal tobacco tax."

"They transport merchandise through New York State without declaring them. It's trafficking."

"I guess they figure that since they are a sovereign nation, they don't pay income tax."

"Sovereign nations don't import goods over federal and state highways."

"They have land on both sides of the St. Lawrence and all this land was theirs once."

"Agree to disagree," she said.

"Okay."

She made a face. "I don't want to win the argument. I want you to understand that some of their members are radical in ideology and could, conceivably, be convinced to assist in a domestic attack."

"Not buying it. I've never seen them bringing in more than smokes. Next?"

"The North Country Riders?"

He nodded. The motorcycle gang did a lot worse than smuggling tobacco. They carried weed from Canada into New York. They also carried illegal pharmaceuticals.

"Possibly. For the right price, I believe they'd carry anything or anyone."

"The Mondellos?"

"Moonshiners? They are all about avoiding taxation and the feds. That family has been in business since prohibition."

"They have property directly on the river, facilitating their illegal distribution. They have the means and the opportunity."

"Motive?"

"Same as for the booze. Money."

He shrugged. "I can't rule them out. Who else?"

"The Coopersmith family. Survivalists are one thing, but what if they feel it is necessary to give the coming Armageddon a little shove?"

"I've known them since I was a boy. They are all about protecting their own, protecting this country. I can't see them doing anything to jeopardize either. Who else?"

"That's it." Her eyes still twinkled, and he felt for all the world like he was in an interrogation room. Sitting here, under the guise of helping her out when actually he was on her little list. She knew. He was convinced. But some tiny part of him did not want to say it aloud.

He shook his head. "You left out the congregation."

"A religious order?" she said, but her eyes narrowed as if just considering them.

He shifted in his seat, realized he was relaying his discomfort and forced himself to sit still.

"You know about them?"

"Some." She gave nothing away.

"They are also on the St. Regis River, between the Mondellos and the Coopersmiths, just a stone's throw from the St. Lawrence."

"That's true."

"Father Wayne heads the outfit. Call themselves the Congregation of Eternal Wisdom." He waited for her eyes to light up with recognition or her brows to lower in disapproval. But instead, her expression remained open.

"Go on," she said.

He didn't want to. The coffee now sloshed in his stomach like waves tossed by an angry sea. This storm's origin came from deep within himself, out of the sight of his DHS observer. Funny how something that had been his entire world for so many years, to her, meant nothing at all.

"It's a cult. They call themselves a congregation but it's a cult. They also live in a fenced compound. You might see some of the men outside the complex. They wear simple clothing. The top is a brown tunic. Bottom is baggy pants. No pockets, just a satchel, if they need to carry anything. Their heads are shaved and most wear beards."

"I haven't seen anyone like that. Is it an all-male order?"

He dropped his gaze to his half-finished coffee. "No. But you won't see the women. They stay put."

"Are they a radical group?"

"No. But their ideas are untraditional. Their leader says he is preparing them for ascension. They consider themselves the chosen and they consider children communal property."

"Many cultures share in raising children."

The small hairs on his neck lifted. "These kids don't know which of the women is their birth mother."

Now she was frowning but her notebook was out.

"They practice polygamy and some of the males undergo voluntary castration."

She stiffened. "What? Why?"

"Preparation for the afterlife. No sex there, according to Father Wayne. You'll know which ones have done this because they shave all their hair away." Axel lifted his mug and swallowed, tasting the remains of the coffee mingled with bitter memories. He should tell her the reverend's last name, but he just couldn't summon the courage.

"They sound like the Branch Davidians," she said.

"Except for the UFOs."

She sat back, leaving the pad open on the table. "Are you pulling my leg?"

He wished that were so. Axel pressed the flat of his palm to his middle, trying to settle his stomach.

"No joke. They live, farm, sing and dance out there on the river. And their leader has twisted theories of UFO visitations with God and scripture. The jumble is confusing but the gist is that reported alien visitations are actual angels sent by God in preparation for the end of the world. Only they call it the Rising."

"How many?"

"Hard to get an exact count. Thirty adults, maybe."

"How many children?"

"Social services go out there to check on them. The cult won't let kids be inoculated or register their births. They're homeschooled, or they tell us they are." He knew that schooling included creationism, their version of scripture and little else. "They collect the necessary textbooks and fill in all the correct paperwork." He locked his jaw so tight there was a distortion in his hearing, so he eased up.

"How do they fund their order?"

"Selling books and junk online. Taking donations and offering religious retreats. They recruit from the guests and once you are in, everything you own becomes theirs. Communal property."

"How do you know so much about them?"

Because I was born there.

"It's my business to know who lives in my county."

She lifted her pen and began writing. "I'll check them out."

And then she'd discover exactly where he came from.

"If you are going out there, you need me along."

"I don't."

"Rylee, trust me. You won't get past the gate without me. Let me help you."

She held his gaze and he held his breath.

"All right. I won't go out there without you."

Chapter Seven

On the third night in Onutake County, Rylee roared into the lot of the roadhouse favored by the North Country Riders on a red Harley Low Rider. The neon advertising for various beers sent colorful light gleaming across the chrome on the line of Harleys parked in a neat row along the front of the establishment, including the handicapped spots.

She parked her motorcycle at the end of the line of bikes and walked it back in preparation for a quick getaway that she hoped would not be necessary. Once the sled was leaning on its stand, Rylee tugged off the helmet and braced it under one arm, keeping her gun hand free.

She had prepared for her meet with the undercover agent from DHS stationed up here, dressing in clothing appropriate for a roadhouse in the territory of the North Country Riders. The tan slacks were tapered so she wore her calf-hugging suede boots over them. Her suede-fringed top covered all her assets and her brown leather jacket covered her service weapon. Under her bike helmet, she wore a black woolen cap.

She paused to take in her surroundings. Or was she just stalling?

That thought sent her forward, as she wondered again if she should have called the sheriff to request backup.

"It's just a meet. Make contact and get out." She tugged

the wool cap lower over her ears, hoping to hide the most obvious of attributes, her blond hair.

No disguising she was female, because of her height. The longer she stood, the faster her heart beat.

"Did you ask for this field assignment or not?" she scolded. Despite the lecture, she suddenly missed her desk and her data with the kind of wistful longing usually reserved for departed friends.

Squaring her shoulders, she marched to the door, paused and then reached for the handle. The interior stank of stale beer and the thumping beat of music assaulted her eardrums. She swept the groups of occupants, seeing that the motorcycle gang occupied most of the tables and the area of the bar closest to that seating. There was a stage at the opposite side with a band playing '80s metal. No one seemed to be paying any attention to them as they shouted in each other's ears and tipped long-necked bottles back.

She made for the area of the bar closest to the band, farthest from the bikers and closest to the spot the servers picked up their orders for the tables.

The sticky floor made it seem she was walking across a surface slathered with glue. She set her helmet on the scarred surface of the bar, beside the heart someone had scratched into it.

As she waited to order, she busied herself looking for her contact. She did not know her, but Rylee's image had been sent to the agent. She still had five minutes to go before the meet.

Reaching into her coat pocket for her mace, she made sure it was close at hand. Then she retrieved her mobile phone and glanced at it because the screen showed she had made a call, connected and had been connected for three minutes. Had her helmet made the call?

She glanced at the caller information and groaned. Sheriff Axel Trace. Rylee lifted the phone to her ear but could hear nothing.

"Trace?" she asked.

"Rylee? Where are you? I was just having your phone geolocated."

"I'm fine. Sorry. Must have pocket dialed you."

"Fine? What's that music?"

"'Bye, Trace. I have to go."

"Rylee, where—" She disconnected and shoved the phone back in her pocket.

"What'll ya have?" The bartender was young with a bushy beard that did not disguise how painfully thin he was, or cover the tattoos on one side of his throat. It seemed to be a wing and the word *blessed*. The tips of the wing flew up behind his ear, which sported a plug the size of a nickel. Above his eyebrow was a musical note.

She ordered what most of the patrons were drinking.

"Glass or bottle?"

"Bottle."

The beer arrived and her server made a nice show of flipping the opener before uncapping the bottle and sliding it across the marred surface.

"What you riding?" he asked.

"Harley. 2016 Low Rider."

"Sweet."

A woman across the bar at the table extracted herself from the lap of a big man with a stomach that left her little room. She knew him. He was Lloyd Fudderman, head of the North Country Riders. But Rylee did not know that woman. The brunette wore a black T-shirt modified with a slice down the center to expose the tops of her breasts and so short her stomach and navel hardware were in full view. She strode away, swinging her hips to the delight of Fudderman, whose full salt-and-pepper mustache lifted on both sides of his mouth. His beard was stained yellow from tobacco, Rylee assumed, and his black leather vest showed various patches.

His woman wore unlaced biker boots and jeans that had been artfully torn and frayed across the knees and thighs. Her long wavy hair bounced with the rest of her as she passed behind Rylee to the bathrooms.

The lightbulb went off in her head at last and she slapped her money on the table, retrieved her helmet and beer and headed to the toilet. That must be her contact.

Rylee passed through the swinging door and into the brightly lit bathroom. At the row of sinks, a heavyset bottle blonde uncapping a lipstick. The T-shirt she wore indicated that she was one of the staff. The young woman had a florid face that clashed with the lipstick she reapplied. The color of the cosmetic reminded Rylee of a dog's tongue. Rylee's contact was nowhere in sight. Rylee dipped to see under one of the two stalls and spotted the brunette's unlaced boots. She glanced to the employee, who eyed her in the mirror and then broke contact to check her phone.

Rylee's contact emerged, checked her hair and ignored the soap, sink and bottle blonde as she refastened her belt, which unfortunately sported a Rebel flag. Then she glanced at Rylee, scowled and headed out.

Rylee blinked after her in surprise.

"Agent Hockings?" asked the blonde.

Rylee opened her mouth and just managed to keep it from swinging open as she nodded.

"I'm Agent Beverly Diel."

"Yes," she managed, cocking her head as her entire system misfired. "Hello."

"That was Queeny. She's Fudderman's woman, though she's half his age. Seems to be a lot of that going around up here."

"In the gang?"

"And at the cult. Fudderman has been in contact with

the head of the Congregation of Eternal Wisdom. You know them?"

"No."

"I haven't been able to contact any of the women out there and the men don't come in here or speak to secular women. I suggest you find out what you can about them. But do not go out to their assembly alone."

"Why not?"

"Because it's a cult. The headman has them all twisted up into believing they're the chosen people and the judgment is coming. They live separately, and they might be armed against what they see as a coming apocalypse. If you go, go with backup."

"I'll do that." She didn't have backup and wouldn't get any without first showing something to prove she was on the right track.

Beverly gave her a hard look.

"I won't."

"All right, then." She washed her hands and yanked down a paper towel from the dispenser with both hands.

"Did you get my report?"

She rolled her eyes. "Thin in evidence, heavy on speculation."

"I'm an analyst."

"I get that." The woman scanned Rylee's outfit, making her words seem like insults. "What I don't get is why you are up here instead of at your computer terminal."

"It was in my report."

"Rylee—" Her tone was one you used to explain to someone dim-witted. "You're fishing, am I right? Trying to get the attention of the supervisors who are ignoring you?"

"My report—"

"I read your personal file. You don't belong here. You don't have the training or the experience. Go home."

Rylee felt like a swimmer preparing to let go and sink into the deep.

"What do you think will happen if I call your supervisor?"

Rylee felt her skin grow cold and a shiver of fear inched up her spine. It wasn't the prospect of losing her job that frightened. It was the prospect of telling her father that she had lost her job that really made her gut twist.

But what if she were right? There was no turning back. She went home and admitted that she went rogue or she finished this and stopped this threat. Rylee narrowed her eyes, preparing to fight.

Beverly's brows lifted and she looked interested for the first time.

"The man who evaded Border Patrol…"

"The man you followed onto Kowa land?"

Her head dropped.

"Yeah. That's something."

Rylee lifted her gaze to meet Beverly's. The woman no longer seemed harmless. There was something of the hunter flashing in her dark eyes.

"He got away clean because someone from Fudderman's group picked him up. Took him back over the border, what I heard."

"What about his cargo?"

"Missing. The Kowa took it and that's all Fudderman's guys know."

"Did you report this?"

Her mouth went tight, and she gave Rylee a "what do you think?" look.

"So, they *do* carry illegals," Rylee said.

"First I've heard. It's been all weed and Oxy, so far as I can tell. I'm a regular buyer."

"I thought they didn't sell up here."

"Ha," she laughed.

Clearly, the sheriff did not know this. Or did he? It wouldn't be the first time a law enforcement officer had been paid to look the other way.

"What if I can get the cargo from the Kowa?"

Agent Diel cast a look that told Rylee she had no confidence that would happen, but then she gave her a patronizing smile and nodded.

"Sure, hon. You do that. But don't come back here dressed like that."

"Like what?"

"Like a magazine version of how tough girls dress." She shook her head as she scanned her from head to toe. "You see anyone in her wearing suede boots?"

"I came on a motorcycle."

"Every last one of them already knows you are here and who you are and what you are investigating. You'll get no help from that crew," said Diel.

"They running their own organization?"

"I don't know yet. Might find out in time. Now ride it out of here and don't come back. I'll contact you if I have anything."

"My number?"

Her face twisted and she lifted her phone. "I have it."

"So you could have called," asked Rylee.

"Wanted to get a look at you. Worse than I thought," she said. Then she capped her lipstick and shoved it in her front pocket before pausing at the door. "You should keep that outfit for Halloween. Maybe add a temporary tattoo."

Beverly left and the door banged shut.

Rylee braced herself on the counter, allowing her head to drop. When she opened her eyes, it was to see the tile comet—a streamer of toilet paper—fixed to the heel of one suede boot.

The commotion outside brought her up and to full alert.

The music had stopped and there was shouting coming from beyond the door. She recognized one voice. Axel Trace was bellowing her name.

Chapter Eight

Dressed in plain clothing tonight, Axel appreciated how quickly his presence inside the roadhouse had been noticed. The jeans, boots and flannel shirt beneath the open canvas jacket did nothing to keep him from being as recognizable as a roast pig at a vegan picnic. *Probably just as welcome, too*, he thought.

The patrons gradually came to rest, pivoting in their seats to face him as all conversation came to a halt. The band caught on last. First, the drummer lost the beat and then the bass player missed the bridge. The singer and lead guitarist opened his eyes, straightened and stepped back from the microphone. Feet shifted uneasily as the gathering cast glances from Fudderman and then back to him.

Fudderman lifted his half-finished longneck to his lips and tipped the bottle, draining the rest. Then he set the bottle down with a heavy crack that made the woman on his lap startle.

He pushed her off and to her feet, eyes never leaving Axel's. A smile came slowly to his lips as he sat back, relaxed, with one hand on his knee and the other on the bottle.

"Evening, Sheriff." He had the courtesy to not ask if the sheriff was lost or crazy, which Axel appreciated. "The fed is in the bathroom."

Axel glanced toward the dark alcove past the bar. Then

he headed that way. A big man with a shaved head stepped before him, bringing Axel up short.

"Get out," he said, leaning in so Axel could smell his breath, stale with beer and raw onions.

"That your sled parked in the handicapped spot, Hooter?"

"You and I going to have a problem?"

"I won't. But you have a hundred-and-fifty-dollar fine for parking there."

"The hell you say." He began a string of obscenities that involved at least three suggestions that Axel perform physical impossibilities on himself. Then Hooter reached back for a bottle and began an arching swing toward Axel's head.

Axel kicked out Hooter's feet from beneath him. Top-heavy and drunk was a bad combination in a bar fight. Hooter went down hard. The smaller man who Axel didn't know jumped in, swinging a bottle. It was like being back on base in Germany on any Saturday night. Axel grabbed his attacker's wrist and drew back one finger, causing his opponent to scream as the finger dislocated. Unfortunately, he also dropped the bottle, which bounced off Axel's forehead before shattering on the ground.

"Rylee! Time to go! Rylee!" Axel shouted toward the women's bathroom as Hooter scrambled to his feet. He didn't get all the way up before Axel brought his knee to the man's gut, sending him to his hands and knees on the beer-soaked floor.

The men at the bar closed in, forming an ever-decreasing circle.

"Rylee! Get out here." Still time if she made a quick appearance.

She did, only she had her gun drawn. This brought the other occupants of the bar to their feet. Weapons of all sizes and types were drawn in response.

"You," said Rylee, pointing her weapon at the smaller man with the dislocated thumb. "Back up, now."

Her voice was cold and her demeanor terrifying. She seemed born for this, with a steady hand, calm control and chilling expression of anticipation.

The man backed up, cradling his finger. Hooter reached his feet with the help of a bar stool that he scaled like a child on a jungle gym.

The circle widened as Rylee stepped beside him.

"Which one hit you?" she asked.

Ah, she was going to defend him. He was touched. But he also wasn't crazy.

"Let's go," he said, heading toward the door.

Rylee backed along beside him, her pistol deterring any from closing in.

Outside, she lowered her weapon and faced him. "Where's your personal weapon?"

"I'm off duty."

They kept moving, her keeping an eye on the closed door to the bar and coming up short as he reached his vehicle. His sheriff's department SUV lay just beyond where he had parked it, only now it sat on its side, driver's door up.

"What the..." His words trailed off. He rounded on Rylee. "I'm done babysitting you."

"Who asked you?"

"You called me from this...this gang hangout and tell me you're fine."

"I was fine until you started screaming."

"I wasn't screaming."

The door behind them banged open and members of the North Country Riders spilled out like floodwater.

"Come on," she said tugging him toward the back side of the bar. He followed, keeping pace as she jogged along.

Behind them, shouts and the sound of beer bottles smashing on the pavement urged them to greater speeds.

"I'm on the other side," she said, leading the way to a Harley Low Rider.

He paused, agog, forgetting everything as he admired the bike, which was all black right down to the fork and tailpipes.

"Wow."

She straddled the seat, righted the bike and rolled it forward off the kickstand. She'd parked the Harley for a quick escape. He eyed the rear seat that was higher and smaller than the saddle she occupied. He'd look like a gorilla riding behind a jaguar, he decided, but when the next bottle landed beside his boot, he made the move.

"I forgot my helmet," she said. Then turned the key. The engine grumbled. "Hold on."

He did, wrapping his arms around her waist and flattening himself over her back like a large bulky coat. She revved the engine and set them in motion, leaving a cloud of smoke and considerable rubber on the pavement.

He finally found the tiny footrests and decided this bike was designed for one person. A glance behind them showed an angry mob in the street.

He felt a pang of separation over leaving his sheriff's vehicle and worry over his SUV's welfare.

"Where are we going?"

"Kowa Nation," she called.

"Bad idea," he said. "They'll take your bike."

"I have to speak to their leadership."

He had to shout to be heard over the wind.

"Then let me call them. Pull over."

"Anyone following?" she asked, glancing in a side mirror.

"No. Pull in up there."

She did as directed, turning into the empty lot of the ice-cream stand now shut up tight for the evening. Drawing up beside one of the picnic tables, she rolled to a stop and braced her feet on either side, steadying the bike as he dismounted.

"That gang of thugs is selling weed in your county," she said.

"How do you know?"

She shook her head. "Can't say."

"Great. Thanks for the useless intel."

"You could use it and shut them down."

"I'm working on that and thanks again for telling me my job. But you see, I must catch them at it and have real evidence. That's how we do it up here."

She made a face and knocked down the kickstand, easing the sled to rest.

"Why didn't you draw your service weapon?" she asked.

He didn't answer but pressed gingerly at the lump emerging on his forehead with two fingers.

"The guy threw a punch. He didn't draw a weapon."

"He attacked a law enforcement officer."

"Just a way of reestablishing his personal space."

"You do know how to use a handgun?"

He blew away a breath through his nose and his teeth stayed firmly locked. His chin inclined just enough to give an affirmative answer.

"Guns, drawing them, shooting them, killing things. It doesn't solve problems. It only makes different ones."

She wondered about that answer. It seemed to come from some personal experience, and she thought of his army service record. Two confirmed kills, she recalled, the line of his personnel records coming back to her in a flash of perfect clarity.

"When was the last time you fired your pistol?"

"Hanau, Germany, 2008."

"You haven't drawn your sidearm in a decade?"

"Not a requirement of my position."

"Was this after you killed two servicemen in Germany?" she said, quoting from his records.

His eyes narrowed, glittering dangerously. "Yes."

"Will you tell me about that?"

"No. But you can read all about it on Google. May 1, 2008, one month before discharge, Hanau, Germany."

"But you would draw your weapon if circumstances demanded it."

"What circumstances?"

"To defend the citizens under your protection?"

"Yes."

"To protect yourself?"

"I don't think so."

She watched him swallow down something that seemed bitter, judging from his expression.

"Was it so terrible?"

"Taking another man's life? It's a scar on your soul."

"Then why pursue law enforcement?"

"More like it pursued me. Sheriff Rogers, the man I replaced at his retirement and for whom I have great respect, asked me to run for sheriff. He said I needed to get back in the saddle and that the county needed me."

"Seems you aren't really back."

"Most lawmen never have to draw their weapon."

That was true. And she really could not judge, because she had never been placed in the kind of situation he had faced.

"But you're not most people."

Axel gave her a long look and she felt, somehow, that he was taking her measure. He used the palms of his hands to scrub his cheeks as if trying to remove some invisible film. When he lifted his gaze to meet hers, he nodded, as if to himself.

"The report said two servicemen were involved in a drunken brawl. That the first serviceman drew his weapon on military police and that I ordered him to put down his weapon. He didn't. Instead, he drew on me and I shot him. Two shots and down he went. His partner charged me and I shot him, as well."

That was exactly what she had read.

Rylee pictured the bar in Germany, the drunken servicemen. The MPs called to restore order. She covered her hand with her mouth and then forced it down. She had asked and the least she could do was listen to him without sending judgment.

"But then there's the part that they don't put in the reports. There is the part that you see at night when you close your eyes. That first serviceman? He was drunk. Really, really drunk, according to his blood alcohol. When I shot him, he fell backward against the bar. He looked at me, and it was as if he suddenly realized what was happening. He seemed to me like a man who had just woken from some kind of a nightmare and into another one, where he had attacked an MP and now he was going to die. He knew it. He started to cry. His partner didn't have the opportunity..." His words trailed off. "He just..." Axel swallowed hard.

Rylee placed her hand on his. He turned his hand palm up and wove their fingers together, squeezing hard. Then he tried again.

"He just died instantly. I found out later, he was a newlywed expecting his first child. He was a boy. They named him after his father." Axel lifted his gaze and held hers. "That's the part they don't put in reports."

Rylee found her voice trembling when she spoke. "But you know that wasn't your fault. You were doing a job, responding to drunk and disorderly. That serviceman raised his weapon. Drew his weapon on you."

"His partner did what any good wingman would do, backed up his friend and it cost him his life."

"He attacked you."

"The price was too high."

"You had a right to defend yourself."

"There are other ways, Rylee. I could have thrown an empty bottle at him. Especially the second guy. He was drunk and he didn't have a weapon."

"He *was* a weapon, trained by the US Army."

"I think, believe, that a gun isn't the only option."

"It's the safest one."

"Safest?" He gave a mirthless laugh. "Not for the person on the wrong end."

He stared at her with eyes that beseeched her to understand. But she couldn't. Not really. Because she'd never faced such a situation. All she knew was that she was in no position to judge his feelings and that killing those two men had taken a toll on him. The urge to comfort overwhelmed. She stared up into those blue eyes and lost her way. Like a pilot flying in the infinite sky, there was nothing to help her recover her bearings.

She stepped forward, taking their clasped hands and bringing them behind her as she used the other to stroke the back of his neck, threading her fingers into his short thick hair. Rylee stepped closer, pressing her body to his.

He lowered his chin as his arms came around her. Rylee pressed her lips to his. Her urge to comfort dropped with her stomach as her body's reaction to his overwhelmed her. She reveled in the pleasure of his hungry kisses, as his strong hands stroked in a steady rhythm up and down her back. His mouth was velvet. She pressed herself to the solid wall of muscle as his arms enfolded her, taking her mouth with greater urgency.

Looking back on that first kiss, she would have liked to take credit for drawing back first. As an analyst, she should have done some figuring and recognized that kissing the sheriff was a bad idea. But it was Trace that eased her away. He groaned as he broke the kiss, as if it cost him something to do so.

The next thing she knew, she was blinking up at him, missing the comforting heat of his body and the new buzz of desire that made her inch closer. He allowed it but simply knotted his hands behind her back and leaned away.

"What are you doing to me, Rylee?" he whispered. His voice was a soft rumble that seemed to vibrate low and deep inside her.

"Making a mistake." She followed that with a half smile.

"No doubt. And it's the sort of mistake that I might just approve of, but you said something about wanting to go to Kowa land?"

Her brain snapped back into action. How could she have forgotten the information she had been given by Agent Diel?

"They have something. That duffel. I need to get it back."

Chapter Nine

"What's so important about that bag?"

Axel waited, marking her indecision by the furrows now appearing on her brow. Apparently, he was good enough to kiss but still not good enough to collaborate with.

She pressed her lips together, giving him a fierce look, and then she dropped her chin and studied the ground. When their eyes met again, he could tell she'd reached a decision.

"That illegal I was after? He was picked up by Fudderman's group after leaving the Kowa Reservation."

"You know this how?"

"I have a contact who also told me that Fudderman's people took him."

"Took him where?"

"My contact believes he was transported back over the border."

"Why bring him over only to take him back?" asked Axel.

"Because he wasn't important. His cargo was."

Axel felt that tingle at the base of his spine. The one that told him things were about to go south. He locked his jaw, not wanting to ask the next question. Turned out he didn't need to.

"Whatever he carried was left behind at the Kowa Nation. They have it. The question is, are they complicit in this carrier's plans or did they intercept him and his goods by accident because of my pursuit?"

"All right, you convinced me." Axel stood before her. The concern that had vibrated along his spine now moved to his stomach, twisting it in a way that told him they needed to move. "I have a friend on the Kowa Nation. We'll give her a call."

Rylee's brow descended on the word *her*. He failed in keeping his smile a secret. Was she concerned with the fact that he had female friends? All sorts of possibilities danced through his mind, distracting him from the task at hand. Primarily, he wanted to kiss her again.

"Her name is Kate Vasta. She's the younger sister of the acting chief of police." He drew out his cell phone and scrolled through his contacts. She answered on the third ring. Her voice was full of light animation and what sounded like delight to hear from him. Kate had been more than a good friend. But that was in the past, at least for him.

"Axel Trace. What can I do for the sheriff of the county?"

"Hi, Kate. I need a favor." Axel went on to explain what he wanted, and Kate promised to allow them in the rez as her guest. She also offered to meet them at the border and escort them directly to her brother.

Axel ended the call and grinned back at Rylee. "We're in."

"Thank you," said Rylee.

Her words showed gratitude. But her voice carried a very different message. He'd known kissing her had been a mistake, but he just couldn't resist. Now all the complications of a relationship, newly forming, were bubbling between them as they faced this new threat. It was baggage they did not need. In his line of work, distractions were dangerous.

Rylee donned her helmet, straddled the bike and kicked

back the stand. She turned over the motor and looked back at him, waiting.

Axel climbed on behind her and tried to ignore the feel of her warm body pressed close to his. He failed. There had been several times in his life when he knew he was in big trouble. This was now one of them.

True to her word, Kate Vasta was waiting for them in a battered green pickup truck at the border of the Kowa Nation. Kate drove Axel, with Rylee following on her bike, taking them directly to her brother's home. Apparently, they were expected because both her brother and one of the executive board members were waiting outside for them. Rylee was off her bike and at his side with cat-like speed.

Kate stepped out of her truck and addressed her brother. "Brother, I brought a guest. You remember Axel Trace, and this is his friend Rylee Hockings."

Her brother looked none too happy as he nodded. "We met."

Kate turned to Axel. "Do you need me?"

Axel spoke to her with his eyes fixed on her older brother. "I don't know. Do we?"

Vasta shook his head and Axel flicked his gaze to Kate. "Thank you for helping us out."

"Anything for a friend. You give me a call sometime. You hear?"

Axel felt a pang of guilt. It was wrong to call a friend only when you needed a favor. He made a mental note to call Kate soon. Then he glanced at Rylee and saw her glaring daggers at Kate as the woman climbed back into her truck and reversed course.

"Would you two like to come inside?" Vasta asked.

Axel motioned Rylee forward and followed her into the Vastas' ranch-style home. They were directed to the living room, where Vasta had to ask his children to leave the room.

Rylee did a good job of briefly explaining that the duffel bag that was, perhaps, in their custody contained something of national interest and possibly posed a significant hazard to his people.

Vasta and Executive Council Member Jeffries exchanged a long, silent look. Then Jeffries rose and asked them to follow him. They returned to Rylee's bike and waited for Jeffries to climb into a new matte black dually pickup. Then they left Vasta behind and followed Jeffries's vehicle out of the drive and past the city center, the casino and through one of the communities where the Kowa people resided. Beyond that, they headed to the St. Lawrence River and several storage facilities, stopping at a nondescript prefab garage.

"It's in here," said Jeffries. He paused only long enough to release the lock on the container door and click on the lights. Inside were storage containers filled with boxes of tobacco and a small desk supporting a computer from the last decade and a phone. Beyond squatted a gray metal filing cabinet that looked to have been kicked down a set of stairs, as the second drawer was too badly bent to close. Jeffries unlocked the filing cabinet with a small key and removed the duffel bag from the bottom drawer. Rylee's entire posture changed. She was on full alert with one hand on her weapon. Axel gave her a nudge and shake of his head. Her hand dropped back to her side.

Executive Council Member Jeffries set the duffel on the desk.

"We confiscated this from the person you pursued here," he said to Rylee. "We let them go. It seems to us that the carrier was Japanese. But I really don't know."

"Could he have been Chinese?" asked Rylee.

"I don't know." Jeffries rubbed the back of his neck. "It's possible."

"Has anyone looked inside this bag?"

Jeffries nodded. "Yes. Executive council and the acting chief of police have all seen the contents of this bag. We are in agreement that we do not want it on our lands but were not in agreement as to what to do with it."

Axel thought of the possibilities. What were the choices?

"Half the council was in favor of destroying it. The other half wanted to deliver it to state officials."

"Has anything been removed from this bag?" she asked.

"No."

She motioned to the bag. "May I?"

Jeffries nodded, extending a hand as he moved away.

"Why now?" asked Axel. "You could have given it to her when she first arrived."

"She didn't arrive. She entered our land without invitation. This negated any option to deal with her. Now she comes with a friend and with the escort of the sister of the chief of police."

Rylee flushed. "I am sorry for my bad manners. If I could, I would have done things differently."

Jeffries nodded. "Do them differently in the future. This is our home. How would you have reacted, if situations were reversed?"

"I would have deemed you a threat. I might not have been as forgiving as you have been."

Rylee turned her attention to the duffel. The way she unzipped the canvas bag gave Axel the chills. She moved as if the entire thing might explode.

"Is it volatile?" he asked.

"No. But if it is what I think it is, the contents are very dangerous."

"In what way?"

"I can't say," she said through clenched teeth, gingerly drawing back the sides of the bag.

Axel glanced in to see a second container of vinyl, rolled with a Velcro fastener. It reminded him of the sort of thing he used to carry lures for fly-fishing, only his version was canvas. Rylee lifted the orange-and-black bag to the desk and released the fastenings. Then she unrolled the container until it lay flat on the desk. The rectangular vinyl was divided into dozens of slots, each containing a glass vial.

"Ampoule transport roll," she said. Her voice had an airy quality and her breathing now came in short, rapid blasts from her nose.

"Get it out of here," said Jefferies.

"The foreign national carried this onto your land?" asked Rylee.

"No. This little guy crossed onto our land and we were in pursuit when we saw the drone with the duffel. Both in the same area, near the river. One of our people shot at the drone and it dropped the duffel, but we lost the thing in the trees near the river. Runner also got away. Recovered the package, though."

"A miracle it didn't break on impact," said Axel."

"Fell through the pine trees. My son caught it. And the guy who was there to retrieve it took off." Jeffries looked grim. "That spy came onto our land to retrieve this," Jeffries motioned at the bag, but now stood well back from the desk.

"Your son is very lucky. It was a good catch," said Axel.

"I was thinking the same thing."

Rylee rolled up the transport container holding the vials and then pointed at the duffel. "Burn that."

The rolled container went inside her leather jacket. She extended her hand to Jeffries and thanked him again. Then she turned and headed out of the storage building like a woman on a mission.

She had been correct, he realized. She had gone against

the odds and gotten it right. But her people were all in the wrong place.

Axel thanked Jeffries and then jogged after Rylee.

Chapter Ten

The ride to Kinsley was a blur.

They stopped at her motel to switch from the motorcycle to her vehicle and collect the drone given to her by Stanley Coopersmith. Then they headed to his office in Kinsley.

As Rylee pulled to a stop at the curb, he saw his battered SUV parked before the station. Pete, of Pete's Garage, had beaten them here, managing to tow his sheriff's vehicle back. Axel paused on the sidewalk to take in the damage. One side looked as if it had slid a hundred yards on gravel. The sheriff's insignia had all but disappeared, along with most of the paint on the passenger side.

Rylee was like a schoolgirl, nearly skipping the distance between her car and his office. He unlocked the door and held it for her, then flicked on the lights.

Her expression was animated; she seemed to have an external glow, like a halo or aura surrounding her. In his office, she paced as she spoke with an excited ring to her voice. She kept the phone pressed to one ear and her finger in the other.

Rylee seemed to have completely forgotten he was even there, as he took his seat and scrolled through his emails. Why did he care if she knew he was there or not? But he kept glancing her way, hoping to catch her eye. He didn't.

She described the cargo they had recovered. Arrangements were made for a pickup. After the call, she came to rest, collapsing into the big chair beside his battered wooden desk. The chair had been in the former sheriff's home, but when the stuffing began to show in one worn armrest, Rogers's wife had insisted it be banished from the house and it ended up here.

"Can you believe it?" She pressed one palm to her forehead and stared at the tiles of the drop ceiling above his desk. "I wish I could call my dad."

"It's not that late."

"He's in Guam again, I think. But, boy, I'd love to call him. I can't, of course. This isn't public info, but..." She smiled and sighed, happy in the prospect of telling her family of her coup.

"You were right." He moved to sit on the edge of his desk, keeping one foot planted on the floor. It didn't help. Rylee at close range still made him feel slightly motion sick. Did she know how pretty she was? "You gotta be pleased."

"More than pleased. Did I tell you that I'm one of seven? Seven!"

"No, you didn't tell me that."

"Oh, yeah. And as the youngest, I have never successfully commandeered my dad's attention for more than a minute at a time."

"Well, this ought to do it." He had lost his need to gain his father's respect the day he had asked his father which of the women in the compound his mother was and been told that it didn't matter.

Not to his father, maybe, but it sure did matter to Axel.

"What's he do, your dad?" *Besides ignore his daughter*, he wondered. Had he ever been that in need of his father's approval? He hoped not, but he admitted to himself that he had been back before he started sneaking off the compound. Only then did he begin to realize how twisted and aberrant his childhood really was. Early on he began to suspect that the warnings about the outsiders being damned had been a lie. A way to keep them all apart from anything that might undermine his father's control over them all. At first, he had sneaked off for attention. But no one had seemed to notice or care. If he hadn't left, would he right now be dressed in brown robes with his head shaved?

"My dad is a colonel in the US Marines, Indo-Pacific Command. All my brothers and my only sister are marines, too. I'm the black sheep, did not follow my marching orders."

"He wanted you to enlist?"

"Of course. He wanted me to attend officer training school and be a marine. He expected all of his children to serve their country."

"You are serving your country, Rylee. Working with Homeland Security would certainly fit that bill. He must know that," said Axel.

"Not according to my dad. You're either in the US Marines or you are not. There is no other option."

"So, your career choice caused some tension?" asked Axel.

"Oh, yeah," said Rylee. "I just didn't want to live my whole life out of the gunnysack. I wanted…wanted to find a place, one place to call home. Mom said home isn't a place. But you know, it could be."

"Except for my time in the service, I've lived my entire life in this county."

"Meanwhile, I didn't even know that there were families who did that. I saw from your records that you were emancipated. Is your family still here?" asked Rylee.

Why had he mentioned his past? Of course, she would have questions, but that did not mean he was ready or able to answer them. How did you even begin to explain the complicated mess that was his family? Let's just start with his mother. No, that was a terrible place to start. His father? Even worse.

"Just my dad. He's still around. I don't see him often."

Rylee's eager expression fell. She glanced away. "Oh, I see."

She didn't, though. How could she?

Axel forced a tight smile and she glanced away.

"I'm sorry about your mother."

He realized then that his words had led her to believe wrongly that his mom was dead.

Of course, Rylee was sorry for what she saw as a loss but she might be sorrier if she knew that his mother lived not ten miles from him and was not permitted to speak to her son or acknowledge him in any way as she prepared to enter Heaven's Door, as they called it. She had chosen his father's religious dogma over a relationship with him. That kind of rejection caused a sorrow that just never went away.

This would be the time to correct her and explain the situation. Axel groaned inwardly. His stomach knotted, and he knew he would not be doing that. Not today, not ever. Many of the good citizens of the county had forgotten that he was the skinny boy brought out of the Congregation of Eternal Wisdom by social services. They had forgotten that Sheriff Kurt Rogers had removed him from the influence of his father and fostered him for five years before Axel had joined the army.

His father had told Axel to his face that if he did not want to follow the true path to Heaven's Door, he could suffer the Desolation with the rest of the unbelievers. Axel's ears still burned at the memory of his father's scalding condemnation.

"Any brothers or sisters?" asked Rylee.

That was another complicated subject. One that he didn't even know how to begin to answer. Surely, he had brothers and sisters. But which ones were his by blood, who could say? The only way to sort that would be DNA testing and that would never happen.

Axel opted to keep his answer vague and truthful and then change the subject. "Yes. But you… Seven, right?"

"Exactly. I have five older brothers and an older sister, all in the marines."

Uh-oh, he thought. Each one would be glad to knock him in the teeth for what he wanted to do with their baby sister.

Rylee continued, "Oliver, the oldest, is a master sergeant in the Marine Air-Ground Force. Paul is a sergeant major in personnel. It burns Oliver up that Paul has a higher rank. Paul is stationed stateside in California. I have two twin brothers, Joshua and Grant. They're both second lieutenants and both intelligence warrant officers in Hawaii. That's a great posting. Those two have done everything together since as far back as I can remember. Marcus is only two years older than me and an assault vehicles commander. Can you believe my only sister, Stephanie, is a gunnery sergeant in communications? She's working as a cyber-network operator in Germany."

"Your mom?"

"Mom worked in the military schools. She taught music. And I play guitar and strings because of her. But she passed five years ago of a lung infection."

"I'm sorry."

"Yeah." She took Axel's hand. "We have that in common—losing our mothers. Don't we?"

They didn't. He frowned.

"I know. It's hard, right? I think Josh and Grant were glad to reenlist, with her gone. Home isn't a home without a mom. Or at least that's how it was for us. We lived all over. Oceanside, Honolulu, Okinawa and then back to Hawaii, but Kāne'ohe Bay this time. We were in Jacksonville, which I liked, and then Beaufort, South Carolina, which I hated. But I was thirteen. Thirteen-year-olds hate most new things, I think, and moving. I detested moving. Maybe I just hate South Carolina because that's where she died. So, Dad got transferred from Guam to Germany. That way me and Stephanie and Marcus could be with him. My older brothers were all up and out, enlisted by then." She straightened as if someone had put an ice cube down her back. "Sorry, I didn't mean to unload all that baggage."

"It's all right. You know, families can be complicated." He set his teeth and looked at her open expression. Maybe Rylee could understand. She knew grief and separation and a dad who was emotionally unreachable. Only difference was she was still trying to reach hers. "Listen, about my father—"

Her phone chimed, and she darted to her feet, removing the mobile and staring at the screen.

"My boss," she said and took the call.

Thirteen minutes later there was a helicopter parked on centerfield of the community baseball field. Rylee jogged out, keeping low. He didn't know what he had expected but it was not to see Rylee, carrying both drone and samples, climb aboard and disappear behind the door. Before he could take a step in her direction, the chopper lifted off, sending the dirt on the infield swirling behind them.

"Didn't even say goodbye," he said, as he covered his face from the assault of rock and sand.

What was he thinking? That she was staying? This was a good reminder that she was on to bigger and better things. He told himself it was for the best. Best that she left before she discovered just where he had come from. Because if she stayed, sooner or later, she'd learn the truth and that was something that he just could not bear.

IT WAS THURSDAY AFTERNOON. After a long night and a few hours of sleep, Rylee was back in her office in Glens Falls.

Somehow, everything seemed different, as if she didn't belong here.

Rylee held her cell phone in her palm, staring down at the contacts list. She had scored major points, located the vanguard of the attack and was just aching to crow about her accomplishment.

Her brow wrinkled as she realized that it was Axel she wanted to call. Not her father, who would likely be unavailable. He'd been unavailable emotionally to her for most of her life. Expecting him to suddenly see her as a competent protector of their country was just irrational. So why had she done all this?

If not for praise and advancement and accolades, why? Confusion rattled inside her like a bag of bolts in a barrel.

She hardly knew Axel. So why was she missing him and wanting to tell him everything that had happened since leaving him last night?

He was a bad choice for many reasons, not the least of which was the way he played fast and loose when deciding which laws to enforce.

For just a moment, she allowed herself to imagine an alternate reality. One where she came home to Axel every night. One where she stayed in one place and made a home for them. A garden with tomatoes and a bird feeder. Neighbors whose names you bothered to learn.

Rylee had spent her life moving and, while she'd believed she wanted something different, every decision she'd made climbing up the ranks had involved a move, and there was no end in sight. A promotion, the one she wanted so badly to earn, would require packing again and a new office, new city, new coworkers. Why had she never realized that in choosing to do the opposite, and not joining the US military, she had nevertheless adopted a transient lifestyle?

She sat hard as the realization hit her. She wasn't ever going to stop moving. She wasn't going to be a team player.

Or be a welcome part of a group task force on anything. She was going to live a rootless existence, moving from one apartment to another with whatever she could carry in three suitcases. Just like her father.

She was never going to have that dog or those kids or that husband that she had believed she wanted. Was she?

Rylee scrolled through the contacts, past her family's names and her friends and her professional contacts, stopping on Axel Trace. Was she really going to pick him?

Suddenly, Rylee's accomplishment frightened her. It was what she wanted. To make a splash. To gain attention. To use her analysis skills and new field experience to move onward and upward.

So why was she thinking of a cool autumn night and a picnic table outside an ice-cream stand in the far reaches of New York State and the man who waited there?

Chapter Eleven

The knock upon Axel's door brought him grudgingly to his feet. Friday nights were busy, and he'd just made it home before eleven o'clock. The hour meant this was not a visitor. Most bad news came lately by phone or text, but some folks, the older ones mostly, stopped by to drop trouble on his door. Usually not after nine in the evening.

He had discovered that the later the hour, the larger the problem. Domestic, he decided as he left the kitchen in the back of the house, thinking the visitor would be a woman carrying her children in her arms, seeking protection. He'd stopped counting the number of such visits he'd taken since being elected as county sheriff.

Axel hiked up his well-worn sweatpants and grabbed a white T-shirt from the peg behind the door on his way past. He had changed for bed after his supper, but he'd cover up before he greeted his visitor. He had the shirt overhead when the knock came again.

He glanced through the window set high on the door and his breath caught. Rylee Hockings stood on his step dressed in a gray woolen jacket, thigh-hugging jeans and scuffed hiking boots. She was looking down at the yellow mums on his steps that had already been nipped by frost. The blossoms drooped and wilted. The angle of her jaw and the overhead light made her skin glow pink. The black knit cap on her head trapped her blond hair beside the slim column of her throat.

His breath caught, and his blood coursed, heated by her nearness. When was the last time a woman took his breath away?

Never was the answer. He'd steered clear of most women, recognizing the trouble they inherently caused and not wanting the complication of explaining the soul-scarring mess that was his family. Why would any woman, especially one as dedicated, smart and pretty as this one, want a man who most resembled the tangled wreckage of a submerged log in the river. He was good for tearing the bottom out of boats and causing other people trouble. So far, his personal life had been nothing but bad.

She lifted her fist, knuckles up, to knock again and glanced up to see him peering down at her.

"Hey! You gonna let me in?" she said, her voice raised to carry through the locked door that separated them.

He shouldn't. Because if he did, he had a fair idea where the evening might lead. She was smiling like a woman satisfied with the world, but he had the feeling he could change that smile, brighten it, perhaps remove the lines of tension bracketing those pink lips.

Axel turned the dead bolt, pulled open the door and stepped back.

"What a nice surprise."

She'd left Wednesday night and there had been no calls, no texts and no emails from her or from Homeland Security. He'd decided that she'd dumped him like an empty beer bottle, and now he didn't know what to think.

"We've assembled a team. They'll be here tomorrow morning. I just wanted to brief you before their arrival on all that's happened."

"Sure." He thought the surprise must have shown on his face. Thus far, she had briefed him on very little.

She breezed inside with the cool air, and he closed the door behind her. She stepped into the neat entry and sank to the bench with his shoes lined up beneath and the variety of coats hanging above on pegs. Above that, the cubbies held his hats, gloves and a softball mitt.

"Boots off?" she asked.

He was happy to have her remove any item of clothing she wanted.

"Sure. And let me take your coat."

He waited as she worked loose the laces while also glancing into the living room. She slipped out of her boots, revealing new woolen gray socks. She was getting the hang of dressing for the weather up here, he thought. But Rylee was quick and used to adjusting to her environment. She must be, after so many moves.

She stood and he took her coat, using the opportunity to lean in to smell the fresh citrus scent at her neck before stepping back. Rylee headed to the living room. He had left it earlier, as he always did, pillows in line on the couch he used only for napping and his book waiting on the table beside his comfortable chair beside the remote.

"You're neat," she said, coming to a stop.

Having things, personal things, was something he never took for granted. Personal property was forbidden at the congregation. He could never have imagined owning a home of his own. Filling it with the overstuffed comforts that were lacking in the austere landscape where he had been raised.

Wooden chairs placed on pegs each night. Floors swept and then mopped. Children assigned tasks on a weekly basis that grew increasingly difficult as they aged.

He'd been approaching that age where he would have been expected to choose the most holy position for males at the compound or the lesser status of men who did not accept the full preparation to be received in Heaven.

"Axel?"

He snapped his attention to her and realized he was clenching her coat in his fist.

"I asked if that was coffee that I smelled?"

The smile was forced but she didn't seem to notice. "Yes. Have you had supper yet?"

"Oh, hours ago, but I'd love a cup of coffee."

He debated where to bring her—the living room with that big couch or the dining room with the large wooden table for a professional conversation?

He motioned to the living room. "Make yourself comfortable. I'll bring you a cup. How do you take it?"

"Black."

He nodded and waited as she slipped into his world in her stocking feet. He was quick in the kitchen, returning with two cups. He tried not to place too much meaning on the fact that she sat on the sofa.

"Do you use the fireplace often?" she asked, gazing at the wood fireplace, screened and flanked with fire tools and a metal crate of kindling. The logs fit in an opening built in the river stone masonry for that purpose. The stone swept up to the twelve-foot ceilings of the old farmhouse and was broken only by the wide mantel crafted with chisels by hands long gone from the living, out of American chestnut back in a time when the tree was a plentiful hardwood.

"Yes, and I keep it set. Would you like a fire?"

"Oh, that's not necessary. It's just I always wanted a house with a fireplace. They don't usually have them in California or Hawaii—or Japan, for that matter."

"Or in South Carolina?"

She laughed, but her eyes were now sad. "That's right. How long have you been here?"

"Let's see, I found this place after I left the service. I

bought the home after I finished my probation period with the City of Kinsley."

"Police Department," she said, quoting the part of his history that she obviously knew, the part that was in the records. But Sheriff Rogers had held back enough. Keeping the circumstances of his claim for emancipation listed as abandonment. The truth was worse and more complicated.

"That's right. So that was, wow, six years ago. And I still haven't replaced that back deck."

He set down her coffee and took a seat beside her. She gathered up the mug and took a sip.

"Strong," she said and set the ceramic back on the slate-topped coffee table.

He left her to set the fire. The entire process involved striking a match and lighting the wadded newspaper beneath the tepee of kindling.

He slipped two logs from the collection and waited for the flames to lick along the kindling, catching the splinters in bright bursts of light.

"That's a pretty sight. Warms me up inside and out," said Rylee, gazing first at the fire and then to him.

An internal spark flared inside him and his heart rate thudded heavy and strong.

He knelt beside the fire and glanced back at her, taking in the relaxed smile and the warm glow of the firelight reflected from her cheeks and forehead. The entire world seemed to have taken on a rosy glow and he wasn't at all certain it was the fire's doing.

"Is it too late for a conversation?" she asked.

Did she mean too late in the evening or too late in their relationship? He'd spent the first few days resenting her intrusion, followed by a pervasive annoyance at the extra work she caused him. But just before she left, when they took that wild ride on the motorcycle, and even before that kiss, he knew there was something different about this woman. Perhaps the threat she posed was not professional but strictly personal.

Was that better or worse?

"No, it's not too late."

"Trace, I think I made a mistake with you. I want to apologize for trying to run you. You don't work for me and it was wrong for me to treat you as if you did. To come in here and tell you what to do in your own county. That's not collaboration. It's my first field assignment and I really want to do well. It's important for my career for me to get this experience. But even more important was finding the package. Finding that case will save a lot of lives."

He came to sit beside her on the sofa. "That's a good thing. But you're back, so I have to assume your work isn't finished." He didn't let himself latch on to the possibility that she'd come back to finish their business. "Do you want to tell me what this is all about?"

He waited in the silence that followed as she laced her fingers together and leaned forward until her forearms rested on her knees. Then she stared at the fire as it caught. He had time to add both logs to the blaze and return to his seat before she spoke.

"Yes, I think you deserve that. There was some trouble this summer—July—in the Adirondacks just south of here and in the city of Saratoga Springs." Her brows went up and she looked to him.

He nodded. "I know the area." He'd even gambled at the thoroughbred track a time or two in August.

"There was a CIA operative there. Apparently, he was collecting intel from a foreign agent on US soil, which breaks about fifty rules that I can think of. Regardless, the meet was made at Fort Ticonderoga and he retrieved a thumb drive full of intelligence. However, they were followed and our man had a difficult time getting the information into the hands of federal operatives. There was a civilian involved. A completely untrained, inexperienced woman, and how she survived I do not know. In any case, the intel leads them to believe there was a small sample of a biohazard, which they recovered. That told us what we were looking for. Unfortunately, the actual sample and the helicopter carrying it were shot down. This material went missing for part of August. Apparently, it was discovered in a downed helicopter by an adventure specialist and a New York City homicide detective, who somehow managed to evade pursuit by foreign agents and successfully brought the intelligence to a state police office outside of Saratoga Springs, New York. The sample went to the CDC in Virginia."

The Centers for Disease Control, he knew, took care of all sorts of things, but as the name implied, they all had to do with diseases.

"Is it a pandemic?"

Chapter Twelve

Rylee's head dropped, and she gave a tired nod. "Yes, a pandemic."

Axel suddenly found it hard to breathe as visions of men and women in yellow hazmat suits cropped up in his mind like goldenrod.

"It's really bad," said Rylee. "What we collected were the samples to be used as prototypes for mass production."

His throat went tight and his breath caught as he remembered the yellow taped vials and the ones capped with red. "We also recovered an active vaccine."

"Vaccine?" asked Axel. That didn't sound too bad.

"The sample is a chemical weapon we have been tracking for months. It's a deadly strain of the flu."

"If it is a weapon," asked Axel, "why bring a vaccine?"

"They would want their people vaccinated before releasing the virus," said Rylee.

"How will it be released?" asked Axel, bracing his hands on his knees as he awaited the answer.

"We don't know," said Rylee. "A subway at rush hour. An outdoor concert. A Renaissance festival. The beach. Anywhere, really, where there is a crowd. It's airborne and does not die on surfaces. Technically, they could dust it on anything—the railing of a cruise ship, the escalator at a mall, a single suitcase on a baggage carousel at Dulles Airport."

A chill went up his back as tiny needles of dread seemed to pierce his skin.

"This is not the average seasonal flu," said Rylee. "It's a whole different animal. A pandemic. Virulent. They compared a possible outbreak to something like the influenza epidemic of 1918, which killed more people than World War I. And it attacked people ages twenty to forty. Not the old or the very young, but healthy adults. It killed fifty million people with a mortality rate of 2.5 percent. The CDC estimates that this strain has a mortality rate of 12.4 percent in unvaccinated populations."

Axel felt sick to his stomach. Why hadn't he helped her from the start?

"My office has been running different scenarios and possible targets. The intelligence that we received indicates that this virus will be used in a biological attack. Prior to the attack, the intelligence collected indicates that the active virus strains would be delivered across the border. We have been on high alert, trying to discover where the crossing would be made."

"And you thought the crossing would be here on my border. And your supervisors thought Buffalo."

"Yes, that's right. We weren't sure if the biological agent would be coming across in a large container or if the terrorists were planning to incubate the virus here within our borders. We now have our answer. They're going to manufacture here."

Axel placed a hand on her knee. "But you found it. You got the virus before they could turn it over to the manufacturing plant."

"Well, that's partly true. We did get it. But we can say, with fair confidence, that they will try again. This size of a load makes it easy to carry and hard to find. The load will likely not be carried in a tractor trailer, train car or ocean liner, as we theorized. That's why we're deploying here.

We think they'll use similar tactics. If they get through, if they put this virus into production, lives will be lost. It would be bad, Axel. Really, really bad."

He sat back in the couch, drew his hands together and wrapped them around his body. His quiet little county had become ground zero.

He thought that he knew this place so well. Now he wondered if he ever knew it at all. His home had become the front line in a war on terror. The truth horrified him. He thought of that virus coming again into his country and getting loose and the lives that would be lost if they did not stop it.

"Who is behind this?" he asked.

"The CIA operative who had secured the intel called the group Siming's Army. Simings are creatures or deities, perhaps, from Chinese mythology. They are referred to as Masters of Fate, and Judges of Life, and as worms—The Three Worms, I believe. These deities are said to enter the body at birth. They are supposed to mark an individual's good and bad actions on earth and use that information to calculate a person's life span. Each worm rules a different body system—mind, body, heart. When your time is up, one of the worms attacks."

"Well, that's terrifying."

"So is this group. Because we had never heard of them before, their motives are murky."

"What do they want?"

"We believe that they think that the US has committed evil on the earth and Siming's Army will exact revenge. Judge us for our actions. We hypothesize that they will attack our heart, mind and body, metaphorically."

"What's the heart?"

"We don't know. Our children. Our citizens. New York City. Congress. The Mall of America. We just don't know."

"The mind?"

"Electrical grid. Internet. The federal government. Again, open to debate."

"This pandemic is the attack of only one of the Masters of Fate. The one on our body?"

"That's right. We believe the virus is the attack meant for that system."

Meaning there were two others, heart and mind, still out there.

"What do we do now?" he asked.

"Go through our suspects again. Find who is helping the motorcycle gang with this cargo."

"You can cross off the Kowa," he said. "At least that's my belief based on their willingness to turn this over to us."

He glanced to her and she nodded. "I agree."

"So, who's on your short list?"

"We are fairly certain that the North Country Riders are involved with the transporting of either foreign nationals, the virus or possibly both. We don't think they're working alone because they don't have the compound or any sort of home base to secure the virus. Also, they have no banking system. Our people can't follow their money because they don't seem to handle any."

"They transport weed. I know they get paid," said Axel.

"Cash, it seems. So who are their bankers?" Rylee blew out a breath in a long audible sigh. "It's my supervisor's opinion that they would be working with someone like the Mondellos."

"The moonshiners?"

"Well, they have a home base and they're well protected. They are an established farm with trusts and way more money than they should have, though we have yet to track it all down. Their money operation was described to me as complicated and sophisticated."

"And they have border perimeter security and boats to

cross the St. Lawrence into Canada," said Axel. "But to attack their own country?"

"They're high on our list."

"What about the survival group? Coopersmith has a compound, as well. And he's not only fortified but heavily armed. And they believe that the end of the world is coming. They'd survive a pandemic. I'm certain."

"Yes, they are also contenders. They might have given us the drone as a way of removing suspicion."

"So you are surveilling both groups?"

"Yes."

And he had been annoyed that he had had to pull her butt out of trouble both times. He should have been helping her. Should have known that there was a credible threat. She wouldn't be here, otherwise.

"I'm sorry, Rylee. I should've been more help. I should have trusted that you had good instincts and good information."

She twisted in her seat so that she was facing him. Her smile was sad and her eyes luminous. He thought of their kiss and wished he could kiss her again.

"Is this a fresh start?" she asked.

"I think so. I'd like it to be."

She reached out and took his hand. He stroked the back of hers with his thumb.

"And you're willing to work with me?" she asked.

"I'll do everything I can to help you."

"Wonderful. One of the groups we are now targeting is the Congregation of Eternal Wisdom. You're familiar?"

Despite the warmth of the room, a chill rolled up Axel's spine and into his chest until his heart iced over. He drew back, leaning against the armrest.

Was he familiar? He was. But he did not want to be the one to bring Rylee to them.

She went on. "They have nonprofit status and are not

required to do an annual report. Every nonprofit exempt from income taxes, must file an annual return, except churches."

"What?"

"It's true. Fraud within churches is a major problem, as is mismanagement and money laundering. Very tough to prosecute with the separation of church and state. Most goes unreported. We believe that little of the money collected by this organization from members' estates, donations, retreats and sale of religious products is being used for the congregation's preservation. Numbers don't add up. That means they have established a banking system. They could be the bankers for whatever group is assisting Siming's Army."

"They could launder money collected by the ones paid to carry the load?"

"That's correct."

"That outfit is dangerous. They're especially dangerous to women. You should not be the one to go there. Send some of your men."

She cocked her head as if something now interested her. "You are the second one who's told me that this outfit is dangerous for women. The first was my colleague with DHS. What exactly is going on out there?"

Axel sat back and rested his head on the sofa. He stared up at the ceiling. He didn't remember when he started talking, but he did. He told her what he knew of the cult. He went on and on, but he left out one important detail. One piece of information that he knew would send her out of his house and break their new collaboration. He just did not have the courage to tell her that he'd been born and raised inside the order of the Congregation of Eternal Wisdom.

Chapter Thirteen

Rylee waited as Trace contemplated her question. She knew about the cult. She had even been out there to speak to their leader, Reverend Wayne. From what she could see, the residents there were of an extreme belief but did seem to be content and grounded. They lived communally and from a quick overview, she believed they had adopted some of the tenets from Buddhism, Taoism, and perhaps the old Shaker communities that use to thrive in upstate New York at the turn of the last century, until their tenet toward celibacy brought the group to the obvious end. In this community, both men and women were covered up. All seemed happy. And committed to preparing themselves for what they saw as the upcoming end of humanity's time on earth.

The reverend had left her to speak to the two social strata of men distinguishable by whether they grew facial hair. And to the women, who did not seem subjugated or threatened. She could see the children but had not spoken to them. Her observation was that they were on the thin side but there were no visible indications that they were not well cared for and developing normally.

"Is there something going on out there, Axel, that you want me to be aware of?" asked Rylee.

Trace scrubbed his hand over his mouth and then turned to face her. The fire had taken the chill from the air, leaving her with a pleasant lethargy brought on by a sudden pause in the frantic preparations and debriefing that had been the last two days.

"People up here give them a wide berth," he said. "We know that the folks who come from all over to join them are very committed to their beliefs that the end of the world is near. The reverend, however, seems more committed to being certain that the newest members of his flock are stripped of all personal possessions and assets upon joining. The reverend seizes these for the betterment of his congregation. I have been in contact with the IRS about this but, as he is a nonprofit and a church, investigating him is tricky. A cursory look came back with nothing suspicious."

"I can ask some friends at the Treasury to have another look," said Rylee. "But if they already came back with nothing… Why are you so certain something illicit is happening out there?"

"A feeling that I have. A bad feeling."

The silence settled over them like a warm blanket. She was growing comfortable with him. There was no pressure to fill the warm dry air with useless prattle. She watched a log roll in the flame, sending a shower of sparks below the grate. The embers glowed orange and gradually faded to gray. She loved the smell of wood smoke. Somehow, in her traveling from place to place, it had always been a comfort. Their home in Germany had had a fireplace and she used to beg her parents to light the fire. They did very occasionally, as her mother did not trust that the chimney had been correctly cleaned.

She caught him staring at her, seeing a different kind of fire in his eyes. The need he stirred in her had gained in strength. What at first had been an annoyance and a distraction, had gathered into an internal storm that was getting out of her control.

She glanced back to the flames. She had told him everything and that felt good. Instead of making her anxious, the information felt like what she should have offered at the start—a collaboration with local law enforcement. If she weren't so suspicious of everyone, she would have done this earlier.

He was a decorated officer with an exemplary military record. True, he had been in the US Army, but she wasn't going to hold that against him. She wasn't like her dad, seeing one branch of the military as superior to the rest. And he had come home and gotten his education, without the help of family to do that, applying for aid and to colleges. Getting that first job right here in Kinsley's police force and then being elected by the county at such a young age. Clearly, his community had faith in him. Unless those same citizens on his watch list had made sure that he was elected.

Her smile waned but she pushed back the doubts.

No, there was no evidence or even speculation to that effect. It was only her problems with trust that made her so reluctant to believe in him.

Trust. And that was the trouble. Or at least what the counselor at school had suggested to her. The free mental health service offered through the health and wellness center at her college. The mental health professional who had advised she come weekly and proposed to her that her tendency to avoid relationships might be due to her experience of losing any friends due to the frequent moves. And that her difficulty forming an attachment with a partner might be due to her father's emotional distance and physical absence.

You don't trust men to stick around, she had said.

Yet, this man had stuck around in his county despite having no family here. Parents listed as unknown on official records. Sheriff Rogers's report listed him as abandoned. Yet Axel said his dad was still around. Had his father abandoned him or was he unable to care for his child? It was also possible that his father had been deemed unfit as a parent, but then there would be a record. The entire thing was mysterious. In any case, how complicated must his feelings for his father be?

That blank spot in his past troubled her. Where had he been before his appearance in official reports? The records yielded nothing. Where had he been for thirteen years?

"Would you like something other than coffee? I have beer and white wine."

"You don't seem like a wine guy."

"Former girlfriend," he admitted.

Red flags popped up before her like traffic cones in a construction area.

"Should have improved with age, because she left it over two years ago."

"Anyone since?"

"No one serious. I'm not in a relationship, Rylee, if that's what you're asking."

"I'm not." But of course, she was, and the reason she cared if he were available made her ears buzz and her stomach ache with dread because it meant that she was considering one—a relationship—with Sheriff Axel Trace. *Not him*, she told herself.

"So, wine?"

"No, not her wine. I'll have a beer."

He chuckled and stood, removing the barely touched coffee and heading out. With both hands full, he could do nothing about the low-slung sweatpants and Rylee nearly fell off the couch staring at the dimples at his lower back and the tempting curve of his butt.

"You should get out of here right now," she muttered to herself. She folded her arms over her chest and sat back in the chair. Her gaze fixed on the fire, burning low and giving a soft crackle as the logs surrendered to the flames.

He returned with two beers in glasses. That earned points. He set hers beside her on the table and returned to his seat with his; only this time, he took the center cushion, closer to her. The proximity brought his scent to her.

Wood smoke, something stronger and new. Had he put on cologne while he was gone? Whatever it was, it was sexy as hell. She leaned to retrieve her new drink and took a long swallow. The bubbly brew cooled her throat. They sat quietly, with the outward semblance of calm. Only her heart was thumping like a rabbit caught in a snare, and his jaw clenched as he held a smile that seemed forced.

"This is such a nice room," she said. That brought a beautiful smile to his face, transforming his usual serious, dour demeanor into something breathtaking. A trickle of excitement moved inside her.

"I picked out everything." The pride was clear in his voice and with good reason. He had an eye for masculine homey touches.

Were they going to do this?

He caught her gaze and held it. He set aside her drink and then his own. Then he extended his hand, palm up, offering himself to her.

"I want to kiss you again," he said.

"Is that right?" she asked.

He nodded, his gaze never wavering from hers. A luscious tingle danced over her skin and her cheeks felt hot.

"It's a bad idea. Long-term, I mean," he said. "I'm staying. You're going. That doesn't give us a lot of time."

"Time is overrated," she said.

His smile broadened. And he gave a dry chuckle that warmed her inside and out.

"Is that a yes on the kissing?" he asked.

She grinned. "That's a yes."

She took his offered hand and he dragged her into his arms. She settled beside him, feet on the sofa and arms hooked around his neck.

"What if we do more than kissing?" he asked.

"I'm open to more."

She waited for him to kiss her, but instead he let his gaze roam over her face, down her neck and then return, retracing his course until his gaze fixed on her mouth. She drew her lips between her teeth and dragged her bottom lip free. She watched him swallow, his Adam's apple bobbing. The room no longer felt warm but hot. The tension between them coiled like a spring. Still, she waited. She hoped he'd make the first move. Instead, he let his head drop back to the sofa and closed his eyes. Squeezed them tight as if the only way to resist her was to remove her from his sight. She took the opportunity to study his features. The thickness of his dark brow. The length of his feathery lashes. The slight flush that covered his cheeks and neck. The strong muscles that flanked the column of his throat. And the interesting wisp of dark hair that emerged from the top of the shirt. She had caught him dressed in little. She suspected he wore only a T-shirt and not a thing beneath the thin sweatpants. When she'd knocked, had he already been ready for bed? Would he consider taking her along?

Waiting was overrated, too, she thought. If he knew that she was not staying and that she knew he was not going, she did not see any reason why they should not spend the evening together. It was not a conflict of interest. They were no longer on opposite sides. He had agreed to help her with her investigation, and she had shared what information she had. They were both consenting adults.

The more she rationalized her decision, the more she had to push down the demons of doubt. Why was she trying so hard to convince herself that sleeping with Axel Trace would not be a mistake?

Somewhere in her heart, she recognized that starting something she could not finish with this man was dangerous. She should crawl off his sofa, find her boots and march herself out of his house. She should go back to the motel and continue reading through the mountain of paperwork associated with this investigation. But she couldn't. Some unnamable part of her could do nothing else.

She ignored reason and her better judgment. She ignored caution and fear. She ignored doubt, as she pressed herself against him and lowered her mouth to his.

Chapter Fourteen

Axel's grip about Rylee tightened as she deepened the kiss. Her insides began a persistent aching to touch his skin. The impulse to drag away every barrier that separated them built to a roar, drowning out the receding whisper of doubt.

This was right. This was perfect, and she wanted all of him. Rylee broke the kiss and felt his resistance in the tightening of his grip before he allowed her to lean back. His confused expression made her smile. She could see the rising beat of need tighten his jaw and burn in his hungry gaze.

She wasn't teasing him and it took only an instant to drag the long-sleeved shirt over her head, leaving her in nothing from the waist up except her white lace bra.

His mouth hung open for a moment and he made a sound in his throat, like a sigh, then he reached for her. Warm hands splayed across her bare back. The contact thrilled, and they shared a smile.

"You really want to do this, Rylee?" he asked.

"Seems so."

"I'm going to need you to give me a definitive answer here."

"Yes, Sheriff Trace, I want to make love to you, right here and now, in front of this lovely fire on this soft leather couch." She ran a finger down his forehead and nose, pausing on his lower lip. "Definitive enough?"

In answer, he took her index finger in his mouth and sucked. The smile fell from her lips as his tongue swirled about the sensitive pad of her finger. Her mind did the rest, anticipating the pleasure he had in store for her. Rylee's eyes fluttered closed and her head fell back. He released her finger as his hands moved to her torso and he leaned her forward, kissing the center of her chest, just below the collarbone. Then his tongue painted tiny swirls on her flesh.

Axel stroked her back as his mouth moved from the top of one breast to the next. She felt the clasp at the back of her bra release. Free from the constraints, she shrugged out of the lace and tossed it aside.

His hands reversed course, coming between them as she straddled his lap. He lifted her. The calloused, rough feel of his palms on her sensitive skin gave her an erotic thrill matched only by the look of longing on his face. His focus dropped from her face to her breasts. She leaned in and he licked one nipple to a hard, aching bud.

This time she groaned. The need that had burned her up now turned liquid and she gave in to the urge to move on top of him, rocking back and forth. Axel sucked one nipple and then the next, taking his time and making her crazy.

She tugged at his shirt, dragging it up to his shoulders and then raking her nails over the exposed skin of his back.

He released her with surprising strength, lifting her effortlessly off his lap and onto the seat beside him. Then he stood and stripped out of his shirt before stooping to strip off her socks. She stood then, and he unfastened her jeans, sliding them down her legs. Dressed in only a tiny scrap of white lace, Rylee waited.

"You're so beautiful," he said, his voice low as if they were in church.

"Back at you," she said and offered her hand. "Rug or couch?"

"Ladies' choice."

Rylee pointed to the sofa. Then stretched out on her back and beckoned to him. He came to her, offering her a small open packet, protecting her again. She rolled the condom over him. He squeezed his eyes shut as he sucked in a breath at her touch. She lay back and he came to her, barrier between them. His body burned. His hot, firm flesh pressed tight to her damp skin. She opened her legs and he glided into her. She savored the steady rhythm and the delicious friction. His spicy scent mingled with the smell of leather and wood smoke.

She wouldn't think about why this was the wrong man at the wrong time. Rylee arched back, closing off all doubts and warnings and, oh, yes… This was what she wanted. Him making love to her here, safely hidden away from the rest of the world and their judgments and rules.

She closed her eyes to savor the perfection of his loving.

And as she moved with him, the rest of her thoughts receded until all she could do was catch the rising wave of pleasure that shattered her to pieces before dropping her safely back between the soft folds of the sofa and the warmth of Axel's embrace.

She dozed. Rousing when his fingers danced up her shoulder as he kissed her neck, humming his pleasure.

They snuggled together on the wide leather sofa, the fire heating the room. Something about the feel of him, his scent and the strength of his big solid body made her feel grounded and at home. She stroked the warm velvet of his back, savoring the feel of his skin when his voice rumbled through his chest.

"Do you like it up here on the river?" he asked.

"It's got a rugged beauty," she said, hearing the languor in the slowness of her voice.

"Would you ever think of staying?"

The languor dissolved, and she stiffened. What was he asking?

"I've got plans, career plans to earn an assignment in New York City."

He made a disapproving sound. "You ever been there? It's noisy and dirty and crowded."

"And a major assignment."

"I thought you said you wanted to stop moving from place to place."

"Well, yes. But after I get promoted."

The rumble in his chest was back, sounding like a growl.

"No end to that. Just like your childhood being dragged from one posting to another. Only this time you are doing it to yourself. Don't you want a home, Rylee?"

She scowled. Her career advancement involved a willingness to travel. Getting to New York would put her in a place to make a real difference. She looked forward to telling her family, imagined the conversation with her father. It was important to do well, more important since she was not in the military.

She lifted to an elbow to look down at his handsome face, marred only by the frown tugging at his mouth.

"Would you ever consider leaving this county?"

His answer was immediate. "I can't."

"Because of your job. Elected official?"

"I know this place. Everything I am is because I was born in Onutake County. There are real good people here and then there's the ones that bear watching. I'm here for them, to be here when things go bad."

"You sound like it's a foregone conclusion."

"It is."

"Anyone specific?"

"The Congregation of Eternal Wisdom."

"Ah," she said. "We talked about them. They're on my watch list."

"They definitely should be."

"You have information on any illegal activities?"

"Just bilking vulnerable people out of their life's savings and twisting their beliefs to Reverend Wayne's version of faith."

"Not illegal, as I've said."

"Immoral, then."

"That's why you stay? Because of that religious order."

"It's a cult."

She swallowed back her disappointment. Was that a lump in her throat? What was happening to her?

She had enjoyed sleeping with him, but she wasn't looking for a relationship. Who was she kidding? Sleeping with Axel had been mind-blowing and now that she could think again, she realized she was in real trouble.

"So, you're needed here." Why did she even want to know and why was she holding her breath?

"I am. Maybe someday I'll be free of this place."

AXEL WOKE IN the gray predawn light, lying on his back with Rylee beside him. She slept on her side, pressed between the leather back of the couch and his body. One arm lay on his chest, with her palm pressed flat over his heart. Her cheek rested on his shoulder and her mouth was open as she gave a soft snore with each intake of breath. Her top leg was coiled about one of his, so that her foot and ankle threaded beneath his opposite calf.

She'd asked him if he'd ever leave the county. Nothing had tempted him so much as her question. The tug to be with her was new, like some invisible cord drawing him to her.

Then there was his father and his promise to see Axel suffer for daring to leave the fold. He knew exactly how his father might do that; he could call his followers together and, at his word, they would all return to their rooms and take their lives. That included the children, his siblings, who had stayed and the mother he could not even name. She was there among the other women, one of them. He'd tried shutting them down and failed. He didn't have the authority. His father knew that and seemed to bask in Axel's powerlessness.

Rylee's skin was covered in gooseflesh. The fire had burned out and the air in the room held the chill that told him the forecasted cold front had arrived. His arm was under her and his fingers splayed over one perfect orb of her ass. He resisted the urge to squeeze. Instead, he lifted his opposite hand and dragged the fleece blanket from the back of the chair, covering their naked bodies. Rylee hummed her satisfaction and then nestled closer.

One eye opened and she peered up at him.

"Hello, gorgeous," he whispered and brushed a strand of blond hair from her cheek, tucking it behind the shell of her ear.

"I've got to pee." She pushed up and groaned. "Freezing in here."

"Take the blanket," he said.

In a moment, he had the fleece around her shoulders.

"What about you?" she asked.

"Heading to my bed. Care to join me?"

"Sounds reasonable." She grinned and then went down the hall toward the guest bathroom as he headed to the master.

They reconvened in his king-size bed, where she dropped the fleece in favor of the down comforter and flannel sheets and him.

"Oh, the sheets are cold," she said, shivering.

"Not for long," he promised.

When they finally stopped warming the sheets and each

other, the bedding was tangled about his waist, two of the pillows were somewhere on the floor and they were both panting. He gathered her in, their moist skin sticking them together like Post-its. He smiled, tucking her head under his chin as he embraced her.

He had known they'd be good together, but Rylee in the flesh was so much better than anything he could ever have imagined. She was bold and more uninhibited than he would have guessed. In her professional life, Rylee was exacting, demanding and a pain in his butt.

In his bed, she was generous, thrilling and the best thing to happen to him in forever. He wondered if she had an early start and if she didn't, if he could manage to keep up with her.

He grinned like a fool at the ceiling of the quiet room as Rylee's breathing changed. His entire body felt sated and relaxed, and he had the suspicion that it was not just having sex with an amazing woman that he had to thank. It was sleeping with Rylee. He really wanted to please her and to give her a piece of himself that he had kept from all the others. He wanted her to know him as no one else had. The smile began to fade.

Why was that?

He wasn't stupid enough to think that if he were good enough in bed, she might not want to leave him. Was he?

He pressed his free hand to his forehead and groaned. That was exactly what he thought. If they were perfect together, she might just change her mind about this case and her promotion and quit everything to live forever in his arms.

He was, in layman's terms, an idiot.

As if to prove his point, Rylee's phone alarm sounded from the living room and she was up and retrieving the device before he could even drag the pillow from his face. He opened his eyes to see the golden light of morning made richer from the reflection off the yellow leaves of the sugar maple that occupied much of the backyard. The next thing he saw was Rylee dressed in her wrinkled jeans and rumpled shirt, still barefoot as she crossed before the bed, staring at her phone. She disappeared into the bathroom without even glancing at him in the bed.

That was bad, he knew. Really bad. He'd made more than a few hasty exits after spending the night somewhere that, in the morning, seemed like a mistake.

He dropped back into the pillows. Morning had come, and he needed to play it cool as if this were just one of those things, except it wasn't. Maybe he should tell her that.

Or never tell her that. The sound of the water running brought him to his feet. Images of Rylee, soapy with suds rolling down her body, sent him to the bathroom door. His hand on the knob, he paused. Then he realized it was the water running into the sink and that a closed door was a clear indicator that she did not want his company.

His hand fell to his side.

"Breakfast?" he called.

"Sorry. I've got to run."

And what had he really thought she would do? Call her boss and resign?

Axel dragged himself back to bed and realized that his hamstrings were sore and that he was still naked. He needed to start running again.

"Run away from Rylee, maybe," he muttered. The chill in the air made him choose jeans and a flannel shirt, which he dragged on over a clean white T-shirt.

He headed to the kitchen, hoping that some fresh brewed coffee would wake him up to the fact that what had rocked his world had clearly not been an earth-moving experience to Rylee.

He didn't like being a workout dummy. Question was, should he tell her so or cross his fingers and hope she needed him again?

Chapter Fifteen

Rylee blinked at herself in the medicine cabinet mirror. Her hands were on the edge of his sink, only inches from his shaving cream, razor, toothpaste and toothbrush that lined the back of the countertop.

Had she lost her mind?

Obviously, she had lost her mind because the sex with the sheriff had been mind-blowing. Hard as it was to admit she had never experienced that sort of a connection with anyone in her past. Note that her past wasn't littered with hundreds of lovers, but she had had enough of them to know that what she and Axel had shared was unique, and that made her realize it was dangerous.

She wanted to get out of there as quickly as possible and find somewhere she could think. Somewhere where her view did not include the wide, tempting expanse of Axel's bare chest. She needed her brain and not her instincts to guide her.

Certainly, she knew better than to sleep with a coworker. Axel was not actually a coworker or a subordinate, but he was a local associate and that made this a bad idea. The sort of idea that could end a career. And here she was so close with a real breakthrough and solid evidence that this place had been used by the terrorists to smuggle some of the biohazard.

The troops were on their way. Her boss was on her

way. She'd already received a text with Lieutenant Catherine Ohr's ETA. And she'd received them while naked in Axel's bed.

She wanted very much to be dressed in a clean, ironed suit when she met her superior, rather than the rumpled mess of clothing that had clearly been scooped up off the floor and hastily donned on her way out.

Coffee. She needed coffee, but she also needed to get out of here first. She did not want to have a conversation with Axel. She did not want to explain her reluctance to continue with something that was so devastatingly wonderful that she could not wait to see him again and wanted very much to crawl back under that giant fluffy coverlet and explore every inch of that amazing body. It was one thing to have a body that was as perfectly formed as Axel's and was quite another to know how to use it to the best effect. And he ticked every box. She was still ticking as a result. Her leg muscles ached with fatigue and yet, here she was trying to think of a way that she could see him without having any of her colleagues find out. No.

"Bad idea," Rylee said to her reflection, wagging a finger at herself for emphasis.

Rylee found his spray deodorant, pressed the button, sniffed and decided against it. What she needed was a shower. She didn't need to add more of Axel's scent to her skin. She glanced toward the shower and then shook her head. She paused only long enough to draw a long breath and close her eyes before emerging into his bedroom. He was, thankfully, fully dressed in his casual clothes and sitting on his unmade bed. White T-shirt, open blue flannel shirt and faded blue jeans. His feet were bare, and she found the sight of his long toes dusted with hair instantly arousing.

She groaned.

"You okay?" he asked.

"I'm not sure." She forced herself to stop fidgeting and stood still before him. "Axel, did we just make a mistake?"

His mouth went tight, and his brow descended. He glanced away from her and then back. Then he rose to stand before her, close enough to touch, but he did not reach out.

"I don't know, Rylee. Only time will answer that. I do know that I don't regret what happened between us. I'm sorry if you do."

Her hands were clasped, and she spun the titanium ring she had commandeered from her brother Paul that encircled her thumb as if it were a spinner. What to say?

"I'm not sure we have very much in common," she said, feeling it a bad start. Her belief was confirmed by the narrowing of his eyes.

"We have this in common," he said, motioning to his bed. The covers looked as if they had been twisted and tossed by the ocean and then cast ashore to dry. "And we have the fact that you cared enough about me last night to share my bed."

"My timing is bad. My supervisor is en route, and I only have an hour before she'll expect a briefing. It's not that I don't want to see you again. It just can't interfere with my work."

He quirked a brow and his mouth twisted as if he were reluctant to admit she'd scored a point.

"Honestly, Axel, I knew she was coming today. I just didn't know she was flying and would be here so soon."

She came to sit beside him. "You must think… Well, I don't know what you think."

He turned toward her and stroked her hair, which was still tangled and as wild as he knew she could be. Then he drew her in and she let him. He dropped a kiss on her forehead before stepping away. He took the opportunity to stroke her cheek with his thumb. His touch sent an electric tingle over her skin.

"Let me know if you need anything from Onutake County."

She held her smile. "I'll be in touch."

Then she headed for the door, one hand shoved in her jeans pocket, clutching the key to her motorcycle. In her back pocket, she'd shoved her nearly dead phone. She needed to get to the motel to recharge its battery and her own.

Something popped into her mind and she paused at the door to his bedroom. He watched her, his dark brows lifted.

"Um, I think I'll be going out to the Eternal Wisdom commune today. Maybe I can find some reason to shut them down."

His expression grew stormy and the blood vessel at his neck pulsed dangerously. "Not alone. We discussed this."

"They might be involved in smuggling."

He snorted. "If they are, you'll never catch them."

"And why is that?"

"Too smart."

She picked up the gauntlet he'd tossed. "We'll see about that, won't we?"

"You aren't going alone."

"I'll have my team with me."

"They don't know these people like I do."

"You can ride along, if you like."

The acid in his empty stomach burned at just the thought of going out there with her because he knew that Father Wayne would instantly pick up the vibe between them. Then he would delight in revealing to Rylee that he was Axel's father.

The only thing worse than having that happen was letting her go out to that place without him. She didn't know or understand how very dangerous Father Wayne could be.

His breathing changed, coming in short angry puffs, and his teeth were locked so tight he'd need the Jaws of Life to get them open.

Axel considered and decided that his shame was small compared to Rylee's safety.

"Axel? You all right?"

He unlocked his jaw. "I'm going with you. End of story."

"Okay, let me clear it with my supervisor. I'll get back to you." She glanced at the screen of her phone. "Jeepers. I have to go."

He walked her out and watched as she drove off, knowing he would have to tell her. Father Wayne was more than a cult leader and con man. Rylee had the right to know. His father was why he stayed and, more specifically, because of what he feared his father might do. Axel was imprisoned here as surely as when he had been trapped behind the congregation's walls. He had to stay, to be here to stop his father from ever carrying out his deadly version of the Rapture, which he called the Rising.

LIEUTENANT CATHERINE OHR waited for Rylee in her rented sedan outside a craftsman-style home painted gray. Rylee checked the address again and pulled behind her boss. The two women exited their vehicles simultaneously.

Lieutenant Ohr swung the leather briefcase over one shoulder as she cleared the distance toward Rylee with her long stride. She extended her hand and the two women shook.

"Right on time," said Ohr. "We are gleaning some interesting data from the drone. Good work on its recovery."

"Thanks," said Rylee. "I had some help with that. Wouldn't have gained access to the survivalist camp without the assistance of the sheriff."

Her supervisor's mouth turned down. Ohr was a tall woman, nearly six feet in height, and she was skeletally thin. Rylee had observed her at lunch; generally, Ohr ate a cup of yogurt at her desk and seemed to leave her computer only to smoke cigarettes. As a result, her complexion was sallow and her brown hair thinning and brittle. The lines around her mouth, always prominent, seemed to harden at the mention of the sheriff.

"Yes. Sheriff Trace. I read that in your report. It's generally a good idea to cooperate with local law enforcement. However, in this case, I think you might have done better to speak to the former sheriff, Kurt Rogers. Better information and less entanglements."

Rylee's brow wrinkled and confusion settled over her, along with a twinge of anxiety. Why would she have spoken to the former sheriff? And what entanglements did she mean? Was she talking about her personal relationship with Axel? But how would she know?

Lieutenant Ohr paused on the sidewalk to face Rylee.

"This is where Kurt Rogers lives," said Ohr. "He has some information on Sheriff Trace that I think you need to hear. Shall we?" Ohr motioned toward the house and did not wait for Rylee before extending her long legs and striding up the walkway to the front door. She ignored the bell and knocked briskly. As they waited, her supervisor tightened the sash on her leather jacket. A deep bark told Rylee a large canine had come to the door. Then there was a voice of someone telling the dog to be quiet and a moment later the door swung open.

The man had a full white mustache, rosy cheeks and hair that made Rylee think for a moment that he perhaps belonged at the North Pole. He was slim, however. But the choice of suspenders to hold up his jeans did reconfirm her initial impression. The man looked from one to the other, swept them each with a glance and said, "I see the dress code hasn't changed. But the last time I spoke to the feds, they were both males, so perhaps we are making some forward progress. Come on in, ladies."

He stooped to grab hold of the collar of his black Lab, whose thick tail thumped against his master's leg. Rogers told his dog to sit and she did, her tail now thumping on the carpet runner as the two women stepped inside. Catherine ignored the canine, but Rylee extended the back of her hand to the dog, allowing the animal to take in her scent.

"This is Ruby," said Rogers. The dog's ears perked up at the mention of her name. Rogers released her and she stayed where she was until he guided them from the entry to the living room, at which time she took the opportunity to sniff the legs of both new arrivals before settling in a dog bed beside the recliner.

After the initial chitchat, they were motioned to a sofa. Rogers chose the well-worn and stained brown leather recliner.

"I understand you want some background information on the current sheriff. That right?"

Her supervisor not so much sat as perched on the edge of the sofa, ankles together and hands clasped on her knees.

"I wondered if you could fill in my subordinate on what you told me on the phone and include any additional details you might have recalled." Catherine tapped her clasped hands together as she spoke.

Rogers drew a long breath and then turned to Rylee. The pit of her stomach dropped, and she felt the tightening of the muscles between her shoulders. Whatever he was about to say, she knew it was not good. What would these two think if they knew she had come directly from Sheriff Axel Trace's king-size bed to this meeting? Rylee repressed a shudder.

"Well," said Rogers. "I told Ms. Ohr here that Axel used to walk to Kinsley whenever he could slip away. He didn't talk much but the librarian sort of took him under her wing." He turned to Catherine at this and continued with, "She's retired now, as well. But I can put you in touch, if you'd like. I'm sure she may have some additional information on Axel."

"Not necessary for now."

Rogers turned his attention back to Rylee. "He didn't really fit in with the people. I could see he was unhappy and it bothered me that no one came looking for him. No matter how long he was gone. That got me to call social services. We all went out and had a look at the compound."

Rylee sat forward as if stabbed in the back. Had he said compound?

"Other than their unconventional living situation, we did not find the children in poor health or malnourished. All of them seemed relatively happy and..." Rogers rubbed his neck. "You know, they just have different ideas. Ideas that I'd call dangerous. And not everyone out there toes the line. One of Reverend Wayne's followers was arrested by Border Patrol for transporting an Eastern European into the US."

"A Croatian," said Ohr.

"Leadership denied knowledge and I found nothing to prove otherwise."

"Do you feel they are engaged in human trafficking?"

"Maybe. Might have been an outlier. I couldn't catch them, but for that one time. If folks at the compound are smuggling or trafficking, I never found any evidence."

Rylee interjected here. "You say *the compound.* What exactly are you referring to?" But she knew. She was certain that she already knew.

Rogers brows lifted. "Oh, I thought you knew. Axel was born on the lands belonging to the Congregation of Eternal Wisdom. His dad is the leader of that group. Man named Wayne Trace. Goes by Reverend Wayne."

"His name isn't Trace. It's Faith."

"Changed it."

Ohr gave Rylee a long, critical look. "Thorough background check would have revealed the name change."

Rylee dropped back into the thick padding of the seat cushions. Wayne Faith was Wayne Trace. Cult leader and Axel's father. If she was such a crack investigator, how was it possible that she had missed this?

The knot in her stomach turned into a whirling sea, pitching so hard that she needed to grip the armrest to steady herself.

One of the men on her watch list was the father of the sheriff. How much worse could it be? She knew the answer to that. She could have slept with the son of a man who was about to go on her list of suspects. That would make it worse.

Rylee's supervisor lifted a brow, regarding her. "Is something wrong?"

Rylee forced herself to release the armrest and managed to give her head a shake. She turned her gaze to the former sheriff. She put aside her emotions, pressing them down deep where they threatened to explode like compressed gas. "Mr. Rogers, the sheriff gave me some information on this group, but I would appreciate it if you could you tell me exactly what you mean when you say they have dangerous ideas."

Rogers thought for a minute. His index finger setting the whisker straight in his mustache.

"Yes, I could do that."

Chapter Sixteen

Axel waited for Rylee on the shore of St. Regis River in a park that was a popular launch for small crafts. He suspected that she'd set the location because she did not want to be seen with him. He didn't blame her. He should have told her the truth, even knowing that this was exactly what would happen.

Most women did not like being lied to, but this omission interfered with her case. Could she forgive him?

Maybe she doesn't know. Which meant that she would find out eventually or that he had to tell her.

He liked neither option. They'd already gone too far. His night with Rylee had made him wonder about things that he had no right thinking about. Like what it would be like to wake up to see her in his bed every morning.

I'll bet she'd be a great mom.

Axel wiped the sweat from his upper lip. That was the kind of thinking that was going to get his heart broken.

What was he doing? He would be a terrible father. The only examples he had of parenting were twisted. All he really knew was what not to do. Could that be enough?

He was out of his unit now without remembering leaving his SUV. He paused in his pacing to look back at his vehicle, the door open and the alarm chiming. He strode back to slam the door. Then he faced the water. The fog was thicker there, rolling toward him like some special effect in a stage production.

This park was too close to the compound of the Congregation of Eternal Wisdom for his liking. The compound was situated on the St. Regis River. Mid-river lay an island belonging to the Kowa tribe, and the shore beyond was also Mohawk land. Beyond that, across a narrower stretch of the St. Lawrence, lay Canada.

Axel shifted, rocking from side to side as he stood between his vehicle and the river. If not for the fog, he could have seen the fence just south of this spot. One had to have lived there to know it wasn't to keep intruders out so much as it was to keep insiders in. He hadn't been back to this spot since the day he'd jumped that fence and walked out that last time.

The cold of the air and the warmth of the water had created a real London-style fog, but the chill he felt had nothing to do with the damp or the fact that he could not see more than fifty feet. He didn't need to see, it was all there in his mind—the layout, the women and children in one building, single men in another and the others, the ones they called most blessed, ensconced in their own house. These were the ones who had made, what his father called the greatest sacrifice, and what Axel called self-mutilation.

The engine sound brought him around. Headlights glowed eerily in the mist. Tires crunched on gravel and he recognized her sedan, the red handprints nearly unnoticeable in the mist. She parked her car at an angle, so her departure would not require her to reverse direction. Her cab light flashed on as she exited her car, shutting her door with more force than necessary.

She paused to lock her car, unnecessarily, he knew. Then she cinched the belt to her coat before marching toward him. One of the large boulders, placed to keep folks from accidentally driving into the river, gave him support as he sagged.

Her expression told him all he needed to know. She knew everything. He could see it in the upward tilt of her chin and the downward tug at the corners of her mouth.

She stopped and glared. Her face flushed. He forced himself not to shift as he held her cold stare.

"I don't even know where to begin," she said.

"I'm sorry, Rylee. I should have told you."

"Yeah! My first field assignment and your father is on my watch list."

"He wasn't. You never mentioned him."

"But you knew that he should be. You knew that one of his followers was arrested by Border Patrol for transporting an Eastern European into the US."

"A Croatian. My father denied knowledge."

"Do you believe him?"

"It doesn't matter what I believe. Only what I can prove."

"It matters to me."

"Part of the indoctrination is to believe that he is one of God's chosen. I believe that none of his followers would take such action without his specifically ordering them to do so. I told ICE exactly that when they questioned me."

Immigration and Customs Enforcement had charged one of Reverend Wayne's followers, William Evers, with human trafficking. The illegal immigrant was deported and, as far as Axel knew, Evers was still in federal prison.

"You lied to me," she said.

"I omitted."

"You were born there, in that compound. I'm looking for a foreign agent on US soil and now I learn that one of your father's followers was engaged in human trafficking. That kind of activity points to the possibility of ongoing human trafficking. The sort of trafficking that might bring my suspect to your county."

"Do you have evidence to that effect?"

"We know a foreign agent carried a deadly virus strain onto US soil. We know that person is missing. Additionally, we know that one of Wayne Faith's followers once transported an Eastern European illegally into this county. And we know that you are the son of Wayne Trace, whose surname was changed to Faith. Do you have any idea what my affiliation with you will do to my career?"

"Who you sleep with is your business, Rylee."

"The trouble is I don't really know who I slept with. Do I?"

He glanced away.

"It's not just that you lied, Axel. It's that I can't trust anything you say, or don't say, again."

He looked back at her. "You ever been ashamed, Rylee? During your years traveling with your family or in college or maybe in your stellar career? You have someone in your past that you'd do anything to distance yourself from?"

"If you wanted distance, why did you move back here after your discharge?"

It was a question he didn't think on because the answers hurt too much.

"Maybe I wanted to be near my mother."

"Who is?"

He looked away again. "I don't know. But if she ever wanted to leave, I wanted her to know I was close. That I could help her if she'd let me."

"Is that all?"

He looked up and then to the river and then to the ground. Everywhere and anywhere but at Rylee.

"Why else, Axel?"

"To stop him. I wanted to be here in case he set a date. I have siblings there. I have childhood friends who never left. If Father Wayne decides that the Rising is coming, I wanted to be here to stop him."

"Stop him from what, Axel?"

"They rehearse their departure to Heaven's Door. That's what he calls mass suicide. Not death, just a door. They have costumes and rituals. He holds their lives in his hand. On his word, they'll all kill themselves."

He hazarded a quick glance to see Rylee's mouth had dropped open.

"Can't you close them down?"

"I told you, I've tried. It's not illegal to believe what they believe. I've had Child Protective Services out there dozens of times. The children show no signs of abuse. And their upbringing is no harder than Fundamentalists or any number of religious subgroups."

"His religious beliefs are crazy."

"But not illegal."

She closed her mouth and gave him a troubled stare. She seemed to be deciding something. Axel held his breath. When she didn't speak, he broke the silence.

"If you have something on him, some law that he's broken, I can help you."

Rylee shook her head. "Perhaps you do really want to stop him. I don't know. But you can't be involved in this investigation any longer and I cannot have anything more to do with you."

"Rylee, please."

"Goodbye, Axel." She started to turn away.

He felt the panic squeezing his heart. He couldn't breathe. Axel's hand shot out and he stopped her, drawing her back.

"You can't tell me you don't have feelings. That what we shared meant nothing to you."

"I can't say that. But I can say it is the reason why this hurts so much. You made a mistake. I can forgive you. But it's over between us. I can't take the chance that you are holding back other secrets or that my association with you won't jeopardize this case. It's too important. Far more important than either of us."

"Then let me help you," he begged.

"Too late for that, Axel. You know it. Now let me go."

He didn't want to. But he did, releasing her and with her, the best chance he'd ever had at a normal life with a woman who made his body quake and his heart sing. Now, both seemed to be burning to ash. What right did he have to a woman like her, anyway?

Axel watched her go back to her sedan. The engine purred to life and she rolled away, looking straight ahead, as if he didn't even exist. In a moment, the fog made her, and her vehicle, disappear.

AXEL STOOD AT his office window in the building that held all city offices, including his. Right on time, the charcoal gray sedan arrived driven by an unknown female agent with Lieutenant Catherine Ohr in the passenger seat. Behind them, a second car pulled in, this one announcing Border Patrol. Two officers exited, one male and one female, in uniform. He knew them both. Captain Sarah LeMaitre and Officer Greg Perhay. They'd worked the Ogdensburg Bridge and the forty-eight miles of US coastline along this posting for as long as he'd been sheriff, and today their expressions were all business.

Ohr exited the vehicle and headed across the parking area with the second agent in tow. He lost sight of them as they rounded the building. It gave him time to return to his desk and the computer and the mobile phone that still had no texts or messages from Rylee, despite his making three unanswered calls to her.

The two women appeared in the hallway, visible from his office through the glass panel, and entered, coming to a stop before him in the small seating area beyond his desk. In the hallway, LeMaitre and Perhay flanked the entrance. Axel's unease grew as he turned to his visitors.

Ohr wore a business suit and black leather trench coat with the collar upturned, bright red lipstick and a low-heeled shoe. She was gaunt, even with the coat adding much-needed bulk. Her cheekbones stood out and the makeup she used did not hide the unhealthy color of her complexion.

The second agent, by contrast, was tall and fit with brown skin and dark curling hair clipped close to her head. She wore a thigh-length blue woolen coat with an upturned collar, gloves and a cashmere scarf the color of oatmeal.

Ohr shook his hand. Her long bony fingers clasping his for the briefest time possible. Then she introduced the second agent, Lucille Jackson.

"What can I do for Homeland Security?" he asked, wondering why Rylee was not here with them but unwilling to ask.

"I understand from Kurt Rogers that you were born on the compound of the Congregation of Eternal Wisdom," said Ohr. She might as well have slapped him across the face.

His cordial smile slipped and he straightened, feeling the need to sit down.

"Yes. That's correct." He motioned to the chairs before his desk. "Would you care to sit down?"

Ohr gave a shake of her head but not a hair moved. She stepped in, crowding his personal space.

It was a technique of which he was familiar, and so he forced himself not to step back. She smelled of ash and tobacco. He glanced to Jackson, who had a pad of paper out and was jotting down notes.

"Are you still a member?" asked Ohr.

"No. There are no members outside of the compound. You are either in or out."

"Emancipated at thirteen?" asked Jackson.

"Yes." Axel did not like being on this side of the questioning.

Ohr leveled him with a steady stare. "We have reason to believe that the individual who escaped capture on Monday, September 4, may be here on Congregation's property."

He straightened. "Your source?"

"I'm not able to share that. The message was received by a Border Patrol agent." She lifted a hand and motioned to the agents behind her without turning her head.

Captain LeMaitre stepped forward and handed over the letter, which Ohr passed to Axel. The page was torn from a lined composition book. He recognized the type of paper from his early schooling on a twisted version of the world beyond the compound walls.

He read the note.

The Rising is near. We are prepared and joyful to reach Heaven's Door. Please tell our son, Axel, we will miss him and have missed him greatly. Ask him to come home to us.

"Where did you get this?" he asked.

"One of the brothers from the congregation delivered it to a border agent. Do you want to tell me what this means?" asked Ohr.

"This congregation believes that they are the chosen people and that a great disaster is imminent."

"And they'll be spared?" asked Jackson, her eyes rolling toward the ceiling as if having heard this on too many occasions.

"The opposite. They believe they will be called to the Lord before the Desolation. They prepare by readying themselves to meet God by living according to their leader's mutation of religious scripture."

"Mutation is an interesting choice of word," said Ohr.

Axel absorbed this gut punch with only a twitch of his brow. She knew about the rituals of castration, then?

Ohr smiled and extended her hand for the note. He returned the page, folded as it had been.

"There's something else," said Axel. "Part of their ceremonies are preparations for the Rising. If Father Wayne tells them the Desolation is near, it is possible they might all take their lives."

"You are talking about mass suicide?"

"I am."

"I'm aware of their beliefs. Unfortunately, shutting down this organization is not our objective. We are not interested in another Waco. My objective is recovery of the foreign agent who slipped through Agent Hockings's fingers." She tilted her head in a way that was birdlike. "Are you certain Wayne Trace is your father? I understand that he gives all children born on the compound his name. Isn't that correct?"

"That is because all the children born in the compound are his. He is the chosen one. The only man allowed to touch the women. That means any and all women of age."

Ohr folded her arms as if finding this unsettling. Her expression showed her disapproval. "Your mother is there?"

"As far as I know."

"What is her name?"

It was such an obvious question. But the answer made him sick to his stomach. He wrinkled his nose and swallowed. Trying not to look at Ohr, he spoke.

"I don't know her name. The women who elect to join the cult, they are not allowed to claim their children. All those born there are separated from their birth mother and raised communally by women who have not yet born children or are past the age to bear children."

Ohr's brows rose high on her forehead. She and Jackson

exchanged a look. He recognized the silent exchange, having witnessed it before—pity mixed with disgust.

"Why is that?" asked Ohr.

"Part of Reverend Wayne's dictates. Children belong to everyone."

"During your time there, did you ever see any illegal activities?"

"No."

"Funding?"

"Donations to his cause and the assumption of all assets from those who decide to throw in with him."

"You know what Agent Hockings recovered here. You know that we are still in pursuit of the person who transported this package. Our investigation leads us to the conclusion that this individual is still in your county. In your opinion, would your father have any reason to shelter such an individual?"

"Don't call him that."

"But Reverend Wayne Trace *is* your father."

Axel lowered his head. The truth was impossible to bury. He knew because he had tried. He took a moment to breathe, the air heavy with the stink of stale cigarette smoke, and then he answered her question.

"He's been preaching the coming apocalypse, the end of the days, for nearly twenty years now. That's a lot of days gone and his followers all willing and wanting to meet their maker. Eager, even. The outbreak of a plague would give his prophecies more credence. Earn points with his followers. Maybe bring in a pile of more followers. So, yes. I believe it is possible that he would assist and shelter such an individual."

"Our findings exactly. We have the layout and all the information on known members within. What I need from you are details on the life inside and the interior layout of buildings to which we might need access. Drone surveillance shows us that one individual never leaves the women's compound. Is that normal?"

"No. Every one of the members have work assignments. The only exception is illness."

"Thank you."

Axel wondered who was ill or injured. Then another thought struck him.

"Do you think this person, in the women's compound, is the one who transported your package?"

"Not at liberty to say," said Ohr. "Now, your congregation hosts retreats for outsiders."

"It is not *my* congregation."

"Yes. In any case, they allow outsiders in for up to three weeks."

"But they are housed in a separate area."

"For the most part. But not during meals."

"If they wish to join the congregation for prayer or meditation or meals, they are welcome," said Axel. "The congregation makes their way of life look ideal. Pastoral, simple. Wayne is a very charismatic guy and he knows how to sell the soap."

"Soap?"

"His lifestyle. The congregation. Most of the converts are unhappy people who have been on more than one retreat. Folks who don't fit in anywhere else, I guess. He makes the unhappiest among them feel a part of things until they just let go of their old life and join him."

The possibility hit him like a fillet knife to his stomach. He braced as he looked from one woman to the other.

"Which brings me to our next concern. We need to identify the residents there. Do you have a list of some sort?"

"I'm sorry, I don't."

"Then we need agents inside. Drones can only do so much. The members never look up, so there is no way to identify any of the residents. Damn bonnets, hats and veils.

And if they are hiding someone, our suspect, we need access to find him."

"You think they'll walk your agents to the very spot where they might be hiding someone?"

"That's the mission. We don't require their cooperation."

"I could assist."

"Your connection with this group makes that impossible. But we will inform you when operations are complete." With that announcement, the lieutenant turned and left his office. Jackson fell in beside and slightly behind her.

"How much personnel do you have up here?" he asked the retreating figures.

"I'm not at liberty to say."

"Because he's got fifty or more. And he's got contacts."

"Who do you mean?"

"The North Country Riders. That adds another thirty. You are badly outnumbered. I'd advise against charging into the lion's den."

"You are being dramatic. They're federal officers. They can handle themselves."

Axel knew his sire was fully committed to his little empire. What he didn't know was what he was capable of, when his kingdom was threatened.

Would he follow through and call for the deaths of all his followers? Would they do as he commanded, go to their bunks and take the cocktail of drugs inducing a sleep from which none would ever awaken?

Axel found himself on the move without even recalling leaving his office. He had to speak to Rylee.

Chapter Seventeen

Rylee looked from one woman to the next. Each wore a brown head covering that allowed her to see no part of her hair color. Their complexions ran the gamut from a deep walnut to a freckled pink. But they all shared the same cautious eyes and rigid posture.

The meeting with Reverend Wayne Faith had not gone well. The man talked in circles, repeating himself and the same quotable truisms.

God's hand will bring justice.

We are the chosen.

This life is the true path to Heaven's Door.

We pray for the souls of the lost.

By the lost, he included Rylee and all who lived outside the walls of his compound.

It was just past 5:00 p.m. on Saturday night and she and Agent Lucille Jackson stood before his stylish desk surrounded by murals depicting people dressed in shapeless brown garments being lifted into the sky. The Rising, he had explained in detail. The mechanics of which seemed to involve the trigger of a great human disaster followed by God welcoming home only these few men and women. She'd have laughed if they were not all so serious and deadly sure. What she didn't know was if the good reverend would be willing to give his predicted apocalypse a little shove forward by helping to smuggle into their country a population-decimating virus.

"We will need to see the living quarters," said Agent Jackson, keeping her voice calm while revealing a bit of the southern accent. She had not removed her mirrored glasses and so the stare down was one-sided.

Rylee's fellow agent stood five inches taller and had clear brown skin with russet undertones. She wore her black hair close-cropped and an impenetrable expression.

The standoff stretched, tight as a stretched rope.

Finally, Wayne spoke. "It would be out of the question to allow two women into the men's quarters."

Rylee had elected to wear a DHS ball cap, in deference and as a reminder of who and what she was. No need to announce or explain to his followers. They likely already knew she was a federal agent. Whether that would attract or repel was an open question.

"We will start with the women's quarters, then," Rylee said and turned to go.

Wayne hurried around his desk. The man was thin with a fleshy face and neck that would make a tom turkey proud. His hair was sparse, but he had grown the back out and wore it braided in some aberration of the elves of Middle-earth. Unlike his followers' drab attire, Wayne's robes were white. The rest of his congregation wore the more practical brown, which was perfect for the thaw that turned the icy roads here into a muddy quagmire.

He managed to get ahead of them as they reached the lobby beside his office and before his church of death.

"You can't go alone."

"Federal officers," drawled Agent Jackson. She waited as Wayne scowled and stared at his reflection in her glasses. Now his gray complexion had a healthy flush. The man was not used to being challenged. That much was clear.

"An escort, then."

"If they can keep up," said Jackson and headed outside.

Rylee was glad for the hiking boots that remained on despite the sucking mud.

Jackson swore as she lifted her pant leg to reveal a shoe and sock smeared with what Rylee hoped was only mud. There were farm animals wandering about.

Before they had reached the women's quarters, a young female dashed up before them, arms raised to stop them.

Jackson had her hand on her sidearm. "You do not want to do that," she warned.

"Sister Della is coming. She's right there." The woman's wave had changed to a frantic combination of pointing and motioning.

Jackson kept her attention on the young woman and her hand on her weapon while Rylee glanced back the way they had come.

Striding toward them from the stables was a tiny stick of a woman who held her skirts high to avoid the mud. The result was a troubling view of her striped socks and rubber clogs below cadaverous knees. She moved quickly for one so small. Rylee judged her to be in her fifties from the heavily etched lines around her mouth and the fainter ones around her eyes. Unlike her pale legs, her face was ruddy and tanned as if she spent every minute of the day out of doors.

"That's her. Sister Della is an elder," said their obstructer. "She'll take you in."

The woman lifted a hand. "Sister Nicole, I am here. What is the trouble?"

"These two demand access to the women's quarters," said Sister Nicole.

"Demand? Not a pretty start. Ask, children. Just ask." She reached beneath her robes.

"Stop," said Jackson.

Della did and cast her a curious expression. Rylee cocked her head as she stared at familiar blue eyes and that nose… She recognized this woman but was certain they had never met. Had they?

"What are you doing?"

"Getting my keys, girl."

"But slowly," said Jackson, her weapon now out of the holster.

The woman's face did not register fear so much as fury.

"You bring weapons into this holy sanctuary?" asked Sister Nicole.

"We are federal officers and we carry guns," said Rylee.

Sister Nicole tugged at her brown garments, looking affronted. Sister Della lay a hand on the younger woman's shoulder.

"I'll take them from here," said Sister Della.

Sister Nicole opened her mouth as if to raise an objection and then acquiesced, nodding and lowering her gaze. She lifted that gaze to glare at the intruders before returning the way she had come.

Sister Della watched her, the smile on her face peaceful as a summer sky. Then she slowly withdrew the keys. "I'll take you anywhere you wish."

Jackson pointed at the women's quarters and Sister Della led the way. Over the next hour, they wandered in and out of stables, gardens, residences and any outbuilding large enough to hold a shovel. Sister Della gradually lost the reclusive reserve and asked Rylee a few questions about herself and her beliefs.

"Are you enjoying your time here on the St. Lawrence?"

"Working, mostly."

"Have you met our son, Axel Trace?" asked Sister Della.

"Our?" asked Jackson.

"Children belong to all of us," she explained. "We were grieved when he joined the army and now, a sheriff, still using weapons to solve the world's problems. What he never understood is that there is no saving the world. Only yourself—your soul must be clean, you see."

"I have met him," said Rylee.

"Have you? What does he look like?"

Clearly, Axel did not visit.

"Would you like to see a photo? I have one on my phone."

"On a phone? Really?"

She looked mystified, as if she had never seen a mobile phone.

"How long have you been inside these walls, Sister?" asked Rylee, as she pulled up the photo she had taken of Axel and Morris Coopersmith on the bench outside the ice-cream stand her first night in town. She wasn't sure why she had kept the shot instead of deleting it. Axel looked relaxed and had a gentle, sweet smile on his face as he sat with his head inclined toward Morris. Looking back, she realized that it was the first moment when she began to fall in love with Axel.

Sister Della moved in as Rylee stared at Axel's kind, handsome face.

"Hockings? You all right?" Jackson asked.

Rylee shook her head and turned the phone, so the sister could see. Sister Della opened both hands and placed them on either side of the phone, cradling his image and Rylee's hand.

"Oh, he's so handsome. Looks just like his father," said Sister Della.

Rylee glanced back at the image. She didn't see the resemblance between Axel and Reverend Wayne. And she was certain that Axel would do anything to change his lineage.

Sister Della sighed and released Rylee's phone, pressing both hands over her heart. "He looks well."

"He's a strong, capable man." *Despite your efforts*, she thought.

"We've only had three leave us. All boys and all to the army. Can you comprehend? We are pacifists. Killing is against God's law."

"What about killing yourself?" asked Jackson.

"Do you refer to the Rising? That's not killing, Lamb. That is responding to the call of our Lord."

Della's placid smile was disturbing. Rylee shifted uncomfortably in the austere quarters.

"Has the sheriff been helping you to find what you seek?" asked Della.

Rylee took a chance. "He is. We are looking for a person. Foreign national, likely Chinese."

"Really? Here? I've seen no one like that." Her face was troubled and Rylee sensed she did know something.

"Axel has been searching with us. It's important to him."

"What has he done, this Chinese person?"

"He's a threat to national security," said Jackson.

"National." She laughed. "There are no nations. We are all one." The sister turned to Rylee. "May I see that photo again?"

"I can make a copy for you."

"Really? I'd like that. Though we are not supposed to have photos of—well, yes, but he's not my old family, so perhaps… I'm not certain." After this conversation with herself concluded, she beamed at Rylee. "I'd like that."

Dark clouds continued to build throughout the late afternoon. As the sun dipped, so did the air temperature.

"Are there any other buildings on the compound?" asked Jackson, now shivering from the cold and casting a glance skyward.

"None here." Despite her small stature, Rylee thought

she noticed the sister straightening, growing and setting her jaw.

"What is it?" asked Rylee.

"Have you been down to the river?"

"Yes. Do you mean here on your grounds?" Rylee was not looking to the north toward the St. Lawrence but to the west, where the St. Regis River glinted steel gray through the trees.

"That river is a dangerous waterway. We only use our boats in fair weather."

"Boats?" said Jackson. "Here?"

"Yes, they are outside of the compound but belong to Father Wayne. Some of the male members of our congregation are lobstermen who use the boats daily to check their pots. One of the men at the boathouse could show you."

"What do you use the boats for?" asked Rylee.

"I'm sure I don't know. I'm in charge of the animals. And the women are not allowed near the boats."

A few more questions and they discovered where the boats were located. Sister Della walked them back toward the church and sanctuary, where their car was parked.

"Right through there." She pointed toward the open gate. "If you are quick, you might find your…man."

Rylee didn't like her impish smile, as if she were the only party privy to some joke.

"The road to the boathouse is on the north side of the outer wall, judging from the engine noise I hear."

Sister Della offered a wave before she turned and walked toward the barn and the animals in her care.

"Why did she tell us that, about the boathouse?" asked Jackson.

Rylee shook her head, perplexed. She had been wondering exactly the same thing. But Sister Della had told them something else. She had told them to hurry.

"Boathouse?" asked Rylee.

"Oh, yeah," said Jackson. "Calling in our position and destination," she said, and with that done, they headed to their car and left the compound grounds, turning north to the dirt road that paralleled the high concrete block walls. The afternoon bled into evening, with the gray clouds making the twilight come early. The lights of some buildings beyond the wall and below their position came into view.

"That's right on the river. How did we not see it?" asked Jackson.

"We saw it, but there is no affiliation between that business and this church. I've checked all their holdings. A marina is not among them."

Jackson gripped the wheel over some kidney-jarring ruts and steered the sedan to the shoulder. "Wonder what else Reverend Wayne left off the list."

"Lots of vehicles for this late in the season," said Rylee.

She took out her binoculars. Below them lay a small inlet, cut from the river, with steep banks. On the concrete pad were several cars and trucks and beyond was a metal commercial garage or small warehouse that was likely the marina. Stacks of blue-and-green plastic crates, used to ship live shellfish, lined the docks before a crane. Below the jetty, bobbing in the water, three brightly colored lobster boats were tied.

"What do you see?"

"Looks like a quay with commercial fishing vessels, wharf, lobster traps and crates to ship seafood." She lowered the binoculars. "We need a drone."

"We need a warrant." Jackson put the vehicle in reverse and glanced in the rearview mirror. The curse slipped past her lips. "We've got company."

Chapter Eighteen

"How many?" asked Rylee as she pivoted in her seat. Behind her, she was blinded by the flashing, bouncing headlights.

"Too many!" said Jackson.

"Can't go back."

"What do you think they want?"

The answer came a moment later, when their rear windshield exploded. Rylee screamed as glass fell all about them, pelting the backs of their seats and flying between them, reaching the cup holders and console.

Jackson did not wait, but stepped on the accelerator, sending them jolting forward down the rough unpaved road to the quay. Their pursuers followed. The distinctive sound of bullets pinging off the rear fender sent Rylee ducking behind her headrest.

"Faster," she yelled. Now more in control of herself, she had drawn her service weapon and removed her safety belt. Pivoting until she faced backward and stared out the shattered rear window at the trucks. The flash of headlights was enough for her to identify four pickups, much newer than the old battered models she had seen within the compound.

These might be from the order or someone else altogether.

A flash of gunfire told her which pickup truck was currently shooting at them. She returned fire and was gratified to see the trucks swerve off the twin ruts of a road and bounce into the wooded area to their right. The crash of metal colliding with the trunk of a tree made her flinch.

The rest came on like wolves pursuing the fleeing deer.

"Both dead ends," said Jackson.

Rylee glanced ahead and saw that Jackson had to either veer to the left toward the concrete pad on which sat a commercial metal storage building or to the right and the opposite side of the canal, where the crane, traps and seafood shipping containers sat on a concrete slab above the three fishing boats moored to the jetty. Between the two and beyond both lay the black water of the channel.

"We can't go back," said Rylee. "We're outnumbered and outgunned."

"Right or left?" asked Jackson.

Both bad choices.

"Left," said Rylee, choosing the metal building and the possibility of better cover.

Jackson turned the wheel, committing them to the side that held the commercial garage. As they approached, Rylee saw that the storage facility backed up to the canal on one side and the channel on the other. The building before them was a two-story structure made of sheet metal. On the front sat two bay doors, each large enough to drive a tractor trailer through, but both bay doors were closed. There were no windows that she could see, except in the side door that flanked the structure. Beside the building sat some sort of scaffolding.

"Aim for a garage door?" asked Jackson.

"Likely locked. Left side?"

"It's too close to the river. We might go off into the water."

"We need cover," said Rylee.

"Going through the garage door?"

There was no way to tell if there's a vehicle parked just beyond that door.

"Side door. Right side."

Jackson's elbows extended as she braced. Rylee could not see why but hugged the back of her seat as the car jolted, scraping the undercarriage. Rylee was thrown against her seat and then into the dashboard behind her. When she regained her position, it was to see the pickup trucks fanning out, surrounding them. The smooth ride marked their arrival on a concrete slab that held parking, the metal building and a scaffolding, she now saw, that held six boats at dry dock, parked one above the other and three across.

"Brace yourself," called Jackson. Rylee had time to pivot in her seat as Jackson swerved, sending them careening in a half circle. Rylee lifted her gun arm, still gripping her pistol as she was tossed against her door. The impact jolted her service weapon from her hand.

They now faced their attackers. Jackson's repositioning would allow their car doors to provide them with some cover as they escaped toward the garage's side door.

Where was her gun?

A glance at Jackson showed blood oozed from her nose, running down her chin and disappearing into the navy blue wool of her coat's lapel.

"We have to get inside."

Jackson and Rylee threw open their doors simultaneously. Bullets ricocheted off the grill as Rylee ducked, her hand going to the floor mat. She flinched as her palm landed on something hard. Shifting, she recovered her pistol. Then Rylee exited through the door toward the back of the vehicle.

Jackson was already at the side door and using the butt of her pistol to smash the window glass. Dangerous, Rylee thought until she saw Jackson slip the safety back off.

Rylee reached her as she stretched her arm through the gap and released the door lock from the inside.

The two women slipped inside. Behind them, machine gun fire erupted, closer now, the bullets shrieking through the metal walls all about them.

"I can't see a thing," said Jackson.

Rylee returned her pistol to her hip holster and retrieved her cell phone, gratified to discover that it worked after the jolting exit.

She swiped on the flashlight app and the beam of light swept their surroundings, disappearing into the cavernous space. The shipping containers beside them were neatly stacked and now she realized they were not shipping containers, but the modern version of the clay pots once used to catch lobsters. The more efficient models were each spray-painted with the owner's number. They rose from the floor to the ceiling.

"They're coming!" Jackson pointed toward the bouncing beam of headlights darting through the open side door.

"We need backup."

"Could we take cover under the dock?" asked Jackson as they backed, shoulder to shoulder, farther into the garage.

"There *is* no dock. It's concrete and the seawall. Only way out of here is across the canal or back the way we came."

"Trapped."

That was it. A succinct one-word summary of their situation.

They were pinned and needed to survive long enough for backup to arrive.

Rylee used her phone to send a text with their situation. Then she hit her contacts list, using the mapping app that would send her location with her message. Finally, she added the names to the group text. First, *Cath-*

erine Ohr and *Sarah LeMaitre* from Border Patrol. She swallowed back her doubt before adding the last name, selecting *County Sheriff Axel Trace*. She held her breath and pressed Send.

"This way," said Rylee.

Jackson hesitated. "If they come through the side door, they'll come through one at a time and we'll have a clear shot."

But their pursuers didn't choose the opening through which they had entered. The sound of their bullet punching through the metal garage door before them and the sound of men shouting confirmed that. Rylee's decision to move became more urgent.

"They're destroying the garage lock," said Jackson.

"That's Wayne Faith," said Rylee. "I'm certain."

Rylee led them with her phone through the cavernous structure, past two boats in dry dock stacked one above the other on metal scaffolding. Beside them sat empty racks and a winch. Construction equipment, including a Bobcat and a backhoe, completed the vehicles. They'd never get out of here in either one, Rylee knew.

At the front corner, beside the door, Rylee noticed a framed office with large glass windows reflecting her light back at them.

"That's just where I'd look for us." Jackson paused, searching their surroundings. "What about those stacked boats?"

"You want to hide in one of those wooden bottomed boats?" asked Rylee. It was the kind of choice that left no option.

"It's cover. Hard to reach. A tower, easier to defend."

"Depends on how much ammo we have. And how much time we have to hold them," said Rylee.

"You walked right by those boats. They might as well.

And it would put us behind them. We might be able to slip past them and to their vehicle."

"We can't slip out of those boats," said Rylee. "The bottom one is ten feet off the ground. The scaffold is metal. We won't be quiet on descent and they have semiautomatic weapons."

"Your alternative?" asked Jackson.

She had none, except the mission. "We need to find the suspect. It's the only proof that this congregation is involved."

"Shooting at us should be proof enough," said Jackson.

"Let's go out the back." Before them were two more large garage doors and a small door to the right.

Jackson glanced toward the rear exit. "No cover. Nothing out there but the seawall and water. Plus, any men that may have come around to block that way out."

"It's dark outside. We might get past them or get out before they block us in."

Jackson gave her a dubious look, but nodded.

Behind them, the front garage door inched upward.

At the back door, Rylee flicked her phone to mute as a reply came in from her supervisor. Then she tucked away her mobile. Jackson called to her in a whisper.

"Help coming?" she asked.

Rylee nodded.

"Look." Jackson pointed to the narrow window flanking the back entrance. "At the boats."

Two of the trucks had peeled off and their occupants were now disembarking from their vehicles. They headed under the floodlight and straight for the boat with the red hull.

"They must have seen us come in here," said Jackson.

Rylee nodded. "So what are they after over there?"

She knew the answer before she saw two men haul the small dark-haired figure from the wheelhouse of the boat.

Their suspect was getting away.

Behind them came the sound of their pursuers, now inside the garage.

FOR THE PAST ninety minutes, Axel had tried and failed to reach Rylee. He had stopped at her motel, called and left messages. With each passing minute, he grew more certain that she was at the compound. He was on his way there when his mobile phone chimed, alerting him to an incoming text message.

He stared at the glowing screen and the message from Rylee. 10-33 Shooting.

He had his SUV turned in the direction of the address listed, an address he did not know. That troubled him. GPS in his sheriff's unit showed a small private quay on the river road near the Congregation of Eternal Wisdom. Axel started to sweat as he depressed the accelerator, exceeding the speed limit on the winding road.

A 10-33 was a call for immediate help.

When he spoke, it was to the empty car's interior. "If anything happens to her, I'll..." *Be lost*, he thought.

Because he loved her.

Why did it take this, gunfire and the possibility of losing her forever, for him to realize that keeping her safe was more important that keeping his secrets?

Axel made one phone call en route. One to his trusted friend Kurt Rogers.

"She called you?" asked Rogers.

"Text. They are pinned down at the wharf."

"What wharf?"

Axel gave him the location.

"Rylee says there are a three lobster boats moored beyond the congregation walls on the river."

"Theirs?"

"She says so."

"What's your plan?"

"I'm going in and getting them out," said Axel.

"Sounds good."

"Call Sorrel Vasta. Ask for boats. I don't want them getting the DHS suspect over to the Canada side of the river."

"I'll ask," said Rogers, his voice relaying his uncertainty.

Axel knew that the cult was unpopular among the Kowa people because of Reverend Wayne's attempts to recruit from among members of their tribe, and the Mohawk people had resources Rogers just did not have. Specifically, they had watercrafts, all sorts, from fishing vessels to tour boats.

"I'm on my way out there now. See you in a few," said Rogers and disconnected.

Axel's car radio crackled to life. Border Patrol was requesting assistance for DHS officer Hockings and Jackson and reporting they were thirty minutes out.

"ETA in five," he replied. He was driving too fast to text Rylee back. He'd just have to tell her when he saw her.

If you see her.

Gunfire. Rylee pinned at a marina he never even knew existed during all that time inside those walls. Why had no one ever mentioned a wharf and lobstering operation?

The answer seemed obvious. No one wanted them to know. He knew from the meals he'd had as a child that shellfish, usually crab, was often on the menu. What he hadn't known was what else his father had carried across the St. Lawrence in their little private fleet.

He turned off his lights before reaching the compound. There was no road between Rylee's location on the GPS and the road where he sat. He crept along the narrow country road, approaching the north-side wall of the compound, scanning the weeds to his right, and then he saw it: the obvious tracks of many vehicles and the crushed and broken grass on either side of a rutted road.

He lifted his radio and reported the location of the road. Then he released his rear door. He took only the time it required to toss out a traffic cone and light a flare. Then he was back in his SUV and rattling along the frozen ruts of the road. Temperatures were forecast to dip to the twenties tonight, frost warning in effect. It was a bad time to be in or near the water.

The glow from below the hill alerted him that he was nearing his destination. His heartbeat pounded with his racing blood and his jaw ached from clenching his teeth. He flicked off his headlights and crested the hill.

The beams from the halogen lights mounted on the roofs of the pickups below illuminated the area, making the wharf resemble a Friday night football field. He saw men on the wharf and jetty, all armed with rifles.

A second truck barreled over the hill behind him and he turned to see the familiar turquoise truck of Kurt Rogers. He stood in the headlight's beam and waved. Rogers was beside him in a moment and out of his vehicle, moving well for a man well past sixty.

"Situation?" asked Rogers, settling beside him with his rifle at the ready.

"Unknown," said Axel. He drew out his field glasses and peered at the wharf.

"Who are they?" asked Rogers.

"Don't you recognize that truck?" asked Axel.

Rogers scanned the wharf using the scope on his rifle.

"Looks like Hal Mondello brought his entire crew. Some on the jetty. Some surrounding that building."

The head of the moonshiners was not visible, but Axel knew his truck on sight.

"All this time I thought it was the North Country Riders," said Axel.

"Makes sense. Fishing vessels would make transport of liquor so much easier. Just meet up with another boat out there and load the crates from one to another," said Rogers, as he continued to scan the area using his scope. "Where's your gal?"

He wished she was his. "Likely inside the garage."

"You best get down there, then," said Rogers, still watching the men through his scope. "You got your gun?"

"Of course."

"You aim to use it?" Rogers gave him a hard look.

"If I have to." But he wondered if it were possible. To again use a gun and kill another man. To save Rylee? He hoped he wouldn't.

"Well, now," said Rogers. "Looks like they are transporting more than booze."

Trace followed the direction of Rogers's attention.

"Look on the jetty beside the yellow boat," said his friend.

On the jetty, two men wrestled a small figure from one of the boats.

"That a woman?" asked Rogers.

The figure was diminutive, dressed in black and fighting for all she was worth against the man holding her.

"The one everyone has been looking for."

"I thought the suspect was a Chinese man," said Rogers.

"Can't be a coincidence."

"They have two choices now. Back the way they came or take the boats." Rogers scanned the scene below.

Mondello's men were all scrambling into one boat.

"Looks like they made their choice," said Axel.

"You gonna let them leave?"

"Absolutely. I'm here for Rylee."

"They're taking that gal," said Rogers, indicating the struggling woman. Two men lifted her between them so that her feet never touched the ground as they hustled her along.

"I'm going down there and finding Rylee."

Axel left the trucks and his old friend, using the darkness to move closer through the underbrush that flanked the road.

Below, the men's captive broke free and ran up the jetty. One man lifted his pistol and shot her in the back. The woman's arms flew up. She staggered, her center of gravity now rolling forward, too far before her legs.

Axel ran through the brush as Rogers swore and started shooting. His friend's aim was good, taking down the man who had shot the woman in the back.

The second man now swept his rifle wildly, moving to find the position of the unknown shooter. He ignored the woman crawling on the jetty, running for cover as Rogers's second shot missed the man who leaped from the quay to the yellow-bottomed boat.

The men on the quay now had Rogers's position and returned fire as Axel moved quickly down the hill. Rylee's text had come from inside the garage, so that was his destination.

Behind him came the wail of sirens. Their approaching cacophony drowned out the shouts of the men below. Border Patrol had made good time.

The men below fired on Rogers, who had moved behind his truck. Their bullets punctured the front grate.

The men by the trucks now moved en masse toward the boats on the opposite side of the canal from the marina. Hal Mondello, past the age of running, paused by the woman, who had made it to her hands and knees. With a mighty shove from his boot, Mondello kicked the woman from the lip of the jetty and into the icy water of the canal.

A door banged open and he saw a familiar flash of blond hair as Rylee ran from the cover of the garage and across the open ground on the opposite side of the jetty. The men, now on the boats, lifted their rifles.

"No, no, no," he chanted as he raced toward the canal. Above, Rogers's shots sent the men ducking for cover.

"What's she doing?" he muttered.

But he knew. Even before she jumped from the jetty, he knew.

Chapter Nineteen

Rylee had left Jackson behind her as she'd dashed out into the cold autumn wind. Jackson could not swim and their suspect, the key to the entire case, had been kicked into the water.

How deep was the water? How cold?

Feet first entry, she'd decided. To be on the safe side. Nothing worse than breaking your neck on a shallow bottom or a piling hidden beneath the inky surface. She saw them, the men scrambling into the boats, as she'd leaped out in one giant stride to nowhere. She'd recognized one of them.

Hal Mondello had stared back at her with a surprised expression as she'd sailed out over the canal. She'd looked from him to the black water before it swallowed her up.

A thousand needles of ice pierced her skin as she struggled with her sodden clothing and waterlogged boots to reach the surface. River water burned her eyes as she realized that this was not like swimming in a lake in July. This water was deadly.

The steel-toed boots and sodden clothing dragged her straight to the bottom. Panic shuddered over her as she fought the urge to gasp against the cold, knowing that one breath of water would be her last. She tipped her head to look back at the surface and saw only deep threatening darkness. The black of a watery tomb. The razor-sharp terror clawed at her, but she forced herself to crouch on the spongy bottom and release her boots. She could not quite feel the laces, double knotted, because of the numbness of her fingers. But one boot came loose and then the next. But now her lungs burned with the need for air.

Rylee tried to release the zipper of her coat, but failing that, she dragged the entire thing over her head and away. The efforts took her sweater with it. Planting her feet, she prepared to push off the bottom when something brushed her cheek.

The blurry image of a woman's face sank before her, the outstretched, lifeless hand gliding over Rylee's chest. Rylee caught the scream of horror in her throat, keeping the precious, nearly exhausted oxygen in her aching lungs. It was her target, the person of interest. Was she dead?

And would Rylee follow her?

She grasped the woman's collar in one fist, locking her fingers around the fabric like the talons of an eagle. She exploded off the bottom with everything she had, kicking toward the surface she could not see. Now she felt the current, dragging her along and out, she realized, to the river.

Sound returned before the light. Gunfire and shouting. The knocking of the vessels against the floats beside the seawall. She couldn't feel her feet or the woman she thought she held. Had she let go?

No time now. Just air, everything centered around that next breath. Now the blackness was punctuated with sparks of light. The surface approaching or her brain preparing to shut down?

She squeezed her eyes shut and kept kicking, willing herself to break the surface, to live, to see Axel Trace again so she could tell him what she should have said the morning he told her about Reverend Wayne. That Wayne wasn't his father and that she was sorry his childhood was so terrible that he felt he needed to hide where he came from. She should have let him know that she didn't care and that she forgave him for the lie because she loved him.

The water gave way to the night and Rylee gasped, inhaling a full breath of sweet cold air. She forgot to kick and just as quickly sank once more. This time she kept kicking, getting her face above and dragging the body of her target with her, struggling until the woman's face broke the surface. Water streamed from the woman's mouth, and she jerked and spasmed as Rylee continued to kick, just managing to keep them both above the surface in the current's pull.

Greedy. That's what the river was. The water making her choose. Take them both to the bottom or just Rylee's prize. A glance to the quay showed they were sweeping out from the mouth of the canal and into the river.

One of the boats left the channel with her, powered by diesel and heading right for them. Rylee realized they meant to run her down. She imagined the propellers cutting into her flesh, shredding her muscle to hamburger.

Rylee stopped kicking and let the river take her again.

AXEL REACHED THE SEAWALL. The gunfire exchange now slowing as those on the vessel redirected their weapons to the river, searching for the woman who had been kicked into it and the one who had jumped in after her.

How cold was that water?

Deadly cold, he knew.

He could not see Rylee, but it was obvious that they could from the shots they unloaded into the river. Each discharge seemed to tear into him.

Mondello's men were aboard the first vessel, now leaving its moorings, and the men from the congregation now drove back the way they had come, back to the compound, where there would be no escape from federal authorities.

A terrible thought struck him. They had an escape. The

Rising. If Father Wayne told his followers that this was the night, how many would end their lives in the way they had so long rehearsed? Go to their bed, take the pills, wait for God to bring them to Heaven.

And remove any and all witnesses.

Terror lifted every hair on his body as he pictured them, and him in the years gone-by, dressing in their white robes, swallowing the placebo and lying on the cots in neat rows, like so much cordwood. The tranquilizers taking them quickly to unconsciousness but this time there would be no waking unless they really did wake at Heaven's Door.

Suicide was against God's will. He had learned this only after leaving—the murdering of one's self was prohibited in the Bible.

Where was Rylee? The lobster boat moved out to deeper water, the men aboard staring back at him and the vehicles from Border Patrol, no longer seeing any of them as a threat. The distraction was why Axel did not see the fast-moving speedboats approaching behind them.

Axel recognized them instantly. The Kowa tribe used these vessels to give tourists exhilarating high-speed rides on the river and perhaps for the occasional tobacco run to Canada. Before the fishing boat was fully underway, it was surrounded by the Mohawk Nation. Gunfire exploded again, and grappling hooks glinted in the air. Axel turned his attention to the water.

A face broke the surface. Rylee, he realized, holding the other woman by the collar of her shirt. Rylee sputtered and struggled to keep her mouth and nose above the surface as she was swept from the boats and downriver. He ran along the seawall, following her course. In a moment, she'd be right in front of him and then, he feared, gone forever.

Chapter Twenty

Rylee saw the orange ring buoy sailing through the air, over her head and past her. But the rope fell across her shoulder. She tried to grab at it, but her arms were so heavy with her sodden shirt and the cold. Her fingers would not respond to her command to clasp. So she hooked her elbow over the rope and held on. She felt the friction as the rope pulled through her jointed elbow, the pain a relief from the numbing death that stalked her. Someone was trying to save her.

After what seemed hours, the ring struck her. She fumbled to get her arm around the ring but it only dunked and bobbed away. She tried again and the ring upended and then shot farther away. Fear enlivened her efforts. If she didn't get ahold of the ring, she'd die. But to grasp the ring, she needed to release her captive.

Was the woman already dead? The hungry, desperate voice in her head told her to let go and that only made her grip the more determinedly against the impulse. She would not let go. Like one of those snakes she had heard of that locked their fangs and would not release even if their head were severed from their body. Rylee held on and watched the ring being tugged away.

She pivoted back toward the receding seawall. Someone was there, gathering the rope, preparing for another throw. But this time, the ring buoy fell short.

On shore, the man tied the rope around his waist. A spotlight illuminated him. It was Axel, stripping out of his jacket and holster. Tearing off his boots and flinging aside his hat. What was he doing?

The answer came a moment later when she saw him back up and then run on bare feet down the concrete pad and dive far out over the water.

Shouting reached her, cutting in and out as she bobbed beneath the surface and then kicked on weary legs back to snatch a shallow breath. The shivering had stopped. Was that good or bad?

A bright light blinded her. A spotlight. If it was the lobster boat, she was dead. Should she let them shoot her or sink once more?

Rylee's kicks grew weaker and she feared that if she sank this time, it would be her last.

AXEL SWAM OUT to Rylee through the freezing water. He could not see her, but he could see the spotlight from one of the boats from the Kowa Nation. He used it like a homing beam, swimming hard and lifting his head only to mark his progress. Behind him, the ring buoy dragged, made noticeable by the slight tug at his waist as he pulled himself along.

He'd learned to swim in the army. A sinker, his drill sergeant had said—too much muscle and little fat. If he stopped kicking, he sank like a stone. But the only way he'd stop was when he and Rylee were safely back on shore. The light danced just before him, so close he could see the entire circle, but he did not see Rylee.

He grabbed a breath of air and dove. Beneath the surface, the light caught the pale glow of her blond hair and skin, now blue in the artificial light.

Rylee reached out her free hand to him as she sank and he grasped her wrist. Reversing course now, he kicked to the surface, breaking first and gasping in the dazzling white light. He dragged her against him with one hand, pressing his chest to hers, keeping her and the second woman before him as he dragged the rope, hand over hand, behind them. The ring buoy hauled closer and closer until he had it behind Rylee. Beside her, the other woman choked on river water and sputtered. Both women had lips the color of raw liver and the shock of that sight was enough to get him swimming.

Shouts reached him. He turned to see Sorrel Vasta waving and motioning him toward the boat. Axel could not even see the shore past the bright light, but he trusted Sorrel and changed course again.

The motor of the boat engine hummed in his ears and then cut abruptly. A second buoy slapped the water beside him and he looped one elbow through the ring. An instant later, he and his charges were gliding along the choppy water toward the stern.

They reached the ladder. Both women were tugged from his arms by many hands. The light flicked off as Axel tried to climb aboard. His hands were stiff with the cold and gripping was difficult. He crooked his wrists and used them, as he might if wearing mittens, to scale the ladder and reach the stern platform. There he sprawled. Heaving and spent.

Vasta kneeled over him, throwing a blanket across his shivering body.

"Axel? We're heading to Kinsley Marina. Ambulance is waiting to take you all to the ER," said Vasta.

Axel nodded. "R-Rylee?"

"She's breathing. The other stopped. We're working on her. Resuscitation. You sit tight."

The engine roared and the boat tipped, cutting through the water like a blade.

"The other b-bo…" His tongue wasn't working, and the

shivering was getting worse. That made no sense. He was out of the water and wrapped up tight.

"We stopped Wayne's men before they got inside the walls of their compound. Father Wayne and eight of his men. Trussed up like grouse. My other boat is taking them in to the Border Patrol guys. Ha! Wait until they see what we brought them. They gonna have to cut us some slack. Maybe have to say thank-you. That might about kill them."

"Rye-lee," he whispered.

"We're taking care of your woman, brother. You just sit tight."

A shout and cheer came from behind him.

Vasta grinned. "We got the other lady breathing again."

RYLEE WOKE UP to the sound of a vacuum cleaner and found that she lay between two air mattresses. Beside her, a freckle-faced red-headed woman, dressed in violet scrubs, checked a machine that blipped and pinged beside the hospital bed.

She noticed her patient was conscious and smiled at Rylee. "You waking up? Good deal. I'll tell your people. They've been in and out of here, checking on you."

"Where am I?"

"Kinsley General Hospital. I'm Tami, your nurse. You're in our ICU. You came in here about the temperature of an ice pop, but we warmed you right up."

"The woman…"

"The one who came in with you?" Tami grimaced. "She's here, too. Bullet wound and the cold. She has frostbite on both feet. Friend of yours?"

"Not really."

"Good, because they have state police standing right at her cubicle. Whatever she did must be bad. We only get that handling when we treat prisoners from Franklin or Upstate Correctional. What'd she do?"

"Not at liberty—"

"To say." Tami rolled her eyes. "Already heard that one. You with Border Patrol?" she asked.

Rylee shook her head. "Department of Homeland Security."

"Well, I'm eaten up with curiosity. You had a near miss."

Rylee lifted the clear covering on top of her that was swollen with air.

"That's a warming blanket. Got one below you, too. Still trying to bring your core temperature up to normal." She tapped away at her tablet and then smiled at Rylee. "Nothing to eat or drink for you just yet. But soon. Your family has been notified."

"My family?"

She tapped on her tablet. "Father, Colonel Hockings." She paused there to make a face that showed the title impressed. "In… Guam. Army?" she asked.

Rylee flinched. "Marines."

Tami smiled as if it were all the same to her.

"Where is Axel?"

"The sheriff? Next door." Rylee didn't like the smile on Tami's face as Tami glanced in the direction of the hall. "On my way to check his vitals next, which I would do for free. But when I'm done, who will check mine?" She laughed. Then she pointed at the button clipped to Rylee's bed rails. "Press the button if you need anything."

Rylee waited until the nurse left to pull down the air blanket. Immediately, she began to shake and shiver again. She had so many questions to ask and patience was not her strong suit. But she adjusted the blankets and closed her eyes, hoping the blanket did its work quickly. She had not meant to sleep, but when she next opened her eyes, only the light above her bed was on and the blankets both top and bottom continued to reverberate like a vacuum cleaner.

At six o'clock on Sunday morning, Axel checked on Rylee and then checked himself out of the hospital against the doctor's orders. Damned if he'd miss the biggest case this county had ever seen, lying in a hospital bed under an electric blanket. He wasn't leaving without seeing Rylee, though. He discovered from a familiar nurse in purple scrubs that Rylee had been moved to a private room for security. From Tami, he learned that Rylee had been awake part of last night. All her vitals were good, and she would suffer no ill effects from her dive into the St. Regis. The woman she rescued had not fared so well. He was informed that she would likely loose several fingers and both feet to frostbite. One lung had collapsed from the bullet wound and she had suffered dangerous blood loss. Whether that had caused brain damage was still unknown. She was currently in a medically induced coma to protect her brain as she healed.

The trooper stationed at Rylee's door checked him in. They'd been on many traffic fatalities together, so the ID was unnecessary.

"Do you have any word on what happened at the compound last night?" he asked.

"None. Been here most of the night," said the trooper.

Axel nodded and left him, pausing when he reached Rylee's bed, wondering if he could touch her. All the wires and tubes made him nervous. Even her finger had a pulse monitor clipped on. He leaned down and pressed a kiss to her forehead.

"I'm here, Rylee. I'm going to finish this for you."

Her heart rate accelerated and her eyelids fluttered. He waited, hoping she would open her eyes. But she did not, and he let himself out.

He was just passing registration when the circus came to him. The flashing blue-and-red lights of law enforcement vehicles bounced off the waiting room walls from the windows overlooking the parking lot. He reached the main waiting area when the double doors whooshed open and in marched the federal and state authorities, moving in formation.

Catherine Ohr led the pack. She was flanked by two men in dark suits and black woolen overcoats. All that was missing were fedoras and they could have been extras in a Bogart and Cagney movie. Behind them, five state police officers stood with sullen expressions and bristly short haircuts, the purple band around their Stetsons matching the purple leg-stripe on their trousers.

"That was a speedy recovery," said Ohr. "They told me you were spending the day." The woman smelled of cigarette smoke.

"Unfortunately, they didn't clear that with me."

"Just coming to see you," said Ohr, pinning him with watery blue bloodshot eyes. Rylee's supervisor had had a long night.

"What a coincidence," said Axel.

"Where's Agent Hockings?" asked Ohr.

"Still in her room, sleeping."

Rylee's boss lifted her thin eyebrows at him, then flashed her shield and ID at the receptionist.

"You have an empty room?"

They were led to a small exam room. Ohr left the troopers milling in the hall. She and her two agents now stood between him and the exit, and for a moment, he thought they were here to arrest him.

"What happened after I went in the river?"

"Quite a lot. The Kowa Nation captured the Mondellos, who were attempting to flee custody in a lobster boat. The Kowa had several boats. The fastest brought you, Hockings and the suspect to Kinsley for treatment."

He remembered that. Speaking to Vasta and wondering if the suspect had died.

Ohr continued her summary. “Border Patrol got the men fleeing the wharf before they reached their compound. My people raided the compound, but Wayne and his council were not among them.”

“They got away?”

“He did not. But he tried. Wayne and his people were in a small motorboat on the river trying to flee the country.”

“You caught them.”

“The Kowa caught them. Initially with Border Patrol.” Her smile was broad. “Wayne is in federal custody along with his council, five men who were with him. Two others suffered gunshot wounds and are here in the hospital. My people are interviewing the men and women from the Kowa tribe. Your retired sheriff is helping with a team at the Mondello property. We have all the Mondellos in custody except the eldest of his sons, Quinton. Still searching for that one. Just about finished up there. We still need a formal interview from Rogers. He seems to know everyone in the county.”

“Did you get to the compound? Did you stop them from taking the suicide pills?”

“We did. Thanks to you. You told Acting Chief Vasta before they took you to the hospital. They got the word to us.”

He vaguely remembered that.

“Seems your father was going to clean house by ridding himself of anyone in the congregation who might have known what he had been up to.”

Axel felt sick to his stomach to be associated in any way with that man. To have him as his father was crushing.

“You saved a lot of lives, Sheriff.”

Most important of which was Rylee’s. Had he saved his mother? The empty place in his insides ached. Maybe now he’d learn who she was.

“Is there anything else, Sheriff? I need to check on the

condition of the woman Rylee dove in to save from the river," Ohr said.

"I've had an update." Axel relayed what he knew about her condition. "I do have one more question. How did Rylee know about the wharf?"

He'd lived inside that compound and didn't know about it.

"According to Agent Jackson, one of the women in the compound suggested they check there for the suspect."

He frowned. It was unlike any of the members to act in a way that would threaten the group.

"Who?"

Ohr referred to her notes again and read. "Sister Della Hartfield."

Della was an elder. Why would she help DHS agents?

"We'll be taking the suspect into federal custody as soon as the paperwork is signed." She motioned to the two agents beside her, who then swept from the room and vanished from his line of sight.

The troopers trailed after them, presumably toward the ICU and their suspect. Axel suspected the doctors and nurses of Kinsley General would put up a fight, but they'd lose.

"Is she the person who carried the duffel?" he asked.

"Yes. Father Wayne confirmed it. He was hiding her at his compound. Waiting, I assume, for the right time to move her. She's the one we wanted. Good work apprehending her."

"I didn't apprehend her. Rylee did that."

Ohr smiled and inclined her chin. "Group effort, then. Retired Sheriff Rogers says that you called him and he called the leaders of the Kowa people."

"That's correct."

"But not Border Patrol. Why is that?"

Axel thought of Rylee's text and his panic at knowing she was in trouble.

"Rylee's text alerted them and you. I called the men and women who I could trust."

"Which included a tribe of Kowa Mohawk and your retired mentor. Not the state police or federal authorities."

"Both too far away to help."

"I should have you fired."

"I'm an elected official."

"Yes. Inconvenient. Likely your county will throw you a parade."

"Probably a pancake breakfast, but I can hope for a spaghetti dinner."

Ohr made a sound in her throat. Then she cleared it and gave him a hard look. "Wayne Faith is your father?"

"So he tells me."

"He's going to prison. Initial overview shows he has offshore holdings and has been playing fast and loose with the congregation's funds for years. In addition to that, as you feared, he called for the followers who remained behind to take some sort of suicide pill."

"But you saved them?"

"Most."

"How many dead?"

"Four. All children. Given the pills before we could reach them."

Axel felt sick.

He turned his back on her and used a paper cup from the dispenser to get some water. The tap water was warm, but it pushed down the bile.

"Additionally, two of Mondello's men were wounded by Rogers. Two Kowas were shot by Mondello's men. No fatalities from the gun battle."

"Who were the wounded?" he asked.

She read the names from a small notebook. He knew each man.

All this, to protect one woman, keep her hidden with his secrets. His father had gone from being a zealot and flimflam man to a federal criminal.

"What will happen to Father Wayne?"

"Espionage charge. It's a capital crime."

Why did he care what they did to him? Was it because he was blood? Blood that had shamed him all his adult life.

"That's why I'm here. Since your father isn't talking."

"Don't call him that."

"Fine. Since Wayne Trace, AKA Father Wayne Faith, isn't cooperating, I need some insight on the congregation. Help sorting and getting those we detained to speak to us."

"He's not even there and he's still controlling them."

"Yes. It's disturbing. He's waiting for an attorney and hoping for some sort of deal."

"Will he get one?" asked Axel, the sour taste in his mouth and pitching stomach now taking much of his attention. Four dead children. He shook his head.

"Not if I have anything to do with it. You all right? You look pale."

He took a few deep breaths, unsure if his condition was physical or a result of being heartsick.

"I'm not all right, but I am willing to help in any way."

She nodded her approval of this.

"We have several members of Hal Mondello's family in custody and are rounding up more of his people. Seems they had some sort of alliance with Wayne Trace. Mondello distributed what Trace smuggled in from Canada, which we, unfortunately, were unable to recover. It's unclear if they knew what they were transporting."

"The duffel Rylee recovered from the Kowa people?"

"That was the second shipment. The first got through. We thought this was the work of Chinese nationals. But that woman you dragged from the river is North Korean. A chemist. We believe Siming's Army was trying to point blame at China, in hopes of increasing tension between nations. That would serve the North Koreans. North Korea would benefit greatly if we lifted sanctions on them while continuing them on China, and even more so if we challenged Chinese control of that region."

"Did you say a chemist?"

"Yes. Possibly here to culture the virus within our borders."

"Culture it where?"

"That's the top question on our list. Most especially if there is a plant currently in operation of this deadly strain of flu as we speak."

That thought chilled.

"But you've stopped them?"

"I'm afraid they don't need the chemist to reproduce what she carried."

"Biohazard?"

"It's a pathogen, Axel. Called a virus seed stock because they use it to propagate more of the virus. Some of it is here. This disease is a powerful killer, the likes of which we haven't seen since the Middle Ages. If it gets loose, we will suffer the worst pandemic ever faced in America."

"A plague?"

"Of sorts. But much, much faster. My experts liken it to the influenza epidemic of 1918."

"But we have the vaccine?"

"Which takes time to produce. In the meantime, we need to find virus seed stock and kill it before Siming's Army can turn that seed sample into an epidemic."

She reached in her pocket, removed a pack of cigarettes

and then dropped it back in place. Axel was certain she longed for a smoke. Who could blame her?

"Now, if you would come with me, you can get me up to speed on this cult on the way."

Chapter Twenty-One

Axel had been back within the compound all day speaking to members of the cult individually, with Catherine Ohr there for each interview. The ashtray before her smoldered with the last stubbed-out cigarette.

"Only a few more," she said. "Let's take a break."

They walked out together into the grassy quad. DHS had set up a mobile operations station complete with multiple trailers within the compound's central courtyard. They had even erected a mess hall between the church and living quarters. Generators hummed, powering the mobile light towers that illuminated their way. The entire area now had a distinctly military feel.

Male members of the congregation were being held in the worship hall and the female members were detained in the congregation's dining hall.

As they continued past yet another trailer, Ohr reached for another cigarette and glanced at her phone. "Seven p.m.," she muttered. "I need coffee." She pointed at him. "Want one?"

"Sure."

"They have pastries and coffee in the mess tent. I'll bring you something."

She strode off toward her people, who moved in and out of the buildings, carrying off computers and other bagged evidence.

Agent Rylee Hockings stepped from the sanctuary beside the main worship hall, where he had just been.

"You're here!" he said, sweeping over her and finding her pale and circles under her eyes.

"For several hours now. I've been interviewing the female members of the cult."

They clasped hands and he smiled at her, his heart dancing a percussive rhythm of joy at the sight of her.

"Rylee, you gave me such a scare." He had so much to tell her, to say. He wanted to rush forward and tell her that he loved her and that he wanted her in his life. Then he saw two of his father's men marched past them in handcuffs. The shame of his association with this congregation broke inside him like a drinking glass dropped on ceramic tile. Millions of shards of doubt splintered out in all directions.

"I need to thank you for coming after me. I was losing to the river," she said and gave his hands a squeeze before letting go. Her smile held. "But we got her. Thanks to you. Who knows what we'll learn."

"Ohr told me she's a North Korean national."

"What? Really?"

"She also told me that Sister Della was the one who directed you to the wharf."

"That's true." Rylee was glancing about as if searching for someone. Her supervisor?

"That surprises me," he said. "It seems hard to believe that a congregation elder would do something that jeopardized the group. Any idea why she would do that?"

"Just a theory. I haven't spoken to her yet."

"What's your theory?" he asked.

"I think she did it to help you."

"Me? Why would she want to help me?"

"Ah… I need to find my supervisor."

And just like that, his opportunity fled. Rylee was back on her mission. It would be easier to stop a runaway toboggan than to prevent her from moving forward with her investigation.

There will be other opportunities, he told himself. Better ones, ones when he rehearsed what to say. No woman wanted to be proposed to in a time and place like this.

He could imagine her telling their kids. *Yes, your mother was just out of the hospital after nearly drowning and on her way to interview human trafficking suspects when I proposed.*

He shook his head, dismayed at the ease with which he produced a mental picture of them together with children. What if he waited and there was no other chance?

"Rylee, I need to tell you something."

She was glancing about them now. No longer looking at him, searching, he thought, for her supervisor among the men and women moving across the yard.

"Take a walk with me?" he asked.

"All right. But I have to get back."

"Just a few minutes."

She fell into step beside him away from the aroma of roasting coffee issued from the mess tent. They walked along the worship hall and sat together on a bench that now faced the back of one of the newly placed mobile operation trailers. At least this spot was not directly under one of the many mobile light towers.

He looked toward the empty women's quarters. Already the conversation had veered off track. Rylee was asking about the living situations for the females in the congregation.

"Yes," he said, in response to her question. "The men lived in one building and the women and young children in another."

"But Wayne kept some women in a private enclosure for himself," she added.

"He insisted on celibacy among the males. As for the females, they were celibate, too, for the most part."

"Unless he deemed otherwise," she said and scowled. "They said it was only so they could bring him children. As if that were some high honor." She shook her head, her expression angry. "A blessing, they called it. For the men, castration was the highest show of devotion. For women to be *most blessed*, they needed to give birth."

"Yes," said Axel. Could he have been thinking of proposing to her during this? He must have lost his mind.

"And the males went along with this," she said.

"*If* they wanted to stay. Father Wayne can be very convincing. Made sure it was a status symbol for the males to lop off their junk and the women to sleep with him. Told his followers that it made them closer to God. Prepared to meet the Lord without lustful, earthly thoughts. But I…"

"Did he tell you that?" she asked.

Axel nodded, head bowed and the palm of his hand pressed to the back of his own neck.

"When I turned thirteen, my own father told me that he wanted me to mutilate myself on my eighteenth birthday. It's why I ran."

"What happened?"

"Sheriff Rogers picked me up. He went out there and my father denied the entire thing. He claimed I made the whole thing up, but I know whom the sheriff believed. He told my dad that Child Protective Services would be out there to check every child and regularly. But despite all that, we haven't gotten more than a few children out of their hands."

"They got you out."

He dropped his hand. "It's why I stay. To watch over the children, help the ones who run and make certain he never called for them to enter Heaven's Door. I come out here and I never say when. They let me in because I was a member, hoping, I think, that I would change my mind and come back. As if..." He blew away a breath and then continued. "I'd file a notice of indication with Child Protective Services at any sign the caregivers weren't meeting basic needs. Then I got out with CPS to check the kids with them, make sure they were safe."

"He knew you were watching him."

"Yes."

"It's why they were never harmed."

"Maybe," said Axel. "But he liked having me come back here. I think he knew how hard it was for me. How much I hated it here. And he enjoyed that my leaving caused me suffering and that he'd managed to trap me in this place despite my desertion. He used me as an example of how you can walk away but you can never leave. He says I'm tied to them despite what I might say or do."

"You know, I always thought I had it hard, trying to earn my father's approval. And he could be exacting, difficult, but nothing like yours."

"A fanatic. A con man and now a terrorist. I came from him. What does that make me?" It made him unable to propose to her. That much was certain.

"I can answer that. It makes you the complete opposite. He takes advantage and you protect. He exploits and you defend."

"With him gone, I won't be tied here any longer, Rylee. I can go."

She blinked at him and for a heart-stopping moment, he thought he'd misread her. That what he'd seen as love was just sympathy.

"What about your mother?"

He couldn't even lift his head. "I don't know which one of the women is my mother."

"What do you mean?"

"We were separated at birth. She could not claim me and stay with them."

"There is no *them* anymore. We've been explaining that to the members. They're starting to come to grips with what's happening. Most of them, thankfully, are innocent in all of this. Just misguided."

"What will happen to them?"

"Reconnect with families when possible. We'll process them and release them. Where they go will be up to them."

"Will you help them?"

"If we can." She laid a small hand on his shoulder and he lifted his chin until he met her sympathetic gaze. "Axel? I know who she is."

His heart beat so loud that he thought it might bruise his ribs. "How?"

"She looks just like you. I met her on Saturday, here at the compound. I thought at first that I knew her. It didn't take long to recognize why she looked so familiar. I asked her and she confirmed that she gave birth to you. Would you like to speak to her?"

"Yes!" Axel was on his feet. He leaped at the chance and then thought about confronting a woman who had had many opportunities to reveal who she was—and hadn't. "Maybe you should speak to her first and see if she wants to speak to me."

"All right." She stood and faced him, offering her hand.

"Now?"

Her smile was sympathetic. "Yes, now. They won't be here much longer." She was nearly to the sanctuary's dining hall door when he called her back.

"Rylee? Which one?"

"Della Hartfield."

He blinked and nodded. "Della." It seemed right, somehow. "Do I just wait here?"

"Yes. If she's willing, I'll bring her to you."

Axel raked a hand through his hair and tugged at his shirt, momentarily dragging out the wrinkles.

"You look fine, Axel. Just wait. I'll be right back."

He sat on the bench facing the compound's dining hall as his legs bounced up and down with nervous energy. The next eighteen minutes were the longest of his life. Finally, the door opened and out stepped Della, small and pale, her head still draped in the brown covering she had worn for more than thirty years.

Axel stood. The word tore from him like a cry. "Mom?"

She nodded and swept forward, holding out both hands to him. He took them in something that was not the embrace he had imagined.

He had pictured this meeting so many times, but he was always a boy and she always held him. Instead, this tiny birdlike woman beamed up at him with a smile that seemed to blend contentment with something like madness.

Della had always appeared to have only one foot on the earth and the other somewhere else entirely, as if her spirit was too light to allow her to ever be completely grounded.

She kept him at arm's length as she stared at him. Why had he never seen the similarities until now? Her color matched his, as did her long nose and blue eyes. He pushed back her head covering, expecting to see his blond hair, but her hair was entirely white.

"I'm so sorry that I never defied him. He told me that God would strike you down if I broke my oath and, God forgive me, I believed him." Fat tears coursed down her wind-burned cheeks. Her hands were raw from working outdoors and her spine bent slightly.

"I'm glad my father is under arrest."

Her eyes went wide with shock. "Father Wayne?"

"Yes. I hate him." Hated that he shared the same blood and that his father's deadly legacy would cast a shadow across his heart forever.

Della clasped one of his hands in both of hers and gave a little shake to draw his attention. Then she looked behind her and, seeing only Rylee, she turned back to him. When she spoke, her voice was hushed as if she still feared the retribution of the man who was gone.

"Father Wayne is not your father," she said.

Every nerve in his body fired. Blood surged past his ears and he blinked in stupefaction at her.

"What?" he whispered.

"He's not your father, not really. He claims all the children, but there were a few that were not his by blood. Claiming them was preferable to exposing our failings."

Failings? Did she mean their failing to remain celibate?

"Those of us not chosen to share his bed, well, some of us wanted children. So..."

"Did he know?"

"In some cases, and suspected in others. But he never admitted it."

Rylee spoke now. "Because to do that would be to admit he did not have complete control of his congregation."

Della turned to her and nodded. "I always thought so."

"He's not my father," said Axel, the words spoken aloud as if to convince himself of what he was still afraid to believe.

"Yes, son."

"You are certain?"

"I never slept with the man and I am your mother. So, yes, I'm sure."

Axel released Della and stumbled back, colliding with a wooden bench. He placed a hand on the seat as he fell and thus managed to avoid hitting the ground. The bench shuddered with the force of his landing.

He stared up at his mother as the icy pain in his heart melted away like frost on a spring thaw.

"Who is he, then?"

Her smile faltered. "Do you remember Jack Pritcher?"

Other than Kurt Rogers, Jack Pritcher had been as close to a father as a man could be. In Axel's mind, the big man came back to life. The father figure merging into a father.

"Jack died when I was ten," he said to Rylee.

"He was our carpenter," Della told Rylee and patted the bench as if this were one of Pritcher's creations. "Came from Schenectady. Wife had died, he was older than I was, but he had a kind heart."

A weak heart, Axel remembered, because it was his heart that failed him.

"He came up here after his wife and child died in a terrible car accident. He was a lost soul. I'm sure he never intended to be a father again, but then you came along."

"He never told me," said Axel.

"Not in words. But in other ways. And you have his build. Very trim and muscular. His hair was quite red as a young man, so he told me. And your beard has red highlights."

Axel rubbed the stubble on his cheek.

"Did you two ever think of leaving?"

"Why, no. I loved my work with the animals. I understand them in a way I never understood people. They are more straightforward and no facial expressions to confuse me. Jack seemed content keeping the buildings in good condition. It gave him a purpose. You know what he did back there in Schenectady?"

Axel shook his head.

"He was a fireman. A protector, just like you."

That made his heart ache all over again.

"Della?" asked Rylee. "Why did you tell me where to find the suspect?"

"Suspect?" Her placid expression changed to one of confusion. "I didn't."

"You told us about the wharf," Rylee said, reminding her.

"Yes." Her peaceful smile returned.

"Why?"

Della gave a chuckle as if the question were silly. "Well, because your friend asked me, child. 'Are there any other buildings on the compound?' Those were her exact words. I merely answered her question."

"Because she asked you?" asked Rylee.

Della nodded, seemingly pleased that Rylee now understood.

"What will you do now, Della?" he asked.

"Well, that's a good question. I'm not sure if my older brother is still with us. Perhaps I'll start there. He used to live in Altamont. I remember his address. Also, I've been considering becoming a nun." She swept the veil back up over her hair, wrapping it expertly to cover her head.

Right back into a structured religious community, Axel realized.

"You don't have to, Della. I can take care of you," said Axel.

"Now you sound like my brother. And I don't need taking care of just yet. And though you were always the sweetest boy," she said, "and I'm proud to be your mother, I never really knew how to be one, or a wife. I'm not sure how to explain it, except that I loved Jack, in my way, but I was not in love with him. I don't connect to people in that way. I'm afraid he stayed, hoping I'd change my mind."

Had his father died of a broken heart? Twice broken, he realized. First, at the loss of his wife and child and then, by Della's rejection.

"And he stayed for you, of course." Della beamed at him, her small hands clasped as if in prayer. "He was proud of you. Do you remember carrying his tools? You were his little helper."

Della patted him on the cheek. "I'll write you when I'm settled, shall I?"

"Della, you don't need to join an order," said Rylee. "Our social workers explained that."

"But I will. Perhaps one with animals. That would be nice. I must be somewhere safe for the Rising. Have to be ready." She was now moving back toward the dining hall. Whatever he had expected, it wasn't this. He followed, trailing her back to the entrance. Della paused at the door handle, only because it was metal and she didn't like metal. He remembered that about her, as well.

Rylee opened the door and the trooper within took charge of Della. She never even said goodbye.

The door clicked shut. "I'm sorry, Axel. She's troubled."

He nodded, his teeth tight together and the muscles at his jaw working hard.

"One of our people told me that she's on the spectrum."

It explained everything and nothing. He looked to the empty place where his mother had been. "Yes. I see."

Chapter Twenty-Two

Rylee managed to catch a few hours' sleep and was back at work before nine the next day. They finished up at the compound at noon. Ohr had one final interview with Axel in his office in Kinsley. When Rylee arrived, they were already in the conference room. When she tried to join in, Ohr told her to head back to their offices in Glens Falls.

Rylee just blinked at the order. Instead of moving out, she held the doorknob like it was her last friend and stood momentarily petrified. This was not how she had pictured their goodbye.

"I'll finish up here," said Ohr. "See you back at the office."

Rylee stared at Trace, who stared mutely back, his look expectant.

"All right," she said and closed the door.

Trace's head bowed.

She made it outside, but her footsteps slowed. She wasn't going like this. Instead, she waited outside in the cold for Ohr to emerge. Then she planned to see Axel alone. She had to tell him thank-you, at the very least. And tell him that she loved him? Not that it would change anything; he was staying and she was going.

Kurt Rogers emerged from the coffee shop across the street and ambled over to her.

"They still got him in there?" asked Rogers.

"Yes. Thought we might get a late lunch, but heck. It's closer to dinner now."

Rylee could not keep from fidgeting. She tapped her fingers and sighed. The longer Ohr kept him, the less time she'd have to say goodbye.

"My cat paces like that when she's on the wrong side of the door from her kittens," said Rogers.

Rylee stopped pacing.

"It's the cold."

Rogers leaned against the bench on the sidewalk and glanced at the entrance of the administration building in Kinsley. Dressed in a lambskin coat and wearing gloves, he looked broader and younger. She could see for a moment the stature of the sheriff he must have been.

"What are they doing?" asked Rogers.

"Final interview."

Rogers looked back at the agent in the sedan waiting to drive Ohr back to Glens Falls. Rylee's vehicle was parked just behind that one. In a little while, she'd be in that car, driving away. She should be so happy and proud. Instead, she wanted to scream.

The thought made her heart ache. But what was the choice? He was an elected official here and she'd already been told she was being promoted. New York City, if she wanted, or DC.

Soon, she'd have her choice of postings. It was what she wanted. Wasn't it?

Rogers ambled over to the agent in the vehicle, who lowered the window so they could speak.

Ohr finally emerged from the outer doors, followed by Sheriff Trace.

"You still here?" asked Ohr.

She nodded and turned her attention to Trace, painfully aware of their audience. Her driver had left the vehicle and both she and Rogers watched them. Ohr looked from her to Trace, waiting.

"HELLO, SHERIFF," RYLEE SAID.

His hesitant smile faded. "Agent Hockings," he said, formally. "Thought maybe you left. What can I do for you?"

"I wanted to thank you for rescuing me from the river."

"You already have. And you're welcome."

She couldn't read him. The tension was clear from his expression and the caution in his eyes.

"So, you got what you came here for," he said.

Had she? It seemed something was still missing. Why couldn't she say it to him? She glanced to Rogers and then to Ohr. Finally, she returned her attention to him. Her mouth was so dry.

"Yes, most of it."

"It doesn't all come out like in the movies," he said.

Ohr interjected here. "Our people will be moving to locate and eradicate the manufacturing site. Meanwhile, CDC is creating and stockpiling a vaccine against a possible outbreak. Our diplomatic channels will advocate pursuit of sanctions against North Korea based on evidence that you found."

"You know where they are manufacturing?" asked Axel.

"We have Hal Mondello and Wayne Trace, and both are eager to make a deal. I'm sure our investigation will turn up that information."

She did not mention that they had not succeeded in capturing Hal Mondello's oldest boy, Quinton, thought to have fled to Canada. That bothered Rylee, because he seemed very much in charge of the moonshining operation during her investigation.

Her supervisor turned to Rylee. "Did you tell him you're in line for promotion?"

Rylee's cheeks burned with what felt like shame. It was in part due to Axel's efforts that she'd succeeded. She could not have done any of this without him and the Kowa people. Without them, she'd likely be dead.

Her supervisor continued, "You have done an above-average job here, Agent Hockings. Proved me wrong and far exceeded my expectations. You've more than earned that promotion."

Rylee felt none of the pride she had anticipated. She'd spent enough time imagining this moment to know that the twisting dread that tugged at her stomach was not the jubilation she should have been experiencing.

"Congratulations," said Axel, his voice flat and his expression strained.

The time had come to say goodbye. To get on her horse and ride off into the sunset. Specifically, she needed to slip into the faux leather seat of the sedan still sporting the handprints of the Mohawk tribe and point her vehicle south. Instead, she lingered.

Ohr shook Axel's hand and swept away as if in a race-walking competition and finding herself far behind.

Trace watched her go. "Does she always walk like that?"

"Yes, except on inclines."

"Smoking. Steals the wind," he said.

The odor of burning tobacco clung to her clothing and hair the way the tar likely clung to her skin.

He returned his attention to Rylee, moving closer until she could smell the wood smoke that clung to his flannel and the enticing earthy musk of him.

"Where will you go with your promotion? Do you have an office in mind?"

"I was thinking I'd like a bigger posting. New York, of

course, or LA, New Orleans because of the port, or Tampa because of the weather."

None of those included the frozen landscape that now surrounded them. And this was only the preview of what winter held in store, when chunks of ice the size of barges would hamper maritime traffic.

"Tampa seems nice," he said with no enthusiasm.

Snowflakes continued to drift down from the blue sky as if confused as to where they had come from and where they belonged. The grass between the sidewalk and curb had become stiff and crunched with each of her shifting steps. But the snow stuck only to the automobiles and the hard cold blacktop of the road surfaces.

Would he ask her to stay? She tilted her chin to look up into his face, blinking at the snowflakes that landed in her eyes.

"No reason to stay here," he said.

She met his stare. "Would you ever leave?"

Had she really said that aloud? The door of possibilities cracked open a bit.

His brows lifted, disappearing into the wool lip of his ski hat.

"I've never lived anywhere else," he said.

"And I've lived everywhere else." She tried for a laugh, failed and cleared her throat. "Funny that trying to get this promotion, and the last one, kept me on the move. When what I said I've wanted was to settle in one place."

"Your job keeps you mobile."

"I might as well be in the army…moving like a migrating bird."

"Maybe the next posting will be a more permanent one."

Rylee felt the tears misting her eyes and choking her throat. Her nose began to run and she wiped it with her leather glove.

"This is all wrong," she said.

"I know. Crazy, right?"

When she imagined a man making a commitment to her, it wasn't in the form of question. As if he were wondering if she could extend her visit for a day or two.

"You can't stay. Can you?" he asked.

He didn't confess his true feelings or express his devotion. His expression looked pained and she wondered if perhaps he'd be happy to see her go and be done with this… Whatever it was they had shared.

They had known each other only a little over a week. It wasn't long enough to fall in love. Was it? This had to be the stress of the case and the danger. Just an encounter.

She scowled. "I should go."

His nod was exaggerated. "Yes, right."

It was looking more and more as if the emotions that were kicking her like a mule were distinctly one-sided.

"Thank you, Sheriff, for all you've done to help me with this case." She extended her gloved hand.

He stared down at it, frowning like a kid who was expecting something specific on Christmas morning and instead got socks.

"Yeah, you're welcome." The handshake was mechanical.

She smiled. "I hope you'll call us if you see anything of which we should be aware."

He held her hand motionless, as if reluctant to let go. Finally, he dropped his hand to his side and then shoved it into his pocket. She could see the balled fist there.

Rylee walked on brittle legs to the driver's side door, gripping the keys as if they were the neck of a snake. She managed to wait until she left the town of Kinsley before the tears began to roll down her cheeks. The sobs came next.

Kurt Rogers came to stand beside Axel as the caravan of sedans pulled out like a motorcade.

"You should go after her," said Rogers.

"Nothing for her here, Kurt."

"Just you, I guess." He rested a hand on Axel's shoulder and squeezed. "You tell her you love her?"

He shook his head, knowing that words were just impossible.

"Never took you for a fool, son. Until now, that is."

"Maybe I ought to follow her."

"Sure. Plenty of nice places to go. You two could make a home anywhere." His hand slipped away and he faced the river. "Still, this place is awful pretty, with the snow falling like glitter in the sunlight." He studied the fast-flowing, wide river. "Never get tired of that view. All that water rolling toward the sea and here we sit on this shore, letting it pass by. That's the job, I guess, watching over the folks up here on this side of the river. But you can watch over folks anyplace, Axel. Doesn't need to be here. Follow her and you two can decide where to settle later."

"The town needs me," he said.

"Sure. But what I'm wondering is what *you* need. If it's a woman, all well and good. If it's *that* woman, you best go after her."

Chapter Twenty-Three

Rogers was right again. Axel was letting her get away. He stood in the road, the flurries bringing a dusting of snow. This was his county. He'd been elected to serve as sheriff, and he'd done his job. But he'd stayed to watch over the congregation and stand between the madman at their head and the flock he exploited.

But now they were gone. The women who had raised him had spread out among social services, returning to families or making a lateral move into the arms of another commune. His mother had said her goodbyes and Axel now believed that she had done all she was able to for him. His mother was smart but that part of her that allowed her to connect with people was simply absent. He didn't blame her, but it made him worry. What if he weren't capable of being the kind of parent he had missed? What if he were too damaged by his upbringing?

"What's holding you back, son?" asked Rogers. "Your father is gone. Taken into federal custody, and with all the charges, the only time you'll see him again is on visiting days."

"I won't be visiting. He's not my father."

Rogers lifted his thick white eyebrows. Axel told him the tale.

"You going to change your name? Make it Axel Pritcher?"

"It didn't occur to me."

"Might make a fresh start."

"Maybe. As to Father Wayne, I'll lay odds that he finds his own following in federal prison, but he can't lure vulnerable folks out here. The man was a regular pied piper."

"That's true. But he's gone. That means you can go, too."

Axel turned to look at the old lawman. "You knew that's why I came back?"

"Suspected, is all."

"I still have two years left on my term."

"If you're hanging up your star, I'm not too old to step in until they can do a special election. But try to talk her into coming on back here, if you can."

"Why?"

"Nice place to raise a family. Make me a grandfather, of sorts."

Axel blanched. "I don't even know if she wants a family. And I'm sure I don't know how to be a father."

"The heck you don't. I taught you all you need. Good sense of humor, patience and love. It's not hard, boy. Not as hard as telling the woman you love that you can't live without her. Now that is a job only for the brave at heart."

Axel nodded, glancing back at the empty road.

"Your military record says you are a brave man. Guess we'll find out if that's so. Get going or you won't catch her until she leaves the county."

THE FLURRIES HAD changed to a light snow that required intermittent wiper blade action. Rylee peered out through the windshield at the precipitation that made visibility difficult. Beyond her windshield, the world looked cold and the road lonely. Time to think about the case and not about Axel. She swallowed the lump of regret, but it stayed wedged like a large cough drop accidentally swallowed.

All the way out of Onutake County, she fought the urge

to turn her car around and go back to him. Tell him that she wanted… What? To live at the edge of a northern wasteland? She wanted a home and she wanted Axel. She wanted to stop moving all over the world, but she also wanted a career. How did she make this work? What compromises would she need and which of her objectives would be sacrificed to get the other? It was seldom in life that you reached a point where you could so clearly see two paths.

When she decided not to enlist, she had known it was one such juncture. When she had finished college and joined DHS, she had seen her path and taken charge. But how many of those choices were made not to please herself but to make her father proud?

All of them, she realized. Every one. And if he was proud, he had certainly never told her. Not even when she called him to report that her investigation had led to the arrest of the prime suspect. She could share little else, as the investigation and details were both classified, but his reaction had been typically underwhelming.

"Just part of the job, isn't it?" he had asked her during the brief phone conversation.

Risking her life, getting shot at, diving into a frozen river, just part of the job? It was. But even her supervisors recognized she had gone above and beyond, offered congratulations. They were also putting in for a promotion on her behalf, showing with actions how valuable they considered her service.

The conversation with her father had crystalized that searching for praise from him was pointless. He didn't know how, didn't understand her need for it or just refused to offer even the merest encouragement.

So why was she still acting to please him?

She wasn't. Would not. From this moment she would make choices on what was in *her* best interest.

The wiper blades couldn't keep up with the snow, so she

adjusted them again to the next higher setting. The other vehicles from her office had left her behind as they sped along, obviously anxious to be home before dark, while she was in no such hurry.

All she knew for certain was that she had made a huge case, her career was on track and she had never been so miserable.

The misery was the clue to the puzzle. Nothing good should make her feel this sad. Why didn't she see before that leaving Axel would not be like leaving one case for another? He was too important to leave behind. And a week was long enough, obviously, because she was certain that she loved him. But uncertain if he loved her.

At the very least, she should have told him that she had fallen in love with him. The risk of finding out he did not share her feelings now seemed less chilling than not taking the risk and never knowing.

Rylee glanced at the road ahead, the southbound lane of the Northway, searching for an exit or a turnaround that would allow her to change direction. A few miles back, the highway had been a single lane divided only by a yellow line. Now the two directions ran parallel with a median ditch between them.

She considered trying her luck on the snow-covered grass, but the possibility of ending up in the ditch between the divided highway kept her rolling along. Finally, she spotted her chance. The green sign with white letters indicated that the upcoming exit for Exit 26—toward Pottersville and Schroon Lake. Her chance to change direction lay only one mile ahead.

Rylee had been so deep in thought that she had not even noticed that the vehicle behind her was a trooper until the driver hit his lights.

"Really?" she said, glancing from her speedometer to the rearview. "I was only five miles over."

The Northway traffic was light on the two-lane highway, and she easily glided to the shoulder of the exit ramp to Pottersville, followed by the trooper.

It wasn't until the man approached her vehicle that she recognized that he was not in a trooper's uniform and was approaching with his handgun out and raised. She reached for her pistol as she adjusted her view in the side mirror to see the man's face.

Quinton Mondello. Eldest son of Hal Mondello, she realized. The new head of the Mondello family of moonshiners and the one suspected of transporting their North Korean detainee over the US–Canadian border. With no solid evidence of human trafficking, Quinton had been released. He had not been present on the attack at the wharf and had also evaded federal custody at the raid of his family's compound, slipping through the net when they had come to make arrests after the shooting.

He took aim, plainly deciding to shoot her from the back before ever reaching her window. Headlights flashed as a second vehicle pulled in behind Mondello's. His backup, she assumed.

Mondello's first shot missed its mark. Rylee had left her seat and scrambled to the passenger's side as the bullet punctured the rear window and then cleanly through her headrest before shattering the windshield. The fractured windshield was held in place by the protective film but was now a mosaic of tiny cubes of glass.

Rylee exited her vehicle with her pistol drawn and the safety switched off. She used the open door as a shield. Mondello had reached her rear bumper. He had no cover.

She aimed at center mass, making a guess on his position because the light made it impossible to see him clearly.

Her shot broke the side window, showing her that he'd moved. Where was he?

She listened and heard only a vehicle's chime, indicating a door was open. His backup, she realized.

No time to call it in. She needed to move. Rylee reached the front of her vehicle, the engine block providing cover.

"Drop it, Quinton." She recognized the familiar male voice.

"She ruined my family. My father is in jail because of her," said Mondello.

"Your father is in jail for human trafficking that North Korean across the border, and for manslaughter for kicking her into the canal. Did you know what she carried could have killed your whole family?"

Quinton Mondello's voice rose an octave, making him sound crazed. "You're on my list, too, Axel, and you just jumped to the number one spot."

"Drop it or I will shoot you."

Quinton laughed. "You haven't shot at anything or anybody since coming home from the Sandbox. Everyone knows you are scared to shoot. A regular basket case, I hear."

Rylee moved to look around the fender. The two men faced off like gunfighters at high noon. Only Axel's pistol was aimed at Mondello and Mondello's was still pointed in her direction.

Mondello spotted her now and smiled. Their eyes met. He had her now in his sights, and the fact that Axel would kill him after he made his shot seemed to make no difference. Mondello lifted his pistol and two shots fired.

She registered the surprised expression as she put a bullet in his chest. The second one, the one that removed the smug expression along with part of his face, had come from Axel's weapon.

Mondello dropped, inert and lifeless, to the pavement with a sickening whack. Rylee flinched.

Axel ran forward, gun still aimed at Mondello. He

reached the still body and placed his foot over the pistol that lay just beyond his curled hand. He stowed the gun in the pocket of his jacket. He made a quick check of Mondello. The sight of his ruined face told Rylee that no one could have survived such a grievous head injury.

Only then did Axel holster his personal weapon and run toward her. She stood to meet him, with time only to slip her gun back into the nylon case.

Then he had her in a crushing embrace. His kisses, frantic, began at her forehead and moved down to her cheek and then to her neck. There he tucked his face into her nape and muttered disjointed words.

"Almost too late… Could have… Almost… My God, Rylee."

"I'm here." She drew back to look at him.

In all the days and all the times they had been together, she had never seen him so pale. He was trembling.

"My hand was shaking. I didn't know if I could make that shot."

And then she remembered that this peace officer had never drawn his pistol since coming home from serving. He had told her he didn't think he could take another life, not even to save his own. Yet, he had done it, to save hers.

"It was my bullet," she said. Trying to take the blame. But they both knew that the way Quintin had dropped, as if his head were no longer connected to his body, meant that it had been Axel's headshot that had killed him.

Her shot had been deadly but not incapacitating. Mondello would have had time to take that shot at Rylee.

Axel seemed to come back into possession of himself. He still looked pale as moonlight, but his gaze was steady as he cradled her head between his two strong hands.

"No. It was mine."

"You saved my life," she said.

"Thank God." He dragged her in for another hug. "Thank God," he whispered into her hair.

"How did you know?"

She drew back, needing answers and to call this in.

Axel blinked at her.

"How did you know Quinton Mondello was following me or that he planned to kill me?"

"I didn't."

She wrinkled her brow, trying to make sense of this.

"Then how did you get here? Why are you here, Axel?"

He let her go and glanced down at the dead body oozing blood onto the road. The thick red fluid oozed along the cracks in the tired pavement.

"Not a good time. Wrong place. Really wrong."

He was muttering again.

"Axel. Look at me."

He did. The trembling had ceased but he looked miserable.

"Why are you here?"

Axel looked at the pavement and the body again. He grasped her hand and pulled her away from the corpse of Quinton Mondello.

"Axel, I have to call this in."

He raked a hand through his hair. "Yes. Call it in. I'll use my radio."

Rylee watched him go. He remained in his vehicle for a long while after lowering the radio. Finally, Rylee headed back to him.

"Climb in," he said. "It's cold outside. Troopers are en route. Be here in ten."

She climbed into the quiet cab and the two waited in silence. Discussing the events would only taint their statements.

"Thank you for coming for me."

Axel nodded but said nothing.

The sound of sirens was almost immediate.

"How is that possible?" she said, spotting the flashing lights of a large vehicle. Her hand went to the handle of her gun.

"There is a voluntary fire company at the southern half of the exit."

And sure enough, the EMS vehicle rolled down the northbound ramp and across a utility road she had not seen beneath the snow cover. Clearly, this was a well-traveled route by the volunteers.

Soon the quiet stretch of road became an active crime scene and Rylee felt grateful that it was not her corpse being tucked in a body bag and rolled into the back of the emergency vehicle.

AXEL OPTED TO spend the night in a hotel, rather than drive back home. He didn't sleep well and woke with that dull throbbing headache that came from too much caffeine and too little sleep.

He made it to the troopers' station, reviewed and signed his statement. That left one piece of unfinished business and the reason he'd come in the first place: to speak to Rylee.

A text message, a reply and a location chosen, he headed to the small pub and bistro in Schroon Lake. Inside, he was nestled in the aroma of bacon and frying foods. The interior was all knotty pine bedecked with snowshoes and skis from another century. Hand-hewn beams stretched above him, and a kayak hung from between the ceiling fans. Rustic wooden furniture sat before a blazing fireplace and several customers occupied high stools at the bar, cradling their drinks. The men's attention flicked from their drinks to the television, before returning to watch the busy woman behind the bar.

"Welcome," she called. "Sit wherever you like."

He scanned the room but did not find Rylee, so he took a place at a circular table near the stone fireplace and beneath a chandelier made of antlers. Out of habit, he took a seat facing the door and the wide windows that showed the parking lot and the road beyond. The light flurry was now making progress in coating the windshields of the cars parked before the bistro.

He had a cup of coffee that had been refilled once before he saw her step from a vehicle. It wasn't the one she'd driven last night. That one was now in evidence, part of an active investigation. His first shooting and his first kill, at least since coming home from Iraq, or as he thought of it, the Sandbox.

Axel didn't recall leaving the table or the room or the restaurant. But there he was in the lot with the snow floating down lazily and his breath visible in the cold air.

She was talking to herself. Then she sighted him and hesitated in her purposeful stride. Her steps became awkward, as she slipped on the icy pavement before she recovered and continued her forward momentum at a slower pace. She seemed in no hurry to reach him and glanced back at her vehicle with a look he thought might be longing.

Was this meeting an obligation for her, a duty to be discharged? The thought cooled him more than the wintery air. His coat was in his hand. He must have grabbed it on the way out. Axel slipped into it and waited.

"Hello, there," she said. "I didn't expect an escort in."

They faced each other, him feeling uncomfortable in his own skin and her waiting. Should he hug her or kiss her cheek?

Instead, he fell in beside her, grasping her elbow and helping her toward the sidewalk. Her boots were gone and instead she wore the sort of shoes that corporate folks wore. She was changing back to the data analyst she had been.

Already leaving him, he realized. He had to stop her. Suddenly, he forgot how to breathe.

"I'm glad you're all right," she said. "I was just rehearsing how to tell you how grateful I am. That's twice in one week you've backed me up."

It was a job he wouldn't mind taking full-time.

"Getting to be a habit."

"Thank you, Axel, for saving my life. Again."

"You're welcome."

They reached the door to the restaurant and he opened it for her. Like many places in the north, this establishment had a double-door system and a small room that was for waiting in the summer and, in the winter, for keeping the warm air from escaping when guests came and went. Here, they paused between the inside and the outside to face each other.

"You all finished here?" she asked.

"For now. Lots of paperwork, you know."

"I imagine so."

"What about you?" he asked.

"I am all packed up."

She glanced past him to the second door, which led inside, catching a glimpse, he knew, of the log and pine interior.

"It looks like a nice place."

It might be the place they would come back to over the years. That special place where he asked her to be his wife. Or, he thought, it might be that place he avoided forever, never to return.

They moved inside and he led the way back to his table and the cold cup of coffee that waited there.

Rylee took her seat beside him at the pine table. She held her smile as she turned her gaze back on him. Her hand snaked out and clasped one of his, her fingers icy. Their palms slipped over one another and he closed his hand. She gave a little squeeze.

"I know you don't draw your weapon. Haven't, I mean."

"Quinton was right. Not since the Sandbox," he added.

"You fired your weapon. Took the necessary shot. Are you going to be all right with that?" she asked.

"I will be, because I had no other option and my actions kept you here on this earth."

"That just makes me doubly grateful."

Gratitude was not the emotion he wished to engender within her heart.

"I wasn't going to let him hurt you, Rylee. I don't want anything to ever hurt you." And if she'd let him, he'd be there for her, to keep her safe and watch her back. Why couldn't he find the words to tell her so?

Her hand slipped away and the heat of their joined flesh melted from his tingling palm.

"When are you heading back to Kinsley?" she asked.

"That depends."

Outside the windows to their right and left, the snow swirled in the gray afternoon.

"I've been wondering something, Axel." She cocked her head, her eyebrows lifting. Did she know how beautiful she was? Just a look was like a dart piercing his heart.

"You said before that you didn't know about Quinton. That he was coming for me."

The jig was up, he realized. Of course, she'd come back around to that question. "That's true."

"Then why were you there?"

"I love you. I followed you yesterday to tell you that. To get on my knees and ask you to marry me."

"You followed..." Her brow wrinkled, and the corners of her mouth dipped.

Panic seized his heart with sharp incisors.

"Rylee, don't go."

"What?"

"I love you. I don't want you to go."

Now it was her turn to stammer and stare. "Y-you… what? Axel, you've only known me a week."

"Nine days."

"It's not very long."

"Engaged, then. Going steady. Dating. Just not going away."

"My job is in Glens Falls. I'll be transferred soon."

"Yes. I know that. And I don't care. Let me come with you."

Her mouth dropped open and she stared.

"That is a very different offer than asking me to stay."

"It is."

"Axel, are you sure?"

"I'll follow you anywhere, Rylee. If you let me."

She shook her head now, as if not able to understand his words.

"What about your job? You're a county sheriff."

He looked north, perhaps seeing the county and the people there.

"Special election. They'll fill the spot." Now he was looking at her again. "Rylee, I went back there after the military, stayed there because of him."

"Father Wayne?"

"I needed to stop him from killing his followers, my mother, all of them. I knew he'd do it. It was part of his personality. The power of life and death, the ultimate test of his control."

Axel pressed his palms flat to the table.

"I don't need to watch him anymore. End of watch. Mission complete." He stared across the table at her. "Do you understand? I'm free. For the first time in my life I can go anywhere I like, do anything I like and be with whomever I choose." He reached out and she took his hand. "I choose you, Rylee."

"But the county. Your home."

"I hate it there. Hate everything about it, especially the memories. Let someone else take the job. Someone who is there for reasons other than duty."

"Is that really how you feel?"

"Yes."

"What about Kurt Rogers?"

"He'll always be a mentor. I'll visit or he'll visit. But I won't stay in that county. No more."

HE'D BEEN THROUGH so much. Raised in a cult and then fostered. Held in the county by fear and obligation. She thanked God for Kurt Rogers, who had helped Axel find his way. Then the military, where he'd nearly lost himself again. Back to his county, a self-appointed guardian, giving himself the impossible job of curbing a madman, a man who, until recently, he'd believed to be his father.

"Rylee? Say something."

She leaned forward, reaching for him until her fingers stroked the red stubble on his cheek.

"I love you, too, Axel. I just didn't know how we could make this work between us. But now I see nothing but possibilities."

"Is that a yes?" he asked.

"Yes to the engagement."

He rose from his seat and pulled her into his arms, kissing her with passion before the great stone fireplace in the middle of a restaurant with few customers to witness their union.

When she drew back, her face was flushed and she beamed up at him.

"What should we do now?" he asked.

"I was hoping to buy you lunch." She smiled and offered her hand.

"Yes. Lunch."

She stood beside him, still holding his hand as she spoke. "And after that, a life together."

Together, they would make the permanent home that she had always wanted and raise the family for which he had always longed. They were together at last and forever, just as they were always meant to be.

* * * * *

COMING SOON!

We really hope you enjoyed reading this book. If you're looking for more romance, be sure to head to the shops when new books are available on

Thursday 14th November

To see which titles are coming soon, please visit

millsandboon.co.uk/nextmonth

MILLS & BOON